The
Lost Girls
of
Foxfield
Hall

GW00642793

BOOKS BY JESSICA THORNE

The
Lost Girls
of
Foxfield
Hall

JESSICA THORNE

bookouture

Published by Bookouture in 2021

An imprint of Storyfire Ltd.
Carmelite House
50 Victoria Embankment
London EC4Y 0DZ

www.bookouture.com

ISBN: 978-1-83888-741-4
eBook ISBN: 978-1-83888-740-7

This book is a work of fiction. Names, characters, businesses,
organizations, places and events other than those clearly in the
public domain, are either the product of the author's imagination
or are used fictitiously. Any resemblance to actual persons, living or
dead, events or locales is entirely coincidental.

To Dad

Prologue

The last day of summer, September 1939

They meet beneath the spreading boughs of the great yew tree which has stood in that spot for even longer than the Hall. Their place, just for them, ever since he had persuaded her to climb out of her bedroom window and reach for the outstretched branch. But she had been too young then, too small, and she had slipped. He tried to catch her, but he was just a child as well and they had ended up in a tangle of limbs and tears.

Fifteen years have passed since then, just a blink of an eye to the watcher, and the children are adults now. But still, so young. Tears flow now as well, but for another reason, another pain. Tears of parting.

This time, leaving the Hall with its lights and comforts, they walk into the twilight and the young woman folds into his embrace.

'It won't be long,' he murmurs, her gentle lover, her dearest friend. 'It can't last long. It'll be over before—'

She presses a finger to his lips. 'They said that about the last war, David. Let's not make the same mistake.'

He kisses her fingertip and smiles as she releases him.

'They need pilots.'

'And you just had to volunteer.' Her returning smile is shaded with heartbreak. 'Any chance to be a hero.'

'Your hero. Always. It isn't forever, and I will come back every possible chance I get.'

'I know you will. I know. I just—' She pulls away, but not entirely, because she can't leave him entirely. She still holds his hand. 'I don't even know what I'm doing here.'

'You're helping your father with the estate.'

'Am I? It doesn't feel like it. I'm lost here. He just wants me home to keep me out of trouble.'

'Keep you out of trouble, Ellie? Whoever could manage that?'

She tries to smile at his joke. She fails. 'I should be doing my bit too. There's nothing for me to do here except play lady of the manor. What use is that?'

'Nothing? What about that ghost of yours? Weren't you going to find out all about her, track her down? That was your plan. Now you have time.'

She blushes, looks away. 'Don't tease, David. Anyway, Father called it a childhood fantasy.'

But David smiles, and gently turns her face back to his. 'I know you still believe in her. Come with me.'

They make their way through the gardens, hand in hand, until they reach the dark walls of the maze, drowning in the scent of yew. But they have no fear, these two. This is their place and has been all their lives. They have no notion of the things that they should fear that linger in this place.

And there in the heart of the maze, in front of the ancient well, she kisses him again. For a time, they lose themselves in each other.

'See? There's no ghost here,' she tells him. She sounds almost resigned. 'You were right. Everyone was right.'

The watcher almost laughs. But all she can do is watch.

For now.

'Here,' David says and pulls a black box from the pocket of his overcoat. 'I bought it for you in London. So you can photograph the Green Lady.'

The young woman glares at him, suddenly suspicious. 'Are you making fun of me?'

He recoils in mock horror, which makes her smile reluctantly. She can't help it. 'I wouldn't dare, Lady Eleanor. I am but a lowly suitor, the Arthur to your Guinevere, a wandering knight errant who is not worthy to—'

'You'll be back by Harvest Festival to win my favour?' She smiles and the teasing tone infects her voice. It is a game they play.

He wants to say yes. He wants to make that promise. He wants to so badly. The evidence is there in his expression, in his earnest eyes. But he cannot make that promise. No one can. The good humour dies.

'I… I'll try…' he whispers, but it's a sound of defeat. He doesn't know what the future holds. He can show bravado with anyone but her. They know each other too well. And the war is coming. It's in the air. It rumbles through the earth and whispers a siren song of heroism and sacrifice, a harbinger's wail of deaths to come. 'If there's any way…'

She pulls him close again, rests her face against his chest, and he struggles to calm his breath. 'You don't have to promise me anything.' She turns the box over and over in her hands. Little glass discs on its front and back glisten in the moonlight. 'This must have cost a fortune,' she murmurs in wonder.

'It's worth every penny. Look, you can be as famous as Harry Price.'

She rolls her eyes at him. 'Oh, can I? Lucky old me.'

He grins, a lopsided, rakish grin. It is charming and endearing, and so filled with love. 'Go on. Catch me a ghost, Ellie.'

She shakes her head, exasperated with his gentle teasing. But she doesn't argue. Instead her eyes fill with tears and she looks up at him. In those glistening blue eyes, the watcher sees the dread, the fear that she will never see him again. She is trying to drink him down, to sear his face into her memory.

'As easy as that,' she says.

'For you, yes. There's nothing you can't do, my love. I have film for you and even a flash. The bulbs are expensive though so don't waste them. They're back in the house, in the bag. But I wanted to surprise you.'

'You did,' she says, and her voice wavers. She pauses for the longest moment before she seems to pull herself together, making herself brave. 'Promise me you'll write.'

He enfolds her in his arms and holds her close, each of them pushing their fears and doubts, their regrets, down deep inside.

'Whenever I can.'

'My champion,' she says in reply, and they laugh at a shared, secret joke. Then they kiss again.

When they part, their fingertips still cling together, like a promise. As if they can't bear to let go.

The watcher felt that once. Long ago. She longs for it. Longs to feel again, to live, to breathe.

To love.

To be a maiden with a champion of her own.

But she refused to betray her love, and she was betrayed by those who should have loved her most, her own blood. She died a sacrifice's death, strangled, drowned, bled dry. A tithe to the land, to power, to the greed of another.

And now, bound by ancient magic to the well, encircled and entrapped by a labyrinth of yew, all she can do is wait until she can walk again. Step by agonising step, she drags herself towards the Hall, under the light of the harvest moon.

But one day she will get home.

Chapter One

Monday 16th September 2019

Owen had made Megan promise she wouldn't live life looking over her shoulder. That she wouldn't fret, or obsess about all the *what if*s, should something happen to him. Move on. It was easier that way, he said. He'd tried to make Mum promise too. She refused, but Megan could never say no to her brother.

Especially not now.

New place, new job, new start.

Passing through a village that looked like a postcard, she let the GPS guide her, noticing that, despite the fact she was supposed to be in the rural heartlands, hers seemed to be the only Land Rover around which had ever been off road. Not to mention that it was about fifteen years older than any of its shiny cousins.

As she imagined the kinds of people who might own these cars – country types in name only – she reminded herself she wasn't here to socialise. Just to work. And Sahar had done her a huge favour by recommending her for this gig. Not to mention arranging accommodation and basically doing everything she could to, quote: 'lure you down here so you can stop me losing my mind'.

It hadn't been a difficult task.

She just needed to get away from home, from family, from everything.

Five minutes beyond the village, just after the back of the pristine 'Welcome to Ashleigh' sign, the road forked. Megan took the left, passing under the dappled shade of a stand of oaks, around a bend, and then she saw the gates. You couldn't miss them. They stood open but were still huge and imposing. They were flanked by another sign – white with a green maze logo and the flowing red line representing a fox. Foxfield Hall.

The long gravel drive wound up through a wooded area which gave way to rolling lawns. She caught a glimpse of something that could have been a ditch or could have been a long-neglected ha-ha and then the house came into view. Beautiful, no doubt about it. Unique. And old. She'd seen the photos Sahar had emailed, and scouted out the place online before saying she'd take the job. There were some aerial photos which showed elements in the land that had given her all sorts of ideas and her research had left her excited. God knew, she needed something to excite her these days.

She parked around the side, away from the gleaming rows of high-end Mercs, Beemers and the others she couldn't name arrayed across the neat car park. The second car park was off to one side and she pulled in by an off-white van and a rather sad-looking Ford Fiesta. Never let it be said she got ideas above her station. If there was a staff car park she had to guess this was it, or else it was very well hidden and this was where the rebels left their vehicles.

Sahar hadn't mentioned the five stars. Or maybe she had, and Megan had been too focused on the prospect of the gardens and the maze to listen. But she shouldn't be surprised. Now that she thought of it she was fairly sure the words 'luxury' and 'exclusive' had been bandied around.

Still, she was in a reasonably smart, if affordable, trouser suit, or would be when she put the jacket on. She fished it out of the rear of the Land Rover, where she had draped it carefully over her bags, far away from the equipment she'd brought with her. Sahar had assured her that everything she would need would be here but there were some things that were sacred. Her own tools, for example.

As she walked back around the corner of the building, a woman appeared at the steps leading to the columned portico at the front, the entrance to the hotel, her midnight hair in a neat bun, her blouse, waistcoat and skirt so well cut that it took a moment before Megan realised they were a uniform. It took even longer to realise it was Sahar. Her oldest friend, ever since they'd met at school.

Sahar gave a squeal of excitement and threw her arms around Megan's neck, pulling her down into a hug. Normally, she'd squirm and complain but, right now, she needed this and she sank into the embrace in relief, and Sahar, always sensitive to the feelings of others, held her as long as she needed. 'I'm so glad you said yes!'

Megan hadn't actually said yes. Not yet. It was just that it was very hard to say no to Sahar at the best of times. And this was not the best of times. Hadn't been for months. But she pushed that thought away.

Seeing Sahar again almost made everything better. Coming here was the best decision she had made in an age. Not that she would admit that to Sahar. She would never hear the end of it.

'I didn't get the impression there was an alternative answer.'

'Well of course there wasn't. Ready? This is just a formality, I promise. With your reputation, references and CV they'd be lucky to have you.'

And they were certainly paying enough. Megan didn't say that out loud. No one had even blinked when she named her price. Restoration of historic gardens did not come cheap.

She pasted a professional smile back on her face. 'Ready.'

The house was beautiful, a sprawling manor of a place, like something out of a fairy tale. It wasn't one style, but looked more like every historical period was represented in some way, a few that didn't even belong at all. Victorian with a touch of Gothic here, and Dutch Baroque there, some Tudor elements buried deep underneath. And under that, even earlier elements. Foundations that went back to time out of mind. She made out half-timbered gables, and twisting red-brick chimneys. There was a dome jutting out of the roof at one point, and a massive conservatory off to one side. The building rambled over the space, wings added on wherever the fancy had taken a particular generation. All of it beautiful and elegant, unique. But unplanned. It was the type of building that had grown organically, as if of its own volition. A house and its grounds usually went hand in hand, or ought to. Matching this would be a trick and a half.

'Gorgeous, isn't it?' said Sahar. There was genuine love in her voice for the place. Sunlight glimmered off the windows and made the red bricks warm and comforting. 'The family, the Fairfaxes, lived here for generations, just adding on bits over the years. I like to think they collected architectural features. Whenever they went travelling, they came back with a new idea and just slapped it onto the house. The interior is the same, modernised now of course and refitted for the hotel, but it keeps its charm. You'll see.'

Megan had no doubt she'd get the full tour as soon as this trial – or interview, she should call it – by the board of trustees was over.

'The apartment's here too?' she asked.

'It's round the back. Just you and me, babes, like old times. Less parties than college though. Oh, and Amir when he visits. That's okay with you, isn't it?'

Megan grinned. Amir, Sahar's boyfriend, worked in the City, and she adored him. The commute down to Ashleigh wasn't too arduous but it wouldn't be a daily thing, not with the hours he worked.

'So long as you keep him in your bedroom at night, I don't mind at all.'

Sahar gave her a wicked grin. 'Not a problem, babes. Right then, you ready to wow the bigwigs?'

The wince was immediate. Megan couldn't help herself. 'Not sure about that, Sahar.'

'Why not? You always do. Come on.'

*

The interior was just as eclectic as the building itself, although the style was more muted, tailored to appeal to a wide audience of visitors, and completely Instagrammable. It billed itself as a boutique luxury hotel, and Megan could see why. It fitted. It was the type of place that didn't scream money because it didn't need to. It had that old-world, eternal quality to it. And Sahar was right at home here, all efficiency and businesslike calm. The moment she stepped inside there was no doubt she was running the place. Megan followed her, a little bemused to see the transformation in her old friend.

But every so often Sahar would meet her gaze and give her a look that made her stifle a giggle, just in case Megan was afraid she had come over all corporate clone. Maybe having your best friend on the periphery of a formal interview wasn't the best idea ever, not if you didn't want to burst out laughing.

The meeting room had more oak panelling on the walls than a druid's grove. The round conference table was a modern piece which had been made from a cross-section of some ancient beech tree, highly polished so the rings made a pattern like ripples in a pond. Sitting around it were three men and a woman. Sahar motioned Megan towards one of the remaining seats and then took a place beside her.

A young woman with bright red, pre-Raphaelite hair and soft hazel eyes behind a pair of expensive wire-framed glasses smiled at her, a smile which took Megan completely by surprise. The young man next to her scowled for a moment and then smoothed his features. He was nearer thirty than twenty, with that kind of physique that said he liked to keep fit, had played something like rugby since school but was enjoying the beer a bit too much these days. He wore a suit that looked more expensive than anything Megan had ever owned, including her Landie. All the same, it hung on him like a cheap rag. The other two men were older, and eyed her curiously, no doubt trying to work out why a young woman would work in a profession like hers, or cut her hair quite so short. Just as well they couldn't see the tattoos really. But then, she didn't let just anyone see them.

Megan pasted a smile on her face.

'Miss Taylor, thank you so much for coming,' said the pre-Raphaelite artist's flame-haired fantasy. She smiled again, her fingertips playing on the edge of the tablet in front of her. 'I'm Nora Grainger, and this is Alan Brooks, Dr James Havesham and Professor Fred Deacon. We form the trustees of Foxfield Hall. We really just wanted to welcome you and discuss the plans for the grounds.'

'Particularly the maze,' said Professor Deacon. He had the distracted gaze of someone who really didn't want to be there.

'The maze,' Mr Suit scoffed suddenly. He'd been introduced as Alan Brooks, Megan reminded herself, and she knew his type. A second later he confirmed her opinion. 'We should just bulldoze the bloody thing and the woods beyond it and turn it all into a golf course.'

It took all Megan had in her not to let her jaw drop so hard it dented the exquisite table. But someone else replied.

'We talked about this, Alan, and voted,' said Nora Grainger, her tone cool. She'd had this conversation more than once, that was for sure. He scowled back at her and for a moment she seemed to wilt, but then the others cut in.

'The house and the maze are Grade II listed and that's the end of it,' said Dr Havesham. 'We are here to speak to Miss Taylor, not to rehash old arguments yet again. Miss Taylor?'

Nora Grainger shuffled through some of the papers in front of her, without making eye contact with anyone. Beside her, Sahar shifted in her seat but said nothing. Megan could sense that she was suppressing the urge to tell Brooks where to go on Megan's behalf. She could read Sahar like an open book.

Why invite her here if all they wanted to do was bulldoze the place? She decided to focus on the others.

'Call me Megan,' she said, relieved to have the opening. And with that she began to lay out her plans for the estate. Sahar had sent her photos and Megan had drawn up plans. She had already sourced a number of key specimens as well as planting that would fill the spaces and mature with time. They wanted this done quickly and were willing to pay for that. Replanting areas with broadleaf native trees on the approach for romantic woodland walks would take longer, but a replica of a traditional cottage garden to provide organic vegetables for the kitchens was easier, as was the most important item: the restoration of the maze, complete with a transformation of the central area to make a secret garden, the kind so beloved of wedding photographers and the Chelsea Flower Show with which she had made her name as a landscape gardener. She had several awards for her small garden designs, and this was no different. A lot of the structure and the necessary elements were already there, ready to be shaped into something magical. She broke the grounds down into sectors, describing the function and atmosphere she wanted to create for each area. She had them in the palm of her hand in no time and, beside her, Sahar beamed. Delighted to be right.

When she'd finished she'd made the case for it financially as well as horticulturally.

That was the deal-closer. Even Mr Turn-it-All-into-a-Sodding-Golf-Course was onside. Or at least, onside enough.

Megan knew she had them from their expressions and also because this wasn't the first time she'd had to do this: persuade people that, actually, the land they took for granted could give them so much if they only took care of it.

And she was interviewing them as much as the other way around, just as Sahar had said. She asked her questions clearly, succinctly, and got the answers she wanted.

The problem was, every time she looked up, she saw Nora Grainger, with her slender face, hazel eyes and alabaster skin, her red hair in rich waves that had to come from a high-end salon. The woman was distracting. That was the problem.

Sahar thanked everyone and invited Megan for a cup of coffee in the drawing room, suggesting the board might join them when they were ready.

Because obviously they needed to dissect everything she had said first.

'Oh my God, babe, you were amazing,' said Sahar when the door shut behind them. 'I mean, I knew you would be, but it was like watching a master at work. Come on, they'll have the coffee ready for us by now. I asked Hattie to time it.' She checked her watch. 'I was only out by five minutes.'

Megan grinned at Sahar, relief swamping her system, leaving her with a buzz that meant coffee wasn't actually needed.

The drawing room was a neat little sitting room off the bar, which Sahar explained had once been the morning room. The door at the end led into a library. A special collection, apparently, and one jealously guarded. Sahar chatted about the building and her plans for the hotel, but eventually the conversation inevitably lurched back towards home and the one subject Megan didn't want to get to.

'How're your parents?'

Megan put the cup down with an undignified clatter. 'They're good. Well, you know. Dad doesn't like to talk about it. Mum… well, once she gets started…'

She didn't want to finish that. It didn't seem fair. She drank some more coffee instead and wished they could talk about the house again. But she owed Sahar an update, didn't she?

Sahar looked down into her coffee cup. 'Has there been any word at all?'

Megan's throat closed on a tight lump. 'Nothing. They're saying absolutely nothing. That's not good.'

'But… they have to keep looking, don't they?'

You'd think. Leave no man behind, wasn't that what everyone said? But Owen had been missing for too long now. Megan knew what that meant. Missing in action just meant they couldn't find the remains. In her heart of hearts she knew her brother was dead, even if she didn't want to say so. Her mother, on the other hand…

'They're doing everything they can.'

It was a stock reply. It usually shut people up. Not Sahar though.

'What does that even mean?'

Megan glared at her. She couldn't keep going like this and she knew Sahar well enough to be blunt. 'It means I don't want to talk about it. It means I'm here because I don't want to be at home any more because… well, you know my mother, right? You've met her.'

Sahar had the good grace to hide the grimace. 'Still campaigning?'

'New campaign. Find Owen, make the army mount a rescue mission and bring him home. She's even been co-opting show tunes.'

Sahar reached out and squeezed Megan's hand. 'You've got to have hope though.'

Hope. Hope was a lie. Hope didn't want to let you rest, or give you a moment's peace. Hope kept you up all night, despair its bedfellow. Hope chipped away at everything else until you were empty inside.

'Hope hurts, Sahar.'

Luckily, that was when Nora and the others appeared and the subject changed back to the more comfortable ground of the job, the contract and handshakes all round.

As Sahar sorted out drinks for everyone, Megan found herself gazing out of the window, across the lawns towards the trees and the gates beyond. A fox wandered across the lush green grass, looking for all the world like it owned the place. Completely at home, devoid of fear.

Foxfield Hall, she thought.

Well, it fitted.

Chapter Two

Monday 23rd September 2019

It didn't take long to settle in. She knew her way around in a couple of days. The apartment nestled at the back of the hotel, a building that once might have been stables or something similar, Megan supposed. Double doors led out onto a little private patio which she knew she'd easily fill with plants in no time – it caught the sun just right and would make a perfect nursery – and from there out into the gardens themselves. It housed just the two of them, her and Sahar, other staff living locally rather than onsite. Some were agency staff but Foxfield Hall made a concerted effort to hire from the area, Sahar said. It made for better relations.

And for rather a lot of gossip.

The board had big plans for the hotel and grounds, according to Sahar. Or Alan Brooks did anyway. The other three seemed to view their role as stopping him from doing anything too drastic, but he had sunk a fortune into the place. Family money, apparently, as well as the proceeds from stock markets and numerous shady dealings.

Nora Grainger had had a tough time with him. They had past history from before he was married. He was a couple of years older than her and their terrible relationship had ended badly. Sahar speculated he had put her off men for life and Megan had to tell her it didn't actually work like that. Still, no one liked the way he pushed Nora around. And anyone else who he felt he could get away with bullying.

Local staff were the key to somewhere like Foxfield Hall. Chief among them was Hattie, who ruled the reception with a rod of iron. And she knew everything about everyone.

'You'll like her,' Sahar said. 'Quite a character. I'm not sure this place would run without her at all.'

According to Sahar, Hattie had all sorts to say about Alan Brooks. She had known his family for years, and the man himself all his life. 'Hattie's Nora's aunt or something. Or cousin. Or… oh, you know, one of those relatives who aren't actually relatives but might as well be? Like my Auntie Sepideh.'

Megan decided all the politics was a bit much, both locally and at the hotel, and so she focused on the grounds instead. Sahar already had a gardening and building team in place, running them in a tight unit. Mostly men, but that was usual. Thank God they didn't have a problem with a woman calling the shots.

Her assessment was going to take a while. Once she'd done that they would really get to work. The lawns were easy, and the cottage garden was essentially new work, so they could get stuck into that quickly enough. The trees just needed taking in hand and she could order in as many more as she needed. She'd already designed the little forest path which would pick its way through them and would get the guys started on the hard landscaping for that. Heading into winter was the best time of year to plant new mature trees anyway, dormant and ready for the next spring. So that was all ready to go.

The maze though… the maze was incredible. It had started life as a labyrinth, not originally intended for people to actually get lost in.

Labyrinths had an objective, a ceremonial pathway, a route through to the middle, the destination that made the journey have meaning. Mazes were just there to mess with you.

The design was a curling path, winding around through box hedges and yew, passing by feature areas where specimen plants could be displayed, or set with sculptures or water features. Unicursal, they called it. A single path. Or at least that was the idea. It was formal, processional, like a ritual pathway through the land.

While once it might have been a single path, the plant life here had a glorious mind of its own. New openings had formed where none had been intended, and others had closed up entirely. Once in there it wasn't easy to keep your bearings. On a basic level, the hedges weren't well kept. They needed regular cutting back and that had obviously lapsed some time ago. Every so often someone had had a go at it with a chainsaw, sure, but that had just compounded the problem.

You had to work with the vegetation, not against it. Megan planned to start that as part of the assessment, just getting it in basic shape and opening it up again. The interior plants were beautiful, but wild.

Dotted along the exterior, huge yew trees had just been allowed to grow unchecked. The hedging itself was English yew as well and appeared to take the height of the trees as a benchmark. The hedges towered over the interior, casting it in shadows and blotting out the sun. Inside, other plants, shrubs and trees had taken root, changing the pathways to their own design. As Megan tried to map it out for assessment, she had to push her way through sections, forcing the branches out of her way as she swore terrible oaths to be back with all sorts of sharp implements. But yew hedging was one of the most dense you could find. It harboured all kinds of animal life. She promised herself she'd be careful.

It carried the scent of wildness with it, of living growing things, the distinctive fragrance of yew, that earthy, rich smell which contrasted with the sharpness of the sap. It was unmistakable. The bright red berries stood in stark contrast to the deep green foliage. They were ancient trees, probably older than the maze that had been created from them. Yews were among the oldest of trees in Europe. She brushed her palm against the bark, brittle like old paper. Reddish-brown, with streaks of purple, it peeled away from the trunks in great strips.

Yews were known as the tree of death. You usually found it in graveyards. Almost every part of it was poisonous, especially the leaves and seeds. And yet, it was revered, long lived, spectacular. The Greeks wove crowns of it to honour Hecate. The Celts planted it in their holiest places. It had provided the wood for the longbows that won at Agincourt. The cancer-beating medicine derived from it saved countless lives. No one considered that when they called yews trees of ill omen.

Megan made some notes and moved on, squeezing through gaps, thankful for her heavy work jacket. It took far too long.

The heart of the maze wasn't a huge area, but it was perfectly proportioned for its design. Megan found it almost by accident, squeezing through an overgrown gap she wasn't even sure was part of the path. She could see why they thought of weddings. Though neglected and overgrown, it was atmospheric, humming with the sense of somewhere special in the late afternoon sunshine, rife with life. Roses tangled around a slightly decrepit bower, old stock, but strong, the heavy blooms full of fragrance. Wildflowers blossomed everywhere, tangles of forget-me-nots and poppies, stately stands of foxgloves and lupins swaying.

The well in the very centre needed some work, but that looked mainly superficial. It was clearly an old structure, and the fact it still remained intact was a testament to its original builders, whoever they had been. The mouth was wide and the shaft deep. She'd probably need to put in some sort of cover for safety. But there was no smell of stagnation or decay from it and the walls looked sound beneath the moss. She could hear the water, deep down there, hidden in the darkness, and when she leaned over, it glittered with silver light reflected back at her. She added a survey for health and safety to the list.

There were old stone benches, slightly curved, surrounding the well. She couldn't put a date on them. They were plain and simple. Not madly old, but by no means modern. Victorian perhaps, or earlier. For a moment she pictured afternoon tea parties out here as well as wedding photos, maybe something with a Regency theme. Her mind quickly sorted through the best planting to accentuate what was already there, and ways to keep the wildflower paradise that already existed. Sahar was right. This place had all the makings of her dream garden. It wouldn't even take much work to bring it into shape. It was almost all here already. The rest of the grounds were wonderful, but this maze...

A shiver ran down her spine, as if a shadow had passed over the sun.

The sensation of someone watching her was sudden and unexpected. It stole the sense of joy and wonder in an instant. From the corner of her eye she saw... well, nothing, but she had a fleeting sense of movement, of something or someone else. She turned around, staring at the well, but there was nothing there. Her gaze trailed on, seeking out the path through which she had entered. But there was nothing there either. Although... she frowned. Was it further over to the left than it had been?

No, she was imagining things. Had to be.

There was another opening, wider than the one she'd come through. That was all.

A rustling behind her made her spin around again and then freeze. A fox stared at her from the bower, as frozen as she was, its coat a bright red, glossy in the way an urban fox would never be. The sharp, almost delicate, face reminded her of Nora Grainger, and so did the hair colour. The eyes were a deep copper, alight with intelligence. Fur bristled up along the length of its back and then, in a flurry of movement, it was gone.

Megan breathed out slowly. The place was getting to her. Just another fox. The guys on her team said the place was rife with them. She just hoped no one was still defiantly – and illegally – hunting around here. Probably not, given how healthy that particular fox had been. Or was it a vixen? She had no idea.

Grinning to herself, almost amused by her own imagination, she made her way back out of the maze, notes in hand already twice the length as when she went in.

As she came out she heard raised voices and in the car park she saw two figures, clearly having an argument.

One was Alan Brooks and the other was Nora Grainger. Megan recognised Nora instantly, that shock of Titian hair and neat figure. It had been a week since they had met and memory didn't do her justice.

Alan, on the other hand…

He loomed over Nora, all expensive suit and bad attitude.

'I thought we had an agreement, Nora,' he snarled. 'You can't keep blocking progress.'

It was the way Nora flinched back. It set off every alarm bell in Megan's head. That and the way, the moment she tried to step away from him, Alan grabbed her arm to stop her.

Megan set her jaw and marched towards them. She knew better than to confront someone like him. That never ended well. She'd heard tales from too many support groups and her mum was forever relating horror stories about various friends. But there were other ways.

She put on her best happy employee face. 'Miss Grainger, I was wondering if I could have a word? It's about the grounds.'

Nora turned towards her, startled, and Alan just glowered. He didn't let go though. That was a bad sign.

Ignore him, Megan told herself. *Ignore him and focus on Nora*. No confrontation. Just cut him out of the conversation and move on.

'Of… of course.' Nora didn't sound sure. In fact she was pale and a bit shaky. 'I'd be happy to help.'

Megan folded her arms, still smiling, although she was aware the grin had turned a little more fixed. Alan Brooks relented, letting go of Nora's arm and shoving his hands into his trouser pockets like a petulant child.

'Fine. You'd better get on with it then. I'll talk to you later.' He turned without so much as a glance at Megan and stalked away.

Nora wrapped her arms around her chest a bit too tightly and watched him go.

'Are you okay?' Megan asked gently.

Something flickered across Nora's face, something edged with guilt and shame. She steeled herself and tried to force a smile onto her lips. It went no further than that.

'Sure. Sorry about that. We… we have history.'

History. That didn't sound good. So Sahar was right. 'I didn't mean to intrude.'

Still not meeting Megan's gaze, Nora stared past her shoulder, back towards the maze. '*Ancient* history. I've developed better taste since then. We were in school together, can you believe it? And he doesn't—' She stopped herself, guiltily. 'Anyway, what did you need to ask me about?'

There wasn't anything. Not really. But Megan needed to think of something fast because she had just waded into a personal matter where she clearly wasn't wanted.

'Um, I… I wanted to get some dates sorted with you. For the excavations and the… the restoration work. I need to book a surveyor.'

'Of course. I can get you a list of local people, if you want? I'll drop it in tomorrow. Unless you have someone specific you work with. Are you settling in okay? Have you got everything you need?'

'I'm… Sure… Yes. It's all good.' Why was she suddenly completely incoherent? What was she doing? 'You're here tomorrow?'

Wait, now she sounded hopeful, like she wanted Nora to be here. Which… no. That would be far too complicated. She raked her fingers through the close-cropped hair at the back of her head and then pushed the longer top back from her face.

Crap.

'I'm here most days. After work anyway. The library here is my… my passion…' Nora pushed her wire-frame glasses back on her nose and blushed. 'I might be on the board, but first and foremost I'm a librarian.'

Another world from a gardener really. And here Megan had had her pegged as some kind of PR maven, or a society fundraiser. She wasn't even aware librarians could look like that.

She frantically searched through anything she knew about libraries beyond the fact that some of them now had computers. 'Sahar said the collection here is special.'

The mention of the Fairfax library worked like a magic spell. Nora unwound right in front of Megan's eyes. This time the smile was positively beaming.

'Oh it *is*. I can show you if you like. The Fairfax family collected books from all over the world and some really rare printings. We're doing an assessment and some of the collection will have to be housed in—' And then she paused, realised she was getting carried away and blushed again, averting her gaze. Did she always do that? Shy away from the things that gave her joy? 'Sorry.'

Megan shook her head, smiling with unexpected amusement. 'No need. You should hear me when I get started on landscaping.'

The laugh was soft and delicious. It did interesting things in Megan's chest.

Too. Complicated. What was she thinking?

Nora checked her watch and then gave a reluctant sigh. 'I've got to run.'

Where to? Maybe just away.

'Sure. I'll see you tomorrow.'

'It's a date,' Nora said blithely.

Megan watched as she made her way towards the Ford Fiesta.

A date. Did she know how that sounded?

'Oh, I see how it is,' said Sahar from behind her. Megan spun around, instantly defensive.

'Sahar! Stop it.'

Her friend just laughed. 'Not that I blame you. If I was that way inclined I might daydream a little bit in that direction.'

'Don't tell Amir that, you'll give him ideas.'

But Sahar just shook her head. 'Not my man. He's all mine. Are you done objectifying the boss for the day? Fancy dinner?'

Megan couldn't help but blush at the accusation but Sahar just laughed.

'Nora's here a lot. Devoted to her special collection, her library. She lives down in the village and her family have been here forever. Like most of them. Ashleigh hangs onto its people, she told me once. So I guess you'll be seeing a lot of her.'

The teasing tone wasn't helping.

'Sahar… I don't even know that she's…'

'Gay? Interested? On the lookout for a hot gardener? Rumour has it—'

'I don't listen to rumours.'

Sahar, who very much did listen to rumours, just shrugged. 'Well, you'll never know if you don't ask. I can always talk to Hattie. No one knows her better. If I wait until an evening shift she'll have sneaked a couple of gins from the bar and she's well talkative then. She'll tell us all about her, you'll see. She might even put in a good word for you. If you're lucky.'

There was definitely a problem with working alongside your best friend who was devoted to matchmaking in all its forms. And the idea of her quizzing Nora's aunt – or whatever she was – about Nora's love life on Megan's behalf…

'Don't you dare,' she said, which was greeted with a howl of laughter.

But as she turned to follow Sahar back inside, a shiver ran down her spine. The rustle in the undergrowth at the edge of the car park made her look. Another fox?

There was no sign of one this time.

And she still couldn't shake the impression of being watched.

Chapter Three

Saturday 23rd September 1939

Ellie loaded the film into the camera with every care, keeping her fingers at the edge so as not to damage the surface. She snapped the back of the camera in place and opened the curtains a little to peer outside. It was late evening and she had already said goodnight to her father. He sat at his desk in the study, head bent over the papers spread out before him. More dispatches arrived daily as the situation in Europe lurched from bad to worse. The declaration of war had shaken him and now his work was everything. The Ministry needed him, his mind, his intellect, his experience. It consumed him and Ellie didn't like the way his eyes had taken on a strained aspect whenever it was mentioned. Sometimes even when it hadn't been mentioned, when she knew he was dwelling on something he had recently received rather than listening to her or anyone else.

It had shaken them all. Everyone. In the village the old men stood around their gardens and allotments and talked about Hitler and Chamberlain, about Poland and the Czechs, about the trains full of children who had arrived from London with little brown cards hanging from string around their necks. Their wives and daughters gossiped as well, and their sons… well, their sons were gone already. Militia training first, then the call-up.

At Ellie's insistence, a group of evacuees came to the Hall.

'We have to set an example,' she said. Not that her father could have turned them away. But all the same, she had no idea what to do with small children. So they stared at her and she stared at them until Mrs Worth marshalled the servants into action.

Seven of them, none older than ten, thin and grimy, exhausted and afraid. They had looked so lost standing there on the platform of the railway station. The last ones left behind, still waiting to be chosen, abandoned. She couldn't walk away. Getting them out of London was wise, she knew that. And there would surely be more to be billeted in the village. If they had looked terrified when they arrived, that was nothing to their expressions when they saw the Hall. Mary and Sarah had shooed them upstairs, to be scrubbed clean, up to the old nursery and the servants' rooms, far away from his lordship and his household. Which was composed in its entirety of one adult daughter.

'Is she a princess?' one of the little ones whispered a bit too loudly from the staircase. Her voice echoed around the hall. Sarah smiled and shushed her.

'You won't know they're here, Lady Eleanor,' Mary had assured her.

There would be more. Once the bombing started – and everyone agreed it would start – the cities would be targets. Not like in the Great War. This was different. Ellie knew it from the way everyone had jumped into action, the lessons of the Civil War in Spain learned with bitter sacrifice, fire and blood. Blackouts and gas masks, evacuation and emergency drills, militia training and the Women's Voluntary Service.

Daily dispatches came for her father, and frequently reports brought in person by charming clever men with sharp eyes, who changed topics of conversation to something innocuous whenever she stepped into view. When she was younger she had asked her father what he did in London. He had just laughed and said something about serving King and Country in any way necessary. Now she had an idea of what that might entail but didn't dare say it aloud.

Ellie wondered where David was – if he was thinking of her, missing her – and then pushed that thought away. It was too painful. And it really wouldn't help. She was a grown woman. Lollygagging after him would achieve nothing. The RAF needed every pilot they had. Especially ones with the flying hours David already had before joining up.

He couldn't let her know where he had been posted or what he was doing, not even now. That was that.

She hadn't asked too many questions. Not when his papers came in. Not when they said goodbye at the well and he gave her this camera. Not when he promised to come back to her. Not when he wrote to her. She couldn't.

Beyond her window, the grounds of Foxfield Hall lay still and quiet beneath the waxing moon. Equinox night, with the moon high in the sky, not quite the harvest moon, not yet. Everything was right. She checked the flashbulb, securing it in place. She wasn't going to get a lot of chances to do this. Just a few nights. By the time the harvest moon set, it would be too late.

The legend was just too enticing. Despite David's teasing. If she could capture a picture of the Green Lady, a real picture of a real ghost… She needed carefully documented evidence. She knew all about that from university, the cornerstone of her work in Lady Cecelia's College. She took out her notebook and wrote the date at the top of the page. She kept track of everything in here: when the lights first appeared, their number, the legends in differing forms, reports from the staff and locals, all her findings. It always began with the autumnal equinox, when night and day were exactly equal, and finished with the harvest moon, the full moon nearest the equinox. It was the 23rd of September tonight and the moon would be full on the 28th, the day before the Feast of St Michael and the Angels, the Ashleigh Harvest Festival.

David had never believed in the Green Lady, not the way she did. It was the only thing they disagreed on. So he had dared her to find proof. And bought her the camera to do it with. It was all a joke to him. Most things were.

But not to Ellie. It was a purpose. A quest. Something she had to do. She couldn't explain why, not really. She felt so lost, exiled here at Foxfield Hall. Useless.

At university, she'd had a place, a purpose. But with the advent of war, her father had insisted she return home to Foxfield Hall. She didn't know why. Perhaps he was just worried about her, evacuating her in the same way other parents evacuated their children. Only they were sent away from home. She was brought back, wrapped up with mothballs and carefully put away.

And she was no longer a child.

Though the moon would give her some light, she'd bring a flashlight as well just in case. She shouldn't. Not with the blackout rules. But who wanted to stumble around in the depths of the maze? And who would see her light in there? Hopefully the camera flash would help too, but she had only a couple of bulbs so that was a long shot.

She packed everything into her bag – including the ubiquitous gas mask which seemed pointless out here but habits had to be formed – with the notebook and pencil on top, and her copy of *The Weekend Problems Book* just in case she got bored waiting. The Thermos flask Mary had promised her sat on the table in the kitchen below stairs.

There were three buttered scones too. She folded them in a napkin and tucked them into the bag. The elderly housemaid wouldn't be so quick to help if she knew what she was up to. Mary's family had always lived in Ashleigh and she was superstitious to the core. She'd mutter darkly about consorting with devils and give Ellie ferociously disapproving looks. She had been like that for as long as Ellie could remember.

Ellie slipped on the wellington boots by the back door and pulled her coat on for good measure. Better to be safe than sorry.

The night felt warmer than she had anticipated. She made her way quickly and quietly from the confines of Foxfield Hall down to the gardens and into the maze. She had memorised the way through it when she was seven. It was a simple mathematical pattern, after all, and numbers always made sense. The most reliable thing in the world. People rarely understood that.

Ellie knew exactly where she wanted to be. The bower at the centre would hide her, give her shelter, and all she had to do was wait for the ghost to come. She had to come.

She settled the thermometer on the wall surrounding the well, noted the temperature, and, as she withdrew her hand, something caught her eye, inside the well, lodged in the ivy spilling over the top. Ellie peered closer. The moss was thick here, a deep lush green with a million little leaves, soft as fur. The ivy stretched across the mouth of the well, but it wasn't so very thick. Far underneath it, she could see water reflecting the light of the moon. It looked like a long way down, deep, still and dark.

Growing up, she and David had dared each other to climb down the well shaft – when there were no adults around, of course. There were crevices and handholds and it was wide enough for a child. The water at the bottom wasn't that far away, fed by a natural spring and flowing on underground. It was possibly even still drinkable, although she'd never tried. It came up to her knees at the time. It had been clear and fresh, dancing around her, and she had been sure she heard a whisper, a sigh, maybe even a laugh. Childish fantasies, of course. David heard nothing at all and teased her mercilessly. She remembered vividly the time he slipped and fell. It must be fifteen years ago. But David had just bounced back to his feet, soaked in freezing water and laughed. She missed his laugh so much.

The last time she'd heard it was that day when he left for war, the one she still thought of as the last day of summer…

'Catch me a ghost, Ellie,' he'd said, just before he left her. Like yet another dare.

They had always caused such havoc together. Even when apart.

'Promise me you'll write,' she'd told him when he was leaving, his head full of planes and flying, of war and what it might mean, her heart full of dread. And he did. Dutifully, for the past few weeks. She replied every day. But letters were not the same as having her fiancé here. And there were so many details missing. Things he wasn't allowed to say. Like where on earth he was and what he was doing.

She was twenty-four years old. Not a child. Not now. She pushed her misery away, smothering her fear for him now war was upon them, and studied the well again for what had caught her attention. Entwined in the ivy in the mouth of the well, she saw something, pale and slender, lit by moonlight, that did not belong. Someone had tried to throw it down the well, but the ivy had caught it instead. It was a twist of knotted straw, braided and wound in on itself in a shape. Ellie reached in, pulled it clear and then saw another, a different one this time. A distinct pattern. She retrieved it too. Frowning, she grabbed the torch and shone it at the offending articles.

Corn dollies, they called them. Little, local fancies, made since time out of mind for the harvest. Offerings. She'd made them herself as a child, with Mary teaching her the patterns and the stories behind each one, until whichever governess it had been at the time had found her and shrieked about paganism and superstitions. That one hadn't lasted long after that. Mind you, they rarely had, her governesses.

A smile flickered over Ellie's lips, the memories of those golden childhood days like a flame inside her, and she brushed her fingertips over the braided straw. She'd have to show the evacuee children how to make them, or get Mary to. The maid was much more deft with them, well-practised. Had they ever seen such things, the little mites? Perhaps they'd just roll their eyes. What did Ellie know about children?

One of the two figures had a central body and braided wings going out on either side. The maiden, sometimes called the queen. The other looked like he was kneeling, a spiked crown on his uptilted head. He was the champion, the king. Tiny strands had been intricately wound together and tied with slim scarlet ribbons at various points. They were beautiful, delicate little fancies that had been made by an expert hand.

Arthur to your Guinevere…

Something about them, about finding them here and now, stopped the breath in her throat. It might be an ancient tradition but no one had given corn dollies to the well in her lifetime.

Could they be old? But no, how would they have survived out here, exposed to the elements? They looked new. It wasn't unheard of to find ancient things in the grounds. People had always lived in the area. Her own family had held the estate of Foxfield Hall since the Norman conquest. The Fairfaxes were proud of that, justifiably. They even had their own entry in Domesday Book, this land granted to them by royal decree, *Le Blond, Guillaume, called Fairfax*. They had found pottery, and once an old pin that had been whisked off to a museum.

And they had the ghost, the Green Lady. Some said she had been the lady of the manor, long before the Normans came to Britain, long before there was a manor, or even a queen. Some of the locals maintained she was the original Guinevere, King Arthur's wife from myth and legend, but as far as Ellie knew King Arthur had never walked the paths of Ashleigh, and this was no Isle of Avalon.

The moon went behind a thin slip of clouds and the centre of the maze plunged into darkness. It was cold all of a sudden. Terribly cold. The feeling that eyes were watching her from the shadows made her shudder. A strong sense of another presence swept over her, sending ripples of cold down her spine. Her breath misted in front of her face.

Slipping the corn dollies into her pocket, she turned around slowly.

There was no one here. There couldn't be. She was all alone.

You came looking for a ghost, Ellie.

A shape slid through the shadows, vulpine and sleek. A fox, she realised. It stared at her, completely unafraid. She stared back, marvelling at it. A vixen, on the hunt no doubt, and lucky to be here on her land rather than off across the village where the colonel's hounds would tear it apart as soon as look at it.

But it didn't look afraid.

If anything it made her feel like the intruder here in the heart of the maze.

A wave of despair, a strange terror that didn't even feel like her own emotions, swept over her and she froze, shivering. She thought of David, far away, probably being a hero. He had a war to fight. And her greatest fear was that she would lose him to it. That she would never see him again.

Her legs wobbled. She needed to sit down. But she was Lady Eleanor Fairfax. She wasn't going to collapse on the ground and lie there like some silly girl in a Gothic novel either. She could only imagine her grandmother's face.

The ladies of the Fairfax line do not collapse with a fit of the vapours, Eleanor dear. We have standards.

She had to keep on going. What else could she do? Sit down there and cry out like one of those pathetic heroines in the flicks until someone came to her rescue? Not her.

That thought was like a slap to the face. She exhaled, a rush of breath, and the vixen was gone in a flicker of movement so quick she barely caught its going, slipping into the darkness and away. Ellie took a deep breath of the night's air, cold and heavily scented with roses and yew.

Pull yourself together, Ellie. You can't let a fox and a bit of chilly air spook you. You came looking for the ghost, after all. Now get ghost-hunting.

The fear dropped away. With all the dignity she could muster she walked back to the bower, where she carefully arranged herself – in a deliberately non-swooning position, despite the location – and checked her equipment. She was not about to run away. This was her home, her world. She had every right to be here. She took out the camera and set it beside her, before opening the Thermos flask and pouring herself a much needed cup of tea. Tea fixed everything. She took a drink and let the warmth and flavour work its magic. It was strong and sweet, the way she liked it. Not exactly ladylike but, to Ellie, it was nectar. That was better. Much better.

It was a long time since there had been anyone throwing corn dollies into the well. Her grandfather forbade it years ago, and no one dared cross Lord Fairfax. Or maybe they did? She had just found them here, after all. Was someone sneaking around here at night, practising ancient folk traditions? One of the servants, perhaps? Mary had taught Ellie how to make them as a child. Of course the locals still made the trinkets as part of the Harvest Festival, but that was all for show, wasn't it? A fake well trundled out on the village green each year around now, stopping only to have the flaking paint touched up. It had been quite the tourist attraction before the war. But not here, not at the Hall, not for years.

The little fancies she'd found were curious though. Much more intricate and delicate than the ones she knew from the local crafts-women or that she'd made as a child. She was about to dig them out of her pocket and examine them more closely, when her breath misted in front of her face, pluming like she was smoking a cigarette. Around her the temperature plummeted again and she knew – she just knew – that something was about to happen.

There was no sense of terror this time. Only excitement. More than that. Exhilaration.

This was it. This had to be it.

The first light flickered into existence at the entrance to the centre of the maze and drove all thoughts of wells and corn dollies from her mind. Another sprang up by the furthest seat, and then more. Little lights, shining in the darkness. Green and bright in the darkness, will-o'-the-wisps or marsh gas or who knew what? They didn't have glow worms in this area, and it would be late in the season if they did. It didn't matter. They were here and they were real. She knew that now. She took a photograph without the flash, the better to catch them, but she knew even as she did it that she was shaking too much. It would be blurred and useless.

The lights moved slowly closer to the well. They flickered and cast an eerie glow on the grass so that it seemed to twist and move beneath them. Ellie's breath shook as she settled the camera on the seat to make it as steady as possible, waiting. She didn't just want a photograph of the lights. David would come up with some sort of explanation for them. He always did – marsh gas, he'd say, reflections, optical illusions…

She wanted the Green Lady. She could only hope the camera would be powerful enough.

A dark figure burst through the entrance, out of the maze beyond the wall, shooting out of the darkness, moving fast. Much faster than she had anticipated.

Instinct took over. Her hand moved by itself, and the flashbulb went off… too bright, blinding. It bleached the whole area before her, wiping away colour and turning night momentarily to day.

The ghost – no… not a ghost, it couldn't be – the figure gave a cry of alarm and fell back, toppling over the bench and crashing onto the grass in a sprawl of limbs.

Then it cursed. Loudly.

Ghosts shouldn't do that, surely?

A strange, pregnant silence engulfed the heart of the maze.

Abandoning her precious camera, Ellie ran towards the struggling form. It was a boy, she realised in a rush of disappointment, just a lanky boy in some kind of baggy tunic and tight-fitting trousers. He lay there, winded, blinking furiously to regain his vision.

And he had ruined everything. Her rage took her by surprise.

'Who the devil are you? What are you doing in my garden?'

Chapter Four

Monday 23rd September 2019

The bloody draught was back. Megan couldn't seem to get rid of it even though she had checked the windows a dozen times now. Every so often her room just turned freezing. Not wanting to look a gift horse in the mouth was all very well but she had never been good with the cold. Even when the prehistoric radiators whined and clattered into some semblance of life, it only helped a little. And then the draught would stop and the whole place turned into a furnace instead.

'Not the most efficient,' Sahar had said by way of an apology. 'Sure, they modernised the public areas of the hotel, but not the rest. There isn't the budget for it, not yet.'

Not the whole apartment though. Oh no. Just Megan's room.

Still, free accommodation was free accommodation and if she sometimes had to pull on a jumper in the middle of the night so be it. The gardens were what mattered, and the project ahead of her. She had already fallen in love with it. This magical beautiful place, the place she saw in her mind when she closed her eyes.

A phone rang in the living room and Sahar answered, her voice all brisk efficiency which told Megan it was work-related. She had a different voice when it came to the hotel, a professional voice that hardly sounded like her sometimes. Last time they'd had dinner and a night out, Amir said he heard it more these days than her own voice. They had been planning to sit down and have a glass of wine. It was meant to be Sahar's night off. Sahar had recorded a documentary with that archaeologist she loved, Dr Faye... Something. Apparently she was filming a new series not far from Ashleigh and Sahar had been beside herself with excitement as she told Megan all about it. In detail.

She didn't sound so enthusiastic now.

'No, it's fine. Did you check the pipes? What about the tap? No. I'll be right there. Give me five minutes.' Sahar hung up, and swore. 'Megan, there's a problem in the bar. I'll be back as soon as possible, okay? We'll have that glass of wine then.'

'No worries,' she called. 'I'm going for a run first.'

'At this hour? You're a masochist!' Sahar replied, blithely heading off to work while she was off duty. The irony didn't occur to her.

'Takes one to know one,' Megan called after her as the door closed.

The bedroom was still and quiet, a pocket of her world that didn't quite feel like her own just yet. How could it? She had piled up her books on the shelves and covered her bed with the throw she'd bought from the charity shop. Once she would have put up some pictures, family photos, but that just felt weird now.

There was no Happy Families any more. Not for her.

She ought to phone them. Just to check in. But the thought of doing that made her stomach twist like knotted rope.

A run, Megan told herself. She needed the air and the exercise. She needed to blow off some steam, get outdoors. She pulled on her gear and stepped out into the night, closing the doors behind her. The sense of relief closed around her like a shroud with the silence.

It was still warm outside – warmer than her bedroom anyway, which wasn't hard – the air thick like honey, but the moon was missing from the cloudless sky. The stars splashed across the dark canvas of the night, brighter than ever. The double doors from the living room in their apartment opened out onto the back of the hotel, into the soon-to-be kitchen garden, quiet and deserted now. The beds stood like empty shells of what they once were and would be again. Mark and Stefan, two of her gardening team, had been digging them out only today. The function rooms and the bar were all at the other end of the building, but she could hear the noise from the wedding party, drifting through the night. They were taking the word 'party' literally from the sound of it. She put her earbuds in and turned her volume up to drown out the eighties revival going on inside.

Running focused her mind, let her put her thoughts in order. Away from everyone else. And it stopped her dwelling on everything – life, Dad, Mum, missing home. Missing Owen, missing in action. What the hell did that mean anyway? It sounded like they'd just mislaid him. Like they'd just put him down somewhere a moment ago, got distracted and couldn't remember where. But it was a euphemism, wasn't it? For gone without a trace, captured and being slowly tortured to death, or killed immediately, blown to smithereens so small that no one could even identify the pitiful remains.

More thoughts to push away, to smother down deep inside her. More feelings she didn't want, fears she couldn't face, but which she could silence for a while as she ran.

A light breeze sped her on her way, around the grounds of the hotel, past the groves of trees, across the lawns, swinging back along the drive. Sussex was a beautiful part of the world, that was for sure. No bleak and featureless concrete here, no unremarkable roads, identikit houses or tower blocks. This place had been grown from meadows, trees and rolling hills.

She used to run with Owen, when he was at home. They'd get up first thing in the morning and head out together. Owen would have loved it here, Megan was sure of that. She could imagine him, up with the dawn, raring to go and explore the countryside. He'd be at Megan's bedroom door, banging on the wall and jokingly threatening her with a bucket of water. Megan had always been a reluctant early bird, getting up for their early running sessions only because he was so keen. She preferred to train at night. Now it was more than a way to keep fit, or to build up muscle and tone. It was a meditation in movement. It kept her sane.

Sometimes it was as if Owen was with her. As if, if she just turned her head at the right moment, she'd see him again, running beside her with long fluid strides. He'd glance at Megan, and grin, and pull effortlessly ahead just like he always did.

She was almost scared to look. If Owen ran alongside her now, she could be running with a ghost.

Megan jogged on through the gardens, down along by the linked ponds and on towards the maze. The light from the hotel bled out into the dark. It illuminated the well-tended formal gardens outside the function rooms, the roses and the topiary, and beyond that the yews that guarded the maze.

Out here in the night, away from the hotel, the grounds were blissfully empty.

Or at least, they were supposed to be.

As she approached she saw it. A pale green light dancing in the opening of the maze, not quite touching the grass, twisting and flickering like a gas flame no higher than the length of her index finger. It hung in the air, maybe half a foot off the ground, without anything to obviously fuel it. Megan came to a hesitant stop and pulled her earbuds out, leaving them hanging from the collar of her T-shirt.

The air shivered around her and her skin tightened on her bones. Though she should have been warm from running, she felt cold again, as cold as she had in the bedroom. Colder.

There were no unusual sounds. The distant noise of the party was very faint now, quieter than the call of an owl in the woods beyond the maze. She could hear the occasional scuffle of night animals somewhere far away, that fox again perhaps, and the tinny rhythm of the music still playing, rising from the forgotten earbuds. Reaching blindly into her pocket she turned the music off and the deep silence swept over her, cutting her off from the world of men. She was used to traffic, sirens and alarms. She had grown up with the music of the city. Not this multi-layered quiet which, now she really listened to it, wasn't silent at all.

Chirps and sighs, rushes of whispered sound like leaves in the wind, a murmuring she couldn't quite locate or identify – all these noises swirled around her. The ancient yew tree at the southern corner of the maze wall, twice the size of any of the others, creaked and groaned like an animal in pain, a low and rhythmic sound that reached inside her and echoed in her chest.

And still the green light hung incongruously in the mouth of the maze.

Impossible. Undeniable.

Megan crept towards it but as she closed to about six feet, the little flame guttered and went out. There was no sign of anything there. And then further along, inside the maze, another one sprang to life. She followed it, stepping between the walls of dark, fragrant leaves.

The hedges of the maze were about eight or nine feet tall, more than two feet taller than she was and so thick she hadn't been able to see through them in daylight, let alone now.

In the shadows of the maze it was even colder and the moonlight didn't quite reach the ground. There was still a light though, of a sort. As she got near to the second lick of green flame, it vanished just as suddenly. To her left, down the path just before it split either way, another light leaped up, casting an eerie glow for several feet around it.

What was it? Marsh-light? Bioluminescence of some kind?

This time she dug out her phone and tried to take a photo, but the screen wouldn't come on at all.

'Okay,' she whispered, even though it wasn't. Her breath misted in front of her face. She was definitely awake. She was definitely seeing this. Staring at them wasn't going to answer any questions. 'Okay, what do you want? What are you?'

If she was expecting a reply, she didn't get one. Not a verbal one anyway. Which frankly would have scared her to death. It was too much like a horror movie already.

The light pulsed in a slow rhythm, like breath drawn in and out, like a heartbeat. Waiting.

Waiting for her.

Megan burst into a sprint, trying to get there in time, to cover the distance before it vanished, but once again the light flickered out just before she reached it. With a growl of frustration, she turned around and saw the next one, waiting for her.

What else could she do? She followed them, one after the other, deeper and deeper into the maze. The path opened, not overgrown at all as it had been when she'd explored it in daylight, but neatly trimmed. Had she missed this part of the maze? She ran, tearing along the path, dodging her way around each twist and turn, never quite catching up with the lights.

As if she had torn through something, the walls fell away around her and the temperature leaped up again. Megan staggered to a halt, breathing hard. It was warm now and she was burning up. She unzipped her hoodie and looked around, searching for the next weird light.

They were everywhere.

They clustered in the middle of the maze around the well, making its walls glow, illuminating the climbing roses, wildflowers and thick green ivy. The circle of stone seats ringed it and the bower with a swing beneath it she hadn't seen before occupied the northernmost quadrant. The rest of the area was grass, lush and verdant.

It was the heart of the maze as she wanted it to be, as it once might have been. Like a dream, like the sketches she had just packed away back in the apartment at the end of a long day.

There was a full moon overhead. Full and bright, huge in the sky. A moon where there should have been no moon at all.

Little lights spread out around the well, danced on the stone benches, flickering and turning.

Megan stepped into the clearing at the centre of the maze, between the benches, and from the bower there was a brilliant flash of light. Blinded, she stumbled back and crashed into one of the benches, going down in a graceless heap. A voice cried out. She heard the noise of someone running towards her as she struggled to right herself and blink her vision back into action.

Another woman stood over her, her thick brown hair cut into a bob swinging on either side of her narrow face. She looked about Megan's age but that was where the resemblance stopped. She wore an overcoat, covering her from neck to calf, and a pair of green wellington boots. Good ones.

'Who the devil are you?' Her voice carried a clipped, refined accent, like something from an old black and white movie. There was no doubting the anger which shook through her. 'What are you doing in my garden?'

Chapter Five

The maze, at night

For a moment, neither moved. Ellie didn't know what to do, what else to say. She wanted an answer and she really was furious. She had planned this down to the last detail and now this intruder had ruined everything.

'Well?' she prompted again.

'Your garden?' And that was when Ellie realised that it wasn't a boy at all. *She* was a woman, albeit one dressed as a man, with her hair shorn like a boy's. She scrambled back from Ellie and struggled to her feet. 'This isn't *your* garden.' She cursed again as she tried to circle her shoulder to check for injury, words a sailor wouldn't dare use in polite company. Ellie took a step back, suddenly unsure. She didn't think of herself as a prude, but really. This was quite beyond the pale.

'Who are you? What are you doing here?'

'I'm Megan Taylor. And I live here. In the apartment.'

Ellie couldn't help but scoff. 'No you don't.'

But the woman just stared at her like she was the deranged one. 'I'm leading the garden restoration team. For the board.'

'What team? What board?' A gardener? Surely someone would have mentioned a woman working on the grounds, but these were strange times. Ellie knew that. The woman's skin was deeply tanned like the fieldworkers' following harvest. The estate manager hadn't taken anyone else on, not without checking with her father, surely? And the woman didn't sound local. Had she come with the evacuees? Someone fleeing London for the safety of the countryside? But she didn't sound like a Londoner either. At least not one Ellie had ever spoken to.

The strange woman bent forward, calming her breath. Her clothes were excessively tight on her legs, and the tunic or whatever it was hung loose around her torso.

'You shouldn't be here in the gardens at night.' Ellie didn't add 'dressed like that' although she was sorely tempted.

The woman, Megan, fixed her glare on Ellie in return. Her tanned skin made her eyes seem even brighter in the light of the moon. She didn't look that much older than Ellie herself, now Ellie could see her more clearly. Not really. Ellie straightened her shoulders, stiffened her back. She refused to be afraid. This was her home. And she was the daughter of a peer of the realm.

'*Who* are you?' Megan asked again. And she didn't sound angry any more. She sounded bewildered.

Ellie belatedly remembered her manners. She offered her hand, the way her father had always taught her, ready for a firm but ladylike handshake.

Always remember your manners, Ellie, he would say. *It shows people who you are as much as what you say. They'll respect you all the more for it.*

'Lady Eleanor Fairfax,' she said, in as crisp and matter-of-fact voice as she could manage. 'My father is the Earl of Ashleigh, Charles Fairfax. And this is our home.'

The woman shook her hand, her palm and fingers calloused from manual work like those of the men who tended the grounds here. So perhaps she truly was a gardener? If the younger men had been called up – and Ellie knew they had – maybe they had taken her on as casual labour. It was damned unusual though. Ellie narrowed her eyes.

Megan saw her expression and smiled. 'This is a wind-up, is it? Who put you up to it? Sahar?'

Ellie shook her head, bemused by her words. 'No one *put me up to it*. And it isn't a… a wind-up.' Such strange turns of phrase she used. Almost American. 'You should introduce yourself as well, you know? It's only polite.'

But perhaps the woman didn't know that. Her manners were… well…

'I told you – Megan.' Then she sighed, and rolled her eyes to the stars. 'I'm Megan Taylor. And I live here too, for the time being anyway. At the hotel. My friend Sahar is the manageress, so I'm staying in the apartment round the back with her while I work on the gardens. I've never heard of you though, your majesty.'

Oh, how dare she?

'I'm not a member of the royal family,' Ellie snapped, affronted that anyone should insult them so, especially with everything they were going through now to do their duty. The poor King and Queen, and the young Princesses… it broke her heart to see them be so brave. 'There's no one here named Taylor. I make it a point to know the names of people working in the Hall. There's no one called *Sahar*. Our housekeeper is Mrs Worth and my home is nothing so tawdry as a hotel.'

Megan sat down on the bench and rubbed her temples. Part of Ellie wanted to say she should never sit down before invited to do so, but the rest of her told it to be quiet as firmly as possible. The inner voice sounded suspiciously like her grandmother too. She couldn't afford to get offended now, though, or cling to propriety. There was obviously something strange going on. Something to do with the lights. They were still here, dimmer perhaps, but still burning with their eerie glow. Ellie glanced around to see them circling the well now. Almost like dancers. Or guards.

She wanted answers. About them, about the ghost, but mainly now about Megan.

'You see them too then?' Megan asked. She sounded exhausted, shaken. Good. It meant she was human too. And if she saw the lights that meant they were real. And she shared Ellie's reassurance in it. 'Thank Christ for that.'

The Lord's name in vain as well. Scandalous.

'Did you think you were hallucinating?'

Megan shrugged her shoulders and instantly looked embarrassed. 'It seemed the most probable explanation. That I hit my head or was having a particularly vivid dream. Rather than… well, this…'

Ellie took pity on her then and sat down beside her. 'But it isn't. And once you've excluded the impossible… Have you heard of Sherlock Holmes?'

'Yeah, saw the films and everything. Downloaded them.'

'Down-what?'

'Streamed them, you know. Watched online.'

Ellie raised her hands and laughed. It was an unexpected sound, even to her, but goodness, it felt good to do it. 'You're using words that seem to be English but I have no idea what you're saying. Do you mean you saw them at the pictures? You saw the Basil Rathbone flick? The new one?'

'Basil Who?' Megan laughed as well, a soft and gentle sound. 'Wow, you sound like something out of Enid Blyton. Which of the Famous Five are you?'

Ellie didn't laugh. This woman still wasn't making any sense. Maybe she had hit her head after all. 'The famous five what? *The Sign of the Four* is my favourite of Conan Doyle's books. Is that what you mean?'

The laugh came again. She did that when she was nervous, Ellie realised.

'No. Enid Blyton. The Famous Five? The Secret Seven? Mum made me and Owen, my brother, read them all years ago. She kept her copies from when she was a kid. You talk like them, all jolly hockey-sticks, pre-war, you know, all 1930s.'

Ellie's stomach knotted inside her. It wasn't *pre-war*. War had just been declared at the beginning of the month and everything was spiralling out of control. The sense of strangeness swept over her again and her hands shook. She balled them into fists to hide it. Of course she knew the lights weren't natural. She'd been counting on their supernatural nature to call the ghost. But the ghost she was after was not this woman. And Megan… she didn't sound like a ghost. Or look like one. She wasn't transparent and her hand had felt as real as her own. They were hands that worked, laboured. There wasn't a trace of ectoplasm or…

Sometimes the simplest solution was the most effective.

She reached out and pinched Megan's arm, hard, just to be sure.

Megan recoiled from her, a look of appalled shock on her finely sculpted face. The longer hair on top of her head fell over her eyes. She pushed it back, her expression instantly defensive. 'Ow! What was that for?'

'Just checking.'

'What? That I'm *real*?'

Was it really so strange a question?

'Well yes. And I sound *all 1930s*, as you so charmingly put it, because it is 1939. What year do you think it is?'

Megan gave her a look of pure disbelief. 'Well, it isn't 1939, princess, I'll tell you that much.'

'Oh for goodness' sake, I told you, I'm not a princess. My father is…' Ellie said it before she saw the glint in Megan's dark eyes, the look of amusement, and trailed off. Megan was teasing her. There was nothing for it but to resort to the truth. Holmes was always right. When you have eliminated the impossible, whatever remains, however improbable, must be the truth.

'It most certainly *is* 1939. September the twenty-third, 1939. Why don't we start again? Would you like some tea? I've got scones too. Cook made them this afternoon. They're rather good.'

Megan stared at her for a moment, studying her from head to foot in a most impertinent way, and then relented. She shook her head and wrapped her arms around her chest, hugging herself.

'Fine, tea and scones in 1939. Why not? I'm game.'

Ellie headed back towards the bower and Megan followed her, muttering. Things like *batshit*, and other words a lady should not be saying at all. But eventually she calmed herself somewhat.

'What are the lights? And what was that big flash? I thought something had blown up.'

'My camera flash. I thought you were the ghost.' Ellie opened the Thermos flask and poured the tea. Then she held out a scone. A peace offering. Megan stepped into the shade of the bower. She picked up the camera with the other to make room on the seat. As she did so, she examined it carefully.

'This is a camera?'

Ellie almost panicked. If anything happened to the camera— 'Don't drop it!'

The thing cost a small fortune and David had saved up for it. She liked to imagine he had intended it to be an engagement present rather than a going-away present. It was all she had of him.

Megan put it down with surprising care and pulled out something small and slim, no bigger than a notebook, from the pocket of her oversized tunic. A wire came out of it and curled up towards her face but she pulled that free. She pointed it at Ellie, the little circle on the back like a blackbird's eye. Nothing happened and Megan peered at it, disappointed. 'Damn, battery's dead.'

'What's that?'

Megan tucked it away. 'My camera. My phone. It does everything.'

Flicking open *The Weekend Problems Book*, Megan stared at the pages, fanning through them quickly. It was too dark to read properly; Ellie wasn't quite sure what she had been thinking bringing it. A lucky charm perhaps. A totem of normality.

'What's this?' Megan asked.

'They're just puzzles. I like puzzles. The mathematical ones aren't too bad, but there are some logic problems in there which are quite the teasers. It's for fun.'

Megan made a face like Ellie had suggested amputation. 'Fun?' She turned a few more pages. 'What are you, a maths genius or something?'

Ellie fought back a wave of defensiveness and offered her a scone. 'Mathematics makes sense.'

'Not to me it doesn't.' Megan smiled and left the book alone. 'Not beyond measurements and soil volumes anyway.' But as she looked at Ellie's tightened features her expression softened. 'Don't tell me you get grief for that?'

Grief. Yes, that was a word for it. Her father might be indulgent and David was used to her. He even encouraged her. But other people... almost everyone else...

No one here understood a woman with a degree in mathematics. She should have stayed in Oxford. They would have kept her in Lady Cecelia's, surely? She could have taken a job teaching, perhaps. But for *her* to do that? What a scandal that would have been. No. It wasn't possible. Her father needed her. The household would not run itself and now there were evacuees and volunteers and Land Armies...

Except it did. Everything would run perfectly well without her.

They all should be pulling together right now. Ashleigh was fortunate to be a sanctuary, a place of safety and peace. But she couldn't help put her foot in it.

The vicar was the most recent, during the summer, simply because she'd pointed out that his stipend had increased by a far greater percentage than the fund for the parish poor. Maybe she shouldn't have said it right after service, outside the church, but that was when she had heard the figures. Only her father seemed to understand, and even then he had rushed to make peace. That was his nature. David had found it hilarious of course, but then David took nothing seriously and found the good in every situation.

Whereas Ellie... Ellie would always find a problem to be solved.

To solve this one, she'd better get all the information she could and carefully document it. Megan might not be a ghost, but she *was* something that didn't seem to belong here. How could she resist a puzzle like this?

Ellie watched as Megan took one of the scones and bit into it, making a muffled sound of pleasure. 'These scones are good,' she said with her mouth full.

Good Lord, she really did have no manners at all.

And what did it matter? asked a new and unexpected voice in Ellie's mind. Everything in her life was about manners and propriety. Megan was a breath of fresh air.

'What year do you think it is, Megan?' she asked carefully, reaching for her notebook.

But Megan didn't answer. She swallowed hard, staring past Ellie in shock.

Ellie's head snapped around.

Green light spilled from the well, illuminating the flowers and leaves covering it.

It was happening. The very thing she'd come here to capture. And she was going to miss it.

'Oh no!'

She grabbed the camera, tried to get a fresh bulb from the bag, fit it in, and aim it all at once.

All the green lights went out at the same moment.

'What was that?' Megan spluttered. 'The lights… *that* light…'

'The ghost, the spirits. In the stories they're elves, or fairies. Local legends. I wanted to get a picture, to prove it.'

'Fairies? Come on.'

'I wanted a picture of the ghost,' Ellie finished firmly, as if that made it all better and couldn't be argued. Clearly not if the expression on Megan's face was anything to go by. So she rushed on, trying to explain, and making it worse, as she always did. 'I hoped she would appear. The Green Lady. It's good luck to see the lights, but for the next few nights the Green Lady walks here too, right up until the harvest moon. It's a local legend. They say that the lights come out to dance for her, to call her. She's a ghost, an apparition. A repeating phenomenon. There are reports going back hundreds of years. But I wanted evidence. Empirical evidence. I don't know what the lights are. I think… some sort of related paranormal event. Or more ghosts. Just not as defined. Linked to her, somehow.'

Ellie didn't know what she thought. She certainly didn't know how to articulate it. Lord above, she was making a fool of herself yet again. She put the camera down decisively and grabbed her cup, refilling it and drinking. The warm and fragrant liquid helped her jangling nerves and quelled her disappointment.

'You came out here at night ghost-hunting, Lady Eleanor Fairfax?' Megan asked, her voice softer all of a sudden. The way she said her name, the way it flowed from her lips, it sounded so strange. Alien. Ellie frowned. She wasn't mocking her, not really. But then Megan had been right there beside her. She'd seen them too.

'Yes? Why not?' she asked, unexpectedly flustered. Most people dismissed it as a foolish whimsy. Mind you, most people hadn't seen the lights with their own eyes. And in Megan, finally, there was someone who had. This strange woman, like part of another world herself. 'Everyone calls me Ellie.' Well, they didn't, but her father did. And David did. And she was rather tired of '*Lady Eleanor Fairfax*' if she was honest about it.

'Ellie. In September 1939. Wait, that's…' Sudden doubt entered Megan's voice. Not just doubt. Concern. 'That's the beginning of the war, isn't it? World War Two?'

Another shiver of ice trailed down Ellie's spine. World War Two? What did that mean? 'It's… it's just the war. Not the whole world. You see, we had an agreement, a pact, and then they… they invaded Poland… What do you mean?'

But Megan looked suddenly horrified. She chewed on her lower lip.

'I can't… I shouldn't say anything. Should I? Oh crap… Am I going to be able to get home? I mean… I ran in here. Can I—?' Her whole body stiffened with the thought and she got to her feet.

'Wait,' Ellie called. She needed to know more. Where was home? What year did Megan think it was? How had she come here and what was happening to bring the two of them together? What did she mean about a *second* world war?

But Megan looked scared now, a strange expression that didn't belong on her beautiful face. 'I've got to go back. I've got to make sure I can get back.'

'Wait!' She couldn't just go. Not yet. She was almost as great a mystery as the ghost. And mysteries had to be solved. 'Will you come back again? Please? Tomorrow night.'

That grin again. Cynical and just a bit wild, as if everything was a joke. She used it to hide her fear. And Ellie didn't doubt that it was fear. 'If I can't get home it'll be a matter of minutes, won't it?'

Ellie thrust her hand into her pocket and pulled out one of the corn dollies she had found at the well. She'd forgotten about them but now they had a use. A token. A reminder. A way of knowing that this was all real.

'Here, take this. Maybe it'll… I don't know, maybe it'll bring you luck. But please come back. It's a reminder. And proof I'm real. So you'll come back. Please? Try. For science.'

'For science?' Megan took it, distracted, and turned it over in her hand without even looking at it. She stared at Ellie, her eyes so very dark, a strange, elf-like figure herself, her bone structure beneath her skin like a sculpture. The smile flickered over Megan's lips as she seemed to make a decision. 'Well since it's for science. Tomorrow… if I can, Ellie. If it's possible and this isn't all some kind of dream. I'm sorry, but—' She stared at the way back into the maze with such longing, such concern. 'I've got to make sure.'

Of course. What would Ellie do under the circumstances? The same thing. She was such a fool, standing there, holding Megan up. If she was in this situation she'd be running back down the path to the house so quickly…

'Go,' she said. The lights had vanished for tonight anyway and there was no sign of the ghost. And Megan needed to go home, to be sure she could. Or she would never come back. Even if that was possible.

'Tomorrow,' Megan said. Then she turned and sprinted back into the maze. Ellie stared, amazed, until she vanished into the night.

Ellie waited another ten minutes, but Megan didn't come back. Had she hoped she would? Had she hoped she wouldn't be able to get home? That Megan would be stuck here with her? That wasn't fair. Look at the state of the world she lived in now. She wouldn't wish that on anyone.

But still, she waited. Just in case. Clouds passed over the moon and there was no further sign of the lights, and no trace at all of the Green Lady.

No, she wasn't putting in an appearance tonight. Fickle thing. Just the lights. But perhaps she had sent someone else. Another kind of mystery. H.G. Wells would be proud.

As she packed her belongings away and finished the flask of tea, Ellie found herself hoping that Megan really would come back tomorrow. That it was not just this one night, or some kind of cruel joke of fate.

It wasn't like Ellie had a host of companions to choose from. She didn't know what to do with the children. This wasn't a time for visitors or travel. Getting herself into Oxford had been her dream and her triumph, but now she had her degree… was she just expected to

settle down in rural gentility, marry David and produce an heir? It
wasn't fair. And without David here, that was impossible anyway. But
her father had wanted her home, to help him with his work, to help
with the estate and manage the house. That was what he had said. But
now… now there was nothing to do. The war had changed everything.
Megan had called it a 'world war'… like the Great War come again.
Only this time… this time it felt worse…

They'd said on the radio that it could last years.

Years of wasting away in Foxfield Hall, no matter how much she
loved it, did not appeal. Years of waiting for David to come back, or to
hear the very worst. Years of nothing, years of no purpose, years lost.

She'd seen the expression on Megan's face when she realised the
date. She certainly wasn't from the past, or the present… which only
left the future. A future where women cut off their hair and wore men's
clothes, and worked men's jobs and thought nothing of it. Where a
phone or a camera was the size of a pocketbook, and where the thought
of September 1939 filled one with horror.

Or maybe it was just the thought of being lost in time, of being
trapped here in this time… at the start of a second world war.

As Ellie left the maze and turned back towards the dark silhouette
of her house, shrouded and lightless for the blackout, she breathed a
sigh of relief to see it unchanged. Her home, in her own time. However
dark a time that might be.

A flicker in the corner of her eye made her glance back at the maze.
There were no lights now, and the shadows were complete, but she
couldn't shake the lingering feeling that someone was watching her.

Chapter Six

Tuesday 24th September 2019

Running out of the maze took twice the time that running in had. Megan's heart pounded in her chest but she pushed down the fear, the panic. She had to. *Run*, she told herself. *Run and keep running.* There were no lights to guide her this time and she could only pray that she was going home. Part of her mind told her she had to be crazy, that she'd been dreaming or hallucinating or something… anything! That she hadn't just sat and drunk tea with a ghost-hunting woman from the beginning of the Second World War. But she knew that she had. Impossible, improbable, and still true.

She stumbled on a lump in the ground and almost face-planted in the hedge. She got her arms under her just in time, the impact of the ground leaving her gasping, shaking. Hauling herself up again, she forced herself to calm down.

I have to be able to get back. I can't be stuck here.

If she didn't get back, what would her family do? What would they say? First Owen, then her.

Megan pushed herself onwards through the dark. Thick branches whipped across her face and she forced herself through them, into a stretch of pathway as black as night, so horribly overgrown that it was like an obstacle course.

From the shadows behind her, the ones that clung to the roots of the hedges and tangled like smoke in the branches of the yews, she heard a growl. It was distinct and clear, echoing through the night and tightening around her chest. It sounded like a dog, a bloody big one at that.

Megan held still, even though every instinct told her to keep going, to run for her life. She knew that much. Growing up, one of the guys on the estate had kept pit bulls. All the kids knew what to do if one of them got out. Never run from an angry dog. Walk slowly, carefully, don't make eye contact. If you ran they had to chase you. And if they chased you…

Eventually the cops had arrived, charged the guy with something or other, and all the dogs were put down. It was so unfair. It was hardly the dogs' fault, was it?

Megan wasn't feeling quite so charitable just now. She turned slowly, looking for source of the growl.

Something lit up in the undergrowth, green and glowing in the dark. She couldn't see a dog though. Just darkness and eyes. Watching her.

More than one pair.

She remembered the fox she'd seen earlier. But that didn't sound like a fox.

Megan backed away, step by step, praying that she wouldn't hit another root and fall. She felt the hedge behind her and edged along, pushing backwards, searching for a way out.

Suddenly the eyes blinked out, all at once, as if they had never been there. The whisper of the last growl faded.

Behind her the branches gave way and she stumbled back, out into the night, into cool, fresh air. She hadn't realised she'd been holding her breath until she released it and her lungs ached like they'd been stretched out too far. She spun around, and the maze was behind her. She could still feel it there, looming, but up ahead…

There was the floodlit hotel, the former manor house. There was the huge yew tree that formed part of the maze wall by which she had entered, still creaking and swaying. She could even hear the noise of the wedding party going on in the bar, and further off traffic from the distant motorway carrying through the quietness of the night, all sounds that she should have been able to hear inside the maze too, but which had been strangely absent.

Megan's heart gave a leap of relief. She was home. Well… not home, but back. Back where she'd come from. The twenty-first century. Turning around slowly, she examined the entrance to the maze again. It was the same overgrown thing she'd seen during daylight. There were no growling shadows now. No hovering green lights. No Ellie.

A digital bleep made her jump, but it was just her phone, coming back to life. She grabbed it and brought up the screen. It was only a little after twelve, and the signal was strong, the battery fully charged. So why had it died? Why the hell hadn't it worked in there?

In the maze… Had it been real? Really real?

If it *was* real, she'd left Ellie in there with those… growling things, whatever they were. Should she go back? Would Ellie be okay? She took a cautious step into the maze again, but nothing changed. Not a sound out of place. No lights.

Nothing. The music from the hotel carried on. Somewhere far off a truck sounded its horn. High overhead, a plane headed for Gatwick airport.

She had to know. She had to find out.

Slowly, Megan walked back to the centre, taking her time, listening to her breath, her own footsteps, using the phone as a torch to light her way. It didn't die this time. The battery didn't even drop. She pushed her way through overgrown branches and briars, making several more promises to return with the shears as soon as it was light. It had been clear when she ran in after the lights but now… now she could almost believe it was trying to keep her out.

It took an age to reach the middle.

The centre of the maze was deserted. There was no moonlight now. No light at all but what she brought with her. And there was no sign of Ellie either. No sign that anyone had been there in ages, perhaps years.

The air was still and thick with shadows. And different. She ran her hands through the lush foliage. The roses were thick and full-bloomed, heavier than they had been when she last saw them, years of additional growth wreathing them. The bower was decrepit now, groaning under their weight, and probably dangerous but she went in anyway. Megan sat down again, exactly where she had sat with Ellie, and something jabbed her side. Reaching into her pocket, Megan pulled out the little twist of straw and fabric Ellie had given her.

It didn't look like much, but it was real and solid. It fitted right into the hollow of her hand, a line of braided straw with shapes like arms twisted behind its back, spikes forming a crown on its head, little ribbons of red silken fabric at the top and the bottom. A thousand questions leaped to the forefront of her mind. What was it? Where had Ellie got it from? What had happened to her? And all the hows and whys in between—

And the growling…

She'd never been so scared as when she'd heard that. A deep, instinctual terror, something that didn't know reason or logic.

The phone rang, the ringtone jarring in the quiet. She jumped, bit back a cry of alarm and then, embarrassed, scrambled to answer it.

'Where are you?' Sahar's voice sounded worried.

'In the— in the gardens. I told you, I went for a run.'

'I'm finished. I'm telling you, he may be pretty but that Ben can't work out how to button his own shirt, let alone change a keg. I thought we were having a drink. Come back.'

'I'm on the way,' she replied.

There was nothing else to stay here for. Ellie was gone and whatever had brought them together had vanished too. There were no lights now and the breeze had turned cold. Megan tucked the straw figure away safely and picked her way back out of the maze.

*

The next day, Megan studied the faded photograph hanging in an ornate frame. It was halfway up the stairs, in an alcove, mostly hidden from sight. But it had still been dusted and the glass polished at least. Sahar ran a tight ship here. Everything was spotless. It had taken Megan ages to find it, peering at each photo in turn, wandering around like she had nothing better to do.

In the photo, an older, distinguished-looking man and a young woman stood on a flight of stone steps framed by an ornate arched door. It was Ellie, she was sure of it. She was as Megan had seen her, in her twenties and beautiful, but the photo was unable to capture something about her. Her spirit, maybe? She looked so still and quiet. Her build was right, the features close enough and her hair bobbed the same way. She wore a cap and gown, like she was at a graduation. The man beside her, bearded and solemn, had to be her father. You could see the similarities.

'How are you doing up there, Megan?' asked Hattie. 'Did you find it?'

With a sigh, Megan made her way back down to the reception desk, where Hattie was sitting, a pair of knitting needles clacking away in her hands and a mug of coffee in front of her. She'd have a cigarette there too if she could get away with it, but they weren't allowed to smoke in the hotel. They reserved that for the spot by the back door to the kitchen when they thought Sahar wasn't looking.

Sahar had told her about it when she snuck out to find Megan in the gardens and have a sly smoke of her own.

Behind Hattie's seat, shelves held a jumble of ephemera, things that looked antique and quaint, someone's idea of decorating the hotel. Sahar hadn't got around to updating that part of it yet. Perhaps Hattie wouldn't let her.

On the top shelf stood a figure made of straw woven together in intricate twists and knots. It was tied with red ribbons at the wrists and neck. Once they might have been as vibrant and scarlet as blood but time had drained them to a sad pink. The whole thing was covered in dust. It caught Megan's eyes for a moment, and her breath stopped in her throat, though she couldn't say why. There was something horribly familiar about it.

It wasn't the same as the one Ellie had given her last night, the one sitting on the cabinet in her bedroom, daring her to disbelieve its existence. This was far more complex and detailed.

But the idea was the same.

All around it was a small display of hooked hand scythes, some with a serrated edge, others smooth and wicked sharp. Old harvesting tools by the look of it. Very old. Megan recognised some of them and knew she would need to get a closer look at them for her own interest alone.

To the right collector they'd be worth a fortune. She needed to tell Sahar that. Out on display like that they could be stolen. She could imagine Sahar's expression at that. *The old rusty pointy things? Who'd want them?* She'd be surprised.

'Megan?' Hattie prompted, jerking Megan's attention back to her.

'Sorry, yeah, just where you said it was.'

Hattie peered past her, as if she could focus her vision to see that far. Mind you, Megan thought belatedly, she'd probably looked at it enough times. Perhaps she knew the pictures from memory. She had worked here for years, longer than anyone else. And someone had polished the glass and the frame to within an inch of their lives.

'Charles and Eleanor Fairfax. They used to own the place. He did, anyway. The last Earl of Ashleigh. Quite the story there. He lost his wife in childbirth, his son and heir too. It was just him – a high-flying diplomat, or a spy if you listen to some, all up with Churchill and that – and the daughter, but she vanished.'

Ellie had vanished? That didn't sound good. It sounded final. Fatal.

'He never recovered from the shock,' Hattie went on. 'Blamed himself, I reckon. And he died shortly after so the bloodline ended with him. It's an extinct title now. Happened right at the start of the war so no one went off looking for relatives, I suppose, or maybe there were none. The house went to the army for the duration. There are photos of the soldiers stationed here on the walls all along the corridor upstairs. Most of their stuff was cleared out years ago though.'

'What happened to it?'

'Burnt, most of it. Someone's idea of spring cleaning. And it was the war. Who knew why anyone did anything. I don't know. People! His work papers and that went to Kew. The library is still here, locked away. Our Nora looks after it. He loved that library.'

Ellie had vanished. Was that something to do with what had happened last night? It didn't sound good. She needed to find out more.

'Is there a local history collection in the library in Ashleigh?' Megan asked. Maybe she could discover something there. The newspapers of the time must have reported it at least.

'Oh I'm sure there is, my dear. What's that got to do with the gardens though?' Hattie laughed at her, her eyes sparkling with amusement. 'Historian now, are we?'

A flutter of panic felt trapped at the base of Megan's throat. Why did she want to know? It was a good question. 'I'm restoring the grounds but I need to know the history of the place to do it justice.' It definitely wasn't just the curiosity of someone who had seen things she couldn't explain. 'I need to find out all sorts. Like local legends too. Do you know about the Green Lady?'

Hattie blinked, her mouth hanging open a little too long. She covered by raising her mug to her lips and drinking. She sounded more than a little cagey. 'Heard about that one, did you? Yes, I know all about the Green Lady. She's our ghost.'

Our ghost. Ellie had been looking for evidence of a ghost. Before she potentially became one. Megan forced her voice to sound calm. There was no way she was telling anyone the truth. They'd think she was certifiable. And Hattie liked to gossip. Sahar had warned her about that too. It paid to get a heads-up about people like her. They might not mean to cause trouble, but somehow trouble just happened. Come

June it could all be rainbow flags, but the rest of the year… well… Especially in villages in the middle of nowhere.

Megan pasted on her fake smile.

'Haunted hotels do amazing business, you know? I was saying to Sahar, we should get it into the brochure and up on the website.'

Hattie didn't look convinced.

'They tried that in the sixties. All the rage. But not now. Not flashy enough, is it? Ghosts are old news. Not like golf courses.'

So Hattie had thoughts about Alan Brooks' plan for a golf course too. Her voice dripped with her opinion.

'There must be some sort of record. Has no one ever written up local stories?'

Hattie went back to her knitting, sorting out the wool, several different colours, all woven in there, waiting their moment. 'There was a whole book about the Green Lady in the fifties. Ghost-hunters galore down here, all them years ago. Repeating phenomenon, they called it. Still get them from time to time. The kooks rather than the ghost. We've all manner of ghosts. Some people see them in the night, in the gardens, like little lights they are. You ought to ask our Nora about that. She knows all about it. Don't you, love?'

Megan turned, her throat suddenly tight, and there she was.

'About what?' Nora asked. Her long wavy hair, today tied back in a ponytail, shone in the sunlight filtering across the reception from the high windows over the staircase. She wore an elegant pair of trousers and a white blouse, and carried a grey jacket over her arm. It was all very stylish and expensive-looking. Megan, on the other hand, was in a pair of jeans and a T-shirt which had seen better days.

'I didn't know you were here,' Megan replied, and felt her face flush a bit. What a stupid thing to say. Why would she have known Nora was here? Apart from wanting to.

'Oh, I just popped up before work. I'm due down in the village library.'

'You work there too, don't you?' That could be handy, Megan decided. If she could get Nora to help her, she might be able to find out something right away.

'A girl's got to earn a living,' Nora smiled at her. 'The day job, for my sins.'

Sins. What sins could someone like Nora possibly have?

Megan cleared her throat. 'I just wanted to find out about the house, and its history. For research.' That sounded like a plan, anyway. And it was almost true. It just sounded so idiotic when she said it out loud. Hattie's reaction had been bad enough.

'Megan's interested in the Green Lady, Nora,' said Hattie now, right on cue, her tone almost teasing. 'Among other things. History, legends and the like.'

Nora gave the older woman a slight frown which clearly meant more than was apparent, but then transferred her attention to Megan, her expression clearing. 'For marketing? Brilliant idea. People love historic hotels. I'll give you a hand if you want. Bits of the house are Elizabethan, I think. Or Jacobean anyway. There's been a manor here since the Norman invasion, you know? Probably before that too. I mean, not a manor exactly, but a house of some kind. They all lived here, anyone in power in this area. We did a project on it a couple of years ago with the local history group. Actually my dad has loads of research on it. He's really into local history. Never shuts up about it. What period are you looking at, or is it a general overview? I think there are some descriptions and drawings somewhere. I'll dig them out for you.'

Megan tried to hide how much she was enjoying simply looking at Nora as she talked. Her whole face was lit up with enthusiasm for the history of the hotel. But since Nora knew all about it, why not get her help? It could be… nice. Megan didn't have to tell her about last night, did she? Not that anyone would believe her anyway.

If she wasn't covered in bruises she almost wouldn't believe it herself. An image of the corn dolly flashed into her mind. She'd put it on her bedside cabinet last night and stared at it until she fell asleep. That was real.

Hattie was watching them closely, grinning to herself. She looked like a matchmaker. Oh God, had she and Sahar been talking? What were they plotting?

Abruptly Megan realised Nora had stopped talking and was waiting for an answer. Damn, Megan had to look like an idiot, staring at her. Hattie cleared her throat and fussed around with the wool.

And Nora looked… nervous. Her fingers knotted together in front of her.

'Megan was asking about the photograph up there on the stairs?' Hattie provided.

'Um… yeah…' *Damn it, Meg, think of something to say. You have words. Use them.* 'The photo of a man and woman halfway up the stairs. I think they were the last owners. Hattie said the woman disappeared? I wanted to find out about them, about her.'

Nora smiled her brilliant smile and her eyes sparkled. They looked more blue today than hazel, as if their colour shifted with her moods. Could someone's eyes do that? Now Megan thought about it, something else seemed different about Nora today. When they'd spoken in the car park after her run-in with Alan Brooks, Nora had stopped herself from getting too enthusiastic about the Fairfax family, as though she'd been embarrassed. But nothing was stopping her joy today. Megan couldn't quite put her finger on it. But it was… nice, nice to see Nora's passion for the place and the history.

'Oh, you mean Charles and Eleanor Fairfax. Of course you do. Easier to research of course. She's a fixed point, a real person. The rest is a bit…' Nora waggled her hand either way.

'No it isn't,' Hattie said in tones of severe indignation. 'I taught you to have more respect for our past than that, my girl.'

'Oh come on, Hattie, some of it is pure fantasy.'

'Like what?' Megan almost didn't want to say it but she'd gone this far. Nora hadn't run screaming yet. 'I heard there's meant to be a ghost?'

She waited for Nora's expression to fix in that patient, understanding way, or for her to laugh right in Megan's face. But she didn't. If anything her eyes grew even brighter with excitement.

'Loads of them, if you believe the stories.'

Loads of them. Not comforting, not for someone actually living here. But more than she had hoped for.

'Loads of them,' Hattie said and cleared her throat loudly. 'Go on then, Nora love. Tell her all the things you *don't* believe in. I taught her all these stories when she barely came up to my knee. Little slip of a thing, she was. And so lost. I used to look after her when her dad was at work. And now she's been away to university and has all those books at her fingertips, not to mention the internet and whatnot, she doesn't believe the like of me any more. But she's still an Ashleigh girl, so she can't deny them all. Nor forget them.'

'Oh for God's sake, Hattie,' Nora sighed. 'Stop.' She sounded embarrassed. Hattie just grinned at her, in that encouraging way elderly relatives did when they wanted you to perform at family events. Nora looked up at the ceiling, as if silently counting to ten to keep her temper. '*Fine…* we have our own local story about the Green Lady, the ghost.' Hattie made a noise, as if to interrupt, but Nora rushed on. 'That she's the original Queen Guinevere, wife of King Arthur… which is a *complete* nonsense because Guinevere, Arthur and all of that didn't really exist to begin with.'

'King Arthur?' Megan asked, surprised. 'As in the Round Table and the Holy Grail? I thought that was all down in Glastonbury and Cornwall and…' well, she didn't know where else so she just gestured expansively and trailed off.

'Exactly,' Nora said firmly, her point made. 'Thomas Malory has a lot to answer for.'

'*Pfft,*' said Hattie, stabbing her knitting needles together. 'Thomas Malory knew nothing. He picked up all the true threads and wove them along with a pile of *furrin* nonsense into a whole new cloth of lies. Gwynhyfer of Ashleigh is not just a story.'

Furrin? Megan wondered. Hattie's accent wasn't that strong, so maybe this was a local word. It sounded like *foreign*. But King Arthur was British, wasn't he?

'You're impossible,' Nora sighed, though the words were tinged with affection.

'Who's Thomas Malory?' asked Megan, now thoroughly baffled.

'Oh.' Nora turned back to her and bestowed that smile. 'Fifteenth-century writer. Popularised the myth of Arthur, and the Holy Grail, and all that, in *Le Morte d'Arthur*. And besides, Hattie' – that exasperated but fond tone was back again – 'even if Queen Guinevere *did* exist, which is a big *if*, it's just that the name sounds the same.'

'Homophobes,' said Hattie, triumphantly, and Nora gave a small cry of shock and dismay.

The ground seemed to drop out from under Megan's feet and her own breath caught in her throat. She looked at Nora, who was staring at her in horror.

Slowly, Nora's lips managed to move. 'Homo*phones*, Hattie. Things that sound the same. People conflate figures or terms in folklore and history because they sound the same.'

'Oh, you and your big words,' Hattie sighed. She was trying to sound like she was fed up with them, but Megan wasn't entirely buying it. In fact, she wouldn't have been surprised if Hattie knew exactly what she was saying and had done it on purpose. 'You come up with all these words after university. Can't expect me to get them all right. Go on then. Tell us why our Gwyn don't exist.'

Nora gave Megan a strained smile and a look which tried to say sorry. 'If she *did* exist, she can't be the real Guinevere. She's from the wrong period, to start with. She's much earlier. Everyone tries to make links to King Arthur but really—'

'Not *him*,' Hattie interrupted again, still not satisfied. 'He's nothing. She's the important one. She died here. They laid her at the well, bound her there. And all she wants now is to come home. Can't let her though.'

Nora cut in again, seeing the look of unease in Megan's eyes. 'You lay a ghost to stop it haunting your house. It's an old tradition. Like exiling it. Then they grew the maze around it to keep her there, to stop her getting back to the house, I suppose.'

Mazes often had ritual aspects to them, Megan knew that. Was this part of it? Had the Fairfaxes planted the maze to keep a ghost at bay? But when you started to say the ghost of Queen Guinevere… yes, it kind of fell apart on the grounds of believability. But who said local legends had to make sense? Definitely not Hattie, it seemed.

'Time was they dressed the well and kept her happy that way, gave her corn dollies as sacrifices and' – she gave Nora a pointed look – 'treated her with respect.'

'Yes,' Nora replied but this time her smile was fond and indulgent. She was beautiful when she smiled. The nervousness drained away. 'Absolutely. And we still do. All the ghosts. Even if they're fictional.'

All the ghosts. Well, that was comforting, Megan thought. She was living in a house known for *all the ghosts.* Then she thought of the growls and the creatures in the hedges and she shuddered. Not comforting at all. She needed to think. Ellie had been looking for one ghost in particular.

'So the Green Lady is the ghost in the well? Guinevere? Or Gwyn… Gwynhy…' She stumbled over the unfamiliar syllables.

'Gwynhyfer.' Nora said the name so it sounded like 'Guinevere' but with a softer accent. 'Yes. So the legend goes. Stories about her go back hundreds of years. Maybe thousands.'

Yes, because Ellie knew all about her when I met her last night. But again, that wasn't something Megan could say. Not and keep the appearance of sanity anyway. And she really didn't want Nora to look at her like she was crazy. Well, she didn't want anyone to think she was crazy but… somehow it mattered more with Nora.

'Is there a book or something about Gwynhyfer, about the Green Lady? I thought, maybe, the local library, that you might be able to show me—'

'Sure.' It was like being pounced on by a puppy. 'We've books. And there are websites. And loads of conspiracy theories. Oh, you wait until you see the conspiracy theories.' Nora's eyes sparkled, hazel again now. It had to be a trick of the light, the way the colour changed.

'Come down to the library with me. I'll show you. There are even some conspiracy theories on what happened to Eleanor, but not a lot of facts, I'm afraid. What with the war, everyone had a lot of other things on their minds. And her dad died so they stopped looking for her really. Her fiancé came back after the war and tried to find out what happened. But he never found anything.'

'Ah, poor David,' Hattie sighed, in a way that wasn't entirely sympathetic. 'He had a bad war, that one. Never recovered.'

For a moment Nora's expression hardened. She'd make a terrible poker player. Every emotion played out on her features. 'I guess. He was my great-grandfather, Megan. He left Ashleigh afterwards, and never came back. Most people end up coming back but not him. I think he had PTSD. His wife left him, and Granddad was raised by his – David's – parents.'

'He never got over losing young Eleanor, I heard,' said Hattie, and started to knit again. 'She was a light in this world. And without her he was lost.'

'Maybe,' Nora replied but she didn't sound convinced. 'The men in my family have never had a scrap of luck. Neither have the women for that matter. The few of us there are.'

'Your family has always run to boys,' Hattie replied. 'That's what makes you special, my pet.' Her knitting needles started to clack away again. Megan felt like they had just been dismissed but was ready to take advantage of that.

The library in Ashleigh. Well, it wasn't far. She could call it research and the guys could work away on the grounds without her for the morning.

'I'll meet you at the library,' she said and Nora beamed at her as if she had promised something else. It made her feel unaccountably warm, and not in a bad way, if she was honest. Nora was a beautiful distraction. But Megan couldn't get Ellie out of her mind. A young woman had vanished without trace in 1939 and, despite the warm glow she still basked in from Nora's smile, Megan couldn't shake a feeling that she needed to do something – anything – to somehow find her.

Chapter Seven

Tuesday 24th September 2019

The drive to the village took Megan along the winding narrow roads. A thin path clung to the verge some of the way but the rest was ditches and thick, ancient hedging. She wouldn't fancy trying to walk it. Gates dotted the other edge, leading to fields and farms, the occasional house. There were probably paths across the fields, of course. That was the way things were done around here, wasn't it? Or had been. There were still rights of way and such, no matter how hard landowners tried to shut them down. Megan wound down the windows for air. She still couldn't get used to the noises here – the quiet that wasn't actually quiet, the distant calls of birds, the cows, farm machinery at work. She was a city girl at heart and always would be. It was different from the quiet she had heard last night though, that deep, expectant silence with swallowed-up sounds.

And the growls.

She shook that memory off deliberately.

The village of Ashleigh nestled in a valley, cut by a river and focused almost entirely on the double-arched stone bridge in the middle and the grey Norman church with a squat tower. Ashleigh Park School was on the far side of the bridge, another half hour's walk uphill again, sheltered from view by the huge elm trees bordering its grounds. Once upon a time it had been another stately home. Houses in the village looked like cottages but had been extended to within an inch of their lives. It was a prosperous place and the wealthy gravitated here. There was a pub, a farm foods shop, as well as a small supermarket, a couple of craft shops and a coffee shop which closed down except for the summer months.

The library stood on the corner on the far side of the bridge, next to the green. Megan had never imagined she would live anywhere with a village green, not even temporarily. An abandoned patch of wasteland where teenagers drank cider and set things on fire, sure. But not an honest-to-God village green. She was willing to bet they had a maypole stashed around here somewhere, and a feral pack of morris dancers roaming the fields.

There was a lot of activity on the green at the moment, all the way up to the church, as the village began to arrange some sort of fête. The lads in her crew had been talking about it earlier but the problem was they all took it for granted that everyone knew everything about it so hadn't gone into details. Megan didn't have a clue and now wished she had asked. But whatever it was, there were stacks of decorations, a row of stalls being constructed and tents being carted around. It had to be happening soon.

Megan parked by the river, wedging the Landie into the space and locking it behind her. She was ready to cross the road at the bridge when someone called her name.

Nora stood on the other side, waving enthusiastically. She had given Megan directions to the best parking place and driven down in her own car.

Megan waved back, then felt like a fool and thrust her hands into her coat pockets. It was the heavy-duty one she wore for work. It probably had mud all over it. She had been elated at the thought of spending some more time with Nora, especially away from Hattie and her knowing looks. But that had been before she'd had some time alone to think about what she was doing. Now she was nervous all over again.

The library was a small, ornate building in the middle of the village. Megan had never encountered a public library with a garden before. Usually they were grey concrete, hidden behind railings, often with bars on the windows as well. Not this one. On either side of the path, box hedging wound its way around a flurry of wildflowers – cornflower, mallow, poppies, meadowsweet, ox-eye daisy, campion, and yarrow. Megan paused, admiring the contrast of the riotous blossoms, all designed to attract bees and butterflies, and the formal lines of the box hedging, hemming them in, and containing them. The gravel beneath gave another layer of contrast; the hard stone, the restraining hedging and then an explosion of unfettered life and colour.

The library and its beautifully kept garden sat in sunlight, picking out little decorative effects over the double oak doors in the way the red bricks were arranged and shining green woodwork around the multi-paned windows. Nora sauntered in like she owned the place, waving to the woman behind the counter. She made a beeline for a bay of shelves marked 'Local history' and without a moment's hesitation pulled out a slim paperback and handed it to Megan.

The words *Mysteries of Ashleigh* were emblazoned across the cover, over a black and white picture of the Hall looking rather more rundown and ramshackle than it did now. Another joined it, an older hardback with a green-grey cover. Megan squinted at the spine to find the title: *The Green Lady of Foxfield*.

'We'll have to ask Marjorie for access to the local history files. She isn't here today so I'll make an appointment for you. But these are a start.'

The study area upstairs was deserted so they took their seats beside each other and Nora opened another book – a big coffee-table tome with glossy pages and colour illustrations. The figure of a lady in a flowing green robe dominated the centre of the two pages, and behind her Megan could see the well from the centre of a maze.

'*Sighted over the centuries in the vicinity of the well, the Green Lady appears only under a harvest moon. Legend says she is making her way back to the Hall, but can only go as far as the length of a cockstride each night,*' Megan read out loud and looked up to find Nora staring at her. 'Dare I ask what a cockstride is?'

Nora held two fingers about six inches apart and giggled. 'Traditional spectral unit of measurement. I have no idea why. But a bound ghost can only move that far.'

Nothing about time travel or 1939, nothing about Ellie. Megan couldn't ask about that. Not without looking demented. 'When's the harvest moon?'

'It's the full moon nearest to the autumnal equinox, which was yesterday.'

Looking at Nora here, in the library, the way she seemed so comfortable and at home, the way she could find everything she wanted with a wave of her fingertips, was like looking at some wild creature in its natural habitat. It was beautiful. She was beautiful.

Megan sucked in a breath. Nope. Couldn't go there. Not here, not now. She had enough to think about with work, enough emotional turmoil with her family. She couldn't drag poor Nora into all of that.

Not to mention, as one of the trustees, the woman was technically her boss.

Nora tutted as she put down some kind of almanac. 'But the harvest moon was the thirteenth, so according to tradition the Green Lady won't appear this year. She only walks after the equinox and before the harvest moon. That isn't possible this year. The harvest moon came first.'

Megan frowned. 'I don't get it.' But maybe that was what happened when you were trusting to old legends. She had to be missing something.

Nora met her gaze reassuringly. 'That's just the way it goes some years. The harvest moon is the one closest to the equinox. It used to be celebrated with a festival. Ashleigh still has a Harvest Fête at Michaelmas. They set it up on the village green and there's food and music and stuff. It's actually kind of fun.'

A fête. That's what they'd been setting up on the green. It should have sounded naff, but not the way Nora talked about it. 'What's Michaelmas?'

'The Mass of St Michael and all the Angels. For the archangel Michael, God's champion, who defeated Satan and all that? It's this Sunday.'

'That sounds… a lot less pagan.'

Nora snorted out a laugh, something which she even managed to make sound attractive. 'You'd be surprised. The fête here runs in the days up to Michaelmas and they bundled the old Harvest Festival into it. A way to keep the pagan traditions alive, even under the guise of Christianity. Scratch the surface around here and you'll always find something older.'

They fell silent again, studying the books once more.

'What about this one?' Nora asked, flicking open the hardback. Its pages were heavy and dusty, but Nora didn't care. 'There are a lot of theories about the Green Lady here. Even the wilder ones. Hattie loves the Guinevere story.'

'Is she your relative?'

'*Guinevere?*' Nora exclaimed and then realised her mistake and laughed out loud. 'Oh she'd love that, Hattie would. No, you meant Hattie, didn't you? We're not actually related, but we might as well be. She's an old family friend. She wasn't joking about raising me. My mum died when I was four. My dad didn't handle it well. Like I said, the men in my family have no luck.' It sounded like it. 'So Hattie was always around. I owe her so much. I just wish she wouldn't treat me like a child though.'

'Families are like that, I guess. You're always the child.'

'I suppose so.' Nora shifted awkwardly and stared back at the book to avoid meeting Megan's gaze. 'Here's something about Eleanor…'

Megan took the book from her and scanned the other page she'd opened, nearer to the back. There was a grainy print of a picture, even less recognisable as the girl she had met last night than the photo on the staircase. She looked younger too, an earlier picture.

Eleanor Fairfax, she read, *the daughter of the Earl of Ashleigh, Charles Fairfax, vanished during the Ashleigh Harvest Festival on the 28th of September 1939. Despite an exhaustive search of the area, Eleanor was never found. In the years that followed various sightings of her were reported, from London to Edinburgh, but nothing was ever confirmed. With the escalation of the Second World War and the death of her father, her case was quietly shelved.*

'Not much,' Megan sighed, unable to hide her disappointment.

'It was written about twenty years later,' Nora replied. 'The newspaper reports of the time would have more. Try the other one. It's newer. A bit on the whack-job side when it comes to the older legends though. Fully buys into the Guinevere-was-a-local-girl-made-good thing. It's a modern book, so you can borrow it if you want.'

'I'm not a member.'

Nora played with the chain of her necklace, a fine length of silver, the pendant of which hid down inside the front of her shirt. Megan's gaze lingered there and she felt her skin heat with embarrassment. She was staring and she shouldn't be. She knew that. She had to drag her attention away. Luckily, Nora didn't seem to notice. She was still smiling at Megan, leaning in towards her.

'We'll make you one, get you a library card. All you need is something with your address on it. That can't be too hard. Hotel stationery maybe? We can probably find a copy of your contract?'

Megan couldn't help but laugh but, before she could reply, a voice called Nora's name from the other end of the study area. The librarian beckoned to her.

'Oh no. Look, I'd better go. She needs me down on the desk.'

'I forgot you're working today. Sorry.'

'Yeah. And I should get back to it.' She gathered together her things as if reluctant to leave and got up, her long ponytail swishing over her shoulder. 'Here.'

She pushed a sheet of paper at Megan, torn out of the notebook she had just shoved into her bag. It had notes about the house, dates, references, newspaper names, book titles, all that she had been scribbling down while Megan had been reading.

'Come and talk to me at the desk? We'll get your membership sorted.'

'I don't have anything with the address.'

Nora shrugged. 'I know where you live, remember?'

She flashed that brilliant smile again and left Megan to sit there alone.

Megan watched her retreating, then shook herself and glanced down at the paper again. A smile crept over her face. Because it wasn't just a sheet of paper.

It was a sheet of paper with Nora's mobile number written in elegant, looping handwriting across the top.

She folded it up carefully and tucked it away safe and sound in her jacket pocket like a sacred relic. A hum escaped her lips as she gathered her belongings together. Then she headed down to the desk to talk to a librarian about membership.

Chapter Eight

Sunday 24th September 1939

The Church of St Michael's in Ashleigh was already beautifully decked for the Harvest Festival. The vicar wasn't looking too happy about the numbers this morning, Ellie thought, but she liked it quiet. Her father had been distracted all morning, his mood sombre.

It was no wonder either. The wireless this morning had reported that Warsaw was under continuous air bombardment. Thousands were dead. The Poles could not hope to hold out any longer. And no one was doing anything.

'Hitler's on his way here next, isn't he?' said Agatha Brooks from their family pew behind Ellie's. 'It's only a matter of time. The French won't stop him.'

'Oh hush, Aggie,' her husband snapped. 'That's the sort of foolish talk we don't need.'

Ellie noticed her father kept his gaze fixed on the pulpit ahead of them, his mouth a thin, hard line.

Bloody Agatha. A busybody and a bully all her life. Marriage hadn't improved her. She was so sour about everything.

After the service, they would normally linger and talk to their neighbours, but today her father made straight for the car, his mood withdrawn. He didn't even stop for the Graingers and Ellie had to throw a quick apology to them and hope for the best. As he passed beneath the shadow of the memorial to the Great War, she was certain his shoulders tightened and his pace sped up.

She had wondered about telling him what had happened last night, had been looking for the right moment, the right way to explain. But back at the Hall he went straight into his study and shut the door.

So that was how he was going to be today, was it? She didn't like it but what could she do? She went to talk to Cook about lunch, pushing Megan and the maze out of her thoughts.

However, less than an hour later she heard another car outside and then Sarah came into the morning room to say her father wished to speak to her. The door to the study was still firmly closed, so she knocked.

'Come in, Eleanor,' he called, his voice softer than usual. He didn't sound well. Just tiredness and stress, she thought. Perhaps the cough was back. She didn't know but it was always a worry. She'd have to ask him to see the doctor again and she could imagine the expression on his face. Honestly, it was like dealing with a small child sometimes.

He'd spoken in the past of the Great War, of all the young men going off to die, of the trenches, the mud, and the gas. But he had stopped mentioning it at all in the last few months. The pain, the horror, the grief were becoming real for him all over again, she knew that. She could see the ghosts haunting his eyes. She'd watched him on that terrible morning when war was declared, when they'd turned off the radio, unable to speak for the numb shock settling around them. He had taken up his newspaper and stared at the pages, turning them so slowly, without reading a single thing. His gaze had been fixed on something else, something from twenty-odd years ago, phantoms and memories. He knew, from recalling the past, what was coming. *It will be worse*, he had muttered, just once. So much worse this time. It wouldn't just be the soldiers. It would be everyone.

Ellie thought of David, of her handsome pilot, her oldest friend, and she closed her eyes, forcing her racing heart to calm. *The Second World War*, Megan had said in the maze. The woman from another time had looked stricken at the thought of what might lie ahead.

It wasn't possible, couldn't be possible. But Ellie still had the corn dolly, and that was real. The events of last night had to have happened. The very existence of the corn dolly proved it. Megan simply had to be real as well.

Unless she had dreamed it all.

No. She couldn't dwell on that. It was real and that was that. She needed to be strong for her father. There was work to be done here, important work, and even if she wasn't allowed to know the details of it she was going to help him. That was that.

She entered the study ready to offer her assistance, but a woman was sitting in the armchair, a woman Ellie didn't know. She could see she was tall, even when seated, and unusually thin, almost as if she had been stretched too far. Her skin was porcelain pale, and her dark hair drawn back into a tight bun. Her eyes, when she turned them on Ellie, were so piercing that she couldn't manage to see what colour they were.

'This is Miss Ava Seaborne,' Ellie's father announced. 'She's been appointed as my new secretary. She'll manage my affairs here while I'm away.'

Ellie's spine stiffened to a steel bar. What was he doing? She could look after his business matters herself. And he knew it.

'Won't Hartley be managing the estate?'

'Naturally. And Mrs Worth will manage the house itself and your evacuees.'

Your evacuees. Of course. She knew what he thought. *You brought them here, Ellie. They're your responsibility.* As if they were stray puppies or something. As if she was a frivolous child who didn't think things through. And even so, Mrs Worth was in charge of them. Which left Ellie where, exactly?

'I see,' she said, even though she really didn't.

'Miss Seaborne is here to look after everything else. My work, my correspondence, my papers, and you, Eleanor.' The tone in her father's voice when he said her name was a warning. 'To act as a companion for you.' He smiled at the strange woman. 'Alone in the house, my daughter can be inclined to mischief. Bright girls often are, I believe.'

'What sort of mischief?' Ellie asked, outraged.

'Wandering about at night during blackout, for example?'

Ellie bit back a reply before she incriminated herself. She didn't know what to say. He couldn't be doing this to her. She was a grown woman, and she had thought she had finally earned some measure of trust, that while he was away he would rely on her back here. But of course he was sidestepping her again. Remembering her manners, she glanced at his new secretary and nodded in a curt greeting. 'Miss Seaborne.'

A smile lifted the corners of Miss Seaborne's mouth, but didn't reach her eyes – a strange dark green, Ellie now realised. 'Lady Eleanor. How lovely to make your acquaintance. I'm looking forward to our time together. I trust you are as well.'

Ellie desperately tried to school her expression but was aware from the gleam in the secretary's eyes that she had failed. 'Quite well, Miss Seaborne. Thank you.'

The woman smiled again, the same calculating smile. The itch in the small of Ellie's back increased as she became uncomfortable. It always did when anyone studied her that closely. She hated it. Like she was being judged.

'I'm sure Lady Eleanor has many skills, your lordship,' Miss Seaborne said. 'She has already achieved an undergraduate degree from Lady Cecelia's, I believe.'

And I should have stayed there, Ellie thought, fierce with defiance. *I was fine in Oxford. I would have been safe.*

Her father made a harrumphing noise, refusing to meet her glare. 'A women's college, but yes. In mathematics. She performed well.'

Performed well. A *first.* Ellie squirmed in frustration. He would never be satisfied. If only she had been a son. If only her little brother had lived. Her father was fond of her, of course, she knew that. But… no son, no heir. When she married David and produced an heir, then perhaps, but until then she was only a woman. Not even that – she was only ever going to be his little girl.

Miss Seaborne cleared her throat softly.

'Do you speak many languages, Eleanor? *Français? Italiano? Deutsch?*'

Ellie bristled at the patronising tone of her question, but all the same couldn't help but answer. It was as if she was compelled to show off to this woman. Her father had always insisted on a high standard of education from her governesses, before she'd gone away to university, and more than one had said she had a mynah bird's ear.

'Yes, of course. Although, I find German harsh on the ear, especially compared to the Latinate languages.'

Miss Seaborne smiled, clearly amused. 'That depends on the speaker, my dear. It can be poetry. English and German are intimately acquainted.'

'That's hardly patriotic right at the moment, is it?'

But Miss Seaborne just laughed. 'It's more important than ever to know what our foes are saying, isn't that so, my lord? That's how we will win this war.'

Her father said nothing, but nodded curtly. Something passed between them, Ellie was sure of it. And she didn't know how to read it at all. It felt like this was some kind of test he had hoped she would pass.

'Have you studied Old English?' Miss Seaborne asked her.

Ellie shifted uneasily from foot to foot. 'My last governess felt it wasn't becoming of a lady.'

She remembered her last governess, the one she'd had when she was thirteen, had said all sorts of disparaging things about the language of the Anglo-Saxons. And then, when Father had fired her, she had used many words from that very language. All the forbidden ones. But Ellie wasn't meant to know about that, so she pretended she didn't. Cook said the woman had been drinking. Mary said Ellie wasn't to mind that, but she'd heard her maid and Cook laughing about it later on.

Her father had employed private tutors after that.

Miss Seaborne glanced knowingly at Ellie's father, who was suppressing an unexpected smile of his own. 'And yet?'

'And yet somehow she manages to recite *Beowulf* from memory. And *Le Morte d'Arthur*. When that fellow in Winchester found the manuscript I thought she was going to march in and demand to see it herself.'

Ellie winced. She hadn't been that bad. Her father loved to tell tales like that.

Miss Seaborne laughed but there was a gleam in her eye. If she decided to march in and demand to see something, Ellie was pretty sure she'd get to see it too. 'But your true calling lies in mathematics and the sciences, is that not so?'

Here it came. Ladies shouldn't be bothered with such things. They were the preserve of men. Whether Ellie had a natural affinity or not. Why would she need to learn mathematics beyond the keeping of household accounts? It was really far too much. The one thing she really took delight in apart from history, and everyone seemed intent on taking it from her. She had been special at Lady Cecelia's. She should have stayed there.

'Miss Seaborne, with all due respect—' she began, trying not to be hesitant, but still, she knew before she even finished the woman's name that she sounded terrified. If another woman was to try to take control of her mind and interests yet again, to dictate what she was and was not to study, *now*, as an adult, she was certain she would have a fit.

Seaborne cut her off before she could finish. 'I feel that young ladies of today need to be fully versed in as many aspects of the sciences and modern mathematics as they can, don't you? I believe you studied with Emma Talbot at Oxford? She had many wonderful things to say about you. Very complimentary. It would appear that there are paths opening in this war to people like you, Lady Eleanor, many ways to be of service. Perhaps we should examine some of them.'

Too stunned to reply, Ellie could only stare. 'Yes, Miss Seaborne,' she whispered, unsure of her voice. Where was this going?

'Are you fond of puzzles, Lady Eleanor?'

'Yes. I especially like the crossword in *The Times*.'

'Then, I think we shall get along famously. Perhaps I could see my room now, your lordship?'

'Of course.' He rang for the butler and gave his instructions in the same clear and succinct tones he always used. Ellie waited until the door was firmly closed behind the new secretary.

'Where did you find her?'

Her father patted her head and laughed. 'She works for me. Although sometimes I wonder if she is aware of that. I need someone here and the Ministry approved her. She has had security-related roles in the past and came highly recommended.'

'Am I not too old for a guardian, Father?'

'Not when you pout like that. Do as she says, Eleanor. That's all I ask. I don't know what's coming. No one does. There are people in this world who may try to threaten you, or hurt you, to use you against me. Miss Seaborne will not let anything happen to you. With David and myself away…'

'Where will you be?'

'London first.' They were expecting bombs to fall on the capital any day now. The terrible pall of dread hung over the city. That was why the evacuees were here. And why her father could not take her with him. She knew better than to ask. 'And then… I can't really say. You understand how it is. We're at war and our country needs me.'

She knew the tone, that look. It was his duty. And they both knew all about that.

God, King, Country, their people on the estate and in Ashleigh beyond – that was who they were here to guard and guide, to serve in their own way. That was what their position meant to them. It always had.

There was nothing she could do. Her father expected to be obeyed in all things. He always had.

'Of course,' Ellie said as calmly as she could. 'Will you write, if you can?' She prattled on, because she knew that the last thing he needed to be worrying about was the feelings of his spoiled daughter at home.

She thought of Megan, alone, independent. She didn't seem to need anyone else. Ellie just had to be the same. Strong. And hope that someday soon this would all be an unhappy memory.

Chapter Nine

Tuesday 24th September 2019

Megan walked back to the Landie, her mind filled with the things she had read about Ellie at the library, the parts of it that weren't running through memories of Nora. And perhaps the odd fantasy or two. Once she got to the hotel and finished a day's work at her actual job, she was going to see what she could find online, trawl through the newspaper reports and a couple of sites she'd found referenced in the books. She had also checked Nora's number a couple of times to make sure it was still there, and that it hadn't mysteriously vanished or something. Back in the car, she put it into her phone just in case anything happened to the piece of paper.

Her eyes fell on the book she had borrowed, sitting on the passenger seat. *Mysteries of Ashleigh*.

Ellie had vanished on the 28th of September, 1939. And last night, when they were talking, she'd said it was September 1939, but the 23rd. So she hadn't vanished yet.

Megan tripped over the thought. Of course she had *already* vanished. The past was the past. But in her time, in Ellie's time… it clearly hadn't happened yet. There were five days to go. What had happened to her? Young women vanished, sure, and that usually meant something terrible. She was sure that was as true then as it was now.

Megan knew about missing persons. Owen had vanished but her family still held out hope. That dreadful burden of hope. She did as well, of course. But it wasn't the same kind of blind belief, the way her mother's eyes shone like broken glass catching headlights when the ghost of his presence slid by them.

Megan preferred to think of herself as a pragmatist. There hadn't been a concrete trace of her brother since that last deployment. At least not one the army was willing to share with the family. Not on or off the record. Whether Owen had been somewhere he wasn't meant to be, doing something they didn't want to admit to him doing, or simply in the wrong place at the wrong time… Megan didn't know. He wasn't AWOL. They hadn't declared him dead. It was like trying to prise information out of a stone. He was just gone. Operational security meant they weren't allowed to reveal anything else. That was what they'd said at the last meeting. So somewhere in Afghanistan, where the British army wasn't even meant to be any more, Owen was missing.

Megan fought to thrust down the knot in her throat, her heart thudding beneath it, tried to make herself breathe. Every time she thought about him she could feel a panic attack building, the inability to breathe, the sensation that her heart was about to explode in her chest and shatter her from the inside out.

And still Mum and Dad went on – *when Owen gets back*, *when they find him*, *when he's home again…*

Megan balled her hands into fists so tight they ached. She needed to focus on Ellie. That was what mattered now, something she could do something about. She could warn her.

Except she couldn't, could she? It had happened eighty years ago. Ellie was dead. Even in the natural order of things Ellie would be dead. Or the proud recipient of a one-hundredth-birthday telegram from the Queen.

Maybe Megan could only find out what happened. Murder? No one had ever been caught. Abduction? Wouldn't that end up with murder anyway, if Ellie was never found? Ultimately, after many things potentially worse. Megan shuddered and pushed that thought away. She didn't want to think of Ellie dead, let alone raped and murdered, any more than she wanted to think about Owen dying in a cave somewhere. Could it have been a kidnapping gone wrong? Her father was a lord or whatever, a bigwig in London society and politics. He was important. All up in the war planning. Ellie had no reason to run away, not from the life she must have led. The Second World War engulfed the world she had vanished from. So everyone had other things to worry about, Megan guessed.

Bit like Owen.

The more Megan thought about it, the more it didn't make sense. No body, no trace, no hint of a trail.

Like Ellie had vanished into thin air.

Like magic.

And if Megan went to the maze tonight, would Ellie be there? Could she warn her? *Should* she? She'd seen enough sci-fi to know about the things that could happen if you messed with the past.

But how could she keep herself from saying anything?

No, she had to. She had to try and warn Ellie. If she was there.

Damn it, she *had* to be there.

Megan started the engine, shoved the Landie into gear, and drove back with a purpose, head down, teeth gritted.

Another wedding party had arrived, filling the reception, the bar and the sunny beer garden outside. The bride and groom posed for photos, ushered around by a local photographer who knew all the best and most romantic spots. One day that would mean the maze and the well too. If Megan did her job right. Apart from the odd smoker, they'd all be back inside by eight p.m. once the dinner finished and they got down to the serious business of drinking and dancing.

Megan skirted around to the back door and into the apartment. It was just gone three. She had lingered longer at the library than she had meant to, both researching the ghost, trying to find out more about Eleanor Fairfax and spending a not-insignificant amount of time imagining her next conversation with Nora. She needed to catch up on her own work and plans for the garden. Sahar would be busy with the wedding party. And by the time it got dark she could go into the maze alone.

If it worked for a second night. If it had really been real. And if Ellie was there.

God, she couldn't think that. She had to warn Ellie, make her understand what was happening and work out how to avoid it. It had to work.

Megan changed into her work gear and went out to talk to her team, to see how the cottage garden was going. Next she checked in with the tree surgeon regarding clearing the yew back in the maze. If she wanted to be able to get in there she might as well try making it easier on herself.

'It's a strange place, this place,' said Stefan. They were standing in the narrow entrance to the maze, thick dark branches crowding in on them, towering over them as if trying to cut off the light. Megan could smell that familiar scent of life, of mulch, of growing things. The maze tapped into the deep green world and the darkness underground.

'You see it in the soil. And in the trees. Those ones…' He nodded at the yews. 'Back home, they're Makosh's trees, the weaver goddess, and it's unlucky to cut them without asking her permission. She doesn't like it and that's not good.' Stefan was teasing her, she knew that. Or at least she thought he was. Half teasing perhaps. If she called him on it he'd deny he was superstitious, naturally. And yet…

Lots of trees had folklore associated with them. Strange things happened in forests, under the greenwood, where the world of nature was still strong. And Stefan was right. This was a strange place. She knew that better than anyone.

'We'd better ask her permission then,' she said. 'Or we aren't going to get paid.'

Stefan laughed and turned to the yew hedging. 'It's for your own good, Makosh. Otherwise no one will visit your home in the heart of the maze and you'll be stuck there all on your own. No one wants such a life.' He put his safety gear on.

Megan smiled, donning her own ear protectors and safety googles before he started up the chainsaw. The noise drowned out everything. She was definitely not thinking of the lights she had seen. Definitely not. Or the foxes, and the growling. Did Makosh, whoever she was, have wolves or dogs? Megan wasn't sure she wanted to know.

Together they cleared the main path in as far as the centre, cutting, stacking, working together in silence.

Stefan arched his back as he stretched. 'Looks good. What a place. We'll make it beautiful. But not today. Time to call it a day, boss.'

It was six already. Megan had hardly felt the rest of the day go by. 'Sure. Bright and early tomorrow and we'll start on the centre.'

He shrugged. 'If you say so.' But he eyed the place warily, not so self-assured now.

'Stefan? Are you okay?'

He shivered, opened his mouth and then shut it again. He looked embarrassed. 'Nothing. Just the feeling… What's the way they say it? "Someone walked over my grave."'

Or maybe, like he said, there was something about this place.

Megan showered after work, pulled on some clean clothes and put a frozen lasagne in the oven. Which meant she had time to go through the stuff from the library and see what else she could find.

Using Nora's notes – but not looking too closely at the phone number for fear it would persuade her to call and make a fool of herself in her monosyllabic way on the phone – she found the archive of the local paper. It wasn't great and the search function sucked big time, but eventually she dredged up a grainy scan of a copy of a report of Ellie's disappearance. She had last been seen at the Harvest Festival service in Ashleigh, and after that… nothing. The photo of her wasn't very clear either, though Megan could make out her dark hair, bobbed and styled, and big eyes.

She checked the time. Not even nine, yet. What sort of time would she be okay to head out there? When could she expect the maze to work? If it worked at all.

What if it had all been a dream?

A noise made her start, from outside, soft and indistinct. She glanced up but couldn't see anything. It was too dark outside. All she saw was her own reflection looking back at her from the window pane.

She got up and crossed to the window but there was nothing outside.

She pulled the thin curtains closed and stood there for a moment, trying to steady her breath. They felt like a pitiful barrier against the dark.

There was another growl. She was certain it was a growl. Clearer now. A threat from the darkness.

A chill ran down Megan's back, long and lazy fingers tracing ice after them. The room had turned cold, so cold that her breath misted in front of her face. Jesus, she had to talk to Sahar about the heating in this place. She pulled on the hoodie from last night and the scent of yew swept over her. She glanced towards the cabinet and saw it still sitting there, the little angular figure made of straw and ribbon. The corn dolly.

The one Ellie had given her last night.

Megan picked it up, the sharp and brittle straw digging into her skin. It was real. Ellie had given it to her. And now she was holding it in her hand. She had to believe it wasn't a dream when she had real, physical evidence of the event in the palm of her hand.

Nora had told her that people gave the corn dollies to the Green Lady as a sacrifice.

Megan went back to the laptop in the sitting room and tried searching for 'straw shapes'. That just brought up projects for kids using plastic drinking straws. 'Woven straw' brought up a load of raffia bags and things made of rattan and jute. Then she replaced 'straw' with 'wheat'.

Corn dollies.

Hundreds of them. All shapes and sizes.

Not this one in particular. Not the same pattern, the same design. But aspects of it. Elements. It sat on the arm of the sofa beside her, a little abstract figure. If you squinted at it, it almost looked like a man.

It was a ritual figure, like a poppet, traditionally made from the last sheaf of wheat at harvest, meant to be treasured for a year and then returned to the earth. From her web search, she learned they weren't actually made of corn, but rather any dried cereal crops like wheat or oats, those most commonly growing in an area. Corn was just a generic word for grain. It meant seed, or kernel, and the corn dolly was a tribute for future harvests, a seed of hope.

But as to what it actually was, who made it or why she had got it from a woman in nineteen-bloody-thirty-nine? Of course the internet did not have any answers for that particular question.

Megan printed the page from the archives and the ones about the corn dolly and waited for the little printer in the corner to whine its way into life. Nothing happened, not even when she went over and prodded the button on it a few times. Checking the laptop again, she found that the default printer had been reset to the one at reception. She didn't know how that had happened. But she had been printing up the invoices for materials yesterday and, as it was work-related, Sahar had told her to use the printer in reception.

'It's a damn sight better than that wonky old thing,' she said. And she was right.

With a growl of frustration, Megan shut down the laptop. She'd have to go over there and pick up the pages. Then she'd head out into the maze.

She picked up the corn dolly almost without thinking about it, the feeling of it in her hand a strange comfort, a reassurance that she wasn't imagining all of this. It was the only evidence she had.

The wedding party had moved on from elegant dining and speeches, to a loud band and dancing. It wouldn't be long before the band finished up and the combination of the DJ and a well-stocked bar took it to another level entirely. No one would be looking for her.

But Megan hadn't counted on Hattie. She perched behind reception, knitting something else complicated and intricate, this time in many shades of blue. She had a glass of something that might have been water beside her, but was more likely gin. That was Hattie. Sahar had not been kidding. She grinned at Megan as she slipped in the side door.

'All right, Hattie?' she asked, trying to sound casual. 'You still on duty?'

'Oh yes. Not a bother here, love. I put in for extra hours. Had my dinner and I'm chipper… there's not much doing now. They're all enjoying themselves in here. What about you? You must be beazled, the work you put in today?'

'*Beazled?*'

Hattie laughed. 'Tired out. Local word. We've loads of them around here. Old as the hills. We have more than thirty words for mud, you know?'

Megan grinned. Because of course they had their own language around here.

'Just catching up on some work. I'm going to head out for some fresh air. Just, um…' There was no sign of printouts on the printer. She cursed under her breath and Hattie chuckled behind her.

'Looking for these?' She had put down her knitting and held up a few pages, waving them like a fan.

'Yes. I think someone reset the default to this one.'

Hattie handed them over, clearly having had a good read of them. 'We've piqued your interest in the corn dollies, have we, dear?'

Megan folded them up and shoved them into her pocket with her phone. 'Yeah, kinda. Thanks, Hattie.'

Hattie took a swig of her suspiciously clear drink. The ice cubes rattled against the glass. 'Goodnight, Megan. Sleep well.' She picked up her knitting again and Megan retreated, leaving the reception while the rhythmic clack of her needles faded under the beat of the music from the party.

Just before Megan left by the main door, she saw, nestled in among the other books on the bookshelves that lined the walls, *An Illustrated*

History of the Twentieth Century. What would Ellie make of that? She'd have to believe her then, wouldn't she? On impulse, Megan almost tugged it out.

And then she stopped. If she really was going to see a woman from the beginning of World War Two, should she bring evidence of how horrific and terrible that war was going to be? What if she changed history? What if—

But wasn't that what she was trying to do anyway? If only on a small, one-woman, Ellie-Fairfax level.

Megan's hand shook and she pushed the book back onto the shelf. One thing at a time.

The music blared around her again as she passed by the open windows of the function room but faded as she turned towards the formal gardens and headed for the maze. By the time she reached the entrance, it had faded behind her entirely. Megan stepped into the thick green darkness of the maze. The sharp resin smell of English yew struck her, and she took a moment, breathing it in. Without the green lights to guide her, it was treacherously dark but she could follow the path from memory. She and Stefan had worked on it all afternoon, and made sure it was clear. She was sure she knew the way through.

But it wasn't so easy in practice.

Megan turned another corner and found a dead end. Cursing, she turned around and retraced her steps back to the last junction. This time she got closer to the middle, she was sure of it, but still ended up in another dead end. It was insane. She had made sure there was a clear path.

'Unicursal,' she muttered to the maze. 'You're meant to be bloody unicursal. It means just one path.'

Obviously the maze wasn't listening. Or it had decided to mess with her, in that way mazes did. She backtracked, wishing she'd thought this through. Maybe she could have got a photo of it from the upper floor of the hotel, or perhaps there was a map.

But it wasn't going to be that easy, was it? Not this maze, not at night.

She shivered. That familiar cold air again. She hugged herself and stamped her feet, trying to warm up, but it didn't help.

Think, she told herself, and turned once more.

A rustling noise came from behind her and she turned.

For a second time, Megan's foot caught on a root and she crashed to the frozen ground. The air burst from her lungs in a plume of white and she lay there, stunned, staring at the gaps in the base of the hedge to a path on the other side.

Just at that moment, someone walked by.

She saw an elegant pair of bare feet, pale and perfect in the moonlight. A long pair of loose, white silky trousers swished around slender ankles, the bones and tendons beneath the white skin defined and pronounced. The grass leaped up behind the feet as they passed, a trail of tiny white flowers blooming in their wake. But even as Megan stared at them, they wilted and then faded, leaving a trace like snowflakes on the grass, lingering just for a moment, before melting away.

Megan scrabbled up, trying to remain quiet. She didn't know why it felt so important that this stranger didn't hear her, or see her, but she needed to follow them. It was probably just someone from the hotel, one of the guests. But why barefoot? And nothing could account for the flowers. That wasn't normal.

Moving as quickly as she could while staying silent, Megan doubled back to the last junction. Up ahead she saw the figure of a woman in white turn the corner. Megan followed her. This time it was like taking a direct line to the centre. She couldn't say what was different. The paths just realigned themselves, as if the vegetation were folding back out of her way. The woman was a pale form up ahead, and Megan herself was a shadow, a ghost, following her, right into the heart of the maze.

The woman knelt in front of the well, her short black hair close-cropped in a pixie cut that only accentuated her ethereal beauty. Her pale clothes shifted in the breeze, and she reached out, holding something over the water. Megan could hear her singing softly, a voice on the edge of hearing which winnowed its way into her mind and lodged there. The moon lit the whole centre of the maze. The moment she turned around she wouldn't fail to see Megan. But she was so intent on her song, and her task, that she didn't move. Carefully, Megan stole around the edge of the seats towards the bower, where the deeper shadows would hide her. Just as she made it, the woman stood up, still holding something in her hands. She lifted it over her head and looked up to the moon. The light spilled across her face, down her long throat, illuminating her.

Her striking features caught the moonlight, which painted them like a marble sculpture. No one would call her pretty, nothing as meagre and frivolous as that, but Megan couldn't tear her eyes away. The woman radiated strength, power. Everything about her sang of magic.

In her long-fingered hands she held another little figure, woven from corn. It looked like pale gold, and Megan could make out the intricate knotwork with which she had made it. It too was tied with slim scarlet ribbons. Another corn dolly. So this was who left them here. But why? Megan's hands trembled at her sides, and she held her breath, sure this was something she was not meant to interrupt or even see.

The woman called out a single word – 'Artrí' – and dropped the corn dolly into the well. She bowed her head as it fell and then folded to her knees again, peering over the edge as if searching for something in the depths.

Megan shoved her hand into her pocket again and felt the small corn dolly Ellie had given her.

She swallowed hard, watching as the woman muttered words at the well, obviously curses, and then pulled her hands away, torn from rose thorns. Drops of blood glistened on her pale skin, the scratches a livid red.

And even as Megan watched – she couldn't have torn her gaze away even if she'd wanted to, not now – the wounds healed, smoothing themselves away as if they had never been there, like watching a film run backwards.

A sharp intake of breath hissed behind her and Megan jumped in alarm.

Ellie grabbed her, pulling her further back into the shadows and clapping her hand over Megan's mouth. 'It's me. It's just me. Stay quiet.'

Chapter Ten

Sunday 24th September 1939

Miss Seaborne was with them all day and it was soon clear to Ellie that she understood her father's work in a way Ellie never could. Whenever Ellie joined them they stopped whatever they were talking about and the subject slid to something innocuous.

Miss Seaborne watched her carefully. Too carefully. She was charming and polite, engaged Ellie in all kinds of interesting topics of conversation. But the woman never answered a question about herself. And her father didn't mind. If anything he appeared to approve.

Ellie wasn't jealous. It wasn't that. It was just…

The three of them ate lunch together, discussed mathematics and science, philosophy and history. After lunch the car arrived to whisk her father off to London.

'Already?' Ellie couldn't hide her surprise.

'Unfortunately yes. I'll stay in my club but I need to be at the Ministry first thing in the morning. I must speak to the Prime Minister—'

'But Father, surely Mr Chamberlain can wait—'

He lifted a hand to stop her. His gaze went past her, catching Miss Seaborne's. Whatever he saw there, he went on after a moment and Ellie fought the urge to turn around to see if the woman had nodded or shaken her head. 'It must be done, my love. Now, let Miss Seaborne take care of all my business here. She will have full authority over my study and library, do you understand? You do not need to interfere.'

'Interfere?' As if she had ever interfered. She helped him. She always had done.

'Ellie,' he murmured, almost as if he was apologising. But it wasn't an apology, she knew that. There was another tone, one of admonition, a warning. He sounded so disappointed. 'I deal in matters of national security. It's not that I don't trust you, but it could put you in a dangerous situation. And if anything happened to you... You mind your own business now, the household and the estate, your evacuees, and I'm sure the fête committee and the WI could do with some help. More than enough to keep you busy. Miss Seaborne will act as your companion and guardian. She will speak with my voice while I am away. Do you understand?'

Like Ellie was a child. This was intolerable. But then, to him she *was* a child. She was his unmarried daughter. No matter what else she had done, it didn't matter.

'Yes, Father.' What else could she say?

Miss Seaborne followed him out to the car, carrying his briefcase for him while his valet loaded his luggage.

Ellie stood in the hallway, listening to their subdued voices. It all sounded very serious. Very serious indeed.

And when her father left what would happen? What about Megan? Was Ellie going to be able to slip out of the house to look for her again tonight? If the things she had experienced last night were actually real.

No, they had to be real. She trusted her own senses. She had the ability to tell reality from dreams or fantasies. Besides, she had the corn dolly. She had left it on her dressing table. It was real, and so was the one she had given to Megan, and therefore so was Megan. She had to be.

Quod erat demonstrandum.

Dinner was a subdued affair. Miss Seaborne made polite conversation and Ellie tried to be polite in return. It was painfully awkward. Afterwards, Miss Seaborne claimed she had work to be attended to, and closed the study door firmly behind her. So Ellie headed to bed and made her preparations for later that evening. Once it was dark enough, she would make her way outside. Hopefully Miss Seaborne either would not notice or would not care.

Mary brushed her hair with the careful patience Ellie always expected of the older maid. Jolly and pleasant, Mary chatted away about the day. About their new member of the household mainly. The staff were all agog at her arrival and his lordship's departure.

'But your papa will be home again in no time. No wonder they need him, a fine gentleman like him, to talk sense to them *furriners*.'

Ellie winced. Anyone from outside Sussex was a *furriner* to Mary. They didn't even have to be actually foreign. Ellie didn't like the thought of her father travelling to Europe, or wherever they would send him. They were at war. Even with this strange situation that didn't seem real, with Germany assaulting Poland and the rest of the continent scrambling to defend themselves or retaliate and no one quite certain what to do.

'The Nazis don't seem the type to listen to reason.'

Mary laughed. Nothing frightened her, not even Adolf Hitler. 'Oh, it'll be over in no time, you'll see. Poland is so far away and the Germans will be finished with them pretty quick, I'm sure of it. There'll be nothing left to fight about then. You'll still get to the Harvest Festival in the village, don't you fret.'

That was the least of Ellie's worries. She and her father always went to the fête. There were games and races, all manner of competitions, and she was supposed to be presenting the prizes. After that she would attend the church service in St Michael's, and then a cup of hot cider and perhaps some of Mr Walters' excellent seed cakes which he always baked specially. Without Father beside her, it would be so strange.

She looked at Mary in the mirror, over her own shoulder. 'Perhaps Miss Seaborne will accompany me, do you think? Unless she thinks it is too quaint. Or too pagan.'

'Too pagan? What balderdash is that? It's a good, honest celebration as old as time, sanctified by the Church.'

Ellie couldn't suppress a smile. 'Not entirely, Mary. There's a study in the library about the origins of the festival. Our Anglo-Saxon and Celtic forebears celebrated it and the Church took over such festivals when—'

'Oh, Miss Eleanor, such things you say. That's scandalous.' Mary still spoke to her like she was a child, but Ellie couldn't bear to admonish her for it. Mary had always been there for her.

'Well, wherever it came from I would hate to miss it,' she said. And then she had an idea. 'Mary, there's a book in Father's library I was meaning to read, but I'm afraid Miss Seaborne might not approve. He has given her full charge of it. Do you think you could check where she is? So I don't run into her. It might make a bad impression, don't you think?'

Not to mention she'd tried to get it earlier, just after dinner, and Miss Seaborne had appeared as if from nowhere and shooed her out of the library with frightening efficiency. Her father had been quite clear about access, the woman told her sternly. There were many confidential documents in his library, containing information vital to the war effort which would be positively dangerous for her to know. Best she didn't go in there at all. Which was strange because her father had never bothered to say that to Ellie himself.

But she needed that book.

Mary eyed her knowingly. 'It might. And what kind of book would it be?'

'Oh, just a book about local customs and such.'

'Truly? Would I not fetch it for you?'

Even better. 'If you could, that would be wonderful. But I don't want you to get off on the wrong foot with Miss Seaborne.'

Mary shook her head, smiling, a look of defiance in her eyes. 'She's not the mistress here, is she? I don't report to her but to Mrs Worth and yourself, my lady. Which book is it?'

Ellie described it and its location within the library. Mary listened intently, still with that strange smile on her face.

Perhaps she didn't realise that Ellie was being defiant too. Or perhaps she approved of a little show of defiance. You never could tell with Mary. Maybe Miss Seaborne had done something to offend the staff already. That never ended well.

Never lose the respect of your staff, Eleanor, her grandmother had said. *They know more about your business and your household than you do, half the time. And they can make existence unbearable if they take umbrage. Good, loyal staff are impossible to replace. Treat them well, and they will reward you.*

'Very well, Miss Eleanor. Now, you get yourself into your bed.'

Mary bustled off, but Ellie didn't head straight to her bed. She went to the window and opened the curtains. Outside, she could just catch a glimpse of the maze. The lights were already there – eerie green glows in the night. They were waiting for her and the mystery at the heart of the well was calling. Megan would be there, beneath that full bright moon. She had to be. Ellie knew it. She just knew it. And she needed to get out there, somehow. She needed to find out more.

The door clicked shut and she jumped, turning. But it was only Mary, holding the thin book, bound in red leather as Ellie had described. She took it gratefully from her maid.

'Thank you. I don't want to get you into trouble.'

Mary looked so innocent it was almost laughable. 'Trouble? Me? I was just cleaning up. That's what I do. She won't call me over, don't worry, pet. And anyway – *we wunt be druv.*' It was what people said all over the county, its motto. We won't be driven like cattle. We won't be forced to do anything against our will. Stubbornness was ingrained deep inside their bones. 'Let her try.' Mary went over and deliberately closed the curtain. 'Now, miss, you should be in bed.'

'I know, I will, I just…' Ellie glanced over her shoulder. Mary's face grew stern.

'The lights are pretty fancies, Miss Eleanor. But they aren't safe. I know what your science says about marsh gas and whatnot, but I also know what the folk here say about them. They're spirits of the lost. And they'll call you to be lost with them, if you let them. They lead good folk astray, everyone knows it. Don't go out there, not tonight or any other when the little green lights are calling.'

In all the years they'd known each other, Ellie had never heard Mary speak about the lights like this. Many people saw them but most dismissed them – imagination, superstition or a natural phenomenon. Sometimes they lingered. Sometimes they were gone in the blink of an eye.

'They're just marsh gas,' Ellie said. 'We know that.'

'Do we?' Mary gave a barely suppressed shudder. 'Aren't we clever. Gas, indeed. They're more than that. Lost souls that wander the world looking for our Lord's grace which they'll never find. Don't mind them. The little maiden there will watch over you.' Ellie glanced at the tiny corn figure by her bedside and Mary smiled. 'You'll remember making them as a little lass. Women in this village have been teaching their daughters and granddaughters how to make corn maidens for Harvest Festival for generations. We make them to lay to rest the ghosts. And to call those we need to us. Now, to bed, young lady.'

Ellie gritted her teeth. Sometimes Mary acted like she was four rather than twenty-four. But it was easier to let her have her way so she climbed into her bed and let the maid she had known all her life settle the sheets and blankets around her.

To lay to rest the ghosts. In all the times she'd sat with Mary as a girl, weaving the corn dollies, she'd never mentioned ghosts either.

'Why do you think the lights appear, Mary? If they aren't gas.'

Mary sat beside her, on the edge of the bed, just as she had long ago when she had told Ellie fairy stories. It dipped beneath her weight.

'Once upon a time, there was a lady lived here.' Ellie knew this story, but she didn't mind hearing it again, not when Mary told it. She had grown up listening to that voice telling this tale, until she drifted off to sleep. 'She loved a knight and she married him even though her people wouldn't have it. She did it anyway. You're a stubborn lot, you Fairfaxes.'

She laughed and Ellie did too. She couldn't help it. Mary always made her laugh. 'Well, not to beat the devil round the gooseberry bush, she bore him children, a son and a daughter, and then one day, while she was worshipping the old gods at her well – for she wasn't a Christian, not all the way through – she was met by her two sisters. They chided her and begged her to come home with them and set aside her husband, but she wouldn't. She told them she loved him and

her children more than her life, more than any life. So they killed her
and threw her body in the well.'

'That's ghastly. And sacrilegious. It was a holy well, wasn't it?' It
had been part of the ritual of the storytelling, ever since she was little.
Mary would speak, and Ellie would ask questions, even though she'd
heard the story countless times before.

'Of course it was, and they were cursed for it, so I heard. Doomed
to walk the earth forever and never know peace. They look for sacrifices,
for others to take her place, or bring her back. Once in every lifetime,
they say, there's someone as could do it. But no one ever has.

'And that lady, all in her fine green gown, lost in the well, lost to
her brave husband and her beautiful children, was lost to the world,
and lost to heaven too. Her power was lost to us. But her family
blood still flows in the veins of the people of Ashleigh, and that still
calls her home.

'So she comes back, the Green Lady, when the moon is right and
full at harvest time. The legend is that she's trying to make her way
home, back here to Foxfield Hall, but she can only walk a cockstride
each night to get here. And if she gets home maybe her power will
be free, or maybe she'll destroy us all in revenge. No one knows, for
a ghost is a fickle thing.'

Ellie settled down against her pillows. Who could resist a story that
included murder, damnation and star-crossed love? But the way Mary
told it made her feel safe and small, drowsy with familiarity. Much
better than some of her other stories.

But as Mary continued, a chill fell over Ellie, bringing her skin out
in goosebumps. There was a new aspect to her story tonight.

'And she's so old and strong, and her magic was so powerful in her
day, that she calls all the other lost souls to her, all those who died

unblessed, or unbaptised, or died in sin, unshriven, all those of her line. They come as little green flames and go to try to free her from the well.'

The little green lights. The ghosts. Called to the Green Lady, trapped with her forever.

'The Lords Fairfax didn't hold with such things,' Mary went on. 'Not even from their Lady ancestor, so they planted the maze, and tended it, trying to put the spirits off, to confuse them and stop them getting in and out. They used yew, the tree of death and graveyards, a poison tree, but still the little lights came. Still they come and wander the maze trying to find her. And still she gets nearer.'

'And what will happen if she gets here?'

'No one knows, my dove. The corn dollies are for her. To appease her. And to lay her spirit to rest. They watch over you. Now, go to sleep and don't go wandering about at night. You stay indoors, young lady. Promise?'

Meek as anything, Ellie nodded and closed her eyes, but once Mary was gone, she threw back her bedclothes, pulled out her coat and boots from the back of the wardrobe where she had hidden them and crept down the back stairs.

Chapter Eleven

Sunday 24th September 1939

It was brighter than the night before but Ellie still used her flashlight, even if she wasn't supposed to. Did it matter out here in the countryside? The fears of bombings and night-time attacks seemed distant and unfounded now. How were they going to see her?

The little lights were waiting, guiding her, and she wondered if Mary could be right, if they truly were lost souls of her ancestors, drawn back here by the harvest moon and the Green Lady. A shiver passed down her spine, one that was both frightening and thrilling.

If they were her family, she had nothing to fear, did she? Fairfaxes looked after their own. Running across the lawns, she sheltered the torchlight with her own body. She had to be quick and pray that Miss Seaborne didn't look for her. Or see her. This would not be easy to explain.

The maze closed around her like an embrace. Deep and dark, the scent of the yew and the night heady and intoxicating. She felt it ripple through her, fear and exhilaration, a sense of the strange. If she closed her eyes, she could make her way to the well. She knew that, she was sure of it. The darkness pressed close around her and with the torch it was like walking through a tunnel. Muffled sounds, distant rustles and creaks echoed strangely in the blackness beyond. As she turned the corner her breath misted in the air, but she didn't feel cold.

Her footsteps faltered and she stopped, standing there in the darkness. The spirit in the well was one thing but no spirit had placed the corn dollies there. They were real and solid.

And the shadows within the thick hedges moved like a wave. She could feel the maze around her, a living thing, breathing, thriving, a thing of life and darkness.

What was she doing? What on earth had possessed her to come here in the darkness, at night?

But what else was she going to do? Just go back and forget about Megan, about the Green Lady, pretend none of it was real?

No. She needed to know. The darkness was not going to drive her away like a frightened child. This was her home, her land, *her* maze.

She gritted her teeth and pushed on, taking the path she knew as well any other. And when she reached the middle of the maze, she realised she wasn't alone.

But it was not Megan waiting in the heart of the labyrinth. Not this time.

A woman knelt by the well, dressed in a curious white trouser suit. She was tall and elegant, and familiar in a strange, ethereal way, although Ellie could not quite see her face. Her head bowed as if in prayer and her black hair was cut even shorter than Megan's had been.

Another person? From another time perhaps?

Why did a chill creep up Ellie's spine? Why did her breath catch in her throat?

Ellie backed up sharply and the woman didn't turn around. Her whole attention was fixed solely on the well. Ellie crept to the edge of the bower, and hid in its shadows while her heart thudded against her ribs. The woman stood up, lifted a corn dolly over her head.

'Artrí,' she said. 'I call on you a second time. You promised to come to her aid. You swore it.'

At the same moment that Ellie recognised her voice, the moonlight fell on her face. It was Miss Seaborne. No doubt about it. Her long hair had been cut painfully short. When had she done that? Or had she been wearing a wig earlier? Some kind of disguise?

She was there now, dressed in strange clothes, neither male nor female in their cut but loose and bohemian, a far cry from the reserved and buttoned-up secretary Ellie had met earlier today. And yet Ellie couldn't mistake her. The woman smiled, a very different smile to that which she had worn in the study. This was delighted, triumphant.

Miss Seaborne thrust her hands into the rose bushes growing over the well and thorns tore into her pale skin. She cursed at her bloodied hands. They were words no polite secretary should be using. She'd be let go if a gentleman heard her.

Her blood fell through the thorns, through the ivy, into the well below.

The green lights surged forward around Ellie; it was like looking at a river suddenly picking up speed towards a waterfall. The shadows twisted around her, and the air turned to ice, like the opening of a great emptiness before her. The breath she managed to grab slid like something solid and freezing down her throat, needles of pain on soft skin. The shadows twisted with the passage of the lights, an after-image forming as if she had been staring at the sun, and she saw a shape form. Something… something the shape and size of a woman, hanging in the air in front of her. And the light rushed there, filling it, making Ellie start to cover her eyes.

Megan appeared in the midst of the light as it rushed on towards the well. Ellie heard her choke back a cry of surprise, perhaps even fear.

She'd give them away, and how would Ellie explain being here? Either of them being here? How could she confess to spying on her father's new secretary engaged in some sort of pagan rite? And that she was here with a strange woman? A woman from the future?

It wasn't possible. She couldn't let them be found.

She flung herself forward, clapping her hand over Megan's mouth. Her body was warm and solid, real. Every muscle tensed and Ellie realised with a surge of alarm that if Megan tried to fight her off, she wouldn't stand a chance.

'It's me,' she whispered. 'It's just me. Stay quiet.' Thankfully, Megan subsided, still breathing hard. Ellie could feel her heart thundering in her chest through her own body, an echo of her heartbeat. 'Ellie?'

Her voice trembled, as if she was struggling to hide the fright Ellie had just given her. Being jumped out on in the darkness of the maze… well, Ellie could understand why.

'Yes, I'm sorry… just shush. Please. If she sees us here…'

And Megan understood. She looked just as wary of Miss Seaborne as Ellie was.

Whatever she was up to, Miss Seaborne finished, getting to her feet and brushing herself off. There was not a mark on her pristine white clothes. No dirt, no grass stains. As they watched, the scratches on her hands and arms wiped themselves clean, like chalk from a blackboard. Ellie and Megan waited in the darkness as the tall woman circled the well like a cat stalking prey, and then turned away with a sigh of disgust and frustration.

She looked like a ghost, drifting off through the gap at the other side of the hidden garden, vanishing into the dark pathways of the maze. A dark spirit, one that really did not belong in this world at all.

Slowly, Ellie let the breath out of her lungs and realised she was still holding tightly to Megan. She released her as quickly as she could.

'Are you okay?' Megan asked in the softest voice imaginable.

Ellie's hands shook, so she balled them into fists in an effort to hide it. 'Yes. I think so. What was she doing?'

Megan shook her head. 'You tell me.'

Ellie glared at her. Did Megan think she was keeping secrets? 'If I knew anything, I would.'

'No, I mean… Oh, never mind. I have no idea. That's all I mean. I followed her here through the maze. Do you know who she is?'

'You followed her?' Ellie shuffled back, staring at her. 'That's impossible.'

'Because everything else here makes perfect sense?' Megan tried to laugh but the sound came out stilted. 'Come on, Ellie.'

'No, because she's my father's secretary. From *my* time. How was she even there for you to follow?'

To her surprise, Megan laughed. Not at her. She couldn't mistake it for that, thank goodness. But a soft, self-deprecating laugh, like the one her father used when he made a joke he thought was funny and she didn't understand.

'How are *we* even here to be having this conversation? Time is screwy in here. You know that as well as I do.'

'I don't…'

'All I mean is, you're from 1939. Eighty years ago, as far as I'm concerned. So let's not get niggly about what goes on in here and what's real, possible or whatever. Ellie,' and her face suddenly fell to seriousness, 'we have to talk.'

She pulled out some sheets of paper.

'What's that?' Ellie asked, suddenly wary. Prickles of electricity ran across the back of her shoulders and shivered down her spine. She'd read her Wells and her Verne. If Megan was from the future – and she didn't doubt that, because to doubt that now would be to risk her mind – she had to be careful. Some things she shouldn't know. Shouldn't ask. She understood that implicitly. Tempting as it might be… she didn't want to know.

'These are printouts about the corn dolly you gave me, and these—'

Ellie seized on the slight change in subject fiercely. 'Oh yes, the corn dolly. I've brought you a book about them. Well, about a number of local traditions, the Green Lady included.' She waved the book at Megan and for a single moment the mounting feeling of dread subsided. Information was evidence. Evidence was good. It was solid and could be checked. She was on firmer ground with this.

Megan clicked her fingers in front of Ellie's face, shocking her into silence. Ellie liked Megan, but she honestly didn't think she'd ever met anyone as rude in her life. But Megan didn't notice her irritation.

'Ellie, listen. *Please* listen. It's important. In 1939 you *disappear*. You vanish without a trace and you're never found.' She waved a piece of paper under Ellie's face. 'When's the Harvest Festival?'

Vanished? Impossible. She wasn't about to vanish.

'That's ridiculous, Megan. I'm here, am I not? Anyway, I'm never alone. Not between family and servants and now Miss Seaborne…'

'You're alone now.'

Ellie laughed, although it came out in a harsh bark that was far from ladylike. 'What are you then? A hallucination?' She meant it as a joke but instantly knew it wasn't, no matter how much she might wish it. This was no joke. A hallucination? If only she was so lucky. The alternative made her shiver deep inside.

She swallowed hard, calming herself. She looked at the crisp white pages in Megan's hand and her stomach tightened. She didn't want to look at them. It was like an instinct deep inside her, scrabbling rat claws at the lining of her stomach, insistent and terrible. She knew she shouldn't look at them. No one should know their own future. If indeed that was what it was. And then, with a sensation like being drenched in cold water, she finally understood.

'Because that's the only thing that makes sense, isn't it? That you aren't from the future but from my feverish imaginings. I'm having some kind of breakdown, or waking nightmare, and you aren't real. That I have somehow gone insane. Is that why he hired her to watch me?'

'Who?'

'Miss Seaborne, that woman. She arrived today and my father gave her charge of his affairs before he left. And me.'

'Doesn't he trust you?'

'Apparently not. The whole world has gone insane so why not me as well? Maybe… maybe they lock me away. Or maybe I just run wild and—'

To her surprise, Megan took her hand in a warm, strong grip. It comforted her and her racing heart slowed. Megan's dark eyes gazed into hers. In that moment they were Ellie's anchor, the one thing holding her safe from a sea of hysteria.

She couldn't vanish. History wasn't written. She had David and a future, a life to live, the two of them together. When the war was over, when he was back home, when… when everything finally went back to normal. It wouldn't be long. It couldn't be. And she just… she couldn't… Her chest tightened and she couldn't seem to catch her breath. It hiccoughed into lungs which couldn't hold it for more than a second.

'It's okay,' Megan said. 'If we can figure it out, we can stop it. We can save you.' Her voice helped, a little, enough, in the same way as her hand did. It soothed Ellie, calmed her, and she fixed all her attention on the other woman.

Her voice shook as she tried to speak again, and she choked. So much for the stiff upper lip. She took a breath and tried again. 'But if it has already happened…'

'It hasn't happened to *you* yet, has it? So it can still be changed. I think. I don't know. But Ellie, we have to try, don't we?'

She nodded slowly. Megan was right. Just give up? Surrender to the inevitable? Never.

'I suppose we do. But I still can't believe—'

Megan pulled out another piece of paper, like a photo of a newspaper article blown up so much that the picture wasn't true any longer but grainy and thick with strange black ink. But she knew what Ellie was looking at, even in the light of the harvest moon. It had been taken from the local paper, the familiar masthead visible along with the month and year – September 1939. The text was blurred and illegible, the words twisted. There were even copies of folds and tears. The same newspaper appeared at the breakfast table each morning for her father along with *The Times* and a number of others, but never in so poor a condition.

Her own face looked back from the photo below. At least, it could have been her face. The image was so distorted that it was hard to tell. But she couldn't mistake her own name printed below it, or the words 'Missing heiress'.

It ran like electricity through her system and she knew, as clearly as she knew her own name, that she shouldn't look, that she couldn't know her own future.

'Put it away. Please.' Her voice didn't sound like hers any more, but distant and hollow. Afraid. No, that wouldn't do at all. She forced herself to be stern, to be the one in control. 'Megan, you have to put it away. No one should know their own future.'

Chapter Twelve

The maze, at night

Megan's stomach sank. She had hoped that Ellie would agree, that she would read it and they would form a plan. But Ellie was not cooperating. She hadn't counted on that. Maybe she should have brought the history book after all and just shoved the whole thing in her face.

Ellie gazed back at her, holding her hand, but Megan pulled it away, folding up the sheets of paper and shoving them into Ellie's book. Ellie just ignored them, moving her gaze so she just stared past her.

Megan took her shoulders, shook her gently. 'We have to do something, Ellie.'

Ellie stared at the pages for a long moment before she drew in a deep breath, a decision seemingly made. 'There's nothing I need to see there. If I vanish without a trace, no one knows what happened. How can I avoid it?'

'I'll find out. I'll work out what happened.'

Ellie shook her head, but a smile pulled at her lips again. 'Do you rescue everyone you come across or just damsels in distress?'

Suddenly Megan felt foolish, but she grinned at Ellie anyway. 'If I can.' For some stupid reason Nora popped into her mind and her skin warmed, her cheeks flushing. She couldn't help herself.

Ellie, of course, saw it right away. Her eyes brightened in delight. 'Who is it?'

'It doesn't matter. You don't know her.'

And for one awful moment Ellie's expression faltered. '*Her?*'

Jesus, she should have guessed it would be like that. Ellie was from 1939. A knot twisted inside Megan's stomach. What did people even think about same-sex relationships in 1939? It could be normal to laugh at her, or worse.

Turn away in disgust, in revulsion.

But Ellie didn't move. 'Does she have a name?'

'Of course *she* has a *name*.' It came out more sharply than Megan intended. She couldn't help it. 'It's Nora.'

Damn, she sounded defensive. She hadn't felt like this since she was sixteen and trapped in that bloody awful school. Her brother had been her shield, golden boy, sports hero, beloved-by-all Owen. And even then it had been a constant game of deflection and secrets. It was only when she left that she'd felt comfortable enough to come out, with his support. Now Owen was gone.

Ellie pursed her lips and paused to choose her words with care. 'Megan… I do know about… um… *sapphic* relationships, you know? I went to a women's college and some of the girls there had… well, special pals.' Megan rolled her eyes. *Special pals.* That was a new euphemism to her. One that sounded old as… well, Ellie, she supposed. 'It's… it's not easy…'

'No. It's not.' *Sapphic*… she couldn't just say lesbian. Maybe that wasn't the right term in Ellie's time or for someone from her background. She'd probably studied classics as soon as she could read. She could probably quote bloody Sappho. In Greek.

'And your… your *friend*? Nora? Is she… is she interested?'

Oh God, it was mortifying. It was worse than trying to come out to her gran. Enough was enough.

'We were talking about you, weren't we?' Megan said sharply. 'The article said you were… are engaged. Tell me about him.'

Ellie sat back, all the tease gone out of her. 'David.' A smile drifted across her lips. More than affection, deeper than a passing infatuation. Megan knew that look. Sahar looked like that when you mentioned Amir. Every single time. 'David Grainger. He lives over in Belleclair House, on the other side of the village. I mean, his family does. He's not there right now. He… he's with the RAF. A pilot. He's my young man.' She blushed suddenly. 'My fiancé.'

And Ellie adored him. That was clear.

Megan fought to keep her face impassive. This early in the war, the life expectancy of British pilots wasn't long, was it? The Battle of Britain hadn't even happened yet, not for Ellie. And David… if he survived that long… he'd be on the front line. Survivors were called 'The Few' for a reason. They had a life expectancy of a few weeks.

David had a bad war, Hattie had said. He survived then, but he never recovered.

'Where is he?' Megan asked.

But Ellie pursed her lips. 'I couldn't tell you even if I knew.'

Megan laughed and quickly apologised when Ellie glared at her. But she couldn't help herself. Ellie sounded like one of those old cinema adverts or a black and white movie. Ellie frowned and busied herself smoothing down the front of her sensible coat. She wouldn't let anyone see her ruffled, Megan thought. She wasn't the type.

And then a pang of unexpected grief snatched the humour from the situation. Ellie was right there, right in front of her. She hadn't gone missing yet, but she still could. And even if they found a way to stop whatever fate had in store, the whole war still spread out in front of her. She had no idea.

And Megan couldn't tell her. She shouldn't. Wouldn't.

'You said you wanted to show me your book?'

Ellie blinked and then smiled, so relieved that the subject had changed. Her whole demeanour changed. 'Yes. Yes of course. I think it could be important.'

She whirled away, a flurry of activity as she fanned through the pages of the red book. 'Corn dollies,' she said. 'They make them to celebrate the Harvest Festival. And they're old. Really old.'

'But what do they mean?'

'They're gifts, offerings. A sacrifice to the land and the water for a good harvest, when people used to believe in such things. An old tradition, that's all. I learned to make them when I was a little girl.'

'But that woman. She put one in the well. And you… you said you knew her.'

'Miss Seaborne. Ava.' Ellie sat down, deflated now and barely listening. 'She's my father's secretary and she just arrived. But how does she know the maze and what was she *doing*? It was like she was searching for something, under the thorns… Could it be her? Could she be the reason I vanish?'

Megan couldn't bear to see her like that. Not Ellie, who until this moment seemed to be someone who could, and would, do anything.

'Whatever the reason, we can change it,' Megan assured her. 'We have to. If I can find out what happened… Maybe I can't change the past, Ellie, but you can change the future. Can't you?'

Ellie smiled up at her, grateful tears glittering in the corners of her eyes. Light reflected there, a strange green glow, and even as Megan noticed it Ellie's eyes grew round with shock.

'Megan, look!' She surged to her feet, just as Megan turned to look behind her.

The words didn't even register with Megan, not beyond a distant noise.

Green light spilled out of the well, and the little green flickers of light surrounded it, like licks of flame above the grass, flowers and benches. In the centre of the main light, a figure coalesced. A young woman, slender as a willow, dressed all in green with a fall of russet hair tumbling down her back, framing her delicately featured face. She was beautiful, more beautiful than anyone Megan had ever seen, although she caught a glimpse of the way Nora turned her head, the way Ellie's blue eyes saw right through her, and the way her mother smiled when she forgot all her worries. Like she'd smiled the last time Owen came home. She hadn't smiled in quite the same way since.

'It's her,' Ellie whispered and her voice shook with excitement. 'Megan, it's her. The ghost. She's what I've been looking for.'

They stood side by side and gazed at the woman in wonder as all the little lights, shining eerily in the moonlight, began to drift towards her. She stretched out her arms, the wide draped sleeves spilling down from her slender wrists, and she gathered the little wisps of light in. Her aura grew brighter, brilliant and terrible.

Tears wet Megan's face. She was barely even aware that she was crying, certainly didn't want to let Ellie know, and she couldn't lift her hand to wipe them away. The sense of something so much greater than either of them, greater and older, all-encompassing. Ageless and ancient, this woman, this spirit, the numinous touching their world and shaking her to the core. This wasn't possible. Couldn't be. And yet—

'Who is she?' she asked, her voice trembling.

Ellie's wasn't any firmer. She whispered, the awe underpinning her words making them quiver. 'The Green Lady. The Lady of Foxfield Hall.

Our ghost, our guardian. But as to who, exactly? There's a legend – my maid Mary loves to tell it – about the first Lady Fairfax. She's trying to get back to the Hall but she can only travel so far from the well each night. She calls the other ghosts to her.'

'The other ghosts? The lights?'

But Ellie didn't seem to hear her, her eyes fixed on the glowing figure. 'Look at her. Look…' Her voice trailed off.

The Green Lady looked directly at the two of them. She could have been looking straight into Megan's soul, searching through her and weighing what she found there. What that might be, Megan wasn't sure. She wasn't sure she wanted to know. Some secrets were too raw to share. Some innermost thoughts were too painful. And the Green Lady looked so sad.

Megan froze, as if something had reached up from the earth and grabbed her feet, holding her in place.

The shadows around them surged up like oil, twisting away from the ground and the edges of the bower. Megan shied back and some desolate instinct whispered icy warnings in the back of her mind. *Go back*, it told her. *Stay out of sight.*

Ellie's face loomed very pale in the shrouding shadows cast by the yew hedges.

'What is it? What's happening?' she whispered, frantically. Megan waved her to silence. Something else shivered through the chill air of the night, another voice, something primeval and terrible.

At first it sounded like a chant, a strangely discordant song which threaded its way through the night and grated against her senses until she wanted to dig her fingers into her brain to silence it. The song got louder and Ellie winced, her hands coming up to cover her ears.

And the shadows danced to it, twisting and warping, swallowing up the green lights until they glowed with it and took on other forms.

Black shapes, fox-like but huge, paced around the well, their eyes a fierce and terrible green glow, like the ones Megan had seen last night. When they opened their mouths, light dripped like saliva from their gleaming teeth.

Megan's knees gave way and she dropped into hiding, Ellie following suit. They crouched behind the seat, praying they couldn't be seen.

The black foxes advanced on the well, their growls ripping through the still night. The woman in green didn't move, though she watched the advancing shadow animals with nervous eyes. As if she couldn't move. As if she was trapped there, too.

'What are they going to do to her?' Ellie said on a breath.

'She's a ghost, Ellie. What can they do to her?'

Megan could vividly recall them following her last night, herding her out of the maze, the sense of threat. They didn't want her in here.

'Then what are they? And what will they do if they see us? We're not ghosts. Not yet at any rate.'

But the black foxes didn't move any closer. They just circled around the well, growling and snarling, held back or holding their ground, penning the ghost in. The Green Lady folded her hands across her chest, and her face grew even more stern. She waited.

The singing voice fell still, and another shape entered the centre of the maze, wearing a black-hooded cloak so its face was obscured. The voice, when it spoke, was that of an old woman, ancient and haggard.

'Time has come around again so quickly, oh gracious Vala. A generation past and the harvest moon draws near.'

The Green Lady didn't speak, but the visitor reacted as if she did. Perhaps she heard voices the hidden watchers didn't. Perhaps her voice was only for the old woman.

'Charming as ever. They'd say hag, these days. Or witch. And then they'd scoff at its use. They've forbidden your worship for a thousand years, so long that they've even forgotten we existed. Traces of our names remain, fragments of stories twisted beyond recognition. Even this place, if they knew what it really was, would have been ploughed into the soil and sown with salt. They don't hold with us any more now than they did then. They've forgotten us, stupid, naïve fools, and think we were just a superstition and a fancy.' She gave a cackle of vicious glee and stretched out her hands. Green light flared in the well, beneath the Green Lady, and leaped towards her enemy. It writhed around her hands like snakes and then faded, sucked into her skin.

Megan glanced at Ellie to see her frantically riffling through the pages of the book.

'Our sister isn't coming,' the old woman in the hood went on. 'She has deserted you. She knows her place. No one is going to help you this time. And what could she do even if she did come? She doesn't have the power. This is the last one, do you hear me? The last one.'

A pause, and a laugh. 'You aren't going home, not now. All your children are gone. Or soon will be. There will be a sacrifice one way or the other and the last of your power will be mine.'

The Green Lady smiled, a disconcertingly knowing smile, and her gaze lifted to the bower.

'A champion? How have you called a champion?'

The cloaked woman inhaled sharply, smelling the air, and she spun around, her cloak whipping around her. The foxes twisted to face Ellie and Megan too, so fast they seemed to turn themselves inside out to do it. All those unnatural eyes searching through the darkness, looking for the two of them, fixing on them and glowing brighter. The Green Lady had given them away.

'Shit, Ellie.' Megan grabbed her hand. It was as cold as a dead thing in her grip, stiff and unresponsive.

Now the stranger was looking at them they could see her face: a mask, golden, shining and smooth. Beneath the hood it gleamed with unnatural brightness and the holes for her eyes were dark and endless. For a moment Megan couldn't move, watching as the figure crept spider-like towards them and drew a hooked knife, like those she'd seen in the reception of the hotel on display. But the blade wasn't dull, abandoned under a layer of dust and neglect. It was mottled and flaking with old, dried blood, but the edge shone.

'Well now,' the masked woman murmured, and although soft as a whisper her voice wasn't comforting. 'What have we here?'

Megan surged to her feet, dragging Ellie after her. She didn't stop to see how close the woman or the foxes were, but plunged into the night and the maze. 'Run!'

The huge foxes surged up behind them, a tide of fluid shadows with terrible teeth.

Chapter Thirteen

The maze, at night

Ellie raced after Megan in the darkness, her feet barely finding their place on the grass before she ripped them up again and ran on. Megan held her hand in a painfully tight grip. Ellie ran like she had not run since she was a little girl, like she was running from monsters. Like she was running for her life in a nightmare. Because she was.

The ground sucked at her leaden feet, pulling her back, quicksand beneath her. She had to hold on. She had to run. She couldn't afford to fall. Her breath came in harsh and painful gasps, grating in her throat. She could hear the foxes, their snarls and growls, the snapping of their teeth, but they didn't make a sound as they ran, no thump or crash like she and Megan made, no pounding feet or crashing against the yew walls. They didn't stumble or skid like she did. The vulpine shapes flowed over the ground. Ghostly black fog with white teeth and glowing eyes, swift and lethal.

And any second now, any second, they were going to catch her.

Megan hauled her forward.

Thank the good Lord for her, because alone Ellie was sure she'd have fallen, and they'd be on her. And then what? She didn't want to know. She didn't want to imagine.

She needed a moment to gather her wits, to work out what was happening. Just a moment. Was that too much to ask?

'Here,' Megan shouted. A shape loomed out of the darkness ahead of them, a deeper dark than the rest of it, arms stretched out towards them. One of the enormous yew trees, right on a corner of the maze – ancient and twisted, with limbs bigger than her whole body – but there was no way to climb it. Even the lowest branches were too high to jump. But that didn't bother Megan.

'Come here.' Before Ellie could argue or protest, Megan grabbed her around her middle and hoisted her into the air, throwing her upwards. Ellie's hands grabbed the branch, and she clung to it for dear life, swinging and kicking until she could get her legs around it too. 'Climb up higher,' Megan yelled. 'Go on.'

Ellie saw her back up, her eyes fixed on the branch overhead, and the shadow foxes streaming towards her, their green eyes all aglow. She couldn't outrun them now.

Ellie prayed she could make it. She had to.

The first fox sprang forward at the same second Megan did, but she was faster. She launched herself headlong, sprinting across the open ground, and then, as if she'd hit a springboard, leaped towards Ellie, who flung out her arms to catch Megan, to help her. They slammed together and Megan slipped down, but Ellie didn't let go. She clung to her, nails scraping her skin.

Megan was heavier than Ellie would have imagined from her lithe form, all muscle, and gravity was not helping either of them. The fox struck the tree trunk below her kicking legs, and fell, but a moment later another jumped, snapping and snarling at her.

'Don't let go,' Megan yelled. As if Ellie had the intention of doing any such thing. Megan's dark eyes were wide and desperate, but she didn't give up, struggling to haul herself up onto the thick branch beside Ellie.

'Don't *you* let go,' Ellie told her. 'You jolly well get up here, Megan, or else…'

Megan's face contorted as she wrenched her body up by sheer force of will, managing to get her shoulders up over the branch. She lay there, slung over the branch, breathing so hard her chest moved like a bellows, with Ellie gripping her arm so tightly she was certain she'd leave bruises.

'Let's not think about *or else*, eh?' Megan clung to the branch as if it was her lifeline. 'Are you okay?'

Ellie nodded, desperately grateful that Megan was there, that she wasn't hurt.

Megan peered down and Ellie followed her gaze. The black foxes were still circling beneath them, their feet whispers on the grass. Not foxes, not really. They were too big, made of darkness, terrible things from nightmare. They were waiting, just waiting, and they weren't going away. They watched every movement the two of them made, eyes like tiny gas lights in the darkness.

Ellie swallowed hard, a lump of fear scraping down her throat. They might be safe for now but there was nowhere to go. On the other side of the maze wall, she could see nothing. Nothing at all. A thick wall of mist pressed close to the edge and then vanished. There was only a grey void, swirling, just out of reach, a wall of fog without shape and form, without anything recognisable. She ought to be able to see the house, but it wasn't there.

It took a moment for her to notice the change. Silence.

The foxes had fallen silent. They were still watching though. Every movement, every breath. Ellie's eyes widened as they locked on Megan's and she lifted a finger to her lips. Icy touches rippled up her spine and she saw Megan shiver. It wasn't cold. Or at least it shouldn't have been cold. But it was. As if instead of early autumn they had plunged into the depth of winter.

The woman stood at the bottom of the yew tree, cloaked and featureless in her shining mask, terrifying. And still smiling. Ellie knew she was smiling even though they couldn't see her face. She looked up at them and it was like being pinned down by a serpent's gaze, hypnotised, prey. Beneath the hood, behind the mask, all was shadows.

Shadows and darkness.

Ellie could feel her gaze trail over them, seeking out their faces, memorising them.

'Well now, two little birds in a tree…' The woman's voice was musical, accented, and strange. But at the same time, almost familiar. There was a disturbing glee in the way she said it. 'You have one chance to fly away. This maze is mine. If I catch you in here again, little birds… There's nothing for you here, and the Green Lady is only a ghost, a cursed memory which won't go away. She'll bring you only pain. Remember this and forget what you saw here tonight. Come back, set even a foot in here before the harvest moon, and my night foxes will have you.'

She spun on her foot and stalked away. But the foxes didn't go anywhere. They rose as one, clustering around the base of the trunk, their growls echoing up through the night air.

Ellie and Megan sat in the darkness, up in the tree, while the breeze moved the heavy yew branches in whispers and sighs. Beneath them, the shadows growled and paced, jumped up snapping ineffectively at the air.

'I left the book back there,' Ellie said at last.

Megan gave a snort of dismissal. 'Well, we had other things to think about, didn't we?'

That made Ellie smile, even though it shouldn't have, and she glanced down at the foxes. They weren't moving now. They looked more like shadows again, slung across the ground. But their eyes still burned. Intense, focused. The smile died on her face. 'Just a bit.'

The light was growing on the horizon, sunrise burning off the mist that swirled around the maze. Her home appeared in the distance, like a faint sketch made with the softest pencil. And Megan's grip softened.

'Ellie?' Her voice was no more than a whisper. She glanced back and saw the fear on her face, her face that even now looked indistinct and washed-out.

'It's dawn,' Ellie said.

Light spilled over the roof of the house, across the gardens, like melting honey, warm and golden, the light of harvest time.

'What's happening to you, Ellie?' Megan's words slid away, quieter now. Ellie tried to catch her again, but her hands couldn't get purchase, as if they were both ghosts now, her hands passing through what had been solid.

'We're from different times,' Ellie said, not sure if Megan could still hear her. Praying she could. 'It's going to be all right, Megan. We're going home. To our homes.'

'Tomorrow… here? … meet me?'

'Yes. I'll try.' Ellie tried to reach for Megan, but her fingers slipped away as she tried. It was like trying to catch the mist, the mist that was even now dissipating. 'If not, look in the library. If I find anything that might help, look in the library. I'll… Can you hear me? Megan?'

'*Which… Ellie?*'

The breeze whipped through the branches of the tree again, and Megan was gone, unravelled like smoke, snatched away from her. Ellie gasped, staring at the place where she had been, and felt the wind turn her tears cold on her cheeks.

With the sunlight, the shadows vanished. Even so, it was a while before she dared climb down. She lowered herself from the branch gingerly, hanging there for a moment, until she couldn't hang on any longer. Her aching fingers gave and she dropped, landing heavily on dew-damp grass and churned-up mud. No doubt the foxes had been there. She could see their prints, the way their claws had torn through the grass.

Carefully, feeling every ache and bruise, Ellie pulled herself up. Her clothes were covered in mud. She'd never be able to explain this if anyone saw her. And she'd still have to get them cleaned. There would be so many questions. Maybe Mary would help her, cover for her yet again. Maybe.

Who had the masked woman been? She'd never seen anyone so frightening in her life.

And Miss Seaborne… what had she been doing, there in the maze? First her, then the Green Lady herself…

Something didn't add up. She knew nothing about the woman, not really. Her father trusted her but what did he really know? She could be anyone. She could be a German spy.

Ellie wished David was there. She was certain he'd know what to do.

Suddenly she remembered the book. Ellie gathered her wits and ran back to the centre of the maze, her senses leading her.

The book was lying on the bench in the bower. Along with all the sheets of paper Megan had brought with her.

The newspaper article about her.

Missing heiress…

Chapter Fourteen

Wednesday 25th September 2019

Megan limped home, taunted by the dawn chorus, her leg and hip in agony from the fall from the tree. Because being up a tree while trying to keep hold of someone rapidly turning to mist in your arms was a sure-fire way to lose your balance and plunge to the ground so far beneath her. Ellie was gone.

The last thing she was thinking of was Sahar, but the moment she saw the lights still on in their apartment, she knew she was going to have a lot of questions to answer.

She let herself in. The only sound was the TV, blaring out the morning news. So far, so good. Maybe if she could sneak into her room…

Sahar walked out of the kitchen, clutching a cup of coffee. She was still in her nightclothes and her hair was all over the place.

'Were you out for a run? At this hour?' She yawned as she spoke, her eyes barely open.

'Yeah, I… What are you doing up?'

Sahar sat down at the table. Papers were spread all over it. 'I've got work.'

'I thought you had a late shift, Sahar.'

'I switched it with Hattie. She needs tomorrow off. What about you? Your surveyor is arriving at eight, remember? I need to get this lot sorted and… Are you sure you're up to meeting him? You look shattered. You'd tell me if something was wrong, wouldn't you?'

No. Not a chance in hell Megan was sharing what was going on right at the moment. But she couldn't say that either. Besides, Sahar would never believe her if she told her about Ellie, the Green Lady or any of the night-time craziness. And then she'd end up having to see someone a lot more serious than that bloody grief counsellor for another round of *let's express our feelings mindfully*.

She had booked the surveyor just after she had arrived at Foxfield Hall, and she had been lucky to get a cancellation slot. Keith Mayhew, a local guy, with the best references she'd ever seen. Before anyone started work on the middle of the maze she needed to know that the well was safe. A wave of exhaustion washed through her at the thought of going back there. Of course, she knew now it wasn't safe. Not at night, anyway.

'The surveyor, yes. Of course. I'll get washed and changed.'

Damn, she was so tired. Too tired.

'Put on something pretty,' Sahar chimed, not looking up from her work.

'For the surveyor?'

'No, for your girlfriend. Nora's working on the books in the library today. She'll be delighted to see you. Hattie said she hasn't stopped talking about you.'

Megan blushed. She couldn't help herself. 'She's not my girlfriend.'

Sahar cast her an arch look. 'Sure. That's why you have her phone number, is it?'

She nodded to the piece of paper with the notes and Nora's number. Megan had left it on the coffee table. She hadn't even thought of that. Not after the night she'd had.

Damn it, she'd left it too long to call. She should have phoned Nora last night. Now it was going to be awkward, wasn't it?

But first she needed to talk to the surveyor about the maze and the well. About making sure those ancient stone walls were sound. She had an actual job to do here.

On no sleep. Of course. But what else could she do? She couldn't sleep now. There was too much at stake. She needed to know about the extent of this problem as quickly as possible. How long would the survey take?

*

Keith Mayhew, the surveyor, walked around the well, staring at the grass and overgrown briars and ivy, sucking his teeth like they all did. Any second now Megan expected him to tell them the well needed a new catalytic convertor or something. She wished with every fibre of her being she had gone with someone she knew instead.

Professor Deacon, one of the trustees she'd met back when she'd been interviewed, couldn't have looked more out of place if he tried. Who still wore tweeds in this day and age? But he'd insisted on coming along, and since the historical significance of the whole site was under his care Megan was happy to defer to him. Keith and he seemed to go way back anyway, which cut her out of most of the conversation, and at the same time made it easier. She wasn't sure Mayhew would have been happy to take direction from a mere girl.

Not that it mattered. She just didn't feel like that particular fight today.

And he had sounded so reasonable on the phone. Perhaps he'd assumed she was just the secretary. Even in this day and age, people still had the power to disappoint.

Sahar came out with coffee for everyone, followed by Hattie who locked her eyes on Mayhew and proceeded to flirt outrageously with him. Megan and Sahar watched in a kind of horrified awe.

As the sun beat down on them, Megan slipped off her jacket and left it on the bench before helping herself to one of the mugs. The professor sipped his carefully, examining the well as he did so. He glanced at Megan only when the ringtone of her phone almost made her jump out of her skin. Nora's name came up and Megan couldn't help but smile.

'Hi,' she said as she answered and instantly felt stupid. She was standing there surrounded by watchful eyes. Hattie glared at her.

'Hi, Megan. Are you with Keith and Fred? Is Alan Brooks around?' Nora did not sound happy.

'Uh… yeah.' She looked up to meet Sahar's gaze. Hattie was watching her even more keenly now, as if she could tell what was being said at both ends of the phone. Megan forced herself to turn away and take a few steps back into the maze itself. 'I'm with Keith and the professor, I mean. And Sahar. No sign of Alan though. Everything okay?'

On the other end of the phone line Nora's voice chirped away. 'I'm furious. He's trying to sell some of the rare books and— Look, the details don't matter. Tell Hattie and Sahar not to let Alan near the library. He'll start taking them. I'm on the way up now. I've got you on speaker in the car.'

She couldn't focus on what Nora was saying. The maze was still and quiet, away from the centre. The yew walls closed in around her, deadening all sound. Overhead there was hardly even a bird. The oppressive silence ate away between them as Megan tried to shake the feeling of being watched. Her chest tightened, her throat suddenly painful. It was cold now. Too cold.

Last night, shadowy foxes had pursued her through these narrow pathways. She could still feel the breath dammed up in her throat, her heart pounding as she dragged Ellie after her.

Stay away, the woman in the golden mask had warned them. *Or my night foxes will have you...*

But here she was, back again.

When Nora spoke again, her voice sounded a bit more brittle. 'Megan? Are you sure everything is okay?'

'Okay? Sure, I guess.' Why couldn't she seem to say more than two words together? It was Nora. She liked Nora. The hedges loomed over her, dark and imposing. And it made the skin crawl up her spine. She shivered as the masked woman's words circled round her head, the way the woman herself had circled the foot of the tree.

You have one chance to fly away. This maze is mine. If I catch you in here again, little birds... But Megan hadn't stayed away. She couldn't. And she would bet anything that Ellie was just the same.

'Megan?' Nora prompted again.

'I'll talk to you when you're here,' Megan said, just eager to get off the phone and back to the company of the others. Something weird was happening. Again. 'You should concentrate on driving.'

'Are you – are you all right?'

Something fluttered in Megan's chest, something uncertain clawing its way back up inside her. The shadows of the maze grew darker, pressed closer. Her throat tightened. 'I'm... I'm tired, I think. That's all. Sorry.'

'We could... we could get lunch later... if you want?'

A bright rush of something else flooded her unexpectedly.

'I…' *Say yes.* It almost sounded like Ellie's voice, niggling there in the back of her mind. *And your… your friend? Is she… is she interested?* That was what she had asked while going on about 'sapphic relationships' and 'special pals'. And Nora did sound interested, didn't she? She could imagine Ellie's stern glare now. *For God's sake, Megan, say yes.* And at the same time something else in her flailed in panic. This felt more real than anything before. From somewhere deep inside, she forced out the words. 'That would be nice.'

Damn it, she sounded so stupid. *Nice.* But, as if the words had freed her from an enchantment, she shook off the oppressive feeling. It was like the sun coming out.

Nora sounded relieved, her reply coming out in a great, hurried sigh. 'Good. Great. The pub in the village does… *shit!*' She was cut off by the sound of a horn blaring. 'You moron! Sorry, not you, Megan. Asshole in a Jeep. He can't drive for— Yes, you! You can't drive for—'

'Nora,' Megan interrupted, unable to keep the mounting affection out of her voice now. 'Concentrate on the road. See you soon.'

Sahar looked a bit happier when Megan came back into view. Hattie was still there, still drinking her coffee, sitting on the bench in the corner beside Sahar where Megan had left her coat. But to be honest, they both looked bored to tears. The two men, on the other hand, were frowning at the well.

But at least Megan was going to see Nora. And have lunch. Somehow that made everything better.

Lunch sounded good.

'I know that smile,' Sahar whispered as she passed, and even Hattie looked up knowingly.

Megan pursed her lips and slowly shook her head, addressing them both.

'Nora wants you to stop Alan Brooks getting into the library. She says he's trying to sell the collection.'

Hattie raised both eyebrows. 'Well, he has no right to do that. No right at all.'

She stood there, torn between the well and Nora's books. Before Megan could reply, Keith interrupted them.

'Well, the exterior looks sound,' he said, his voice cutting through the frosty silence. 'Cursory visual inspection anyway. It's old. I don't know how old. Ancient. Fred might need to take a look at that. Been cared for, she has. I'll have to dig down a bit to check the foundations though, see what else is there. Then there's the interior as well. But on the surface she's sound. Looks positive.'

'Our ancestors venerated wells.' Professor Deacon joined them too, moving reluctantly, as if he had to drag himself away. 'And the spirits that inhabited them. They made a place holy with sacrifice, with ritual, and with votive offerings. So they built them soundly and took care of them.'

'Funny old tradition really,' Keith said. 'Chucking perfectly good stuff in the water. Speaking of which, I'll need to bring in the equipment to drain the well.'

A jolt of alarm went through Megan, a mirror of what she saw in Hattie. The well was part of the magic of the Green Lady, and linked her to Ellie.

Hattie lurched back towards him. 'Drain it? Why would you want to do that, Keith?'

'Tough to examine it properly if we don't. And given the age I want to be careful in case there's anything archaeological down there too. Fred would never forgive me if I arsed up his precious well, would you?'

Professor Deacon, who didn't look for one moment like anyone had called him Fred to his face in years or used the word 'arsed' in his presence, just laughed.

'Don't take on, Hattie,' he said. 'We'll be careful.'

Hattie didn't appear to be in any way mollified though. From the look she shot at Megan, this was clearly her fault.

'What do you think could be down there?' Megan asked, eager to look at anyone but the formidable receptionist.

'Bloody Excalibur, isn't it, Fred?' Keith laughed.

'Hardly,' the professor sighed. Clearly this was an old joke and one he had grown deeply tired of hearing. 'We aren't excavating here, Hattie. We don't have the resources anyway. But it was once a holy well and there have been treasure troves found in such cases. It never hurts to be careful. It would make the hotel famous. You've heard of Sutton Hoo, haven't you? And La Tène?'

'I thought that was Celtic,' Sahar said.

'Traditions pass on through cultures,' Professor Deacon continued without missing a beat. 'And often an invading force will take on the beliefs of the local people, overlaying them with their own. Look at the Church. Forever stealing mythological heroes to become saints and making sure holy days coincide with pagan festivals. Harvest Festival, for example. Makes the transition easier. Before the Normans, the Anglo-Saxons lived here – for a time part of the great kingdom of Wessex – and before that the Romans made this land their own. Before that it belonged to the Atrebates, the people of the land, possessors of the soil. They were Celts, an offshoot of a Belgic tribe. And before that… well… who knows? They found teeth and bones in Boxgrove in the nineties that predate modern humanity, *Homo heidelbergensis*. The history of Britain is one of settlement, after all, and that goes both ways. Wave upon wave of people arriving here. It's what happens, the way this place, this land, was formed. It's eternal. Without new people, new blood, it would wither and die.' The professor sounded like he was lecturing.

Hattie still looked like she'd been licking nettles. In the distance they heard a car roaring up the drive, which seemed to shake her into action. But not without some final words.

'New blood,' she scoffed. 'It's not new blood we need around here. There's *old* blood in Ashleigh, in all of them born here. You know it as well as I do, Keith Mayhew. People know this land, and know what that well means. None of you ought to be poking around in it. It's bad luck.' She swept out of the centre of the maze, back towards the hotel to protect the books for Nora. She didn't exactly hurry but neither did she hesitate on the way, not as far as Megan could see, absolutely certain in her path. No one knew this place like Hattie.

'You're all in trouble now,' Sahar murmured. 'Hattie has spoken.'

'Not as much trouble as Alan Brooks is in,' Megan replied.

'Oh Hattie, she takes on,' said Keith, dismissing her. 'She'll get over it. Especially when she lets loose on Brooks. She's old-fashioned, that's all. Superstitious.'

'A lot of people are,' Megan said, and decided not to add that they could be right. She turned to Professor Deacon instead. 'I read that Sussex has evidence of the earliest inhabitation on the British Isles. There must be a wealth of history buried here.'

The older man suddenly smiled at her, either charmed by her interest or relieved that Hattie had gone.

'This area, and this house, has been occupied for most of our recorded history, that's true. It's special and it draws special people to it. It's never been excavated before. Not for want of trying. But while it was private land, the family wouldn't allow it. Perhaps old superstitions lived on longer than we thought, and not just in the likes of Hattie.' He rolled his eyes and the glint of humour made Megan's lips quirk into a smile.

Sahar shuddered, wrapping her arms around her chest. 'I'd better go back in. Especially if there's about to be a showdown in my reception.'

'I'll come with you,' Megan said. She had other things to do and she clearly wasn't really needed here. She'd be better off just letting them get on with it. 'Let me know if there are any problems,' she told the professor, perhaps a little too pointedly.

'You girls go on back in,' Keith replied, irritating her even more. 'Tell old Hattie I'll swing in for a pint when I'm done. That might mollify her. We'll take care of it here. Funny old place, this maze. It can turn the head.'

Girls. Great. And neither Sahar nor Megan had their heads turned. Nor, Megan suspected, had Hattie. They set off through the maze together, following her path.

'Wow, that's better,' Sahar finally said as they stepped out onto the lawns again. She drew in a deep breath like she had been starved of oxygen. She shook her head as if trying to clear cobwebs. 'I seriously don't like that maze, Megan. It's creepy AF. Maybe I do need a day off… But not today, obviously. There he is.' She nodded to the front of the hotel where Alan Brooks had just roared up in an extremely shiny Lamborghini. 'Do you think he's compensating for something?'

'This is going to be ugly, isn't it?' Megan remarked as Nora emerged from the hotel reception and bore down on him, her face a picture of fury. Gone was the timid victim Megan had first taken her for. It must have been her car they had heard earlier rather than Alan's. Behind her, Hattie stood in the doorway, her arms folded in front of her like a proud mother, beaming. Megan frowned.

'Is that the same Nora?' she asked.

Sahar laughed. 'Someone's had enough of him. Finally. Want to stay and watch? I could ask the kitchens for popcorn.'

While it was tempting, the weight of exhaustion was making Megan see double at this stage. 'I think I'll head back to the apartment for a bit. I'm supposed to be having lunch with Nora.'

Whatever Nora had just said to Brooks, he recoiled, shock painted all over his features. Suddenly, he was the one with his hands spread wide in supplication, trying to explain himself. He would, of course. His kind always wriggled out of it. All the same, the transformation in Nora was incredible compared to the first time Megan had seen her talking to Brooks.

'Ah yes, the big date. Might want to be careful now. Hattie's been teaching her. It looks like the little vixen's learned how to bite.'

Megan walked away before Sahar could elaborate on that.

Hattie was truly put out by Megan getting Keith to excavate there, even that little exploratory trench. Why were people so protective of this small patch of land?

The image of that cloaked and masked woman from last night flickered to the forefront of her mind again and Megan shuddered. Even now, it felt like someone, or some*thing*, was watching her, like a shadow falling over her as she retreated.

Chapter Fifteen

Monday 25th September 1939

Ellie had just finished her breakfast when the footman came in to tell her that there was a phone call for her.

David. It had to be David. Who else would be calling her at this hour?

She would have run to the study if she could but that would have been unseemly. She had so much to tell him. She snatched up the receiver from the desk where Travers had left it for her and turned around, looking at the door. It closed silently behind her, giving her the privacy she needed.

'David?'

'Hello, my gorgeous girl,' he replied and something inside her flipped over, loop the looping through the sky of her heart. And then panic replaced it. Why was he ringing?

'Are you all right? Where are you?'

The words were out before she thought about them. David chuckled softly.

'Can't tell you that, old thing. You know how it is.'

'Of course. But you're well?'

'Cracking, I promise. But the good news is I've got my papers. It's all go now.'

All go. That was one way to put it. He was going into active combat. That was what he meant. That swooping thing inside her plummeted to the pit of her stomach instead. She might never see him again.

And if what Megan said was true, that she would vanish at the Harvest Festival… it was doubly true.

She swallowed hard. 'Oh, David…'

'It'll be fine, Ellie. Don't fret. And I have a surprise for you.'

'What?'

He laughed then, that deep rumbling laugh she knew as well as her own heartbeat. 'I can't tell you that either. It wouldn't be a surprise then, would it? But it's good news, Ellie. I promise.'

There was a noise behind him, shouting voices and something that could have been a roar or a cheer. 'I've got to go,' he said. 'The postings are up and there are any number of chaps here, waiting to telephone home. I've sneaked in two calls now so I can't stay.'

No, she had to tell him what was happening. He would know what to do, wouldn't he?

'But David—'

'I'll ring again. As soon as I can. Keep the chin up, my love. And I'll see you soon. I promise.'

She swallowed hard, crushing down everything she wanted to say, all thoughts of Megan and the maze evaporating. The fear of last night was nothing to this. He shouldn't promise.

The line went dead and Ellie stood there, staring out of the window at the gardens. It was a misty morning, though the sun would soon burn it off. Could be a scorcher of a day, especially for September. Perfect flying weather, David would say.

And she was going to vanish. Somehow, somewhere, she was going to go missing and never be found. That woman in the maze had threatened them both. Perhaps Megan was in danger as well. She shivered and wrapped her arms around her chest, wishing it was David holding her instead.

David had sent her a photograph – him in his RAF uniform, so handsome, the strong line of his jaw and his dark hair falling over his mischievous eyes. He must have had it taken for her. He had signed the corner, writing in his familiar hand.

For Ellie, with all my love, David.

It sat on her bedside table. He watched over her when she slept and as she closed her eyes, his face would be the last thing she saw. As it should be already. If only they had seized the opportunity and said propriety be damned.

She had put the little corn dolly from the well beside it. The little maiden, her Guinevere to his Arthur. Her hero.

Tears stung her eyes now. He'd sounded so excited, so pleased with himself. But he'd be in harm's way every second of every day.

Don't think about that, she told herself sternly. *Don't ever think about that.*

She glanced down at her father's desk where a file and some notes lay scattered around. Miss Seaborne's hand was beautiful but Ellie didn't understand whatever language it was written in. She frowned at it, trying to make out the meaning. It looked like… like a code…

Not linguistic though. Not another language. Mathematical, perhaps? Or a combination of both? There was a pattern there – had to be really. A repetition in the symbols. She could see it but the characters seemed to blur as she tried to make it out.

You always have to look for the patterns, Professor Talbot had often said. *And how they are disrupted.*

Miss Seaborne had claimed to know Professor Talbot from Lady Cecelia's…

Ellie's life here had been calm and ordered. It had been disrupted with two things – meeting Megan in the maze, and the arrival of Miss Seaborne.

Ellie pursed her lips. For all anyone knew she was still talking to David in here. They'd leave her alone, let her have her privacy. And she really did want to know more about Ava Seaborne, after seeing her in the maze last night.

It took only a minute or so for the college to answer and, luckily, Ellie's former tutor was in her office.

'Professor Talbot speaking.' The voice on the other end of the telephone was crisp and businesslike.

Ellie heaved in a breath and tried to make her own voice sound bright and professional. 'Professor Talbot, hello. It's Lady Eleanor Fairfax here. I hope I'm not disturbing you.'

The Head of Mathematics at Lady Cecelia's college gave a brief laugh. 'Goodness me, no. Of course not, Ellie. It's delightful to hear from you. How are you managing down there in Sussex?'

Ellie smiled, the familiar sound of her mentor's voice like a balm. 'Not too badly. As well as everywhere else, I'm sure. And you? Everyone at the college?'

'Well, hardly anyone here at all these days. Everyone seems to have other things to do. They're digging up the front lawn to make a vegetable garden, can you imagine that? We'll have to get the students to tend it. It'll be the nearest thing to hard work some of them have ever seen. What can I do for you, Eleanor? You haven't just called to catch up with news here, I'm sure?'

No. No, she had not. She just wasn't sure how to broach this particular problem.

'It's… it's a slightly delicate matter, actually. I wanted to ask you about someone who recently came into my father's employ and mentioned you as an acquaintance, a Miss Ava Seaborne.'

'Ava Seaborne?' Professor Talbot paused for the longest moment and Ellie held her breath. 'I can't say I recall the name. Was she a student here?'

Strange. Very strange.

'No. At least I think not. She said you spoke highly of me?'

The professor laughed again, but there was a hint of strain buried in the sound. 'Well, I always do that, my dear. You're one of our finest graduates in the last few years. I hope to have you back here for a doctorate in no time. As soon as this blasted war is over. But I really can't recall a Miss Seaborne. Is she one of the Hall girls? Perhaps it was at an inter-collegial event?'

'Perhaps. It just seemed a little odd.' *Odd* didn't cover the things she had seen last night, and Miss Seaborne walking barefoot and shorn-headed through the maze was the least of it.

There was another long pause. Was Professor Talbot lying to her? Ellie wouldn't have thought that possible. And yet—

'Are you… are you all right, Ellie? Is your father there?'

'No, he's in London.' She tried to sound crisp and efficient, unconcerned. 'He's bound to be back soon. I'm sure there's a simple explanation. I'm probably being a bit of a silly old thing.'

But the voice at the other end of the telephone line didn't laugh. Not this time. 'I doubt that, my dear. I can check the name here and see if anyone else recognises it. It's probably just slipped my mind and will come back to me at any moment. You know how it is when you try to recall something too hard. And in the meantime, you will be cautious, won't you? These are trying times.'

Trying times. That was one way to put it. Ellie wound the cord from the telephone between her fingers, tying it in intricate knots which fell loose when she pulled her hand free. 'Of course.'

'I want to talk to you about an opportunity for a posting, actually. Nothing too arduous, although it might take you away from home a little. A great opportunity for a girl with a mind like yours. And a chance to do your bit. Would you be interested?'

For a moment Ellie wasn't quite sure what the professor was saying. She was still trying to work out what had happened last night and who Miss Seaborne could possibly be. A chance to do her bit? Of course she wanted that. 'I'd – um – I'd have to talk to my father. There's a lot to do here on the estate and…'

Professor Talbot clearly gritted her teeth and exhaled slowly.

'Naturally,' she said at last. 'I can always run it by him as well, so he understands it isn't just some frivolous whim.'

'What isn't?' asked Ellie, bemused. 'The frivolous whim, I mean.'

'I can say no more at the moment, my dear. I'll be in touch though, I promise.'

They said their goodbyes and Ellie gently replaced the receiver. Probably a secretarial role, or maybe even some teaching hours. If she was lucky it would be at the college.

Well, she wasn't needed here.

Behind her, someone cleared their throat, that pointed and determined sound that indicated they wanted her attention immediately. Ellie turned sharply to find Miss Seaborne at the door of the study, her dark eyes fixed on her, her face unreadable.

'Lady Eleanor, is there something with which I can help you?' Her voice sounded clipped and frosty.

How much had she heard? How long had she been there? Ellie tried to reel her way back through the conversation to see what she might have said. Did Miss Seaborne know she'd been checking up on her?

'Nothing, thank you,' she replied as lightly as she could manage. 'I was just talking to Professor Talbot about some opportunities.'

If she made it about her, rather than Miss Seaborne, then maybe… maybe…

'Indeed,' murmured the secretary, still watching her. 'Although, I'm not sure this is the time to be away from Foxfield Hall.'

There was a long and awkward pause. Ellie stared at her, trying to work out if she was wearing a wig or a hairpiece, and Miss Seaborne stared back.

Ellie decided to grasp the nettle, as it were. 'Did you enjoy your walk last night, Miss Seaborne?'

But Miss Seaborne looked mystified. 'My walk? You must be mistaken. I retired early last night. Now, if you don't mind I have work to do in here, Lady Eleanor.' Was it Ellie's imagination or was there an emphasis on the title?

Ellie nodded and left. A flat-out denial then. Nothing. But she couldn't have been mistaken, could she? It was only afterwards, when sitting in the morning room with the tea service laid out for one on the gleaming surface of the walnut inlay side table, that she realised she had been dismissed from her own father's study.

*

Ellie walked the gardens, tracing her footsteps from last night, looking for any hint of what happened. Of Miss Seaborne, of the night foxes, of the cloaked woman who had threatened them. Of Megan.

But there was nothing. It was as if it had never happened.

If it *was* all her imagination, perhaps the danger of her going missing was also an illusion. It was a tempting proposition, a way to escape from the constant dread hanging over her.

But she couldn't bring herself to believe it was all an illusion. Megan had been so sure. She had brought evidence.

Admittedly evidence which shouldn't exist but, still, it did. As obstinate as the woman who had brought it.

Ellie had to take this seriously. And she had to do something.

She circled back to the centre of the maze but there was nothing magical about it today. Not in sunlight. She came back via the rear of the house, intending to enter through the kitchens and have a quick work with Cook about dinner. But in the middle of the vegetable garden, Mary was sitting on a low stool, the evacuee children arrayed before her, cross-legged on the grass. Butterflies and bees flitted around them and the fruit hung heavy on the boughs of the trees. The abundance in the garden was shocking compared to the emaciated state of some of the children but it didn't seem to bother them. They laughed together, listening to Mary's stories, shouting out familiar patterns or suggestions. She had always had a near miraculous way with children.

Ellie remembered well the way she could spin a tale, or calm a terror. Mary had been the one person she was always sure would be there for her. She still was.

Now, she was teaching the children how to make corn dollies.

'And this one's the maiden,' she said, twirling the plaited stalks of wheat with her fingers. 'She's a princess and a sorceress, see? She's the queen.'

One of the children noticed Ellie then, standing there, watching them, and suddenly they were all whispering.

Mary got to her feet. 'Lady Eleanor, will you join us?'

'I didn't mean to interrupt you.'

'Not at all. Peter, there's a good lad, go fetch Lady Eleanor a seat from inside.'

One little boy, head newly shaven thanks to the nits Mrs Worth had found on a number of the evacuees, raced off into the kitchen and returned with another three-legged stool.

Ellie thanked him graciously and he turned bright red before muttering some kind of thanks and retreating to his friends. They all pulled him down into their midst. Ellie sat down and smiled at Mary who grinned, delighted to see her there.

'You remember how to make a corn dolly, don't you?' Mary asked her.

'I'm from Ashleigh,' Ellie replied with a smile. 'Born knowing.'

Mary laughed. 'I was showing them the maiden. We made foxes and hounds together earlier.'

'You called the maiden Lady Gwen when I was little.'

Absently, Ellie picked up one of the little fox figures scattered around at Mary's feet, the simple three-strand plait forming a wave, with a couple of artful twists to give it the impression of a running fox. This had to be one of Mary's. It was too good. The children's efforts showed more enthusiasm than art.

'Lady Gwen, that's right.' Mary hummed to herself, as if remembering something from much longer ago. 'She loved a knight and she died for that love. It says so in them old books of your father's. She was a queen, a Vala, and this was her land, hers and her people. They held it long before the Romans or anything. She had two sisters and they were queens too. And they ruled with magic and with wonder.'

The children leaned in, wide-eyed.

'Were they witches?' one little girl asked.

'Some called them that.' Mary's face grew grim. The child shrank back among the others. 'But they suffered for it. Back in the old times, before King Arthur and the like. It never does anyone any good to cross a Vala.'

'Vala' was the old Ashleigh word for witch, Ellie remembered, or more specifically for the witches of Ashleigh, both singular and plural. One of those odd local words that never quite made it off the South Downs. Another stamp that made the place unique.

'But then King Arthur pulled the sword from the stone and became the rightful king and everything was fine again,' Ellie finished as lightly as she could. They were facing enough pain and hardship. They didn't need any more nightmares in their life. And Mary's stories could be frightening and harsh. She remembered more than a few nightmares of her own had spawned from them.

She had grown up on tales of witches and monsters. Of Vala and their foxes. And somehow she had put them all away, locked them up in the back of her mind and turned to science and mathematics instead. Because those things made sense. They were predictable. They were safe.

Mary shot her a surprised glance. 'If you say so, Miss Eleanor. The story says he'll be back to save us in our darkest hour.'

Ellie rallied, wondering where she was going with this. 'It certainly does.'

Mary snorted. 'He'd want to hurry up then, surely?'

Childish giggles filled the air and Ellie had to smile. The old woman wasn't wrong, was she? There were dark hours aplenty ahead. The darkest, if Megan was to be believed, and Ellie had no reason to doubt her. 'We can't just give up, Mary.'

'Did King Arthur live in the maze?' a little girl asked, her lower lip wobbling.

'No, bless you, he wouldn't dare go in there,' Mary teased. Every little eye turned towards the dark walls of the maze across the green lawns and the maid frowned, clearing her throat sharply to snap their attention back to her. 'Mark my words though, with the blackouts and invasion looming we have enough worries. Stay out of the maze. It belongs to the Vala. No one should stray in there after dark, lest the night foxes get you.'

'What's a night fox?' the girl asked, suddenly pale.

Mary leaned in, looming over the child. 'Terrifying things, black foxes made of shadows. They gobble up disobedient children, out after dark. They were the guardians of Avalon, back in the day, where King Arthur himself lived. And it was only when the king turned against their mistress that—'

'Mary, enough,' Ellie tried to say. Talk of invasion was bad enough. These children didn't need mythical monsters as well as the real ones. 'Ashleigh isn't Avalon and scary stories are hardly—'

'I didn't say it was Avalon, my lady. The queens of Avalon took Arthur to his rest, and the Vala of Ashleigh… well, they had their offerings too. Why shouldn't they be the same thing? They were more powerful than any other. So powerful they wove people's lives like threads.'

'Maybe we should ask them back rather than old King Arthur,' said Peter.

'Now really,' Ellie interrupted before Mary could say something potentially treasonous. 'We love our King, don't we? Three cheers for King Arthur and for good King George, isn't that right, children?'

For a moment she thought they'd just stare at her as if she was a madwoman. But then they gave her a bright hip-hip-hurray that was actually more heart-warming than she would have thought. Maybe she needed to listen to herself.

'Who wants to make another corn dolly?' Mary asked as if she hadn't just been talking of witches and night foxes and scaring them all half to death with her wild tales.

They made more enthusiastic sounds and every one of them grabbed more straw. Mary handed some to Ellie.

'Speaking of King Arthur, why don't we make the champion?' But she didn't get any further. One of the girls gave a squeal of excitement and pointed.

Beyond the garden in all its colours, the dark mass of the yew hedges marking the edge of the maze dominated their view. Suddenly they were all babbling at once.

'It's a ghost! Look, it's a ghost!'

'It's a night fox!'

'Can't be. It's white!'

'So it's a ghost!'

'Nonsense,' Ellie replied because she didn't know what else to say. But they were right.

It was a fox, but one as white as snow. An albino.

How she got to her feet, she didn't know, but she stood there, transfixed, as the white fox froze, staring back at her. Their eyes locked together, human and animal, and Ellie felt a chill sweep through her.

It wasn't a ghost and yet… it wasn't entirely of this world either. She was sure of that.

Someone coughed, a violent, racking noise, one of the children, and the fox shot off, a streak of white light vanishing into the depths of the maze. Cheers and clapping, sounds of excitement and plans to chase it roared around her and suddenly a pack of ragged children was racing out of the garden and across the lawn towards the maze, roaring and shouting.

'Well, I'll be jiggered,' Mary whispered. 'Old Reynard's gone stark white. That's an omen, that is.'

But an omen of what? Ellie wondered.

'We'd better get them back before one of them gets hurt.'

'They're children, Lady Eleanor,' Mary sighed. 'The risk of a few cuts and bruises is what makes them alive. We'd better stop them for the sake of that poor fox though. Pack of little hounds, they are.'

*

After lunch, with the children rounded up, fed and taken on a long tiring walk to the village, Ellie took over the library. It was a small act of defiance and she wasn't sure anyone actually noticed. She was determined to make her way through the book on Ashleigh. It wasn't easy going. Hours passed.

Ellie blinked, trying to drive back the threatening headache and concentrate on the words. For a moment the page of the book blurred and then swam back into focus.

> *Under Canon Law enacted by King Edgar the Peaceful, heathenism was outlawed, along with well worship and magic of all kinds, including necromancy, divination and the songs of the dead. The holy groves were torn down, the wells stopped and broken. Edgar died soon after and from that time until the arrival of the Norman conquerors, not a single royal succession was uncontested.*

What was she to take from that? That despite the subject matter, it was the most boring drivel ever put on a page? That someone should have learned how to form a simple sentence if they wanted students to remember their words?

Her fingers brushed against the strangely smooth paper that Megan had given her last night. She still didn't dare to look at it. Not really.

'You look engrossed, Lady Eleanor. I'm sorry to disturb you.'

Miss Seaborne's voice broke her concentration and sent a spear of alarm through her. She hadn't expected her to come into the library this afternoon. The secretary had been locked away in Ellie's father's study ever since their awkward encounter this morning.

'What can I do for you?' Ellie asked.

'For me? Oh nothing. Not yet, anyway. I wished to discuss the situation this morning, your ill-advised telephone call to Professor Talbot.'

'Ill-advised?' Ellie narrowed her eyes in a glare. 'My father is a senior member of—'

'I know full well who your father is, my dear. I work for him, and for the same people as he does.'

'And what work do you do, exactly?'

Miss Seaborne smiled a thin smile. 'Classified.'

'Of course. How convenient.'

'I must insist you do not discuss what happens here in Foxfield Hall with anyone else. No matter how trusted you might think they are. You can never tell who might be listening.'

Well, quite, Ellie thought and glared at her. She had been listening, hadn't she? Must have been. 'It's almost as if someone could listen through walls. Like magic.'

Miss Seaborne reached for the book on local legends, a curious smile flirting with her lips.

Ellie slid it back, out of her reach. Petty, perhaps, but she wasn't feeling magnanimous right at the moment.

'Are you enjoying it? The book about Ashleigh? Tales of magic and witchcraft right on your doorstep. Did you know, there are some people who believe that magic will finish this war for us. That they can curse Hitler and put an end to it all.'

Miss Seaborne sat down, steepling her fingers in front of her face, waiting for a response.

Ellie blinked. She had meant her reference to magic as an insult and expected little by way of a response but Miss Seaborne had called her bluff. She spoke of magic as if it was real.

'What people?'

'Oh, they're around. Up in the New Forest for one, nearer to home as well.'

'Do you believe in curses?' Ellie asked, curious to see what the secretary would say. Ellie knew she'd seen Miss Seaborne in the maze last night, though her hair had been shorn like a boy's and now was coiled in an elaborate bun, clearly so long it would fall the whole way down her back if loose. But Ellie knew what she had seen.

A pained smile flickered over Miss Seaborne's face. 'Many people believe in curses. Especially once you're away from the cities and all their modern ideas. And curses come in all shapes and sizes. Look at the fortunes of this country in the last twenty or so years.'

Suddenly Ellie thought of all the women in the village who had lost sons or lovers, the fatherless children, the widows and old maids. 'And you think that's a curse?'

It was a stupid question. On the 30th of June, 1916, more than a thousand Sussex men had died in a single day at the Battle of the Boar's Head. The day Sussex died, they said. Husbands, fathers, sons, brothers, all lost. And that was just one day. The Great War had to have been a curse, and rumours of another one terrified her. But no one person had caused it. Not really. Monstrous machines of national pride and alliances that should never have been made, expansionism and opportunism…

'Don't you?' asked Miss Seaborne quietly, looking at Ellie as if she knew what thoughts were inside her head, as if she could read them, or even as if she had planted them there. 'Have you reached the section on King Edgar's curse yet? One argument is that King Edgar took rule and religion out of the hands of the Vala, the wise women, wanderers who knew the land and its power and could command kings. He hated them for it. And when that happened, it all began to fall apart. No succession from that time to the Norman invasion went uncontested. Kings fighting kings. This country, it seems to me, has only ever prospered with a queen on the throne.'

Ellie listened in amazement. She had seen Ava Seaborne in the maze last night. Had it really been her? Or a ghost, a memory? Someone like Megan, travelled from another time? And now it was clear that Miss Seaborne knew all about the Vala, the maze, believed in all of it. What *was* she?

Her voice flowed on, hypnotic, enchanting.

'And now, here we are, pitching headfirst into war again. The Nazis are the same. They treat women as no more than breeding stock for more Aryans – as if there ever was such a race. Whether they would have children or not, whether they want men or not. Can you imagine such a future?'

A future like that? No. It didn't bear thinking about. But that couldn't be what lay ahead. She had met Megan and Ellie couldn't imagine her enduring such a world.

Miss Seaborne reached out again for the book Ellie had been reading, the book which held the pages Megan had brought, folded up inside. Pages which talked about her going missing, about her vanishing forever. She hadn't dared look at them, but now she wished she had. Whatever happened, she knew she couldn't allow Miss Seaborne to see them.

She pulled the book back towards her before Miss Seaborne could touch it. The secretary didn't argue, just gazed straight at her, unperturbed.

What if she was behind Ellie's disappearance? What if she was behind it all?

'The future isn't written yet,' she said. 'It can still be changed.'

'Can it? Forward, backward… it's all the same,' murmured the secretary. She looked bemused for a moment, then scowled. 'You should know all this. Why don't you know this? What was he thinking?'

What was she talking about?

They stared at each other in silence for long minutes. Long, painful minutes. It was as if Miss Seaborne was searching for something in her, some recognition or secret. Should Ellie tell her what they'd seen last night? That they'd seen her in the maze?

The urge to just ask her was strong but somehow Ellie couldn't bring herself to do it. Was she afraid of the answer?

As they looked at one another it was as if a mask fell over the woman's face, leaving it hard and impenetrable. Which made Ellie think of the golden mask the figure in the maze had worn. They had the same air about them. An otherness. Ava Seaborne eventually turned away, trailing a fingertip along the edge of the shelf as she stared at the spines of the books. Ellie seized the opportunity to slip the pages out and hide them under her own notebook. Miss Seaborne stopped at the ominous gap where the Ashleigh book belonged.

'That book is a rare volume,' said Miss Seaborne. 'It would be a tragedy if something happened to it. Libraries used to carry curses too, curses on those who took things to which they had no right.'

'It's my father's library. I'm entitled to take whatever I want.'

'Including rare books on folklore? I doubt that very much.'

'Doubt all you want, but it's true. Besides, it's right here. No one has taken it.'

She held it out and Miss Seaborne tilted her head to one side, like a predator, examining her.

'So I see. I think, in future, you should keep out of the library altogether. Your father has many valuable items in his collection. And his papers are now considered classified. No one should be in here.'

'Not even me? My books are in here too.'

Miss Seaborne smiled. 'I hope, in future, that might change. But nevertheless, for the time being, yes. Even you.'

'I will speak to him about this.'

'Of course you will,' she sighed, the sigh of a long-suffering martyr. 'Nonetheless… You're a bright young woman, Eleanor Fairfax. You have so much to offer the world. We have plans for you, so many plans. But for the time being you really need to learn obedience.'

Obedience… to her? Ellie fumed. And who was this *we*? Her father? Whoever the two of them worked for?

The urge to ask about last night rose again, this time fierce and determined, but, as she opened her mouth to speak the words, Ava Seaborne turned around and left the room. The words never came. The door closed between them.

*

Ellie tried three times to escape the house that night. She had to go back to the maze. She needed to see Megan again, to reassure herself that it was real. And despite the threats from the woman in the mask and the terror of the night foxes, she would not be deterred. This was her home, it was her maze.

Each time she tried, however, Ava Seaborne appeared. It was never a confrontation. Just that when she made her way towards the back stairs, Miss Seaborne was at the foot of them, talking to Mrs Worth. When she headed for the door in the garden room, the secretary was sitting by the fire in there, reading a book, far later than would have been normal.

'Can I help you, Lady Eleanor?'

For a moment Ellie didn't know what to say. So she said the first thing that came to her mind, which was always a terrible idea.

'What are you reading?' It was a stupid question. She couldn't help herself. The woman had some kind of effect on her, deflecting her intent, making her forget what she was planning just long enough to put it off. It was infuriating.

It was deliberate, and Ellie was absolutely certain Ava Seaborne knew exactly what she was doing.

Miss Seaborne turned the book over in her hands, as if surprised to find it there. 'I found it on the shelf over there. A book from 1922, *Mazes and Labyrinths*. Have you read it? Quite fascinating.'

Was the blasted woman taunting her?

Ellie was tired and irritated. She just wanted to get out of the house and she didn't have time for this. 'I thought you wanted everything from the library to remain in the library.'

'I do. But this wasn't in the library. Perhaps your father left it in here. Perhaps you did. Not that it matters. I don't think it's a particularly valuable copy. Interesting though. It covers Egyptian, Cretan, Etruscan, and then on to hedge mazes, like your own. The Romans probably used yew as well. Henry II hid his lover, fair Rosamund, in a hedge maze at Woodstock to guard her from the wrath of your namesake, Eleanor of Aquitaine.'

'I think that's a legend rather than fact.'

Ava Seaborne closed the book gently and set it down on the side table. 'And yet many legends hide facts. Didn't you know that? Living here, I would have thought it was obvious. It's very late. Perhaps you should retire.'

'And you?'

She smiled, and Ellie realised that Ava Seaborne knew exactly what Ellie was planning to do and intended to thwart her at every turn. She needed to speak to Megan again, to see if her friend had discovered anything more about her disappearance. And simply to know that she wasn't just losing her mind. Besides, she had promised.

'It is so dark and quiet out here in the countryside. I'm more used to noise all around me. City life, you know. I find now I hear even the slightest floorboard creak. I think I'll keep reading about mysterious labyrinths for a while longer. Goodnight.'

And that was that. Ellie was trapped inside the house.

She went to bed, seething inside. Sarah appeared with a warm drink.

'Miss Seaborne suggested you might like it, that it might help you sleep, my lady.'

Like a fool she drank it and sleep took her quite unexpectedly.

Chapter Sixteen

Wednesday 25th September 2019

A sharp knock on the door woke Megan up. She hadn't meant to nod off but, once she'd sat down on the bed, she couldn't help it. Sleep had just swallowed her up, a well of darkness closing over her head, and there was nothing she could do about it. She had been dreaming about the maze, and foxes, and Ellie, of Ellie drowning in dark shadows. She reached out to her, their fingers tangling and tearing apart, and her screams were desperate but made no sound.

She stared at the little figure sitting on her bedside locker, the corn dolly of the kneeling king. It blurred in front of her and she reached out to hold it, cradling it in her hand.

She felt a bit better, just a bit. The nightmare dissolved, like the shadows of foxes.

The knock came again.

'Megan?' It was Sahar's voice. 'Megan, are you awake?'

'I am now,' she groaned.

'Nora's here? You're going out, remember?'

Awkward. That's what it was. So awkward. All the same, Megan felt a wild surge of delight.

'Just give me a second.'

She dived into the bathroom to freshen up and then pulled on clean clothes, before stepping out into the courtyard in front of their apartment.

Nora was sitting on one of the dilapidated garden chairs and just seeing her there, in a pale blue linen tunic and white capri pants, her glorious hair spilling around her shoulders, made Megan catch her breath. Beautiful, elegant… and Megan looked like an alien creature beside her. Nora wasn't wearing her glasses today. And her eyes looked different. Brighter.

'Sorry I'm late,' Nora said softly. 'It isn't really lunchtime anymore. Early dinner maybe? I had to deal with Alan. I swear, he'd sell the land out from underneath us if he could. If it's not one thing it's another. At least he's agreed to leave the books alone. He has some scheme with a TV company now and he wants to bring them here to film.' She nodded to the other chair, where Megan's coat was neatly folded over the back. 'Hattie said you left it in the maze. The prof brought it in. How is it all going?'

Megan didn't remember leaving it behind, but she must have. She picked it up and slipped it on, welcoming the warmth. 'It's… it's weird, to be honest.'

'Weird? How?' Nora smiled, but it was a tight, uncomfortable expression.

This was ridiculous. She wasn't going to spill all to Nora about the maze and the well. 'Just… oh, you know. Old places. Strange vibes. Keith's going to drain the well and check the foundations. I'm sure it will be fine. Hattie didn't seem too pleased about that.'

'I know. She told me. At length. I calmed her down. Told her the last thing you'd do was damage the well. It's just a little hole in the ground, right? Nothing to worry about.'

Megan smiled, heartened by Nora's faith in her. 'You still okay for lunch?'

Nora got to her feet. 'Absolutely.'

As Megan followed her, she shoved her hands into her jacket pockets to check for her keys.

'Ow!'

Something sharp dug into her palm. She dragged her arm out, and a spot of blood stood out in brilliant red on her palm. But when she reached back into her pocket, there was nothing there. Nothing at all.

For a moment she thought of the little corn dolly Ellie had given her, but that was back by her bedside, wasn't it? Besides, this had felt different, like a knife.

'Are you okay?' Nora asked.

Megan shook her hand and the ache dissipated. 'Yeah, sorry. I think my keys are inside.'

'That's okay. I'll drive.'

*

They piled into Nora's little Ford Fiesta which rattled and bumped them all the way down to the village. As they rounded a bend, a fox darted out of the undergrowth and Nora deftly swerved, avoiding it. She didn't even flinch, just adapted and carried on. It was impressive.

'I thought… I thought I saw a black fox the other night,' Megan said tentatively.

'A black one? They're rare. We don't get many around here. People used to say they were bad omens. Night foxes, they call them.'

Megan didn't believe it. She'd thought it was magic. But…

'There are *actually* black foxes though?'

'A few. We even had a few albinos in the breeding group over the years. Even rarer. But we're all about foxes here anyway.'

'What do you mean?'

'Well, Foxfield Hall, obviously. And there's no foxhunting in the area so they just keep breeding. Even before the ban. Drives the local farmers up the wall, but I like them.'

'No foxhunting? Not ever?'

She changed gear and threw a somewhat wild grin at Megan. Nora was mercurial, her moods, her eyes, her smile. 'I suppose the Fairfaxes didn't like it. Their coat of arms had a fox on it so the symbolism of it wouldn't be good. And the Hall's name as well. And… okay, this is going to sound odd but nothing good ever came of harming a fox on Fairfax lands. That's what they say around here.'

'Really? I suppose there's a story behind that too?'

Nora laughed. 'In Ashleigh? Oh, yes, there's always a story. So, back in the 1800s, Matthew Goodwin was a landowner on the far side of the village and he wanted to establish a hunt. Put the place on the map, encourage the aristocracy to move here, murder some innocent creatures, I don't know. The Fairfaxes said they'd have nothing to do with it and half the people in the area agreed. But Goodwin organised it anyway and invited all his London friends down for it. They had a massive party, legendary stuff. Next morning the hunt sets off and there's this black fox. A big old Reynard, the old folks call them, black as soot. Like a shadow, they say. Matthew takes off after it like a man possessed and falls from his horse the minute he crosses the boundary onto Fairfax land.'

Megan's whole body went cold. Her hand started to ache again. She tried to clench and unclench it to relieve the pain. It didn't help. *Like a shadow…*

'What happened?' she asked, her voice shaking.

Nora didn't seem to notice, or perhaps she thought it was the rattling of the Fiesta. She slowed as they reached the village. 'Matthew Goodwin broke his neck and died instantly. The fox was nowhere to be seen, and no one ever suggested foxhunting around here again.'

Nora cast her a curious look, noticing her discomfort. 'It's a local legend, that's all. We have almost as many of them as we have foxes.'

She parked outside a row of pretty cottages and locked the car, shoving the key deep into an invisible pocket of her flawless clothes.

On the village green there were more little tents and stalls set up now, although hardly any sign of anyone working on them.

'When is this festival?' Megan asked.

'Starts tomorrow. It'll run over the next few days and there's a huge party on Saturday night. Used to be just a day or so but anything that gets the paying public in, I guess.'

'You don't sound too thrilled.'

'I like things simple. Besides…' Nora sighed and pointed to the pretty cottage in front of them, right across from the square. 'I live there. You can't imagine what we find in the garden the morning after any piss-up around here.' Megan grimaced and Nora shook her head solemnly. No one wanted to dwell on the details of that. 'Anyway… Pub grub okay?' she asked lightly. 'Tom will call us a taxi to take you home, if you want? I mean, if you drink.' She flushed a little. 'Sorry, I should have asked.'

'That's okay. I do. I mean… a drink would be nice.'

They ordered two pints of the local cider and sat outside in the afternoon sunshine, in the beer garden, a patio behind the pub where the lawn rolled down to the river's edge, under a canopy and framed by hanging baskets filled with flowers of every colour. It couldn't have been more picturesque if it tried.

'It's lovely here,' Megan said as they studied the menu. Or rather she studied it. Nora hardly gave it a glance.

'Yeah. They do a great job. Quiet today though. I wonder where everyone is?'

A guy in a branded T-shirt came over with a notepad. 'They heard the TV programme was filming up near Fernhurst, didn't they? That archaeology one with the hot doctor? Half the village is up there hoping to get a look at her. How are you surviving, Nora?'

She smiled up at him, clearly old friends. 'You know me, Tom. Always got to be different. Have you got the steak sandwich on today?'

Megan was about to say she'd have the same, and was wondering what on earth Tom was referring to by talking about filming going on, when her mobile rang. The surveyor's number showed up on the screen. This… this couldn't be good. She apologised even as she answered it, grateful that Nora just shook her head and smiled.

'Keith? What's up?' She tried to sound bright and professional, and not like she had skipped off for a sneaky meal with her boss.

'Megan, we have a problem. A huge problem. I talked to Fred and he's made some calls already. He has people on the way. There's some woman who can help, filming nearby. Once the police clear it.' Keith sounded shaken. Not just shaken. He sounded completely freaked out.

'Police? Clear what? What's going on?' Megan asked softly and Nora's eyes grew wide.

'There's a body. In the well structure, in the foundations. There's a bloody body down there.'

Megan's stomach twisted and bile rose in the back of her throat. One thought overtook everything else, dark and terrible. Shattering.

It was Ellie. Who else could it be?

She had vanished in 1939. She must have gone back to the well, maybe to look for more corn dollies or to put back the ones she'd already found, and that woman... the one with the mask and the foxes... with the hooked knife and its bloody blade...

The masked woman had told them not to go back to the well. That they'd suffer if they did.

All Megan had wanted was for Keith to write a quick report and give her the go-ahead to begin the reconstruction work. It was a health and safety exercise, wasn't it? Nothing more. It was intended to cover them for insurance purposes. It was just meant to cut down on red tape.

Instead, he'd found Ellie.

Chapter Seventeen

Wednesday 25th September 2019

There were cars everywhere. Police cars, vans, some kind of huge truck from which men were unloading equipment. How it had all got there in the short time she and Nora had taken to drive back up, Megan couldn't say. It was like a circus had descended on the Hall.

There was a low-level hum of excitement around the hotel which immediately set Megan's teeth on edge. She couldn't say why until she got to the centre of the maze, found Sahar and saw what was going on.

Though dressed in a smart trouser suit, her short dark hair tapering to a point at the back of her neck, there was no mistaking the new arrival. She was the woman in white, the first woman they had seen at the well last night, the one Ellie had said was her father's secretary.

The excitement that surrounded her was palpable. Everyone craned around the trench which had been dug up to the well, where she paced around the edge, talking animatedly into her phone. Flashes from the photographer's camera lit up the scene, washing it of colour, casting terrible shadows on the looming hedges of the maze.

The woman's voice rose over the hum of interested chatter.

'No, we need to get her out before dark. I want the equipment here now or we risk degradation. Yes, absolutely. Well, see what you *can* do.'

Her. Megan swallowed hard and sharp claws sank into her chest. *We need to get* her *out now.*

As Megan approached, the woman turned and looked at her, eyes huge and dark, long-lashed, utterly compelling.

The gaze nailed Megan's feet to the ground, made her breath seize up in her throat. She squirmed until a smile flickered over the woman's face and suddenly Megan could move again. Her exhausted body complained with every step she took forwards.

'Oh good, here she is,' Sahar gushed enthusiastically. 'Megan, this is Dr Faye Seaborne, from *History Now*, on the TV? I'm sure you've heard of her. This is Megan Taylor, Faye.'

History Now… that archaeology show? It had to be, because Sahar was almost vibrating with excitement.

In person, Faye Seaborne was so much more, a force, a sun drawing all those around her into orbit. And she was beautiful.

Megan drew in an unexpectedly shaky breath. This wasn't like her. She wasn't the type to get star-struck. That was all it was… wasn't it?

'Megan,' Faye Seaborne said. 'Fred told me you were working here. I've been looking forward to meeting you and hearing all about the reconstruction.' She held out her hand and Megan took it, shaking it firmly, surprised at the strength behind her grip. 'I loved your garden at Chelsea last year.'

Megan said hello awkwardly and released Faye's hand. Her skin was strangely cold, but her grip was firm. It sent a shiver through her, something Megan couldn't quite define, or shake off. Faye just examined her as if she was some sort of find. She remembered seeing her on TV now, marching around some Mediterranean country, enthralling her viewers with tales of the past. Archaeologists weren't meant to be beautiful, were they? Not beautiful like her. They should be old and serious like Professor Deacon. Sahar was obsessed with the show. Even Owen had watched *History Now* when he was home on leave, though not, Megan suspected, for the history.

The thought of Owen sent a sharp pang through her body. She didn't want to think about her brother, about where he could be, about what could have happened to him, not standing here over what was, in effect, a grave. It brought thoughts of dark and desolate places, where hope was a faint memory. She'd felt that way last night, clinging to the tree with Ellie, desperately trying to hold onto her. Megan blinked, forcing the feeling away, and focused instead on the woman in front of her.

Why couldn't she shake the feeling that she shouldn't get too close? Because she'd seen her in the maze? Because it was far too much of a coincidence? Because she suddenly couldn't seem to think straight?

And if she was here, now, how had Ellie recognised her? She'd said the woman was her father's secretary. And the name was the same – Seaborne.

Ellie would know what to do, how to get out of this situation effortlessly and without any offence. Megan just had the feeling she was being reeled in like a fish on a line.

'I thought Professor Deacon would be in charge of any archaeology here.'

Faye Seaborne smiled, that glittering, celebrity smile. 'Oh Fred, yes, he's such a pet. I needed something for my show, the new series, you know? Our national heritage is a huge deal right now. And the house touches on so many aspects of English history. It's serendipity, really. I was filming just down the road. I'd already been talking to Alan Brooks about the site anyway, just in passing. So when this happened, Alan phoned me, and put me in touch with Fred. I explained we had funding already in place and could get here immediately. Given the condition of the body, it's a matter of urgency. And when I talked to the coroner, the police agreed too. Aren't they darlings?'

'*Darlings*,' Nora said icily. When they'd arrived at the hotel, Nora had made straight for the police to get a report and then gone to talk to the other members of the board. Now, she'd reappeared with the somewhat sheepish professor in tow. 'Right. And the body? What did the police say about this—' She gestured to the whirlwind of activity around them.

Nora was not impressed, intimidated or enchanted by Faye Seaborne, it seemed. A weird little sizzle of pride warmed Megan's chest.

Slowly, listening to the wide range of complaints and debates between Nora and Faye, Megan was able to piece together what had happened. The local police had already arrived and examined what little had been unearthed so far. They'd cleared the excavation to go ahead, although they were still watching everything with keen interest. Keith had departed for the bar, cursing the whole fiasco, and Hattie was in there too, in a foul mood, apparently. And after one phone call from Alan Brooks, Faye Seaborne and her team had swooped in, along with the entire circus that accompanied her.

She didn't feel right. She didn't feel right at all.

Overtired, perhaps. Stressed and exhausted. All those things, and something else too. Her hand ached. Maybe she should get someone to look at that. Maybe she needed a tetanus injection. She didn't know what she'd cut it on.

'We need a room inside,' said Faye.

'In the hotel?' Nora said, too loudly. Her voice carried over the noise. 'You can't bring it inside the hotel.'

Faye's hands went to her hips. Celebrity she might be, but she was more than that. It shone through now. She was not to be argued with. Not even by Nora.

'I need to get her inside and under controlled conditions as soon as possible.' Why did she need to do that? If it was Ellie… surely the coroner would take the body. But Megan couldn't find an opening to ask. And what could she say anyway? She just kept listening, praying someone would say something to answer any of her questions. Including the most pressing one of all. She just didn't dare ask it herself. 'I can't get her to the university tonight. I have the equipment coming, Nora. I just need the room. If you can't manage that much… Alan said it wouldn't be a problem.'

'Oh, Alan did, did he?' Nora muttered darkly. Alan Brooks had spoken and all the minions had to scurry to obey. She sighed, with the hint of a growl underneath it, and Megan felt her frustration. 'Fine. I will see what we can sort out.'

'It's so lucky you were here,' Faye said sweetly. 'Thank you so much. You're a pet. I told him that you'd never be so unreasonable.'

Nora muttered dark words about Alan and Alan's promises and Alan's projects and what she'd like to do to Alan if she had the chance. 'Sahar, can you give me a hand?'

Which left Megan standing there, all alone with the woman she'd last seen in the centre of the maze. She was about to back away. She wasn't going to get any answers now anyway. But Faye stopped her.

'I'd like your professional input on the maze and the well, Megan,' she said, her grin turning wolfishly eager. 'So we don't damage any of the surrounding landscape in the excavation.'

What could Megan say? The land was her responsibility. 'Yes. Sure. Of course.'

Faye raised her eyebrows in a knowing way but said nothing. Megan couldn't help but feel that the archaeologist could see right through her, as if she could open her up and read her like a book.

She let Faye lead her off, through the group of archaeologists, past the police who were looking on in distracted fascination. They'd given over responsibility for unearthing the body to Faye's team but they hadn't left. Not yet. If it was a recent body, or even a cold case, they would be needed. A cold case like a woman missing for eighty years…

Faye moved through the onlookers like Moses parting the red sea, Megan following her. She didn't want to look, didn't want to see her friend cold in the ground. But there was nothing she could do. And she had to look. She had to know.

It didn't look like a body. A lot of it hadn't been uncovered yet, but Megan could make out a blackened, claw-like hand reaching out from the earth at the bottom of the trench dug up against the base of the well's wall. There was still skin on it, and she could see the nails. A hundred zombie movies lurched, groaning, to the forefront of her brain and Megan wished she'd never seen one. Or this. She really wished she hadn't seen this, before she had even taken a proper look. It was different when it was real, different when there was a chance you knew the person. Even if that in itself was impossible. Under all logical circumstances.

But logic didn't seem to apply on the grounds of Foxfield Hall.

The face was turned away and still half buried, but visible from the ear to the cheek, just as well preserved as the hand. Three of Faye's team clustered around their find, peeling back the remaining soil and spraying a fine mist on the body. Megan stood with Faye above them on the edge of the wedge dug into the rich black earth.

'What are they doing?'

Faye smiled. 'The air could dry her out and destroy her. Look at the way she's preserved. The boggy ground mummified her. I'd call it a miracle if I believed in such things.'

Megan didn't either. But she believed in peat. The earth here, formed from generations of dead things, layer upon layer, cool and wet, close enough to water to keep saturated without a stream running through it and disrupting everything... Nature's formaldehyde, one of her lecturers had once called it. But better. Moss grew over things, cut off the oxygen, soaked up acid, blocked all the things that broke down living matter. It was a living time machine.

Megan knew all the properties of the soil here. She'd looked it up before starting work on the gardens. Part of her job. You had to know the earth in order to persuade it to grow what you wanted.

And now she was looking at a very different thing being drawn from the ground.

She swallowed hard and finally managed to ask the question she had wanted to ask all along. The one she didn't really want to hear the answer to. The one choking her. 'And she's... Do you know how she died? Who she is?'

'Not yet. But we will. She wasn't any older than thirty, probably more like twenty-five, I'd guess. As to how she died...' Faye Seaborne breathed out in a long low hiss. 'Her hands were tied. Look, there are still fragments of the ropes. And there's more around her neck, I think, and if I'm right – Davie, can you clear there? Yes, just there. It looks like a deep cut.' They changed the focus of their attention as if they were extensions of Faye's own hands, doing her bidding, carrying out her work.

'She was murdered then?'

'More like a sacrifice. For the well. Do you realise what this means?'

No, of course Megan didn't, but she had the impression that Faye wasn't really talking to her any more. It was more like she was talking to herself, or scripting something for the TV show, writing the scene for her next bestselling history book. Megan found herself looking around for a camera and, sure enough, there were two of them, capturing and documenting everything that happened. 'She could be a *genius loci* sacrifice. Richie, make sure you get some pictures there. Where's that gurney? We need to get her out of there.'

Finally Megan found the words, heaved them out of her mouth, asked that question she was dreading. 'Is it – is it Eleanor Fairfax?'

'*Eleanor Fairfax?*' Faye looked away from the body for the first time, and stared at Megan as if she'd asked if it was a giraffe. 'Megan, this body is thousands of years old. Eleanor Fairfax didn't vanish until 1939. This poor girl was killed and thrown down here before the Romans arrived on our soil. Look at her clothes, the ornament on her jewellery. *Look* at her.'

They'd cleared most of the mud off the girl's face now. It almost looked as if it had been bronzed. Her features were perfectly preserved, finely boned and beautiful. Megan could even see the remains of a frown, a deep line between her eyebrows. Her hair, slicked with earth, still curled against her high cheekbone. It looked as red as Nora's. Her eyes were closed and Megan could make out her eyelashes, too. Her mouth was slightly open, as if at any moment she might take a breath and get up.

But she wasn't Ellie.

Megan's stomach heaved and she turned away, giving in to the sudden fear that she'd throw up. She covered her mouth, which also served to keep her from yelling with relief.

Faye caught her arm, helped her to step back safely. 'It's okay. Here, just sit down. It can be a shock. I didn't think. I'm sorry. You've probably never seen a body before.'

Megan nodded weakly and took a deep breath. 'Who was she?'

'We don't know. We might never find out, but we'll try. There are local legends that might give a clue. We may even try to do some DNA matching. The lucky thing about somewhere like Ashleigh is that generations of the same families lived here. You can help if you like, to give her name back to her? Or at least to give her an identity. It's part of what we do, you know?'

A *genius loci*. The Green Lady, that was what Faye Seaborne was implying. Or at least, that was Megan's guess. Ellie would know for sure.

I could tell her, Megan thought. *She might not believe me, or call it wishful thinking. But I know what I saw, the light in the well. The Green Lady.*

But the thought of telling Faye about all that stole her voice. She wasn't feeling right, not really. She kept losing track of her thoughts, as if Faye Seaborne's proximity was confusing her. She couldn't find the words, even if she'd been brave enough to speak them. Instead she watched the archaeologists, stepping back and sitting on the sidelines, letting them do their work. They were an amazing team. Faye had them drilled in every aspect of the job. They knew what to do before she had to say it. She was like a general in charge of an army. Megan watched everyone scurry about at her command. The cameras documented everything, but skirted the edge of the dig, never getting in the way.

When they finally were ready to move the body inside, Faye ushered Megan along by her side. Megan helped to lift the equipment, Richie loading her down with rolls of plastic sheeting. They processed through the hall below the main staircase, past reception, like a scene from a horror movie, the few remaining guests and all the staff present trying to see what was going on while not getting so close as to be in the way. Sahar was waiting for them in one of the lesser-used meeting rooms, a high-ceilinged space with open beams above grey flagstones, one of the oldest parts of the building.

Megan helped Richie set up a table and line it with the plastic sheets. The archaeological team laid the body out with surprising reverence. Or maybe not that surprising, given their veneration of the past and the lost, the thing which drove them to do this job in the first place.

'Set up the tent and get the humidifier running,' Faye was saying, in that calm controlled way which made everyone there jump to attention. 'Let's make sure we keep her safe and stable. We can get her back to the university first thing in the morning. Okay, people, you all know what you should be doing.'

'Notifying the press?' someone shouted, which elicited a roar of laughter.

'Glory later,' Faye replied with a wry smile, humour making her voice rich and beautiful. 'Archaeological best practices first. Now, out. All of you. If you don't have something to do, we'll see you in the morning. She's safe and she's back home.' Her hand rested on the edge of the table and she looked down on the face from a thousand years ago. A strange expression of intimacy flickered over her own features. 'I'll keep watch over her tonight.'

*

It was after nine before Megan got back to her room. Somehow the whole afternoon and evening had been sucked away by the dig and subsequent chaos, all wrapped up in the aura of Dr Faye Seaborne and swept along in her wake. They'd eaten burgers and chips from the bar, Megan only realising after she had devoured hers that she had never actually had lunch. She wondered if Nora did. She hadn't seen her since the body had been moved. Sahar had retreated to her office in the hotel, with a stack of paperwork, to be on hand in case Faye Seaborne needed anything.

It wasn't Ellie. That was the first thing. No matter what happened, Megan clung to that thought. It was only when she was away from Faye and her carnival of archaeologists that she found she had time to gather her thoughts. She didn't doubt for a moment that somehow she and Ellie had seen Faye Seaborne in the maze last night. Perhaps she had been scouting out the area behind Fred Deacon's back? Maybe Alan had invited her? It didn't make any sense, but since Megan was dealing with a woman from 1939, monstrous shadowy creatures and death threats from a masked psychopath with a reaping hook, when did things not making sense stop her?

There was no sign of Nora. They hadn't even said goodbye. That was when Megan realised she had hardly even thought of Nora since they had got back here. From the moment she had come within Faye's orbit, nothing but the archaeologist and her dig had existed. It was a thought that sent a cold pang of dread through her. Something was wrong here. Terribly wrong.

Megan wondered if she should just message Nora, see if they could rearrange the abandoned lunch for tomorrow and…

Her phone began to ring in her hand, loud and shrill, one word glaring at her from the screen.

'Megan, love?' her mother's voice wavered from the other end of the line.

Something was wrong. Desperately wrong. Dread made Megan's chest tighten and her skin shrank in on her bones.

'What happened?' she asked at last.

'I had some news about Owen. Someone from the Ministry… They found some… some remains. They say he… he's dead.' Mum choked as she said the dreaded word.

Megan's stomach took another one of those lurches, one that left her wobbly and sick. The world spun around her in the wrong direction. The horrible symmetry of her own day took her strength away.

'Remains? What sort of remains?'

She could picture her mother the last time she'd seen her. She'd looked so pale, like all the blood had been drained from her face. They'd argued. Megan couldn't stand to see her like that, or to hear the same despair in her voice again.

'They used DNA testing.'

She didn't answer so her mother went on, her voice fast and desperate, shaking, barely coherent.

'How can they even say he's dead from DNA? DNA only tells them so much, doesn't it?'

No one else in her family had thought Owen was dead. Only Megan. She was the only one who had said it was possible, who had thought it. That was why she had left, why she was here in Ashleigh. Because all she had done was upset her family.

'Megan? They… they have to be wrong, don't they?'

Megan shrugged in the most appalling impression of nonchalance anyone had ever seen. Luckily there was no one here to see it but herself. Her shoulders rose and fell like sacks of potatoes, and she thought, for a terrible moment, that she would cry. She couldn't cry. Not for Owen.

If she cried it would be over. He really would be gone. She just… she couldn't. And still, she couldn't find the words. Not the right ones. Not to make this go away. Her head swam with the madness of it all.

'Megan, love?'

'Yes, I'm still here.'

'Their tests aren't going to be haphazard, are they?' Mum whispered and it sounded so final. Like she wanted Megan to argue. Like she wanted Megan to regurgitate all the things her mother had said since Owen had vanished. When there was no reply, Mum sighed and her voice was even quieter. 'Maybe he is dead. You said that all along. You were right.'

The sense of betrayal made Megan's stomach twist again. She fought the rush of bile in the back of her throat. She didn't want to be right.

'But *you* can't believe it, Mum!' she protested, the pain in her voice too powerful to disguise. There was a long pause. Far too long.

'No.' Her mum's reply was hushed and hesitant. 'Not in my heart. But when they say it so many times…'

Was this what heartbreak sounded like? Was this how it felt?

'I don't… I don't know…'

'I can't believe he's dead.'

That's what her mum had said when Megan left. If she didn't believe it, if she didn't feel it, Owen couldn't be dead. Megan had been too angry to reply. Now she just felt like something had hollowed her out inside.

'You're a good girl, Megan. You really are.' But then her voice wavered and Megan didn't feel good at all. Not good to anyone or good for anything. 'I'll let you know. If I hear more, I mean. I've got to go.'

She hurried herself off the phone, too upset to talk any more, and Megan just stood there, holding on as the line went dead.

Then she couldn't hold it in any longer. The sob burst out of her, loud and violent, tearing through the silence of the apartment, wrenching itself free until she doubled over in agony.

She waited until the sobs subsided. Because they always did eventually. No one could cry forever, no matter how they might want to.

She had tried to be the realist in the family, tried to brace herself and prepare the others for this moment. But in this moment, she realised that, in spite of all she had said, she had never *really* believed Owen was dead. The gut-wrenching pain hadn't been quite so gut-wrenching as it was now. Because a tiny voice had always whispered that he *might* be alive. And when the rest of her family believed with such conviction that Owen was still out there, that tiny voice inside her had never truly died away. Despite everything she'd said to them. Despite the fact she'd left. But now…

She had known it would end like this.

Whatever happened to 'no man left behind'? That was what they said in all those cheesy old war movies, in the same plummy accents that Ellie carried off so well.

She had to do something. Anything. She couldn't save Owen, but maybe there was one person she *could* save.

If Megan stayed here now, went to bed and went to sleep, she'd be leaving Ellie behind, giving up on her too.

She wouldn't do that.

Ellie wasn't dead yet. Not in her time. And maybe Megan could still warn her, stop it.

Or at least she hoped so.

She pulled on her jacket and headed off into the night.

*

It was colder with the fall of darkness. A fine mist was already covering the ground, the first hint of winter around the corner. Megan slipped by the open windows of the bar, where the archaeology team were living it up and celebrating their find. Curiosity took her further around the side of the Hall, to the place where Faye was watching over the body. She could see her inside, only one light on. She was reading, her head bowed over her book, her skin pale and perfect in the gilded light.

Faye looked up suddenly, as if hearing a noise. Megan hadn't made a sound, she was sure of it, but flinched back behind the shrubbery as the archaeologist glared at the windows. Such a fierce look. It belied the character she displayed to the world. There was murder in those eyes.

Megan retreated silently as Faye got to her feet and stalked towards the white tent holding the mummified remains. She reached out her hand, fingers splayed wide, and held it there, as if feeling vibrations or heat.

'Hush,' she whispered, so softly that Megan could only just make out the words, but not so quiet that they were lost entirely. They drifted on the evening breeze, as if someone or something wanted her to hear them. 'I'm here now. I have you. You're home. Finally home. It will be all right. I promise, my sister. Sweet Vala, my dearest Gwyn, I'll keep you safe. I promise.'

Gwyn. 'Gwynhyfer', Hattie had called the Green Lady. Guinevere.

Megan burned to speak to Faye, to know who she really was, to keep watching from the shadows as she in turn watched over the skeletal shape. But Ellie, alive and warm and flesh and blood – at least in 1939 – needed her. Megan crept away, as quickly as she dared without making noise. The mist was heavier as she neared the entrance to the maze, hiding her from the world. The house itself became a ghostly silhouette behind her, the lights from various windows diffuse, like an abstract painting. As she stepped into the enveloping walls of the maze, the mist closed behind her and the house vanished.

The green will-o'-the-wisps sprang up as she walked, and she followed them inwards. There was something furtive about their progress this evening. She couldn't say what it was, but it echoed in her chest. Fear, perhaps, or nerves. More than a case of the jitters, though. What if the foxes and their gold-masked mistress were there again? What if she made good on her threats? What if, by removing the body of the Green Lady, the woman Faye Seaborne called Gwyn – her sister, she'd said – had upset the balance of it all? Broken the spell?

The centre looked as it always had. The trench had vanished, and the area around the well was intact. The benches surrounding it still stood in their familiar positions. It was untouched, as if the dig had never taken place. They couldn't have put it back so quickly, nor so perfectly. Besides, they were meant to be digging again tomorrow.

That wasn't the problem. Megan was alone.

Ellie wasn't there. Megan called her name once or twice, but it was hopeless. She couldn't push away the fearful dread that she was too late after all, that something had already happened to her, or that the magic wouldn't work again. She squirmed on the swing seat in the bower, wishing the other woman would just appear as she had the previous times. She even tried closing her eyes and willing Ellie to join her, but nothing worked. It felt like praying and prayer had never served her. Not even for Owen.

She was too late.

Maybe the body *was* Ellie's, despite what Faye said. Maybe the paper had it wrong about when she vanished, or maybe their fragile understanding of the way this time thing was working was at fault. Whatever reason, Ellie wasn't here.

Of course she wasn't here. Eleanor Fairfax had disappeared eighty years ago. Megan knew that. She had always known that. She was an idiot. Sitting in the dark, looking for ghosts, believing in magic, counting on it. Trying to make it so that someone who went missing could be found again. So that someone everyone said was dead, wasn't.

Just like Owen.

Megan dropped her face into the palms of her hands and closed her eyes to stop them burning. But it didn't work. The tears just kept coming.

Chapter Eighteen

Tuesday 26th September 1939

At least a night of unbroken sleep did her some good. All the same, Ellie stared at the maze from her bedroom window the following morning and prayed that Megan hadn't missed her. That she didn't think the worst. Ellie still hadn't gathered up the bravery to read those papers. She didn't want to.

She didn't dare.

Ellie had appointments to keep with her neighbours today so no one stopped her leaving. She set off on her bicycle, all the better to preserve petrol, and called on the elderly sisters, the Miss Bellamys, over on the far side of Ashleigh, then stopped in on the vicar, promising him faithfully that she would be ready to hand out the prizes for the fête and would be delighted to help out however she could. Her father normally did it. She suspected that she was something of a second choice. The vicar still hadn't warmed to her after her observation about the church finances.

She wondered what the children staying with her would make of the Harvest Festival. They'd love it, surely. She always had as a child. Still did, if she was honest. All that life and music, dancing, the celebration, the games, the prizes. Races and cricket, and donkey rides for the little ones. Yes, they'd love it.

The Hall was strangely quiet when she returned. Far too quiet. Ellie hadn't realised how comfortable she had already become with the sound of the children in the gardens or thundering around upstairs.

On the hall table lay a note written in Travers' neat script, telling her that David had telephoned again. No other details than that.

Damn it, she had missed him. She heaved out a sigh. Poor David. She hadn't written back to him yet either, entirely consumed with the mysteries of the Green Lady, the maze and Megan Taylor. There he was, ready to risk all for King and Country, and she didn't have time to put pen to paper for him.

It wasn't fair. She would have to do better.

There was no sign of Travers either, which was strange. Ellie took off her coat and hung it over the back of one of the chairs in the hallway, before going in search of one of the household to see if David had left any further message or, better yet, a number she could use to ring him back.

Sarah was dusting in the drawing room and, when Ellie entered, she spun around. Her eyes were red, her face flushed, and she had clearly been crying.

'Whatever has happened?' Ellie asked.

'Miss… Miss Eleanor… Oh, Miss Eleanor, it were awful.'

'What was? What happened?'

'She sent the children off. Called up the evacuation officer and had them take the poor little things to new billets. Turned them all out just like that. And then… then… Mary gave her such a call-out over it, that woman gave her marching orders and all.'

Mary?

Mary had been here forever. She couldn't be gone. She'd been a fixture in the house for as long as Ellie could remember.

'Where has she gone?'

'I don't know, miss. I don't know where she could go. This house is all she's ever known.'

And the children, uprooted and cast out just when they were starting to settle in. A cold anger settled over Ellie. No matter who she was or might be, Ava Seaborne had no right.

'Where is Mrs Worth? What did she have to say about it?'

The household was Mrs Worth's domain, nothing to do with Miss Seaborne.

'Downstairs and she's fit to be tied. But what could she do?'

Right, Ellie had to make a stand on this and quickly. This was not on at all. 'Tell them both I want to see them. Now.'

But when they arrived, Mrs Worth just stood there sullenly while Miss Seaborne looked wholly defiant.

'Where are the children?'

'The evacuation officers are taking good care of them,' said Miss Seaborne. 'They will be certain to find the best homes for them, where they can have individual attention rather than being treated like something from an orphanage. Having them here really wasn't appropriate, not with your father's work. We can find another way to make this house useful for the duration.'

'There is no *we* about this, Miss Seaborne. This is my home. You had no right to dismiss Mary. Where is she? Where did she go?'

'I really have no idea, nor do I wish to know.'

Anger burned like acid in the back of Ellie's throat. 'You just turned her out?'

'Eleanor, Mary was not all she appeared, you must realise that. She had views that were not in keeping with your father's position and his work. It could have been very dangerous. She had entered the study without permission and was reading papers that are highly confidential. And sometimes, even if we know and trust a person—'

'Are you saying Mary is a spy?'

Still Mrs Worth said nothing. Nothing at all.

'Mary Hatten?' Ellie said, for emphasis. 'You know her, Mrs Worth. She worked here even longer than you. I've known her all my life.'

'My lady,' said Mrs Worth at last. 'Mr Travers found her, rifling through the papers. By rights we should report her.'

'That's in hand,' Miss Seaborne said curtly. Mrs Worth lowered her gaze, unable to meet Ellie's furious stare.

'Have you even informed my father? Or are you taking all decisions in his absence?'

Ellie dodged by the startled women and strode down the hall. She reached the door to the study and, flinging it open, she darted inside. The door slammed behind her on Miss Seaborne's appalled but impotent protests. The key was in the lock still. Ellie turned it with a triumphant click and took it with her.

She wouldn't have much time, she knew that. It wouldn't take long for Miss Seaborne to have Travers come up with his set of keys, a duplicate for everyone in the house. She seized the phone and picked up the receiver.

'Hello, operator? Please connect me to the Percival Club in London,' she replied, thinking it sounded painfully vague. She didn't know the number. Did that matter? She prayed it didn't matter.

'Just a moment, caller,' the operator chimed. 'Please hold.'

The line hummed and buzzed. Ellie imagined the operator plugging the cable into the right jack, making the connections, and willed them, prayed for them, to hurry up.

'Good evening, this is the Percival Club.' The voice was all Oxbridge, clear and crisp, just like her father's, all control and politeness.

'I need to talk to the Earl of Ashleigh. This is his daughter, Lady Eleanor. I believe he's still there.' She had to sound like a lady, not an upset girl.

'I'm afraid he's not at the club at this moment, Lady Eleanor.' She sucked in a breath that physically hurt. He couldn't have gone. He couldn't have left yet. 'I can take a message and bring it to him myself the moment he returns.'

'Yes. Please.' But what should she say? What on earth should she say? 'Please tell him that he needs to contact me as soon as possible. There's a…' What? What could she say? That his secretary had dismissed her maid for no reason? That she had turned out the evacuees he hadn't wanted there in the first place… When he was preparing for war? No, not that. It had to be rational with her father. It had to be about Miss Seaborne and Mary.

Mary wasn't a spy but there was every possibility that Miss Seaborne could be. That was one of their tricks, wasn't it? To blame someone else and throw suspicion off. She had access to all his papers, and full control over this house all of a sudden.

Ellie couldn't let this go. And she had to make it sound urgent. But not so urgent that it would worry her father. Just enough to make him telephone her as soon as possible. 'There's a situation at home. I believe it to be a risk to the security of the Empire. Please ask him to ring and talk to me. Only to me. That's vital.'

'Yes, Lady Eleanor.' The man sounded so reliable, so perfectly stolid. She had to trust that he would do as he said. Honour was the first thing to everyone at his club, just as it was with her father. Honour above all else. Perhaps even family. So if the situation called for it, Father would leave her stranded at home. He had to. His duty was to his country. He thought she was safe with Miss Seaborne.

But Ellie knew what Megan would say – that on Thursday night she would disappear. And who on earth was the prime candidate as her abductor? The woman her father had left in charge, dismissing the servant she trusted. Cutting her off from the world she knew. Making sure she was all alone. Who else?

'Thank you.' What else could she say? 'To whom am I speaking?'

'Andrews, my lady.'

'Thank you, Andrews. Goodnight.'

'Goodnight, my lady.'

She settled the receiver back onto the cradle and stood there, in the darkness, listening to the silence. What had she done? Was it going to work? Where was he?

Outside the door, she heard voices – Miss Seaborne raging and Travers, his voice deep and filled with reservations, telling her to calm herself. And then the key turned in the lock and Ellie knew it was all over.

The door opened and Miss Seaborne descended on her like a fury from Greek legend.

'Lady Eleanor is overwrought,' Miss Seaborne decreed and, to Ellie's horror, no one argued. They just stood there. 'Travers, please help her to her room and make sure she does not leave it.'

'You can't do that!'

But she could. Because her servants weren't doing anything to help her. Travers and Mrs Worth were utterly compliant with Miss Seaborne now.

'I think you'll find I can. I didn't want it to come to this, Lady Eleanor, but your father left specific instructions regarding your safety.'

Ellie stared at Travers and he nodded solemnly. 'Please, Lady Eleanor, this way,' he said in his gentle, sombre tones.

She had to find a way to escape her room for the night. Because otherwise, if she didn't appear for a second night, Megan would think she was already dead.

Chapter Nineteen

Thursday 26th September 2019

Megan hadn't meant to sleep so late. That was the first thing she thought when she woke up to the rich golden light of the September mid-morning sun streaming through the windows. She hadn't even had the energy to draw the curtains last night. She'd slept through her phone alarm, and presumably Sahar getting up and heading off to work. She had slept through everything.

The exhaustion was getting worse. It didn't feel natural and she didn't like it. Stress might account for it. Her mum always said stress was her undoing. But it had never hit Megan so badly before.

Mind you, she had never known stress like this before.

She made her way outside and found her team already at work. The gossip was all about the body in the maze and who or what it might be. And the maze, when they managed to make their way into it, was a mess.

'They'd better fix it up for us,' said Stefan. 'Poor old Makosh, she won't be happy with this.'

Neither would the Green Lady. Or the witch with the golden mask.

How would archaeologists react to a pack of shadowy monsters bearing down on them?

'What do you want to do, boss?' asked Mark, the three others looking on expectantly.

She had to make a call. 'Back to work on the cottage garden, I suppose. I'll make sure they don't leave it like this, I promise.'

They looked happier with that and headed off. Megan lingered, looking at the trenches like open wounds, the scoured earth, the mud and dirt, and the lines of tape marking it all into regimented squares. The archaeology crew had trampled down all the roses around the bower. She could prune them back and probably save the plants but it would be touch and go. They were old roses. They'd been there in Ellie's time. And before that.

Now they were almost destroyed, crushed into mud and dirt.

Last night she had seen them covering the bower, beautiful and in full bloom. So whatever magic that allowed her to touch 1939 was still intact. But there had been no sign of Ellie. She had waited. She had stayed far too late. Exhaustion dragged at her even now.

Maybe it was the maze itself, sucking all the energy out of her. Her hand ached as if she had thrust it into a fire. There were no marks on it now, no swelling or any indication of any injury, but she couldn't shake the idea that it was infected.

She left the shadowed labyrinthine pathways and headed towards the cottage garden. But before she reached it, she saw Nora.

She was standing very still on one of the gravel paths, frozen in place. For a moment, there were two of her, two women almost identical, but at the same time, not the same. Subtle differences, shades and nuances. Her eyes, her jawline. A wave of dizziness swirled around Megan's head.

But then she blinked and it was just Nora again.

Except it wasn't. Not just Nora. On the grass beside her, a fox gazed up at the red-haired woman, its fur white as snow.

As Megan watched, Nora crouched down and stretched out her left hand, the fingers softly curled underneath. The fox crept towards her, slowly and cautiously, sniffing her skin and then, so gently, it rubbed its head against her hand, like a cat.

Transfixed, Megan could only stare as the wild animal let Nora caress it, moving her hand down its back and scratching its ears as if it was a beloved pet. Nora smiled, her expression beatific, as she communed with it.

'Boss? Can you take a look at this?'

Stefan's voice broke the silence and Megan spun around, shocked at this male sound intruding on something private and magical.

But then, by watching, she was intruding as well, wasn't she? Whatever she had just witnessed, it wasn't meant for her to see.

When she looked back to the lawn, Nora with her shock of luscious red hair, pale skin and luminous, ever-changing eyes had vanished. So had the fox.

Stefan was waiting for Megan, pointing at the beds where the veg was growing. It was trampled down.

'Who do you suppose did that?'

'Could be anyone,' she replied.

'Looks like bare feet did it,' Mike grumbled. 'Who would be out here barefoot? Went right through it. We'll lose those tomato plants.'

There was nothing so disgruntled as gardeners who saw plants abused. Especially so close to harvest.

'See what you can salvage and tie them back up. We'll just have to do what we can.'

Someone walking barefoot across the garden, out towards the maze. Megan knew who she'd seen doing that, walking in the maze at night, in the dark. But what could she say? She wasn't sure about

Faye Seaborne or what she might be up to, what her entanglement
with Foxfield was and what she'd been doing in the maze at night.
And each time she tried to wrap her mind around what all this might
mean, the thoughts seemed to slide away from her, like mist in her
fingers. There was an answer to this. There had to be. An explanation.
She just… couldn't find her way to it.

The voice came out of nowhere.

'Hi, Megan, how are you doing?' Megan almost jumped out of
her skin. But it was just Nora. 'I wanted to show you something. In
the library?'

What on earth was in the library? Nora sounded so distant, so
formal. Megan frowned, a dull headache throbbing behind her eyes.
She felt fuzzy and… wrong. She couldn't focus properly.

'In the village?'

'No, the special collection here. The Fairfax collection.'

Confused, she followed Nora towards the hotel. Once they were
clear of the gardens and crunching along the gravel path, Nora turned
to her. 'I was worried about you,' she said.

Worried about her? Why? No one knew about Owen. She hadn't
even told Sahar.

But her head ached, and they hadn't really spoken yesterday after
they'd got back to the maze, and everything had kicked off. 'I… I'm
fine. What did you find in the library?'

'Well, it's a bit of a mystery really. Have you… have you ever read
Malory?'

'Malory… you've mentioned him before. The King Arthur guy?'

Nora snorted. 'Yes. Well. *Le Morte d'Arthur*, specifically. A 1906
edition. Beautiful binding.'

Megan followed Nora through reception to the locked door on the far side of the staircase. She'd never seen it open but now Nora produced a key, one of the original ones from the house, clearly, and fitted it into the lock which turned with a clunk.

The library wasn't large, but it was crammed with books from the floor to the ceiling. There was nothing else on the walls but bookshelves. On an antique desk in front of the window was a small black book with gold decoration on the cover and spine.

The cover had an art nouveau pattern, featuring a lion. Decoration coiled up the spine as well. And beside it was an old envelope.

Nora closed the door behind them quietly, and turned the key again.

'You ought to read it. It's addressed to you.' Her voice was cold and so unlike her.

Megan dragged her gaze from the book up to Nora, who stood with her back to the door. Her expression was unreadable, all gentleness seemingly gone.

'What?'

'The letter. Look at it.'

Sure enough, in a flowing script, she could see her name – 'Megan Taylor, Foxfield Hall'.

She didn't want to touch it. It felt like a dare. 'Where did you find this?'

'I know the handwriting. It's Eleanor Fairfax's. But how on earth did she know about you? Or that you would be here?'

Megan could only stare. 'You know the *handwriting*? This is… this is a wind-up, is it?'

But looking at Nora's face, she knew it wasn't.

'Is it?' Nora asked, her tone even darker. 'Some kind of practical joke?'

'You think *I* did this?'

'Tell me,' Nora insisted. 'Megan, this makes no sense and I hate things that don't make sense. Did you plant it in here? I know you're interested in her but if this is some kind of sick joke I want to know about it and I want to know now. Eleanor Fairfax vanished eighty years ago. Am I supposed to believe that she left you a letter in a book about King Arthur and it has remained undiscovered all this time?'

Was she? Because that was what Nora was asking Megan to believe, too. It made no sense. People must have used this library.

'I didn't do anything, Nora. I haven't been in here.'

'Well someone has.'

Megan's patience snapped. 'Eleanor Fairfax, clearly.'

'She made notes too, wrote them in the margins, look!' Nora opened the book, handling it with care despite the trembling in her hands. '*There is a sacrifice to be made. And a champion… Morgan le Fey, Muirgen, born of the Sea, Seaborne…* What does that even mean?'

Muirgen… Sister… Vala…

The whisper was so clear Megan felt the air move against her ear. She stiffened, the temperature plummeting around her so suddenly that she felt frozen to the spot.

'Nora…' she tried again, but Nora wasn't listening. She snapped the book closed with a loud bang. Megan jumped. She couldn't help herself.

'And no one looked at that book in eighty years? No one saw that there was something shoved in the back, distorting it? Damn it, Megan, what are you up to?'

'Nothing. I've never been in here. The door's locked, isn't it? I don't know what you're talking about or how that got there.'

'Open the letter. Tell me what it says. Then you can tell me what you're up to.'

Megan grabbed the letter. The paper was old and thick.

But it had already been opened. Neatly, with a letter-opener.

'You already know,' she said, her voice shaking. 'You've already read it.'

If it was from Ellie, and Megan had no reason to doubt that, Nora had opened it first.

A shiver ran through her body, something that crawled under her skin and shook the core of her like a terrier with a rat. Nora looked away and Megan felt another wave of dizziness wash over her. This wasn't good. Something was in this room with them, something old and dangerous, acting on Nora's emotions, her anger. It didn't seem real. Because while she was airing her own grievances and fears, the emotions were too wild for her. This was an old anger. Ancient.

'I thought… I didn't know what to think. Damn it, Megan, I liked you. I can't believe— Did Hattie put you up to this?'

'Hattie? No – Nora, I don't know how the letter got here. But I… I know Ellie. I mean…'

'*How?*'

She had to tell her. She tried.

'In the maze, at night… Nora, this place, it's special. It's magic. Ellie said, it's the Green Lady and the harvest moon… And the maze—'

Her throat tightened and her eyesight blurred. She felt sick, desperately sick, like she had a fever, and not just flames of embarrassment licking up inside her. She didn't want to ask this of Nora. She'd sound at best delirious, if not completely insane. Her vision twisted with the flares and auras of a migraine. It was like looking up from the bottom of a pool of water, trying to see through the shifting light. A figure loomed behind Nora, overlapping her, a woman in green, or bathed in green light, a woman who should not be there. Her skin was leather, her red hair slicked with mud. A noose hung around her neck and shreds of rope encircled her wrists. A gash on her neck gaped wide, right where the artery would be. Her eyes blazed with an emerald luminescence.

The ground rumbled beneath their feet and the temperature in the room plummeted. Megan saw her own breath mist in front of her face, freezing in that watery light. Nora took another step forward, holding the book like a weapon, her head lowered, that unnatural glow of the ghost bleeding through her.

'Nora, this isn't you. Please…'

The door shook, as if someone rattled the handle, trying to force it open. Outside, a voice shouted. Megan couldn't make out the words but they sounded… old. Ancient. And they rippled with power. The door opened suddenly, the lock giving way without a key. Faye Seaborne stalked forward into the library.

She didn't speak but another ripple of power reverberated through the air. Nora spun around to face it and, like a shimmer of heat haze on a summer day, Megan's vision cleared. She moved without thinking, automatically pushing the envelope deep into her jacket pocket.

Nora swayed on her feet and then gathered her wits, staring at the archaeologist.

'You can't come in here,' she said.

'And yet here I am. Myself and the Green Lady, back in the Hall after so long.' She locked eyes on the book. 'And just what is it you think you have found there?'

Nora stepped out to block her. When she spoke it was as if nothing had happened. Nothing at all. 'A rare art nouveau printing of Malory's *Morte d'Arthur*, isn't it fabulous? A bit out of your period I would think. Megan's something of a fan.'

Faye looked decidedly unconvinced.

'She doesn't look like a fan. I heard raised voices. What are you up to, Miss Grainger?'

'Up to? Nothing at all. I'm just doing my job.'

'Your job? You're doing the bidding of someone else, that's what you're doing, whether you know it or not. You're a fool, gullible and easily led.' Faye snorted, and then pushed by the outraged younger woman as if she was no more than an irritant, bearing down on Megan. She was terrifying, all fury and strength. 'You don't look well. Do you need to sit down? You've gone quite pale. Let me see your hand, Megan. Please…'

Megan's skin tightened around her bones, crushing in on her. She balled her hand up into a fist, and it shook like a leaf in a storm. In the centre of her palm an invisible thorn dug into her skin, burning like acid. She couldn't breathe and the cold ate into her bones, spreading up her arm and throughout her body. She'd been fine before she'd come in here, before she'd seen the letter. Before she'd fought with Nora. Before she'd seen… what had she seen? A hallucination? A ghost? The Green Lady come home to Foxfield Hall at last?

Well, she hadn't been fine, not really. Not since she'd been at the well, before the digging began. And now…

Faye had brought the Green Lady, Gwynhyfer of Ashleigh, back here, back to her home. And last night Faye had spoken to her like… like a sister. *Seaborne…*

'Who are you?' Megan asked. But Faye didn't smile this time. She pressed her fingertips against Megan's palm and closed her eyes, as if concentrating on a problem. That same pulse of power came again, but this time focused on Megan alone.

The world swam like syrup. Faye swore softly under her breath and released her. Sahar grabbed Megan's arm but she hadn't even seen Sahar come in.

'Megan?' her friend said. 'You look terrible. Come with me.'

Both Nora and Faye watched them retreat, like vixens following prey.

*

The backs of Megan's knees hit the side of the bed and she crumpled. When had they got back to the apartment? Sahar pressed her wrist to her forehead.

'You've a temperature, and your glands are like golf balls. I'll get some paracetamol and ring the doctor. Get out of those sweaty clothes and into your bed. Now.'

'Yes, Mum.' She tried their usual joke. It fell flat. Sahar wasn't playing. Which meant she was really worried.

Megan's body ached as she stripped out of her clothes and left them puddled on the ground, carefully removing the letter and tucking it out of sight beneath her pillow. It seemed important to keep it hidden. She pulled a clean T-shirt out of the drawer and dragged it on. Then she got into the bed. The sheets felt blissfully cool, and she realised that Sahar was right. She was burning up. Her head pounded, and her throat felt raw. The ceiling blurred, and she had to close her heavy eyes.

Sleep took her unexpectedly and all too quickly.

*

Megan felt even worse when she woke up again. She could hear the birds outside, and beyond them the noise of the archaeologists digging up the maze, looking for other treasures. There was a jug of water, and some fruit and crackers beside the bed, along with her mobile and a note from Sahar.

Dr Havesham says sleep and liquids best. Fever's down but to call if needed. Ring me if there is any problem. I'll be back later to check on you.

Megan had only a vague recollection of Dr Havesham hovering over her but she'd thought it was a nightmare. At least she wasn't burning up any more. Or not as badly as she had been. Her temperature was all over the place. Dipping like a false dawn and then climbing even higher. Everything was a blur. Her body felt leaden, like something had broken it and glued it back together. The pieces didn't quite fit together, grating against each other. And it was almost two p.m., according to her phone. The symbol for a text message flashed at the top of the screen too, so she hit it, more automatically than out of need to read it.

Nora.

She drew in a breath and opened it as quickly as she dared. *You ok?* And a sad face.

Sick. Megan typed it with slippery, shaking fingers, taking far too long to form so short a word. She could ask the same question. What had happened back there?

Faye Seaborne had seemed to know something was happening in the library. She had… what? Tried to help Megan? Why?

Myself and the Green Lady, back in the Hall after so long. What did that mean? Did she know what the Green Lady was?

She waited but nothing came back immediately so she put the phone down again.

Megan had tried to tell Nora about the maze and Ellie, about the Green Lady. She'd been so flustered that she'd just blurted it out. It had sounded like nonsense.

It was like something had stopped her talking. The Green Lady, or the house itself…

But then Nora hadn't been making a lot of sense either. Nora… Nora had definitely not been herself. And that meant so much more than the usual euphemism.

Megan pulled out the letter from Eleanor Fairfax. The printer paper had not aged well. It was crumpled and cracked, yellowed. The letter itself was better, written on thick cream paper, heavy with linen, in pale blue ink which had never seen the sun. Ellie's handwriting was like artwork, looping and elegant.

Her letter made Megan want to scream in frustration. It was dated the 27th September.

And Ellie had left it there for her. Left it, impossibly, to wait eighty years for discovery.

Somehow.

Dear Megan,

I'm not sure how things will resolve themselves, but I fear Miss Seaborne is not to be trusted. I think she may well be a spy and no one will believe me. Not even my father. She dismissed Mary without references. There's been a Hatten here for generations but no more. Now I am alone.

I will try to reach the maze tonight if I can. The harvest moon will not last much longer and I do not know what, if anything, will happen then. Just know that I am still here. That for now I am safe. I will leave the book and the papers here, trusting that you will somehow find them. I know it's a long shot but I don't know what else to do. I can't let anyone else find the papers you gave me. And yet, I can't bring myself to burn them.

There is a connection between the Green Lady and the corn dollies. The first Lady of Foxfield was a Vala – that is, a priestess of the old religion they practised. There were three of them, sisters, enchantresses whose names twisted over time to become Guinevere, Morgan le Fey and Morgause of Orkney, from the legends of King Arthur. Their true names, or as far back as I can trace them, are Gwynhyfer, Muirgen, and Gwyar. Older names. But they aren't just ornament in the stories. They were powerful. They chose kings and champions, they ruled the people here.

And Seaborne knows this. She knows far more than she should. She is one of them.

Muirgen means 'born of the sea' in the old language.

Megan thought of Faye. Of course she knew this. She had to be the same person, in both Ellie's time and her own. There was no other way to explain it. Except that meant she was immortal, or something like it. She wasn't sure what to make of that. But maybe Ellie knew. Maybe she could figure it out. She was the clever one.

I'll try to get to the maze again, but the Harvest Festival is fast approaching. And if you're right, that will mean my time is done. May the Lord have mercy on me, but I am scared, Megan. I don't know what to do.

There is a sacrifice to be made. And a champion. Maybe they are the same thing. I don't fully understand it but believe me when I say that you must take care. I fear the danger is not just to me, but to you as well. To those we love.

Ava Seaborne says she is here to protect me, but it doesn't feel that way. She wants something of me, something to do with the Vala, and sacrifice, and so much more. I have no idea what that might be.

Except that word keeps coming back to haunt me. Sacrifice.

Ellie hadn't been there last night but she promised to try tonight. Maybe… Megan needed to be there, to do something, to find a way to help her. They needed to talk. She had to go there. Now.

When she tried to haul herself up, her head began to swim in that endless, too-sweet honey of delirium. She couldn't walk, let alone make it out to the maze. Helpless, desolate, she fell back onto the pillow.

Her mobile beeped again and she pulled it to her, trying to focus on the screen. She opened the text.

I'm sorry. I don't know what came over me. Nora. It was Nora.

She could have wept with relief.

Dragging her finger across the screen she managed, eventually, to draw out a message. It seemed to take forever, and her arms ached with the effort, her head pounded. But she kept going because it was all she could think of. *Go to the maze tonight. You'll see then. Help her. Tell her everything. Please.*

The phone was too heavy to hold any more. She let it drop onto the bed and, no matter how it beeped and chimed, she didn't have the strength to pick it up.

Chapter Twenty

Wednesday 27th September 1939

Ellie paced back and forth. She had been awake for most of the night, unable to get out of her locked bedroom, unable to sleep, quietly fuming when her shouts and screams got her nowhere.

Somewhere before dawn she had finally dropped off, although her sleep had been disturbed and restless.

Now morning had come and she was awake again, earlier than most of the other people in the house. She watched the thin light of early morning give way to the brighter September sun, like honey in the air.

The sound of the keys in the door made her jump. She could run, push by whoever it was and make a break for freedom. But where could she go? There was nothing to do, not now.

'Your father is on the telephone for you, my lady,' said Travers.

Ellie pulled on her dressing gown even as she made her way downstairs, her fury at the injustice of all this reignited.

Miss Seaborne was nowhere to be seen and the house was desperately quiet. The door to the study stood open, however, and the receiver lay on the desk.

She snatched it up.

'Hello? Father?'

'Eleanor, what the devil is going on down there?'

She blurted out all she could, about Mary and the children, about Miss Seaborne. Not about the maze or the ghosts, not about green lights, and most of all not about Megan.

She tried not to think about what Megan must have thought when she didn't turn up again last night.

And her father said nothing. Nothing at all. At least not until she finally trailed off, her indignation spent.

He was silent for a few more agonising seconds. 'It was a mistake telling you Professor Talbot recommended Ava, I grant you. She works for me, Eleanor. Not just as my secretary but in a very special capacity. The unit I have a hand in establishing here may well win us this war, or at least shorten it by a significant number of years. Ava is a vital part of that. She identified a threat directly to me, through you. A threat to you, in fact. That is why she is there and there is where she will stay.'

'But Father…' Ellie began.

'Mrs Worth and Mr Travers have been informed and as such they did nothing wrong. I would have not believed this of Mary but at the moment we cannot take any risks.'

'But Mary took the book from the library for me,' Ellie blurted out. 'It's my fault. I… I asked her to.'

He sighed. She'd never heard him sound so exhausted and wrung out, at his wits' end. 'She wasn't found in the library. I don't care about the library, Ellie.'

She couldn't have been more shocked if he'd declared himself the Emperor of Japan. Her father's library was everything to him, his collection unique and his joy.

For a moment she had to force herself to breathe calmly. If in the face of what had happened he didn't care about the library, then it was serious indeed.

'Father?'

'Eleanor, this is for your own good. Do as Ava says. She is there to protect you, to help you, to keep you safe. She knows far more about our family heritage than anyone else. The special unit here would be lost without her. I trust her implicitly.'

'But I don't.'

'Well, you had better learn to immediately,' he snapped and Ellie flinched. 'Now do as you're told, young lady, and she won't have to keep you locked up for the duration of this blasted war. You might even find a way to serve as well. If anyone can teach you it is Ava. Are we quite clear?'

She didn't know what to say. 'Y-yes Father.'

'Good. Now see to your duties in the parish, hand out the wretched prizes in the village to pretend that everything is fine and do as you are told.'

Her eyes stung with tears and her throat went too tight. She wouldn't cry. She simply wouldn't. She couldn't. She swallowed hard and smothered the growing sob down deep inside her.

'Eleanor,' her father said, his voice softer now. 'This really is for your own good. Please, just trust me. I lost your mother far too soon. I could not cope if anything happened to you.'

And that was it. The final straw.

'Yes, Father.' Her eyes burned. 'I'm sorry.'

'Now, off you go. Be a good girl.'

She replaced the receiver on the telephone and sank into his chair, sobbing into her hands.

*

Sometime later, her face washed and fully dressed, Ellie made her way back downstairs to the breakfast room.

Travers opened the door and the footmen wheeled in a serving trolley. As the aroma of a cooked breakfast, freshly baked bread and a pot of tea drifted towards her, Ellie's stomach made a loud and volatile rumble. She was almost ready to fall on it like a savage, but Miss Seaborne appeared in the doorway. Ellie sat back, her hands folded in her lap. Was this the last meal of the condemned? Even in ancient times, that was the tradition, wasn't it? The butler frowned, his forehead lining in worry. Though he clearly had his orders he wasn't much happier about this situation than she was. Well, anything which upset the ordered running of the Hall upset Travers. Ellie knew that. She just kept her hostile gaze on her father's secretary.

'You should eat, Lady Eleanor,' said Miss Seaborne. 'We have a busy day ahead of us.'

She didn't like the sound of that. She did not deign to answer.

'Please leave us, Travers.' Miss Seaborne crossed to the door, holding it for him. Travers didn't look in any way impressed, but what could he do? 'Eleanor, I presume you still wish to attend the meeting of the fair committee in the village? You are expected, after all. The vicar telephoned. There was mention of giving out prizes tomorrow, I believe? And the evensong service in St Michael's, naturally.'

'I wouldn't have thought you would want me out in public. Aren't you worried I'll make a scene?'

'No. I don't think that will be a problem now, will it?' There was no arguing with that, no matter how much Ellie wanted to. 'Don't scowl, Eleanor. The wind will change, and you'll be left with that sour expression. We have much to discuss.'

'You know about the Vala. I saw you in the maze. Is that why you're determined to keep me out of it? What were you doing? What were you looking for?'

Miss Seaborne peered at her, the intense glare of her eyes like a crow's. 'In the maze? Why on earth would I be in the maze?'

'The night after you arrived. I saw you. You had a corn dolly and threw it in the well. You shouted something – Artrí.'

Ava stepped in closer. 'What does "Artrí" mean, Eleanor? Did you find that in one of your books? You've been reading about the local customs, about corn dollies and all the old stories. You know so much all of a sudden. Tell me.'

Ellie flushed, her bluff called. 'I don't know.'

'I think you do. Try again. What did your book tell you about the Artrí?'

Maybe the best way to get information out of Ava was to answer her infuriating questions. Ellie ground her teeth before she answered. 'It's a Celtic name, an early form of Arthur, the earliest, according to the book. The bear king. Taken by the Romans and the later Britons, transformed—'

'The bear king or the high king, a mess of words and sounds blended over thousands of years. It became Arthur… the once and future King of the Britons. The hero, the champion, the one who will come again to save us all. But where did he come from to begin with? Perhaps we made him from our harvest and tied him in ribbons of red, like the blood he shed. The warrior, and the sacrifice, he who gave all he had and all he was for duty. We give the champion to the blade, the waters and the darkness to beg forgiveness, to call our protector to watch over us. Over all the Fairfaxes and those they love.'

Ellie blinked, listening to the words. They rang with poetry, echoed through her mind with power and meaning. '*We give the champion…*' she echoed. 'It was you. But why?'

If she expected Ava to deny it or to laugh, her reaction surprised her even more. The woman's expression didn't flinch. She nodded solemnly.

'One day I may show you. If you can prove to me that you can be obedient, as well as brilliant. If you can do as I say. Eleanor, listen to me. I can keep you safe. The harvest moon is dangerous. Especially for you.'

She had just admitted it. Just like that. Ellie couldn't hide her shock. She didn't think. 'So I've been told.' The words rushed out unbidden.

'By whom?'

She couldn't mention Megan. For one thing Miss Seaborne would never believe her. And if she did, it might be a whole lot worse. Maybe she could be trusted, maybe not. Ellie wasn't sure.

'Who are you? *What* are you? Why should I trust you to do anything, let alone keep me safe?'

Miss Seaborne reached out and stroked Ellie's hair in a surprisingly maternal gesture, leaving her startled. Something rippled through her, bone deep, and Ellie shivered, unable to pull away.

'Because I'm here to protect you, Eleanor. I always have been. It is my one and only true purpose. Not your father's papers. Not really. And even if you fight me at every turn, I will protect you.'

She said it so fiercely that Ellie couldn't doubt her sincerity, or that every single word she said was true. She wanted to deny it, to argue, to shout… but she couldn't. The emotions trapped inside her stayed there.

'I'd like to use the library.'

Ava nodded indulgently. 'Do you want the book on the legends of Ashleigh and Foxfield Hall?'

'Yes. Among others.' What was she saying? She wanted answers about Ava, but not from a book, not when she had as good as admitted that she was a Vala herself. But the words would not come out. Instead, she calmly sat there, waiting for permission.

'I don't think you'll find the answers you want in there, Lady Eleanor.' Ava searched Ellie's face for the longest time but at last she seemed resigned to what she saw there. She sighed. 'Very well. I will unlock the library after you have eaten. Just so long as you promise not to leave the house without me. Or to stray outside at night.'

Ellie wanted to say no, to refuse. But the words would not come. 'I promise.'

There had to be another way to get a message to Megan. To tell her that Ava Seaborne was not to be trusted, that she was somehow tied up in all this. She had her suspicions, but she needed to check the book to be sure… And if the answers weren't in the books, where were they?

Why couldn't she argue against this woman any more? What was going on?

Ellie served herself breakfast and ate as quickly as she could while maintaining her manners. She refused to panic. She would not give in to fear. At least, since Miss Seaborne was finally talking to her, she might as well get some information from her.

'What do the corn dollies mean, Miss Seaborne?'

She stood by the door, her hand on the frame, and looked back over her shoulder. Had Ellie surprised her at least with the question? 'If you can figure that out for yourself you truly will be worthy of being a Vala.'

A witch? Why would she want to be a witch?

'And what if I don't want to be a Vala?'

She smiled, a thin and unamused smile. 'There isn't really a choice, my dear girl. If you are chosen, you are chosen, and that is that. You have the heritage. You have the mind. I think you would be an excellent Vala, if you tried.'

'And what does it mean to be a Vala? What are they?'

'Wise women, my dear. Women who stand outside a man's world, with a power all their own. The keepers of secrets, the holders of the grail. From the earliest days, we've stood between the darkness and the light. We govern fates, we direct lives. We keep our people safe. We appear as queens, as priestesses, as goddesses. We are rewritten as whores and fallen women and we don't care. Strength, wisdom and destiny – they are all that matter. They are the birthright of a Vala. Come then, do your research.'

So… she was a Vala. And she wanted Ellie to tread the same path? Was that even possible? What did it mean?

But nothing else was forthcoming.

The forced obedience grated inside her, but she couldn't seem to fight it.

Ellie followed her to the library and took the book on Ashleigh off the shelf. But when she turned to the writing desk, Ava was holding another book. It was a beautifully bound reprinting of Thomas Malory's *Le Morte d'Arthur*. She set it down on top of the Ashleigh book, patted it, and then walked away.

They said nothing more.

Ellie read all morning. She made notes – it was her book after all, and her library. And finally she wrote a letter. She slipped it and the pages Megan had given her into an envelope and put the whole thing inside the cover of *Le Morte d'Arthur*. She didn't shelve it back in its proper place though. She slipped it into the end of a floor-level shelf, below the window seat, almost as hidden as it could be. It was the best chance she had that it would be overlooked.

Then all she could do was hope for the best.

Chapter Twenty-One

Friday 27th September 2019

Megan drifted in an uneasy sleep, in which black foxes with glowing green eyes chased her through a maze which never ended. She tore around corners only to find another path opening up, and another, but she couldn't find the way out.

'*Run,*' the voice of the Green Lady whispered in her dream. '*Run, my champion. She has marked you but you cannot let her win. It will mean your death.*'

What did the Green Lady mean? Who had marked her?

The next corner brought Megan to a dead end and she turned around, panting. The foxes filled the pathway back. She was trapped, staring at them, but they didn't advance. They just stood there, watching her, their eyes lighting up the night.

Something tugged at her leg. For a moment she didn't dare to look down, but it was insistent, almost painful. A twig of some kind poked out from the hedge and, even as she watched, it moved, twisting like a snake scenting the air. She stumbled back, away from it, but too late. Briars burst from the yew hedging and from the ground beneath her, ripping up through the rich, dark earth. As she tried to wrench herself free, they coiled around her limbs, thorns tearing through clothes and skin. They wound tighter and tighter, pulling her down to her knees, to the earth. And when she screamed they surged up to fill her mouth.

Her right hand burned with a fire she couldn't put out. It raced along her veins and surged with her breath. It devoured her from inside.

Darkness welled up around her again.

Megan stood at the edge of the well now, the green light spilling out over its low wall and swirling around her feet.

Flames licked at her body, green flames, dancing on the surface of her skin. She tried to brush them off but that just made more of them appear.

'Help me,' she whispered, her voice hoarse and weak.

Soft lips brushed her cheek and the flames receded, just for a moment. Megan could still feel them coursing through her, the fever worsening. Time was running through her fingers like water.

'Come with me,' whispered the Green Lady.

She wore the same long dress, but Megan could see her more clearly now. This wasn't the mummified monster she'd seen in the library. The Green Lady was just a girl, no more than twenty. Her hair was plaited at either side, but left long at the back, and she wore some kind of veil over it. Despite the greenish tinge to everything, Megan was sure it was red, the colour of fox fur. The world faded around them, or maybe the spirit just became brighter and brighter. The Green Lady's lips were moving and Megan realised, belatedly, that she could hear singing. The tune was timeless, but the lyrics were in that same unknowable language.

Abruptly her song broke off. The world shimmered again and they were somewhere else, a garden, with a well. The same well, but there was no maze now. The Green Lady looked up as two other figures appeared. One was hooded, a bent form made of darkness, the woman who had called up the night foxes. The golden mask gleamed, reflecting the eerie green light. Strands of white hair caught the moonlight. The other, tall and perfect, a vision of beauty and fierce intelligence, was Faye Seaborne, not as she was now but how she had been, once upon a time. Long hair, the colour of midnight, fell down her back and she was clad all in white.

They were like ghosts. Or memories. And Megan moved like a ghost among them, a shadow herself, an unseen witness. Here, trapped between dreaming and waking, between lucidity and delirium, the Green Lady was showing this to her. But why?

'Little sister, what have you done?' asked Faye. 'This was not our plan. You were to ensnare him, Gwynhyfer, not be ensnared yourself.'

'It is not a trap if you enter it willingly, Muirgen,' said the Green Lady. 'He is a good man. He will be a good father to our child, a good lord to our people.'

'Our people do not need a lord,' the older woman replied in scathing tones. 'They have us. They always have. Since they first settled this land and called us out of it. The Vala. What need they of a master?'

'Time is changing, Gwyar. If they do not appear to conform, they will be wiped out. This is what we have always done, made the invader our own, made our ways appear to be their ways. Adopt and adapt. If we fight, we will lose. We are already losing. Our old ways are dying, cut down by their swords and prayers. This way we will survive.'

The old woman, Gwyar, turned away, cursing, but the one who would become Faye just shook her head in disbelief. 'And you would do this?'

The Green Lady lifted her head. 'I bear his child. I feel her inside me, changing me. I am no longer the maiden in this triad.'

'This is sacrilege and you will pay for it,' cried the one called Gwyar, spittle spraying from the mouth of her mask. She gestured in front of the girl, who folded her hands protectively over her stomach.

'It *is* sacrilege, my sister,' Faye whispered. 'The sacrilege is yours and must be accounted for. And the price will be terrible.'

The Green Lady's face hardened. 'Vengeance begets vengeance and I am more powerful than you. By the ash, by the waters and by all the powers within us, I swear it. Anyone who harms me or my children will never know peace. Cowardice is no excuse.'

And with that, Megan realised, the Green Lady had cast a curse on those who threatened her line. On this woman, who looked like Faye, and her mysterious masked sister.

They faded, the images of the women fixed like light-burn on Megan's retinas for a moment, and then fading. The darkness filled the centre of the maze and she heard a scream, terrible, haunting, a man's voice stretched with a pain beyond bearing.

It was the sound of someone whose heart had been ripped from his body. The sound of someone who had lost that most dear to him. Dearer than his own life. The day the letter had first come about her brother, Megan's mum had made that noise.

The Green Lady was dead. No doubt about that entered Megan's mind. And that was the voice of her husband, her lost love, her champion, echoing through eternity with the pain of his loss.

Megan gasped for breath, her chest aching, her body shivering with shock. Cowardice was no excuse, the Green Lady had said. Not then and not now either. Megan stood in the darkness, shaking from head to foot, trying to force herself to keep breathing, not to collapse or run away.

'Three deaths,' the Green Lady's voice whispered from right beside her. Megan leaped to her feet, her heart launching itself right up into the back of her throat where it hammered for escape like a captive in a dungeon. 'A threefold death she gave me, just to be sure, to steal my power and bind it for her use. But she waited until my child was born, to try to win my mercy. I never saw my baby grow to adulthood. A boy, not the daughter I expected. But I never saw him grown. Gwyar, my eldest sister, took my life. Muirgen, my other sister, saved my champion and our son, guarded the boy and did what she could, but it was not enough. Gwyar has preyed upon our line, squatting like a toad in our place of power since then. She kept me bound and keeps my sister out. Until now. My death was terrible. But so many deaths have followed. All my daughters…'

She circled Megan's frozen form, her pale green gown the colour of waterweed and moonlight. Her hair was wet, Megan realised, and water fell down her mummified face with her tears. This wasn't the young girl, pregnant and trying to bargain for her life and the lives of those she loved. This was the thing the archaeologists had pulled up from the depths of the well, where the water and the soil of Foxfield and the curious conditions had preserved her intact. The creature that had overwhelmed Nora in the library, now back in her home and all the more powerful for that. Her face was stained to something like bronze or leather. And still weirdly beautiful, though at the same time horrific. Her eyes were twin green glows deep inside the empty sockets. Her teeth, Megan saw as she spoke, were perfect.

'How… how did she…?'

The Green Lady lifted her hands to her neck. A ragged gash was still visible there and below it was a rope. 'My sister, my own sister, strangled me. Then cut my throat with a reaping hook. Then she drowned me in the well. A perfect sacrifice, in the oldest way. It sapped me of my magic. I was meant to stay dead. But how could I do that? Especially when she buried me here. This is my land. And it is full of life. They killed me in my place of power, the land that made me a goddess. I did not die. I could not. I became more.'

'What… what do you want?' Megan managed to ask.

'What you call Michaelmas is the time of the champion, the hero, of Arthur. And *you* are my champion, chosen by the blood of my blood, beloved of the blood of my blood. My champions are always drawn back, for the time of trial and sacrifice. The moment when they must triumph or fail. You must not let fear stop you now. Gwyar has marked you, cast her hex upon you, cursed you, but you cannot let her win. She would make you the sacrifice.'

'I don't… I don't understand…'

'She laid a hex, hidden in your clothing. Poisoning your blood, draining your strength. When you called your man to dig at the well, you opened a way for Muirgen, my sister, to return to the Hall, to bring me home at last, and Gwyar could not let that stand. Ah, she is enraged now, Gwyar is. And she punishes you for that. Even Muirgen cannot stop that, though she tries. Gwyar has grown hard and heartless. She has her ally, another to take my place and take my power. And if she cannot have her compliance, she will kill her.'

Megan shivered, unable to stop herself. 'Do you mean Ellie?' she whispered. 'She'll kill Ellie.'

Gwynhyfer rolled her shoulders back in a curiously human gesture. They made a terrible clicking sound. 'Not if you stop her. You, who have brushed death's hands with your own, who has given up that most dear.' Did she mean Owen? No, she hadn't given up Owen. She'd never give him up. But before Megan could speak, the Green Lady went on. 'Save my child.'

Ellie. She wanted Megan to save Ellie.

'But I can't. She's in another time, another place.'

The Green Lady laughed, a bitter, tragic sound. 'All times are one time, all places are one place. Here, the laws of place and time do not apply. Not beneath the black moon. You already have the information you need. Humanity never learns. All those wars, all those deaths, slaughter after slaughter. That is the way of men. But *we* are not men. You must awaken. You must fight back.'

Megan opened her eyes to find her room illuminated by her glow, green light and the ripples of well water thrown up onto the ceiling. The Green Lady stood at the foot of the bed, her arms spread wide. Her light fell everywhere.

Everywhere except the corner nearest the door, where she had left her work coat. As Megan watched, tendrils of shadow thrust their way out of the pocket. They writhed like living vines, like the briars from her nightmare, hissing and recoiling as her green light fell on them.

'In there. She has hexed you, Megan. It lies within. You have to find it and destroy it.'

Megan pulled herself up from her bed, though her body protested and her head pounded like the inside of a steel drum. She couldn't just lie there. If she needed saving she would have to do it herself. But every breath was a hiss of pain, every muscle ached as if it was twisted on a rack, ratcheted with agony. Sweat dripped into her eyes, its salty taste filling her mouth. She plunged a hand into the coat pocket.

It was like reaching into the maw of a shark.

Barbs ripped into her skin, like the briars in her feverish dreams, needles of steel and ice which lanced up her arm, but her hand closed on something that shouldn't have been there. A knot of string and straw, wound together in an intricate weave. It made a shape, one which twisted in her head, digging spikes into her. She didn't want to touch it. But she couldn't let it go.

'Her hex,' the Green Lady whispered. 'A corruption of the champion's inner fire. A curse, bringing pain and suffering, making you burn. You must drown it.'

'It hurts.'

'It will kill you if left here. She bound it with hatred and loathing, and her power is old and mighty. Put out the fire inside it and inside you. Hurry!'

Megan's hand spasmed, as if even now the curse was acting on her, trying to preserve itself and destroy her. She couldn't let it. Not for a moment. She had to destroy it.

Her fist crushed the hex, but it still sizzled against her skin, malignant and terrible. Megan winced, swallowing hard. That wouldn't be enough. She could feel it alive with power.

'Drown it,' Gwynhyfer said.

She knew where. She just didn't know if she had the strength to make it.

But she had to, that much was clear.

She made for the door, forcing herself to run. The cold night air closed over her and her body ached, but she pushed herself onwards, out across the grass and into the maze.

'Quickly, Megan,' the Green Lady urged, drifting beside her like a mist, cold but undeniable. 'You are running out of time.' She held out her hand and threaded her insubstantial fingers through hers, pulling her forward.

Give it to the well, it was the only way. Let the waters there, sacred and blessed, purge it. It all came back to the well, didn't it? Ellie had found the corn dollies there to begin with.

For time out of mind the people of Ashleigh had given their offerings to the well, their sacrifices, their champions.

Megan lurched down the paths of the maze, heading relentlessly for the centre. She wasn't even picking her way with care, just trusting blindly to Gwynhyfer. Her strength was almost gone, her pounding heart echoing through her along with that voice.

'You can do this,' the Green Lady said. 'You must.'

Megan staggered forward.

'Megan? What are you doing here?'

Nora. It was Nora. She'd know her voice anywhere. She sprinted towards her, trying to intercept her, and Megan's body almost betrayed her.

What was Nora doing here? Why was Nora trying to stop her?

And then another realisation struck her. Nora had brought back her jacket from the maze, the jacket with the hex hidden in the pocket.

Nora's hands almost closed on her but from somewhere Megan found a burst of speed she didn't know was left in her. She dodged aside and threw herself across that last cockstride of ground.

With a sob of pain, she fell to her knees at the edge of the well, the far side of the trench.

The hex fell from Megan's hand into the depths and the water boiled at its touch, throwing up a harsh red light for a moment. Steam billowed up, mist flowing over the edge of the stones. A long low hiss followed it, making the air shake and the temperature of the air around them skyrocket.

Megan could barely breathe, her body stretched thin by pain, her tendons strained beyond bearing. The air simmered around her and her vision swam.

Nora's cool hands pulled her back, arms wrapped around her and held her tight. It shouldn't be comforting, not suspecting what she did. But it was. God help her, it was. 'What are you doing out here? What was that? Megan? Talk to me. Please.'

The hex was gone.

The fire left her, but her body was wrung out. She slumped against Nora, unable to move, and tears covered her face. Icy cold tears. She'd done it though. She could feel the difference. And though she ached all over, though her head pounded, she knew at once that the poisonous magic inside her was gone.

For a moment they were both there, Nora and Gwynhyfer, both holding her, real and supernatural. Blended together in the same way as they had been in the library.

'You have done well, my champion, my Arthur… You have done very well.' The voice was a whisper and Nora shivered, tightening her grip on Megan's body as if to protect her. But if she heard the voice or not, Megan couldn't tell.

Megan wanted to answer, to tell the Green Lady she couldn't be a champion, couldn't be a fictional, long-dead, very male king, but her voice wouldn't work any more. The Green Lady began to fade in front of her eyes, blinking out like one of those marsh-lights, the little ghosts of the maze.

It was dark and it was cold. Blissfully cold.

And Nora held her.

The next thing Megan was aware of was Nora's voice, talking into her phone frantically. And then Sahar was fussing over her, chiding her for getting up, threatening her with the doctor again as the two of them brought her back to the apartment behind the hotel. Back in her bed, Megan slipped back to a peaceful, dreamless sleep, the fever broken at last.

Chapter Twenty-Two

Wednesday 27th September 1939

The parish fête committee held their last meeting in the church hall. Mrs Pitt had provided scones, an absolute treat. Ellie made a mental note to thank her in person later.

Jennifer Farnham poured the tea and eyed Miss Seaborne very suspiciously indeed. Ellie had introduced her, of course, but even around the table Miss Seaborne sat apart from them, aloof and untouchable.

'They'll have to surrender, you know,' said Agatha. 'The Poles. Warsaw is rubble. The Jerries on one side, the Soviets on the other, they don't stand a chance.'

'May God have mercy on their souls,' murmured the vicar and spread some of the homemade jam on his scone.

'Oh, enough of that,' Mrs Pitt said. 'We're here to discuss the Harvest Festival, not depress ourselves with things we can't control.'

'They're reopening the schools,' said Jennifer, trying to lighten the mood. 'That's what I heard anyway. About time. Although how they're going to manage with all the evacuees I don't know.'

Agatha cleared her throat. Clearly she already knew.

'A staggered system, I believe. Even then they'll have to take over this hall. Local children in the mornings and the others in the afternoon.'

'The others?' Ellie asked, knowing exactly what she meant. Snobs like Agatha Brooks always had a problem with *others*.

Agatha waved her hand dismissively. 'The evacuees. You had a whole gaggle up at the manor, didn't you, my dear? Until yesterday anyway. You'll be glad to get them out from under your feet.'

Ellie just smiled and tried not to glare at Miss Seaborne. 'Oh, they were no trouble at all. Rather sweet really. And it was so lovely to hear them playing outside. You should take one or two in yourself, Agatha.'

Agatha looked like she'd rather poke her own eyes out.

'So why did you have them billeted somewhere else?'

Ellie sipped her tea and tried not to spit it in her face. She set the cup down silently. 'My father has other plans for the house.'

'Good gracious me, what?' Jennifer said, leaning forward.

'Who knows?' The temptation was too great. She couldn't help herself. She just wanted to see their faces. 'Refugees from Europe perhaps?'

The look on her face was worth it.

'Oh, Lady Eleanor,' Ava Seaborne said, before Agatha could vent her outrage, 'Don't tease your friends. His lordship said quite clearly that the medical corps would have access to the house the moment it was needed. A staging area between London and the south coast. A retreat for officers and suchlike. It's such a peaceful place, Ashleigh.'

'A hospital?' asked Agatha. She looked even more horrified at that prospect. Ellie could imagine what she'd say in private. *Wounded people. How ghastly.*

Miss Seaborne didn't even falter. 'A vital service. I'm sure you understand.' She flexed her hand under the table, though Ellie was sure she was the only one to see it. She felt the air warm ominously.

Agatha smiled somewhat mindlessly. 'Oh, of course. That sounds eminently suitable.'

Ellie stared at the secretary but Ava just let a ghost of a smile play on her lips for the moment and said nothing. A Vala… was this what it meant? Manipulating people? Changing their opinions? Even people as weak-minded as Agatha Brooks. It wasn't right.

And… was that why Ellie had been unable to defy her? Was that the reason she felt obliged to obey even though it was the last thing she wanted to do?

It was the first Ellie had heard of this hospital plan but she decided not to reveal that. Mind you, she didn't seem to have much of a say in anything these days. If the house was to be a hospital what did they intend to do with her?

Reverend Blake finished his scone and nodded sagely. 'I'll be happy to help in any way, Miss Seaborne. I'm sure his lordship knows that.'

'I'm sure he does. Now if you don't mind, our time is a little short. I would like to have a full list of Lady Eleanor's engagements tomorrow, just to be completely clear.'

She was so firm, so self-assured, that they all just fell into line, instantly obeying her. Perhaps there was something to learn there. Ellie knew she would never be able to get them to cooperate quite so quickly. To them, she was just a girl. An unmarried one at that.

But Miss Seaborne was doing something else as well. Something not entirely natural.

Miss Seaborne was folding up the page on which Jennifer had written out all of Ellie's supposed duties for the fête. She put it carefully in her handbag without letting Ellie have so much as a glimpse at it.

What did that matter anyway?

'Miss Seaborne? May I have a word?' said the vicar.

'I'll wait outside,' Ellie said, brightly. Anything to get away, if only for a moment. To escape her influence, her control.

Miss Seaborne just glared at her. 'Don't go too far.'

It was just a brief respite, and Ellie seized upon it. She grabbed her coat and hat, bid everyone goodbye and stepped out into the village. She didn't even pause long enough to put her gloves on.

It was like being able to breathe freely for the first time in days.

They were already erecting stalls and trestle tables. There would be a tombola, a coconut shy – if they could still find the coconuts from last year – and stalls selling jams, pickles and cakes. On the other side of the green, Ellie would be judging the baking competition and the bonny babies. In between it all, where the green was left open, there would be morris dancing, races and a tug-of-war. There would be a band to play music. It would end early, of course, this year.

It would be different this year. She knew that. Even though everyone else was ignoring it, trying to make it the same as last year. *Last year.* That was a joke. Everything was different now.

But who knew if they would ever have one again after this?

It was just one last desperate stab at normality and it was already failing miserably.

She wondered briefly what Megan would make of it. Did they still have such frivolities in her far future time? Just thinking about her made her shiver.

It would have been nice to say that she had been resolute and brave. She wanted to be brave. She had said that people shouldn't know their own future.

But in the end she hadn't been able to resist. Just before she had hidden the papers and the letter for Megan, she had read them. And what she saw had scared her half to death. Reading about herself were bad enough. Looking at her own face and reading how she disappeared… But she knew now, she needed to be far away from Ashleigh and the fête before nightfall. This was where she vanished, in the middle of the crowded festival. No one even saw her disappear.

Who could she talk to about it? Miss Seaborne? No. It would give her another excuse to lock her up. Her father? He was already furious with Ellie. Miss Seaborne had admitted she was a Vala, like the beings in the maze, that terrifying masked figure and the Green Lady. Ellie was certain that Miss Seaborne was manipulating her, controlling her. And she knew from Megan that she was going to vanish tomorrow, never to be seen again. Were the two connected? Was Miss Seaborne the reason she disappeared or was she, as she said, protecting her? And how much did her own father know?

Ellie stopped at the war memorial, reading the names without really reading them. She knew them all far too well. Her uncle and both her cousins were quite near the top. Her father was lucky to have made it back from Ypres, if the stories were to be believed. He wouldn't talk about it but people gossiped.

A war hero. A champion.

'Better not be looking for me up there, Eleanor Fairfax,' said a rich and familiar voice that made her heart tear itself up into her throat. It wasn't possible. It couldn't be.

She twisted around, gasping, and almost dropped her handbag and gloves.

A man stood on the edge of the green, so handsome in his blue RAF uniform, a vision that she couldn't quite believe to be real. How was he here? How was he—?

And suddenly her mind caught up with what she was seeing.

'David!'

She crossed the space between them in such a rush she wasn't even sure if she moved or the world sped around her. David's arms were strong and gentle, that intoxicating combination. He held her close and bent to kiss her, his lips on hers like a dream made real. She couldn't think, couldn't breathe. He was here, really here, her David.

'How's my gorgeous girl?' he murmured, his mouth still brushing against hers. She could smell his aftershave and the Brylcreem styling his hair so sharply. That was new. She preferred it ruffled and messy. 'Missed me?'

'Missed you?' She laughed and pushed him back so she could look at him. 'Of course I missed you. And look at you, David! How are you here?'

'I've been posted. Tangmere, if you can believe it. What luck, eh? I'm only just down the road. Borrowed a motorbike. Here I am.'

'You didn't tell me.'

'I wanted to surprise you. It takes a lot to get one over on you at the best of times so I couldn't resist. Come on, I've got a forty-eight-hour pass and then I'm back to it. But I had to see you, my darling. And I'm home for the fête, isn't that good luck? Just like I said.'

She threw her arms around his neck again, kissing him. 'I can't believe it. I can't – David, I have so much to tell you.'

David being in Ashleigh with her had never been covered in the reports. Surely they would have mentioned that, those future journalists, writing about her like a woman already dead. They'd said he was her fiancé, that he was distraught, but they'd never said he was here.

And he *was* here. Something had changed. It had to have changed. And if this had changed, everything could change. She would change it. Her eyes stung with tears.

'My darling? What's wrong?'

'Lady Eleanor!' Ava Seaborne barked, marching towards them like a fury. 'What the devil is going on here?'

'My fiancé, David Grainger. This is Father's secretary, Miss Sea—'

David stepped back and snapped to attention, saluting Miss Seaborne even as she reached them. He transformed right in front of Ellie's eyes, from her David to an officer of the RAF. She wouldn't have believed it if she hadn't seen it herself. 'Flying Officer David Grainger, ma'am. We met in London with Lord Charles at—'

'I remember. At ease, Grainger.' Miss Seaborne's whole tone had transformed. She was used to command and David knew it. Ellie stared at him as if he had somehow betrayed her. 'Eleanor, we should be going. Time to get back.'

No. She couldn't be dragging her away from David as well. It wasn't fair. And how did they know each other? When had David been meeting up with her father in London?

'David's father is a close friend of my father's,' Ellie added. It was almost true. If the two men ever found more than a brief moment to become further acquainted, Ellie was sure they would be. As it was they were good neighbours and that had to count for something. 'Colonel Nathaniel Grainger of Belleclair House.'

David picked up her cue perfectly, of course.

'He wanted to invite you to dinner this evening. Both of you, naturally. Surely you could come, Miss Seaborne. It would be such an honour.' He was at his most charming, trying to get on the right side of the harridan. As if anyone could do that.

To Ellie's surprise, Miss Seaborne graced David with the most beautiful smile imaginable. His eyes widened in surprise and he returned it with his own, but not the usual confident expression. This one was filled with wonder and slightly shocked. One might almost think he had been struck on the head and left stunned. Ellie suddenly didn't like that look one bit. When Miss Seaborne shook his hand she gripped a little too hard, and he only reluctantly let go.

This could not be good.

'So lovely to make your acquaintance again, Flying Officer Grainger. We have to decline his most gracious invitation this time unfortunately.'

Ellie's heart sank and it must have shown on her face because David looked similarly glum.

'He only has a little leave,' Ellie protested.

But, to her horror, David was the one who answered. 'No, don't worry, Ellie. I'll see you soon. I promise.'

'Soon?' There wasn't any soon for the two of them.

Miss Seaborne had already turned away and was heading back to the car, her slim, imperious figure moving far too quickly.

Ellie was about to protest when he leaned in, kissed her on the cheek and whispered, 'Catch up, my darling. I'll see you *later*. After dark.'

She clung to him. 'But David—'

She'd never get out. How could she with Seaborne guarding her every second?

'Remember the tree? Our old friend never let us down.'

To Ellie's horror, Miss Seaborne's voice barked across the village square. Everyone would hear. It was just another humiliation.

'Eleanor, you have duties, promises to keep. You can see each other at the fair tomorrow. Come along.' It felt like a wire between them went taut, one that threaded through Ellie and wound around her, making her… not compliant but forcing her to obey, nonetheless.

Ellie had no choice but to tear herself away from David and follow the wretched woman back to the car.

Tears burned as they filled her eyes and spilled over the lashes, tumbling down her cheeks. She didn't even try to hide them but she couldn't make a sound. She hated the woman. Hated her.

David just watched her go and, when Ellie glanced back before getting into the car, she saw him still smiling after her.

'I told you, Eleanor.' The woman's hand closed on Ellie's shoulder in what was perhaps meant to be a comforting gesture. It was not. Ellie raged and raged inside as Ava Seaborne spoke quietly. 'It's simply too dangerous for you to be out of my sight.'

*

Ellie made sure she was as good as gold the entire evening. She had to be, in order to avoid raising suspicion. The enchantment Miss Seaborne had woven was not constant. It waned when she thought Ellie was obedient. So Ellie behaved. She ate quickly, yawned theatrically and then claimed she was exhausted and should go to bed.

'There's so much on tomorrow, after all,' she said.

Miss Seaborne didn't look impressed. But she didn't look overly suspicious either.

Ellie performed the whole pantomime of getting ready for bed. She dismissed Sarah. Clearly, the poor girl was exhausted from all her extra duties since Mary's dismissal. Carefully, Ellie changed into a rather smart pair of tweed trousers she rarely had the nerve to wear – especially not in front of her father – a blouse, and a sleeveless pullover. It might not be feminine but it was eminently suited to tree climbing. Besides, this was all David's idea so he could put up with it. She tied back her hair and then pulled up the heavy sash window.

Outside, the tree was still there, still as far from her room as it had been thirteen years ago. Back then there had been a large branch which almost reached the window ledge, but when her father had realised the use she had been making of it, he'd had the gardener saw it off. She could still see the scar.

But if she climbed out and edged along the windowsill, she could drop onto the crenelated little outcrop above the Green Room where they often housed guests. And from there…

The tree wasn't that far. She could jump. It would be fine.

Just like with Megan in the maze. But the other way around. Leap out and down. She'd be fine.

At least she hoped so.

It was windier than she had thought, especially once she was out there, perched on the windowsill. She twisted around, grabbed the edge and lowered herself down. For a moment she just hung there and realised it was a terrible idea.

Go on, a voice whispered.

She dropped and landed deftly. This was fine. It was going to be fine. She'd get there. First stage accomplished. She turned around and the tree was there. Further away than she had thought, but still.

She could do this. She had to. *Carpe diem.*

This was for David.

She crouched, trying to judge it, and then ran for the edge, leaping out like a bird taking flight. She grabbed the branch and hung there, safe. Well, as safe as she could be.

'Down here,' David called softly.

He was right underneath her, jacket open now, his arms outstretched. Like Romeo under the balcony. But you'd never catch Juliet dangling in a position like this.

Ellie smiled in victory and let go. He caught her as if she weighed nothing at all, laughing and spinning her around as he did so.

The kiss left her breathless and elated, her heart thumping against her ribs in joy.

'I can't believe I did that. I can't believe you're here.'

'A chance to rescue my damsel in distress from her tower? How could I pass that up?' David let her down, her feet touching the ground, but he still held her against him, admiring her. 'You look like Katharine Hepburn in that outfit. What do you want to do? Go dancing? I have the bike. We can head off down to—'

Ellie put her fingers to his lips and he fell silent, but his lips moved under her touch, kissing her fingertips. He released her and would have pulled her into a closer embrace but she grabbed his hand. 'Come with me. I have to show you something. We have to go now.'

'What? Ellie, what's going on?'

She didn't answer. Just pulled him after her.

She ran for the maze, David running with her. Just like they had when they were children.

But now the maze was dark and dangerous, lit by green will-o'-the-wisps and the yews groaned and creaked over them, and the walls seemed to close in as they passed through.

The centre of the maze was empty. No Megan. Only the almost full moon and the well like a mouth open wide, ready to be fed.

'Ellie, the lights!' David gasped as they came to halt. He stared around them wildly. 'Do you see them too? Are they... they aren't gas, are they? Or— Ellie, what is it, love? What's wrong?'

The disappointment slammed her breath out of her. 'Megan should be here.'

She turned around to face him, to begin the arduous task of explaining. She didn't have proof, not of anything really. David had always tried to believe her. But he'd wanted proof of the Green Lady. So did she. And with Megan she could finally offer it.

He stood there smiling fondly at her, even if his bewilderment was evident. He had such faith in her, and was waiting, ready to indulge her, ready to listen, ready for anything.

And a wall of shadows rose behind him, spilling out of the maze. In them, the night foxes coiled together, tangled with one another, twisted, falling over themselves as they surged towards him.

'David, look out!' But her scream came too late.

One moment he was there – her David, her love – and then they fell on him, a surging mass of darkness, enveloping his startled face, quelling his struggles, sucking him into their nightmarish embrace.

The shadows spilled onwards across the grass towards her, crawling now, threatening and ominous, and the woman in the golden mask followed.

'I warned you, Eleanor Fairfax. I warned you what would happen if you came back here at night and meddled where you don't belong. If you want to change your future there will be a cost. Do you understand that yet?'

'Let him go,' she screamed, trying to claw the shadows off herself. 'What are you doing to him?'

David struggled at the sound of Ellie's voice, tearing one arm free. But the shadows coiled around him like oil, drowning him in their depths. His eyes widened in horror, and he opened his mouth to call out her name, but they rushed in to silence him.

'Your champion is mine now. And tomorrow, under the harvest moon, we'll sacrifice him. And you'll join us. We'll change your future, you'll see. We will be three once more. Three Vala. It only takes a life. Then this will all be over and done with.'

The shadows twisted in on themselves and the woman was gone.

And so was David.

'Eleanor!' It was Ava's voice, coming through the maze. She sounded panicked. Afraid. And that frightened Ellie more than anything. If Ava Seaborne was afraid… 'Eleanor, where are you?'

But Ellie dropped to her knees, howling in pain and loss, clawing at the ground where he had been.

No trace at all remained. David was gone.

Chapter Twenty-Three

Saturday 28th September 2019

It was afternoon before Megan woke again, the golden sunlight falling on her face. The fever really had broken, and the pounding in her head had finally eased. The pain that had lanced up her arm and threaded throughout her body had finally abated. The events of the night before felt like a strange dream – the Green Lady here, in her room, the hex that had been planted on her to make her ill. She thought for a moment she'd been hallucinating. She could still feel the dry rough straw of the hex in her hand, and she could see the scratch it had left on her skin. And she remembered Nora outside, waiting, Megan's coat folded over the back of the chair. She didn't want to but she couldn't get the image out of her mind.

Nora had brought it back to her.

And in the library, Nora had found the envelope. She knew about Ellie. She'd read the letter.

Nora knew far more about this than she had let on. About all of it.

Megan dragged herself out of bed and into the shower, which made her feel a hundred times better and ravenously hungry. From there, she pulled her clothes on, went to the kitchen and started loading as much food from the fridge onto a plate as possible.

The sound of someone singing drifted in to her, that tune, the same tune, and Megan turned sharply, her breath lodging in panic inside her throat.

The back door was open and Nora was sitting in the afternoon sunshine on the patio, a mug of tea on the table beside her. She looked perfect. She always did.

'Hey, how are you feeling?' Nora said as she came outside. Spread out on the garden table were bits of straw and ribbon. She was making corn dollies. There were about a dozen of them, different designs, small and delicate. And all of them terrifying.

Megan almost dropped the plate in shock.

'What are you doing here?'

'Sahar said you were feeling better. So I came back up.' She nodded at the food that had been so appealing just a moment ago. 'Hungry?'

Megan put the plate down on the table, trying not to get her hands anywhere near Nora's straw creations. Her appetite had gone.

Last night she had realised that Nora had been the last person to touch her jacket before she'd been hexed, the hex itself hidden in the pocket. Was it really possible that Nora had done it? That Nora was the other Vala? She knew about the legends. She knew about witchcraft and corn dollies, about the moon. She knew about it all.

Nora pursed her lips, staring at Megan as she got to her feet. Her eyes were the colour of cornflowers in the sunlight and her hair shone like fire.

'So… the maze last night,' she said as if reading Megan's mind. 'You asked me to help someone.' Megan looked at her, still suspicious. 'I'm sorry, but… there was no one there, Megan. No one but us.'

'No one?' Megan's legs went weak. It wasn't possible. Why wasn't Ellie there again? With the letter…

'No one. I waited. Until you appeared. You almost gave me a heart attack.' Nora pulled a pile of books and printouts from her bag and held them out like a peace offering, an apology. 'I thought you might like these. The books were in the collection here, or my own. I contacted the local archives for you and spoke to a friend. She emailed me more details of Eleanor's disappearance. Police reports and interviews. There's a fair amount of unpublished stuff. I thought… Are you sure you're up to this? You look pale.'

'But the book, the letter…'

Nora's expression grew stern. 'I don't know. But something is going on here and I want to get to the bottom of it. I think Faye Seaborne is involved. And probably someone else. Then and now. It's very weird. Almost like— Look, I've never found that letter before and I've been over every inch of that collection. And last night, in the maze… what did you think I'd see there?'

'I – I didn't. I just—'

Nora sighed and pursed her lips. 'Or should I say *who*? You called out Eleanor's name, you know? You were looking for her, weren't you? And you threw something in the well. What was it?'

She didn't wait for Megan to answer, as if she knew that there was no answer to give. Or if there was, not one that Megan was willing to voice. Nora opened three books, each one marked with Post-it notes, and spread out a host of printouts, portions of which were highlighted in bright yellow. She even had a map.

This wasn't the rageful Nora Megan had seen in the private library, the ghost of the Green Lady superimposed on her. Or the gentle Nora who had helped her last night…

'Fine,' Nora said, arranging her research. 'Don't tell me. Just look at this. We always thought Eleanor Fairfax was last seen at nine o'clock, in the village, here at the church. She went to the evening service with her father's secretary.' She stabbed at the map with her finger and then traced a line through the market square. 'There were all kinds of stalls here. Cakes and hot cider, and corn dollies, traditional crafts, same as they still do.'

All right, Megan thought, *I'll bite.*

'It's Michaelmas, isn't it? Today.'

'Tomorrow. But the fête is today. Ashleigh's always held onto some older traditions. The Harvest Festival starts on Michaelmas eve. Tonight. It's older than Christianity, of course. It used to move around, coincide with the full moon. The harvest moon this year was too early in the month anyway. About ten years ago we switched to have it on the twenty-eighth. It's easier for the parish council to have a fixed date anyway when they're planning it.'

'Of course.' But Megan doubted the parish council had anything to do with it. Ashleigh and Foxfield Hall in particular were shaped by the Vala, by their actions long ago. And some things lingered on more powerfully than others. Older than any of the people who settled here, older than anything, older than mankind.

The people of Ashleigh remembered. Whether they knew it or not.

'It's going to be a great one this year,' Nora went on. 'Dancing, food, fireworks, everything. I walked through it on the way here, retracing her steps.'

'Her steps… *here*? She didn't vanish from the village? I thought she was last seen at the church?'

'No,' said Nora. She pulled a slim paperback over and flicked it open to a page with a pink Post-it sticking out from the side. 'This is from an account by one of the kitchen maids, Sarah Matthews. Never saw it before.' She raised an eyebrow. 'If I didn't know better I'd say it just popped into existence, like a certain letter.'

'*Popped?*'

'Look, archives get lost and misfiled. And things in books get overlooked. But the timing is… well. Just listen.'

And she started to read.

'*It was nigh on ten o'clock when I left the house that night. I passed the young mistress on the road from Ashleigh. When I asked where her companion was, she simply said she had gone on ahead, wanting to be home early. I was about to offer to walk her home again when Miss Hatten, as was dismissed, happened along and did so in my stead.*'

'Miss Hatten?'

'Another maid in the house.'

'Mary? Mary Hatten?'

'I guess so. It doesn't say. Have you seen the full name elsewhere? I could only find this reference. They didn't take it seriously, I think. Sarah was fifteen years old and distraught by Eleanor's disappearance. I think she thought she'd be blamed.'

'Mary was a maid in the house. Why didn't they question her?'

Nora pursed her lips. 'And there you go again. How do you know she was a maid?'

'I just…' There was no way to explain it, no way to prove it. All she had was Ellie's letter. And she wasn't sure how to explain why a missing woman from so long ago had written a letter to her. 'Mary was let go without references a couple of days before. The letter said so.' Nora gave her an arch look for which there was no reply.

'Well, that's a motive for revenge,' she conceded, although she didn't look entirely convinced.

Mary Hatten. Now Megan had a name, something to go on. And confirmation that Ellie hadn't vanished from the village. She'd come back to the Hall. 'Why didn't anyone follow up on that when Ellie disappeared?'

Nora shrugged. 'An oversight maybe? If Mary had already suppos-edly left the area, maybe they didn't think of it. Maybe they weren't able to find her.'

Maybe. There were suddenly a lot of people missing from Ashleigh and Megan didn't like it.

'Anyone else?' Megan asked.

'Well yes.' Nora pulled out a photo of a young man in an RAF uniform in a slip of clear plastic. It was scuffed and faded, but you could still read the handwriting in the corner.

For Ellie, with all my love, David.

'David, her fiancé?'

Nora ran her fingertips along the edge of the photo casing. 'Yes. David Grainger. My great-grandfather.' She looked up from the photo then and Megan saw her eyes had done that strange thing again, more hazel in this moment. Still beautiful. They were always beautiful. Just not that startling blue they sometimes were. As they had been in the library when she was angry. Nora squinted in the sunlight, as if she had a headache setting in. She wasn't wearing her glasses, Megan realised. She hadn't worn them in a while, but now she fished them out of her bag and put them back on before turning her attention back to the photo. Contacts, Megan thought suddenly. They could make eyes look more blue. Had she been wearing contacts? And why was she looking for explanations when it came to Nora?

Because she was afraid Nora was somehow involved in all this madness and she… she didn't want her to be.

'He was stationed not far from here, when it happened,' Nora said. 'We have his war record. He went from losing her pretty much straight back into active duty and from there into the Battle of Britain. Shot down, but survived, badly wounded… I guess that was his war, really. I don't know if he ever recovered. He came back looking for Ellie, but never found her. He married – obviously, or I wouldn't be here – but it wasn't happy, according to Dad. When his wife left him in the late forties, he sent Granddad back to Belleclair, to his mum. She raised him. But David never came back here again.'

'I thought everyone came back to Ashleigh.'

She winced. 'Yeah, well. We lose some.'

'What happened to him?'

'Died in '53. He was only forty. He'd suffered since the war with PTSD.'

She didn't offer any more than that and Megan didn't dare ask. It was clearly a dark part of her family history, something that Megan knew from her own family it was never a good idea to poke at. Looking at the handsome, carefree man in the photo, her heart ached. What could David's life have been if Ellie had survived? She'd loved him, Megan was sure of that. But without her, it sounded like he had just fallen apart.

Or maybe it was the aftermath of the war. PTSD did terrible things and David had been through more than most people would survive.

The next page Nora pulled out caught Megan's attention immediately. A familiar name was scrawled across the top in Nora's handwriting and underlined three times.

'Then, there's this. Ava *Seaborne*. Interesting coincidence, isn't it? I wonder if she's related to our Faye. It would explain a lot. Why she's back here, for one thing. How she got here so quickly when the body was found. Like… like she was waiting for it. And Ava Seaborne herself? Well, wait until you get a load of her story. What we know of it, anyway.'

Faye and Ava… They could be related. If they weren't the same person. It was impossible but still…

Megan knew what she'd seen, what she'd experienced. Impossible didn't begin to cover it. And there was something about Faye Seaborne. Something magical. She didn't want to say that to Nora. It would sound wrong, like an attraction. And it was more than that. It was dangerous.

'Her father's secretary.'

'Her father's something. Secretary would have been a demotion for her. But they worked together all right, in the SOE.'

'The what?'

'The Special Operations Executive. Of course, *that* didn't exist in 1939. SOE was formed from a few different groups. Department EH, Section D and MI(R) are well documented, or as well as they can be any more. What's not generally known is that there was another group too and Ellie's father was involved with its foundation. I don't think it even had a name. He was one of those people who brought all those groups together, forged the organisation that would shorten the war by years. And Ava Seaborne was beside him, right up until he died. She was in Bletchley Park as well, with the cypher school. And after the war, she just vanished. Not a trace left of her. It's generally assumed she died in action somewhere and was never found.'

There were papers on Ava too, but only brief, blurry pictures. She was a tall, slender woman with dark hair. It was impossible to see if it was the same person. The same frame, the same impression, if you squinted at the images. But she could definitely be related to Faye. And if you believed in such things… She could *be* Faye.

All times are one time, all places are one place, the Green Lady had said.

The thought sent another chill through Megan. She'd seen Faye with the Green Lady, in her strange fever vision, and their other sister. Was she immortal? Was that even possible?

Megan's gaze fell on the corn dollies Nora had been making and a cold grip clamped itself around her throat. Little knots and twists of straw, little figures, random abstract shapes, all tied with red ribbons, red as blood. When Nora saw Megan's eyes on them she grinned. So innocent an expression, but Megan couldn't help but suspect something else lurked behind it.

'They're a hobby. We all make them this time of year because you can never have too many. They sell them to the tourists to raise funds for the church. Some chuck them in the pretend well. More take them home as souvenirs. I have a pile of them to drop down to the village for this afternoon.' Nora swept them into the fabric tote bag she had taken the books from. 'Offerings for the Green Lady. That's what I was taught. Sacrifices. I always believed in the ghost, really I did. I wish… I wish I had seen her last night, Megan. Her or Ellie. But that's not possible, is it?'

She sounded so wistful, and just a bit disappointed. Like a child finding out once and for all that Father Christmas wasn't real.

'Me too.' It would have been easier. Nora didn't believe her. That much was clear. The disappointment shook her.

'Maybe we could sneak in and see her now, the Green Lady? She's back in the hotel after all. That's part of the ghost story, isn't it? That she's just trying to get home again, to find peace. I wonder if she's happy now.'

She isn't, Megan thought, remembering her last night. She really isn't. And Nora should have known that. Had the ghost been trying to possess her? Is that what was going on here?

She hesitated.

'If you're up to it?' Nora added suddenly. 'Are you sure you're feeling okay? I know you aren't feverish any more but…'

'Yeah, nothing like a night-time walk to fix a fever.' It was a terrible attempt at a joke and neither of them laughed. But whatever Nora thought Megan had been doing at the well, she didn't ask.

Like she didn't want to know.

But Nora had been there. Because Megan had asked her to go. Despite Ellie not putting in an appearance, Nora had been there to help when Megan had all but collapsed at her feet. That had to count for something.

She was quicksilver, that was the problem, a mystery to be solved. And just a little dangerous herself.

They packed up the books and headed to the main part of the hotel. Hattie was behind reception again, giving a somewhat suggestive wave as they crossed the hall. Megan ignored her, making every effort to avoid eye contact while Nora flushed and hurried on, head down. She'd have some explaining to do, and clearly wasn't looking forward to it.

Richie was manning the room where the Green Lady's body had been housed, but she wasn't there any more. The tent and all the associated equipment had been removed. There were boxes with lumps of clay and oddly shaped things in them.

The photos were pinned to a board, big glossy prints depicting every detail. Nora stood in front of it, hugging her arms around her chest, enthralled.

'How did she die?' she asked eventually.

'She was a sacrifice, we think,' said Richie. 'It's very late for that, of course, so it's going to be controversial and we've definitely never found one dating as late as this one. These people were meant to be Christian at this stage. Or mostly, anyway.'

'This was one of the last areas in the country to convert,' Nora said, distractedly.

Richie nodded. 'Well, we have to go with what's in front of us. The facts as presented. See the rope around her wrists and her neck? It's like some of the Bronze Age bog bodies. First they strangled her, then they cut her throat – see, there's a gash here in the skin. Amazing preservation. And then, before she was dead, I guess they threw her in the water so she drowned as she bled out.'

Nora listened to every word, fascinated rather than repulsed. 'How do you know that?'

Another voice broke through the quiet of the room, making both Richie and Megan jump like startled rabbits. Nora turned more slowly, her jaw tight as if anticipating an argument.

'Her lungs were perfectly preserved. Basic forensics.' Faye stood in the doorway behind them, her hands on her hips. 'Good to see you're better, Megan. From what Sahar said, I was worried that you'd caught something nasty.'

Megan shifted uncomfortably.

'Is it her?' Nora asked bluntly, before Megan could be forced by politeness to reply. 'Is it the Green Lady? Have you brought her home?'

'The Green Lady is a myth.'

'Have you told her that?' Nora snapped, bristling as she always seemed to do in proximity to Faye.

A blast of wind tore through the house, slamming doors and windows one after the other. Megan caught the scent of dampness in the chill air, and then it was gone. The Green Lady was here, just as she had been last night, or an echo of her anyway. The body might be gone but the ghost remained. Megan knew it. She could sense her as if Gwynhyfer stood behind her, breathing down her neck. The ghost had been brought home. And she wasn't happy.

Richie scrabbled around, trying to catch the papers that flew everywhere like demented butterflies, and a moment later everyone in the room was dashing about, trying to grab the ones that got away.

As Megan handed back the sheets she'd gathered and Richie cursed and swore, trying to put them back in order, one caught her eye. She stared at it, unable to move. 'Where did you find this?'

It showed a computer-generated picture of a hooked blade with a simple wooden handle. Megan remembered it too well, although she couldn't say anything. The woman with the gold mask, the one called Gwyar, had threatened her with it.

'We didn't,' said Richie. 'It's what we think cut her throat.'

'It's a reaping hook,' Nora said, glancing at it. 'Or a sickle. You use it for the last sheaves of wheat. There are some outside in the hall, mounted behind the reception, with the corn maiden. Been there for years.'

Something cold and clammy crept its way up Megan's spine. The corn maiden, made in the same way as the hex she had destroyed last night, as the little champion figure Ellie had given her, and as the small army of them Nora had made that she still carried in the bag on her shoulder right now.

She dreaded it. Those things had power. She'd felt it crawling out of the hex last night, malignant, dangerous power.

Faye started to reply, as though she couldn't resist a bit of Ashleigh history. 'They're made of straw, rather than actual corn, of course. But they're known as corn dollies or, this particular type, the Ashleigh corn maidens. The spirit that lived in the crops had to be appeased when they were harvested, so the last sheaf was taken, dried and woven into something beautiful, something to please the spirit. And when time came for the ground to be broken again, the corn maiden was buried again, or drowned in the water source which fed those crops.'

Drowned in a well. Just like the Green Lady.

As though Faye was reading Megan's mind, she carried on in a gentle voice. 'And this lady…' she ran her fingers over the still fluttering photographs, 'she was a sacrifice too.'

Megan had seen Faye throw a corn figure into the well too, a different one, not a maiden. She'd called her figure Artrí. The champion. The word the Green Lady had used to describe her.

'Could the two be tied together?' asked Nora. 'If she died by the same sort of blade, the sickle that cuts the crops, and drowned in the same well, even the knots in the ropes holding her could be seen as the knots that wove the corn maiden together.'

Faye pulled the sheet from her hands. 'It's an interesting theory, but too much of a coincidence. We deal in facts, not speculation.'

'Why not?' asked Megan, bristling that she was dismissing Nora's theory so quickly. 'You said that the traditions in this village are very old, and unique to the area. No one knows as much about them as Nora.'

Nora caught her arm, pulling her back. Her face flushed with embarrassment. 'Megan, it's okay. Dr Seaborne is the expert here. I'm just… it's a hobby, that's all. Don't worry.'

Faye gave them both a glare that blazed finality. 'It's getting late.'

Megan wanted to tell her to go to hell, but Nora all but pulled her from the room.

'Let's go and have another look at it, the Ashleigh corn maiden,' she said hurriedly. 'It'll only take a second.' Something inside Megan really didn't want to look at another corn dolly as long as she lived. But she'd rather go with Nora than stay here with Faye. Or have to deal with the feeling that with the Green Lady finally back in Foxfield Hall things were about to change.

And not for the better.

Chapter Twenty-Four

Saturday 28th September 2019

Looking at it again, the Ashleigh corn maiden looked somewhat pathetic in comparison to the fearsome thing Megan had built up in her mind. No bigger than her forearm, wider at the base, tapering up to a head, it wound in spirals, knotted together to form the vague shape of a woman. Its arms were folded behind its back and a string of knotted corn hung around its neck. It was tied with faded red string. The more Megan looked at it, the more she got the feeling that Nora was right.

And the more she got the impression of the sacrificed body of the Green Lady.

'Turfed out, were you?' asked Hattie, her needles clacking away as she knitted. 'Those people have no class whatsoever. Think they own the place. You didn't want to take that lying down, young Nora.'

She didn't look up at the two of them, just carried on knitting.

'Have they been giving you grief too, Hattie?' Nora asked.

She laughed. 'No one gives me grief, my dear. You know that. *We wunt be druv.*'

Nora had moved to the foot of the stairs now, gazing at the pictures, resting her hand on the bannisters as if touching a rare object in a museum. Megan joined her.

'What's up? Sorry she was so rude.'

'Oh, she wasn't. Not really. She's Dr Faye Seaborne, Megan. She's known for being brusque, and I was kind of stepping on her toes in there. I just get carried away. I love our old stories. Anyway…' Nora gave a sigh. 'I'd better go and catch that bus. I don't fancy walking all the way home in the dark and I've got to drop these off to the fête committee for the stall.' She indicated her bag of corn dollies.

'You didn't drive up?'

'No, can you believe it? Couldn't get the car out this morning thanks to the fête traffic. Stupid truck blocking me in. Hattie gave me a lift up.'

'I'll drive you.' Megan responded without thinking, pure instinct.

'You shouldn't. You've been sick since yesterday.'

Megan shrugged. 'I'm better now.' She didn't want Nora to go, not yet. She still needed to figure out if Nora was involved in all this and, if so, whose side she was on. She had brought back the coat with the hex in the pocket. But she had gone to the maze last night because Megan had asked her to. Nora had helped her, hadn't she?

She couldn't let her go. Not now.

Nora just grinned and wrapped her hair around her fingers in an intricate and mesmerising fashion. 'If you're sure…'

Megan desperately tried to think of the right thing to say. A way to tell her what was happening. A way to explain. Any of it.

She still hadn't figured it out by the time they reached the Land Rover.

*

As they neared the village, a skinny teen in a hi-vis vest tried to direct them into a field, where a hand-painted sign on the gate said 'Parking'.

Nora rolled down her window. 'It's okay, Paul. It's me. Megan's just taking me home. We'll park around back of the church. Tell you what, could you drop these over to the committee for me?' She handed him the cloth bag of corn dollies.

He all but tipped an invisible cap at her. 'All right, Miss Grainger.' His face turned the colour of beetroot.

'How do you do that?' Megan asked.

'Do what?'

'Have people jump whenever you say so.'

'I do?' Nora laughed. 'I wish. I used to babysit Paul and his sisters. Hattie says he's had a crush on me since he was eleven. It's just down there.'

The village was crammed with people. They spilled out across the narrow roads. The pub was heaving and so was the green. A sound system had been set up and music rolled out across the crowd. There was even a coconut shy.

'I know,' Nora sighed. 'It's corny. But it's home.'

'It's… a bit chaotic.'

Nora smiled fondly. 'A bit. But it's only once a year. Have you seen the church, by the way? It's Norman.'

'Is it still open?'

'It's hardly ever locked but, if it is, I know where they keep the key. Besides, it's harvest day. Of course it's open.'

With this many people around, Megan wouldn't leave anything unlocked. But Nora didn't see it that way. Clearly no one in Ashleigh did.

They crossed the road and Nora led her into the church, pushing open the door without any effort at all. She didn't even pause. Perhaps living so close she thought of it as part of her home, somewhere she was so used to being that she didn't hesitate for a moment. The lights were on inside, soft and golden, and Megan stopped, surprised at the beauty within.

The stained glass dominated everything, a woman in green with two others. Someone had tried to disguise them as Mary the Mother of God and two angels or something like that but Megan wasn't fooled for a moment. By now she knew the Vala when she saw them.

'Wow,' she breathed.

'I know, right?' Nora reached out and took her hand, fingers very cold as they entwined. She pulled her forwards. 'And that's Guillaume Fairfax's tomb over there.'

She pointed at the effigy of a knight, lying as if in slumber. Ellie's ancestor, one of them anyway.

'He was the first Lord of Foxfield. Wasn't he?'

Nora grinned. 'The first Norman one. Before that, well… the records are sketchy.' She shrugged but then laid her hand on his stone cheek. 'Half the village is meant to be descended from him.'

'Is that possible?'

She arched her eyebrow. 'Small village. People don't tend to move far away. Especially in the past. Even today, we tend to gravitate back. There's nowhere quite like it.'

'So are you… are you related to Ellie?'

Nora shrugged. 'Somewhere, way back, I suppose.' It wasn't like her to be so vague. She knew her family history and the village history inside out. Megan frowned. Something chilly crept over the back of her neck and she looked back at the glass. Above the figures of the women was a full moon. And below them, clustered around the altar, were all the fruits of the harvest.

It was the night of the harvest moon in 1939 when Ellie disappeared. All those years ago.

And here in 2019?

'What's the moon doing, Nora? Tonight?'

Nora grinned at her, bemused. 'It's the second new moon in the calendar month, a black moon, the evil twin of a blue moon.' She grinned, enjoying her joke. Megan didn't find it funny though.

Here, the laws of place and time do not apply. Not beneath the black moon.

When she didn't laugh, Nora's smile faded.

Nora was still studying her, like she was waiting for something. Her eyes had taken on that blue shimmer again, instead of hazel. It must be the light, Megan thought. And then… then she wondered again. She kept dismissing it. What if it was something more?

'Nora? Are you—' She couldn't say *Vala*. She just couldn't. She didn't know what to say.

Nora took a step closer. She held out her hand, the same hand she'd touched the effigy's face with.

'It's okay, Megan. Don't be afraid. I don't bite.'

'Are you a witch?'

Her smile turned coquettish. Megan wasn't sure if that was the question she'd been expecting but it didn't matter. Nora turned it to flirtation instead. 'I'm not a wiccan, if that's what you mean. But there were cunning-folk in my family, a long time ago.'

It wasn't an admission. Not really. Megan wasn't sure what it was. That captivating blush bloomed in Nora's cheeks again. Megan wished she had the nerve to just lean in and kiss her like they did in the movies. But then what? It would be awkward and strange. She'd get it wrong. And besides, she didn't really know how much Nora knew. Or how she was involved in all this. Or if she was at all.

'That's not what I meant.'

'I know. Look…' Nora's expression fell, and she folded her arms around her chest, withdrawing from their sudden intimacy. 'There's family history, that's all. And in a place as small as Ashleigh, where we're all related anyway, everyone knows everyone's business. So a word like *witch*…' Her eyes fluttered closed and she sighed before she smoothed her expression and looked up at Megan again. 'Let's just say I got called Hermione a lot in school.'

Of course she did. The look of torment that flickered in the depths of her eyes tugged at something Megan knew far too well. She'd spent most of her school life knowing she was gay. That hadn't been easy either. Kids could be cruel about the smallest things.

And about the big things, they could be unbearable.

Megan didn't think. She reached out and caught Nora's hand in her own. It felt very small and cold. Their fingers interlaced again, as if they fitted together, belonged there.

'I always liked Hermione. She's awesome.'

Nora glanced down at their hands, then looked back up into Megan's face, but she didn't pull away. 'So do I.' Nora smiled gently and her cheeks heated. 'There's all this stuff going on. All this crazy stuff. You say something like that… and it… it doesn't seem as bad any more.'

A shiver like electricity ran over her skin. Megan inhaled, held the breath for as long as she could and then let it out again.

Before she knew what was happening, Nora had leaned in and kissed her, not on the cheek. Full on the mouth.

Megan's mind broke apart and reformed. Nora's touch was soft and gentle, and she smelled of summer. Nora's lips and tongue teased and cajoled, and she framed Megan's face with her delicate hands, caressing her skin. Megan ran her fingers up Nora's side until she found the gap between her jeans and her shirt, and the warmth of her bare skin, and Nora gasped, breaking the kiss. Her eyes fluttered closed in pleasure.

'We'll scandalise the village,' Megan murmured.

'Story of my life,' Nora sighed. 'And in the church too. Whatever will the vicar say? Probably something like…' and her voice dropped into a brilliant imitation of a man of the cloth: '*Dear God, Nora Grainger, not again.*'

Megan laughed. She couldn't help it. How did she do that? Nora charmed her at every turn. Even if she wasn't sure where she stood. This woman was enchanting, quicksilver. Being with her was like trying to catch a beam of light. All Megan wanted to do was keep on kissing her.

They left the church and all the stars were out, scattered carelessly across the moonless sky. The music was still going on, but the party appeared to have moved into the pub and the village green was deserted now.

'Want to get that drink?' Nora asked.

There was nothing Megan wanted more in that moment. But… she thought of Ellie. Tonight was the black moon, when the laws of place and time did not apply, according to the Green Lady. She had to get back. This was her last chance to try to find Ellie in the maze of Foxfield Hall.

And… Nora had brought back the coat with the hex in it. She knew so much. Too much. For all Megan knew, she knew everything. She could be the other Vala.

She hadn't exactly denied it.

At the same time, all Megan wanted to do was kiss her again, to wrap herself up in her and never let go. She was an addiction.

It made her dangerous.

'Tomorrow? I need to—'

'I'm sorry, of course. You're driving. And you were sick. Don't mind me. I'm just being selfish. Tomorrow it is.'

Megan smiled as she made her way back to the car and then turned. Nora was still standing at the gate to her house, watching her. She smiled from her garden, perfect, beautiful, smart, funny Nora, surrounded by flowers of every colour, her fox-red hair gleaming in the porch light.

Megan lifted her fingers to her lips where the kiss still tingled and sparked. Like a ghost's touch. Like magic. Like she had been marked.

Chapter Twenty-Five

Thursday 28th September 1939

They took the car down to the village for the second time in two days, even though Ellie and her father usually walked, especially on so warm and fine an afternoon. Even though petrol was in short supply. Ellie wasn't sure she could have walked anyway. She couldn't seem to fill her lungs with air. Her heart ached as if someone had cracked open her ribs and ripped it out.

It didn't matter. Nothing mattered.

Not without David.

And if she didn't do what the Vala wanted, David would die tonight. Perhaps he would anyway. She felt trapped.

They passed stalls and a group of local musicians already playing. There were girls dancing in the market square and a cricket match taking place on the green beside the church. Even in the midst of normality the telltale gas mask boxes were visible in the crowds, and a couple of military uniforms as well.

For a moment there was a flash of blue in the crowd and she thought of David.

A spear of hope shot through her, but it wasn't him.

He was gone. Swallowed up by shadows. Taken.

Noise erupted as the car door opened, making Miss Seaborne twist as if searching for something unseen. Her hand closed on Ellie's wrist like a band of iron.

'Stay with me,' she said.

Last night, Ava – why bother with formalities now? – had almost carried her back to the house, while Ellie screamed for David until her throat was raw. She'd poured her a large brandy which scorched its way down Ellie's throat and made her head spin.

'Where is he?' She had forced the words out. 'How do I get him back?'

But Ava shook her head. 'We can try, but not now. You have to wait. Tomorrow night, the full moon. That's the only time when I can rescue him, when the Green Lady walks and my sister will be in the maze. She'll have him with her, in the shadows between, where no one can touch him. I'll go and get him back, I promise you, Eleanor. But you must never go in there again.'

At least Ava didn't seem to feel the need to exert her strange control over her now. The threat to David was doing that.

Ellie should have listened. She knew that now. Ava had told her all along she wanted to help her and now... now she was the only hope Ellie had, if she wanted to get David back. And she *had* to get him back.

He was hers. He always had been. Her fiancé, her love, her everything. He couldn't be gone.

Ellie dutifully climbed out of the car and rearranged her clothes so that they looked neater. But Ava grabbed her shoulders and pulled her back against the car.

A girl tore by them, wearing a white dress and a crown of straw set with white flowers. She was laughing like a demon and a group of the village lads chased her.

'What on earth?' Ava exclaimed.

Well at least she didn't know everything. It was good to see her shocked by something. If she could feel anything at all, Ellie might have felt smug.

'She's the Harvest Maiden. Like the May Queen, only not as…' Ellie looked for the right word. 'Pure.'

'No. Nor indeed, I suspect, *chaste*.'

'She looked pretty chased to me,' muttered Ellie but Ava glared at her and she was forced to school her features to innocence. David would have roared laughing. Ellie knew that.

And the thought of David made all humour drain away.

The day ploughed on, each minute dragging by. She tried to be pleasant and kind, tried to talk to her neighbours and the other villagers, tasted the cake, even though it was like sand in her mouth, and cooed at the babies who screamed back at her. As the evening came, her head pounded like a drum and her stomach twisted in a knot.

Ava seemed to take pity on her. 'Shall we go for a walk? Perhaps you would like to show me the church. I believe it is quite historic. Your father spoke of it frequently.'

'The church?' Her father rarely had time for religion other than what was expected of him each Sunday.

'It's also cool and quiet. Come along, Eleanor.'

The Church of St Michael in Ashleigh was the oldest building for miles around, a squat Norman church built of flint and rubble constructed not long after the Normans settled there, before the first version of Foxfield Hall was begun. But parts of it were older. It had a rounded apse, and a wooden roof. The windows had been widened and stained glass added much later, although they were still unbearably old. Now the interior was alight with candles and the first fruits of the harvest spilled around the altar. Simple corn dollies tied with ribbons decorated the end of each pew, little traditional designs. With everyone else still outside, the church had an otherworldly quality Ellie had never noticed before. Ava stopped in the aisle, reaching out her hands to touch the nearest pews on either side, her fingers tracing the woven straw ornaments.

'This is more like it. True reverence for the land. Look, Eleanor.' Coloured light from the stained glass painted Ava's features, adding to her otherworldliness. She lifted her face towards it like a flower drinking it down.

Above the door through which they had entered, the windows were aglow with the golden light of sunset. A thousand green and gold shades fell across the floor. Saint Gwyneth, their local saint, or so Ellie had been taught, stood decked in green, her bare feet standing in a pool of water. She lifted her face to the rays of light from above where the dove flew from the clouds and she held up a cup. On either side of her two angels knelt.

A curious unease crept through Ellie. It made the headache even worse.

'Even now, she manages to transform into something else,' said Ava. Her voice was a breath, a whisper. 'Ah, my sister. My Vala. *Gwyneth, Gwyn, Guinevere.*'

Wind whipped through the church, sending all the candle flames into a wild dance, and Ellie was sure she heard a voice beneath the wind, crying out in loss.

'What's happening?' she asked, but Ava didn't seem to hear her. She was lost in a trance, staring at the woman in the window, talking not to Ellie but to the image before her.

'I will find her champion and preserve them both. I swear. On blood and breath, I swear. I will free you. I will bring you home. And you will finally forgive me.'

Abruptly the wind died and the door to the church slammed behind them. Ellie jumped, but there was no one there.

Ava looked at her as if seeing her for the first time. She reached out a long-fingered pale hand, like a corpse's in the light. When Ellie took it, her skin was cold and dry as old parchment.

'I am a Vala,' she whispered and the word bounced around the chamber of the little church until it returned like a chorus of sighs. The word she kept using like air or water or fire. 'Just as I told you yesterday. Guardians. Keepers of fate. Sisters. Enchantresses. We were all powerful and we wove the lives and destinies of kings and slaves. All men bowed before us. We entered into legend and we were forgotten. Soon we were no more than the women on the periphery of stories. My youngest sister was Gwynhyfer, faithful, constant, who spun out threads of lives and tended them, the maiden who waited and lost everything.'

The candles flickered, sending their light dancing wildly all around them. But there wasn't a breeze, not one Ellie could feel. Ava stepped in closer, her voice dropping to a low rumble that ripped through the depths of Ellie's stomach.

'I was Muirgen, born of tempest and wave, weaver of fate, maker of kings and destroyer of fools. And our other sister, Gwyar, the walking death, the harvester, who cuts the thread, who spilled the blood of sacrifice and gathered the power within each life back to the source. Maiden, mother and crone. We called ourselves the Vala and so did all who followed us. This island was ours. This land. All ours.'

Her words echoed around the church, bouncing back at them like a chorus of whispers from another time.

Ellie couldn't quite find her voice. It seemed like a sin to break the spell of this place, of Ava's voice. She knew she ought to run. But she needed the answers. She needed to know, to get David back. And here was Ava Seaborne, or Muirgen, or whoever she really was, dangling those answers in front of her like carrots to a donkey. Logic warred with what she was hearing, no matter what Ellie herself believed. It was too much, too terrible. She might know it was true… but she didn't want it to be. Not now. Not any more. All she wanted was David back safely.

'But they're just legends – Vala, whatever you call yourself. Might as well say King Arthur and the Matter of Britain. They're just stories!'

'Stories? We are more than stories. Surely you understand that now, *you* of all people. Before time and history. Before Rome, before the Celts, before the Atrebates and their kin, before any kind of written word, our people spread far and wide across Europe,' said Ava. 'Not just this island, though it is our stronghold. As for King Arthur, there was no Round Table and those knights and heroes were thugs and murderers. We chose them. We made them. Our names changed, that's all, but the story was the same.'

'So you're what? Morgan le Fey?'

She smiled slowly, knowingly. 'It's a curious name, isn't it? Morgan or Morgana, from Muirgen, born of the sea, le Fey, out of Faerie, Ava out of Avalon… I do so love these names. But here I am… and look what they made of me. The villain of Arthurian legends. An evil enchantress, a wicked witch. But we are so much older than that, my sisters and I. We are as old as the chalk of the Hill, as old as the bones of this land itself. There were so many tribes, so many names. Pagan hordes…' She laughed bitterly. 'And when they turned from us, when we fell, they despised us. They would call us witches. All of us. You included, I fear. Let us look at these carvings before the ones outside give up their pagan rites and find religion again, shall we?'

'We need to go back for David.'

'The moon hasn't risen yet. You will not find him there while there is still daylight.'

'Where is he? Where is your sister keeping him?'

'In nightmares and darkness. In a place we cannot tread. But he is strong of mind and faithful. He might even survive. Until the full moon rises. Gwyn's beloved did. For a time.'

The champion and the Vala… Gwynhyfer had been killed but her ghost was trapped in the well. She had been separated from her champion, her husband, forever. Even in death they were kept apart.

Ellie swallowed hard. She could argue forever, but what choice did she have? The Vala were real. She had to accept that. And she needed Ava's help.

'You will… you will get David back, won't you?'

But Ava didn't answer. She turned away, looking up at the stained glass again.

This was no good. Ellie couldn't wait here. She had to get back to the Hall. She had to find David herself. Ava, Morgan le Fey, could not be trusted. She had her own agenda and if sacrificing David paved the way for whatever it was she wanted out of this, Ellie feared she would do it in a heartbeat. And Ellie too.

She had to find him herself. In the maze, by moonlight, tonight. Under the harvest moon. Megan's papers said she vanished from the village, but if she left that couldn't happen, could it? If she made it back home and found David first…

Before she could move, the doors to the church opened and the whole village blocked her way, entering the building, joyous in their celebrations. They filed in, just a few at first, the elderly, those for who this church was as much a part of their home as their hearth. Ellie couldn't push by them.

Ava's hand fell on her shoulder for just a moment and, with that, her free will fled. Ellie had to stop and greet people she'd known all her life, shaking hands, answering questions as to news of her father, as if nothing was wrong. There was nowhere she could run now, not without making the kind of scene that every fibre of her being was designed to avoid. Ava was not going to let her go. Her hawk-like gaze fixed Ellie in place and there was no wriggling free.

Mr Mayfield settled himself in front of the rickety organ, a once fine instrument in dire need of refurbishment – something that wouldn't happen for years now, if at all. He adjusted his glasses on the end of his nose before he began to play. Ellie retreated, turning like a sacrificial victim towards the front of the church where Ava was waiting in the Fairfax family pew. She could protest, denounce the woman, name and shame her, but…

They'd never believe her. How could they? The tale was impossible for modern ears. She'd sound like a hysterical child, spinning fancies to get her own way. Like a madwoman. She was trapped. Completely and perfectly. And Ava knew it. So many people, watching her, surrounding her, keeping an eye on her. How could she vanish from this?

Music swelled around them and Ellie closed her eyes, feeling it vibrate through her. Light streamed in through the windows behind her, touching the back of her head, the sun falling fast. Fingers of light trailed through her hair, caressed her skull. And the voices began to sing.

Come, ye thankful people, come,
Raise the song of harvest home.

Music and voices swelled around her, the most primal way to touch the divine, to lift praises from mere human bodies and send prayers and glorification swirling out into the ether. Ellie opened her eyes again to light, to the figure of the woman in the stained glass aglow with candlelight and adulation. She was holding a grail. The grail. The twin figures on either side of her weren't angels as she had always taken them for, but women as well.

Three women, three Vala. In Ashleigh.

Witches. And so much more than witches.

Guinevere, Morgan le Fey, Morgause; she knew their names like her own now after poring over the books, and hearing it from Ava. And now the earliest forms. Gwynhyfer, Muirgen, Gwyar…

The Britons, the Romans, the Saxons, even the Normans… all peoples who had arrived to these islands, but their influence and rule took time to extend across the land, the way sunrise and sunset did. And there were places where older ways lingered long in the shadows cast by twilight. It had before and it would in the future. All through time. Such places clung to their past, dug in their soil-black nails and clung on for dear life.

Places like Ashleigh.

The Green Lady had been an integral part of an older tradition, one which lived on even today. How old, there was no way of saying. Ellie just had to look around her. Harvest Festival was a quintessentially English fête. But it didn't feel very Christian.

None of this did.

In other villages, the Harvest Festival was held on a Sunday. Here, it followed the moon. So there would be a service here tonight, a Thursday, and another for Michaelmas, the festival of God's own champion the next day, the 29th.

A champion. *Artrí*, Ellie realised. *Arthur.*

And David was hers, her champion. Just as she had said when he was leaving. She remembered his joking smile the day they said goodbye, his words… *I am but a lowly suitor, the Arthur to your Guinevere.* It seemed so long ago, although it was only a few weeks. And he had come back for harvest, just as he promised. And she had lost him.

David. Her David.

But she hadn't given him the little champion corn dolly she had found in the well. She had given it to a woman from another time. From the future. The woman who knew what would happen to the war, to all the people here. Who had tried to warn her of her fate. Who had tried to protect her from the very start of all this.

In 1939 you disappear. You vanish without a trace and you're never found.

Ellie couldn't rescue David by herself. And she couldn't rely on Ava. She was a Vala too. She had more at stake here than Ellie knew, and her own plans. Ellie could not trust her. No. She had to find Megan. She'd help. Ellie knew that she would. It's what she had been trying to do all along.

Ellie fought back tears, crushed her hands into fists and forced herself to keep going, to be strong. Because she had to be strong.

The service ended and the faithful poured outside, wishing her good evening and asking after her father. They were very keen to talk to Miss Seaborne and plied her with questions. As a new arrival in the village, she was being grilled for her every opinion and all the web of lies she called her history. They weren't going to catch her out. She was a master of deflection, her stories so convincing, her tone so sure.

She lied as easily as breathing.

And then Ellie realised that no one was paying any attention to her at all. They didn't even seem to realise she was still there. Even Ava was too distracted to notice her right now.

It was getting dark now. The moon would be up soon, the harvest moon. If she hurried home now, she could get to the maze, meet Megan and find David. She needed to trust that, trust herself, and she couldn't wait any longer. If the masked woman called Gwyar had him, was keeping him wrapped up in her shadows and nightmares, Ellie had to find a way to free him. Perhaps he wasn't just her champion. Perhaps she was his.

It was growing dark. It was almost time. The moon was rising.

Ava wouldn't be able to stop her once she was inside the maze. Of that Ellie was sure. The magic of the maze, be it born from the land on which Foxfield stood or flowing through her own veins, wouldn't let her.

Whatever plan Ava had, Ellie wanted no part of it. She just needed to get away from the woman. Although she said she would protect Ellie, there wasn't a lot of evidence to support that. Protection appeared to mean imprisonment and Ellie wasn't having that. And given the choice between saving David and freeing the Green Lady, there was no doubt what Ava would choose. Ellie believed in empirical evidence. It was the scientific method. She should never have forgotten that. Ava twisted everything with her charisma and powers of persuasion. Even if she was in some way trustworthy, she wasn't telling the whole truth. There were things she was hiding yet.

And in every story Ellie had ever heard, Morgan le Fey always looked after herself first.

Ellie stepped back into the bustling crowd outside the church, keeping her eyes on her father's so-called secretary. She edged further away, until she reached the depleted cake stall, which she slipped behind. Out of sight. Hidden. Then she turned and sprinted across the village green.

If only she had worn the trousers from last night. Her skirt was practical, but not that practical. And these shoes were not made for running. It didn't matter though.

In minutes, she was beyond the boundaries of Ashleigh and running along the dark country road which led home. She just had to get back to the Hall.

And no one even noticed she was gone.

Chapter Twenty-Six

Saturday 28th September 2019

Megan shifted down a gear as she headed uphill, towards the bend. She was almost back at the Hall and it was dark now. Her headlights picked out the narrow tunnel of road between the thick hedgerows.

She just had to get back there.

If Ellie came to the maze tonight it meant she was okay.

Megan might have lost Owen but she had warned Ellie. And she couldn't shake the feeling that whatever they had done, the two of them in their own times, it was all changing. Her history, Ellie's future, Ashleigh itself…

The other car came around the bend in the middle of the road at high speed. The full headlights seared into her retinas and she swerved blindly to avoid it. The next thing she knew, branches and hedgerows tore at the windscreen as the Landie came to a crashing halt in a ditch. Her head slammed into the steering wheel.

Everything went quiet. So horribly quiet.

A low growl rippled through the air. Something rustled in the bushes to her left. Branches like emaciated fingers scratched against her face. Megan reached for the seatbelt which had probably saved her life. But the growl came again. She stopped, her heartbeat growing even louder in her head. The same nausea she'd felt in the maze swept through her. It twisted her gut and made beads of sweat prickle on her skin.

Nothing, it was nothing. She'd hit her head.

Back down the road, the other car had stopped, its brake lights bright, its hazard lights pulsing, a migraine rhythm beating behind her eyes. The engine rumbled… the growl she'd heard. Megan unclipped the seatbelt and tried the door, but it wouldn't open, wedged into the bushes. She cursed and climbed across to the other door, forcing it open against its own weight. The front of the Land Rover was stuck in the ditch, wedged into the hedgerow. Megan clambered up from the vehicle onto the grass verge and then stepped onto the road to Foxfield Hall.

The sound came again, deep and threatening. Not the other car this time. It was still there, engine rumbling. But that was definitely a growl. A breeze moved the leaves of the hedge, stirring them like whispers. And the shadows moved with them.

From deep in the bushes on the other side of the road, she saw a green light, like the will-o'-the-wisps that had led her to the maze in the first place. No, not one, but two. Two small green lights. And another growl. A snarl. In the shadows.

The black fox surged out of the darkness, ripping itself from the shadows to land in front of her. Sharp, silvery claws clattered on the tarmac.

Megan sucked in a breath, ready to cry out, but she couldn't. She stood transfixed as the night fox crept towards her, one step at a time. It was much bigger than any normal fox, more like some kind of mastiff. She remembered the first time she'd seen one. Now it looked even bigger. She took a step back, then another, but the fox kept pace. When she tried to skirt to the right, it matched her, driving her back towards her wrecked car. If she ran it would be on her. She knew it, could see that in its eyes. It was just waiting for her to run, daring her.

How had it got out here? They'd been in the maze. With the golden masked woman. How was it here, now?

The fox bared its teeth again. They glistened in the dwindling light and Megan staggered back a few more feet, onto the tarmac.

The roar of the car engine took her completely by surprise. She turned to see headlights on full beam bearing down on her, the sound of the vehicle deafening. Tyres tore up the road, screeching as the car sped up, barrelling down at her.

Megan threw herself out of the way but not fast enough. Something hit her a glancing blow, sending her spinning off into the bushes. She landed heavily and pain shot up her side, blossoming in her hip to agony. Branches and stones dug into her face and hands.

Darkness welled up around her and almost swallowed her, but she heard the car stop. Someone got out, slamming the door behind them. Footsteps crunched on the road surface and a shape loomed over her.

'You want to know when to stay down, to stay out of it.'

Megan was sure she knew the voice. But her hearing didn't seem to be working properly. She was drowning in wave upon wave of white noise. It distorted everything. Shadows ate at the corners of her vision and when she tried to move her head it hurt so much she couldn't see at all.

'This *has* to happen,' the woman said. 'I won't tell you again. The hex was a warning. This has happened already. And it must happen again. Stay out of it or face the consequences.'

Whoever it was walked away, got back in the car and drove off, leaving Megan in the darkness. She tried to pull herself up, but her arms gave out and she slammed back into the dirt. At some point, she passed out, growling shadows swallowing her whole while the moon laughed overhead.

*

She came to again to hear someone shouting for help, the glowing light of a smartphone illuminating her face. It was Faye Seaborne.

She crouched down beside her, her hand on her forehead. 'Megan? Just lie still.' Megan tried to struggle up. 'No. Listen to me. Don't try to move. Help's on the way.'

'You don't understand…'

'I do. Please, let me help. We've got to get you some medical attention now. I've called an ambulance.'

An ambulance? No. They'd take her to hospital. She'd be there all night even if she was lucky. That gave her the incentive she needed. She hauled herself up onto her feet, shaking Faye off as she tried to stop her, ignoring her protests.

'I'm okay.' She just wished she wasn't swaying as she said it, and that everything would stop moving in and out of focus.

Faye grabbed her arm.

Wind came out of nowhere, making Faye stumble back from her. Leaves and twigs, all the rest of the assorted debris of nature, skittered up the road. Megan pulled free and Faye cursed.

'Megan, stop.'

'I have to help her.'

'You're hurt. I think you hit your head. If you're lucky, that's all. You aren't in any condition to help anyone.'

'That's exactly what you want, isn't it? I know who you are. I know what you are. You want Ellie dead, but I don't know why.'

Faye's face went very white in the moonlight, pale as bone. Her eyes widened – green eyes, Megan realised – the greenest eyes she had ever seen.

'Ellie?' she said slowly. 'Eleanor Fairfax? Megan, she vanished eighty years ago. Of course she's dead.'

'You'd know, wouldn't you? You're probably the only one who would know. You and your shadows and your ghosts. Did you plant the hex on me?'

Faye bared her teeth in obvious disgust.

'I did nothing of the sort, Megan. I tried to help you. And if you can think clearly for a moment, I never would have had the opportunity. Someone else did that. Someone with access to you and your belongings. When did I have that?'

She wouldn't have. Megan tried to push her away. 'I *know* what you *are*!'

'And what do you *think* I am?' Faye took a step towards her again and the wind gusted, pushing her back. She snarled in frustration. 'Has Nora Grainger been filling your head with stories? Her and her aunt Hattie, or whatever that woman is pretending to be this time. Or has a dead girl been telling you tales?' As Megan's eyes widened, Faye's eyes narrowed with understanding. 'Eleanor wrote you a letter, didn't she? Hid it in the library, I suppose? That was the scene I walked in on.' She laughed, admiration and frustration vying for dominance. 'Eleanor Fairfax, I should have known… What did she say?'

'That you… That you never age, just change your name. That you were a spy in her time and God knows what else. That you're a Vala. You're a witch. That you're Morgan le Fey.'

This time Faye didn't laugh. Megan wished she had. It was so much worse to have her just accept so fanciful a notion.

'All this from Eleanor? Really?' But Faye didn't deny it either. She didn't react at all. Just studied Megan like a cat with a mouse while moonlight glinted in her eyes. She smiled slowly, her teeth so very white. Her voice came, curiously quiet over the wind and the raging bushes. No argument, no questions. 'And what if I am?'

She hadn't denied it. Any of it. She just asked 'what if I am?'

Megan didn't have an answer for that. It stole her breath away. The world fell away beneath her, leaving only her and Faye standing in a void.

'I'm not going to let you kill Ellie.'

'Eleanor's already dead, Megan.' Faye tried to say it kindly, in that irritating, patient way people always used when trying to explain things they thought would cause upset. The same tone they'd used when they told her Owen was missing. 'She ran away from the Harvest Festival in the village all those years ago – 1939…' She sighed, lowering her gaze, guilt and regret flickering over her features. 'I couldn't…'

And she looked up again, straight into Megan's face. Faye studied her, examined her as if trying to work out how much to tell her. The struggle played out on her perfectly sculpted face. In the end, she just gave in.

'I got David out but he was never the same. Whatever he saw in there, whatever happened to him… The trauma of it all… I couldn't help. I wasn't able to stop it.'

She looked so defeated. So broken. It tore at something inside Megan's chest, made her doubt everything. But Ellie hadn't vanished from the village. She'd gone back to the Hall, to the maze. Megan was sure of it. Which meant she'd be there now. She had to be.

'Well, I can,' Megan told her, and dodged by Faye, running as hard as she could up the open road. At the gates, she ducked across the lawns, through the trees, covering the land she knew as well as she knew the lines on her own palm now. She could hear Faye trying to keep up, to follow her in the darkness.

'Stop, Megan!' Faye yelled but Megan could hear the breath catching in her throat as they ran over the uneven ground. 'It isn't what you think. It isn't Eleanor that's in danger. Ellie's dead. You risk changing everything. You've changed things already. You can't mess about with time. If you go in there, you could kill David as well. Nora wouldn't ever be born. Do you want that? Or worse. Those green lights, those ghosts, they're the girls who died. The ones murdered by Gwyar when they failed to become Vala. They're all the lost girls of Ashleigh.'

Faye was lying. She had to be. Knowing there was no way she could trust her, Megan didn't hesitate as she reached the lawns and tore through the rose garden. The maze was a dark wall on the far side, the huge yew tree at the corner standing sentinel. It wasn't far now. And once she was inside, she'd lose her in seconds. The maze would take her away.

The first green light appeared at the entrance, dancing a little above the ground, beckoning her in. A ghost. One of the lost girls, the line of Fairfax, the daughters of Gwynhyfer. Those who could have become Vala, but died instead.

Ellie would be there. She had to be. And this time Megan was going to save her. No matter what.

Chapter Twenty-Seven

Thursday 28th September 1939

The long grass swished against Ellie's legs, whispering warnings, but still she pressed on. The hedgerow at the edge of the field formed a black, uneven line of threat. Ellie put her head down and forced herself to keep going as quickly as she could. She passed through the gap and gnarled branches caught her hair. As if the land itself was trying to stop her.

But the moon, full and bright overhead, summoned her.

Ellie was almost home when a figure came into view, walking along the path through the south field. Remembering the hooded and masked woman in the maze, doubts began to rear in her mind and she slowed her pace.

But the figure ahead slowed too, hesitated, and stopped a little way off.

'Lady Eleanor?'

Sarah. Ellie recognised the parlourmaid's voice – as shy and unsure as ever.

'Sarah? What are you doing out here?'

'On my way home, my lady. And begging your pardon, I could ask the same of you. It ain't right, my lady, you being out here on your own. Wherever has Miss Seaborne got to?'

'Miss Seaborne will be along presently,' Ellie replied, a little too haughtily.

Sarah's shoulders tightened and her smile faltered slightly. She recognised trouble when she saw it. 'I'd be happy to walk you back home, my lady.'

And though offended, she was still Sarah, still a heart of gold. Even though it meant she would be even later getting home herself.

'Don't you have family waiting for you, Sarah? It's harvest after all, and the fair's on. Aren't you walking out with Thomas from the bakery?'

Sarah blushed furiously. 'And here's you knowing far too much again, Miss Eleanor. Spying on us, is that the way of it?'

Ellie laughed. No one would need to be a spy to work out why the young man brought the deliveries up so promptly, or why Sarah hummed to herself when she thought no one was listening. 'No, Sarah, of course not. I apologise.'

'Then I'll walk you home, Miss Eleanor,' the maid replied with gracious dignity, making her sound much older. 'As is right and proper.'

This wasn't good. Sarah would deliver her back into the house and she'd be bundled off inside and watched over like a hawk until Miss Seaborne got back. She had to get to the maze to find David.

Ellie was still desperately trying to think of a way out when they heard footsteps coming up the path towards them and a figure tore itself out of the shadows of the hedgerow and into the field with its well-worn path like a scar running through it.

'And what are you two doing out here lollygagging?' said a familiar voice.

'Mary?' Ellie could barely believe it. Her old maid was wrapped in a long black coat, with a headscarf covering her head, but she was instantly recognisable.

'Lady Eleanor? What are you doing out here, pet? Where's that wretched Seaborne woman?'

'Oh, Mary, I missed you so much. I told her she couldn't let you go but she did. I tried to tell my father, and I will sort it out. You'll get your job back. I promise.'

Mary tutted and smoothed the back of Ellie's head with a surprisingly affectionate gesture. 'There now, lass, don't make promises for others. And don't fret either. It doesn't matter to me. I was just heading up to collect my things and be on my way. Time to move on, any road.'

'But you can't go, Mary.'

'Of course I can, my pet. Nothing's permanent. Except the bones of this land and the land itself. Come along now. I'll take you home. Sarah can head on her own way. That young Thomas must be worried sick waiting.'

Sarah bobbed into a curtsey, clearly relieved, and said her farewells, as eager to be off as Ellie. Mary didn't know Ava Seaborne's orders to the staff. And if she did, she wouldn't care. Luckily Sarah didn't say anything to enlighten her.

They made their way quickly across the dark fields to the grounds of Foxfield Hall. It was so much quicker this way than following the road and the light of the full moon was enough to guide them. It didn't seem far with Mary beside her. Ellie told her about being locked in her room, about seeing the Green Lady and about trying to ring her father. And about his reply.

'Oh well,' Mary huffed gently. 'Men are always so preoccupied with their own affairs. A war here, an indiscretion there, a scandal or a crime… it never changes. They don't pay any mind to us. We have to just get on with it.'

'But David… Mary, something happened to David. I have to get to the maze. Tonight. I have to find him. Mary, David is in danger.'

'Young David? I'm sure he's in no more danger than anyone else. Calm yourself. Do you trust me, Ellie?'

Trust her? Of course she trusted her. She had known Mary all her life.

'Yes.'

Mary beamed, holding out her hand. 'Good girl. Come with me then. Let's finish this. For once and for all.'

Like someone in a trance, Ellie took her hand. So strong, so firm. So reliable. A hand she had always been able to reach for, a hand that was always there to help her, no matter what.

But now Mary's grip felt cold and hard. Too tight.

Mary strode across the open ground, Ellie trailing along beside her. The maze appeared behind the house, a dark wall looming out of the shadows. The yews creaked and sighed, sang their ancient song. The scent of them was heavy on the air. Ellie struggled forward, her legs leaden with a strange sort of tiredness. The maze opened up in front of her and the green lights were already appearing, calling her.

But as she reached the entrance, she had to stop. A wave of wooziness swept over her. The lights grew even brighter, iridescent in the twilight. More and more of them surged towards her.

'Don't you know what they are?' Mary asked, a laugh underpinning her voice. 'The ghosts. They are truly ghosts, you see? They're the ones who failed. The girls, like you, who walked this path, hoping to become a Vala. Hoping to take my sister's place. But they couldn't do it. They wouldn't pay the price.'

Ellie dragged herself free and fell, her hand closing on yew branches, crushing the leaves so that the heady aroma rose around her. She couldn't hold on. She fell into the maze and landed heavily on her knees. Mud soaked her skirt and stockings. Pushing herself back to her feet, Ellie tried to calm her breathing, tried to clear her vision, but a terrible trembling invaded her limbs. She couldn't stay up, couldn't see, and all she could hear was a high-pitched whine like a scream.

'What have you done? Mary? What's happening?'

Mary smiled at her. It should have been comforting. It should have put her at ease.

But now something inside Ellie's chest fluttered, that thing deep down inside her that knew she was prey. Mary smiled and all her teeth were bright and sharp as broken bones in the light of the harvest moon.

'Don't blame me. It's the maze. Doesn't want you here, she doesn't. Knows what it means for her and for you, I suppose. Oh, of all of them you're the brightest, the most likely, the strongest. Don't you want your beloved, David? Your fiancé. Your champion? Well… I've got him.'

'Mary?'

'Such an innocuous name, isn't it? Everybody trusts old Mary. No, I'm not your Mary. I never was. She was just a mask I wore. I prefer this one.'

From her bag she took a slim, golden mask and fitted it to her face, dropping the bag at her feet, no longer needed. In her other hand she held a reaping hook.

'Who… who are you?'

'You can call me Gwyar. It's closest to my first name though I have worn too many to recall. I was Orcades, and Morgause. I am the last thing a sacrifice sees, the crone, the destroyer of champions. I break them and bring them low at the end. They kneel gladly before me to offer up their lives. Now, if you want to see your beloved again, you'd better get up and do what I say right now. Do we have an understanding?'

Ellie stumbled to her feet again. She wouldn't be afraid. She was determined. David needed her. Whoever this was, *whatever* she was… Lady Eleanor Fairfax was not going to show fear.

'Where is he?'

'You know that. Don't you? Go on. Find him. Then we'll begin.'

In the middle of the maze. He had to be there. That was where Ellie had seen him last. Gwyar didn't move as Ellie bolted away from her, running as fast as she could towards the middle, trusting the maze itself to take her there, to help her. Even if it didn't want her there. Even if the Green Lady was trying to keep her out.

'Please,' she panted under her breath. 'Please… don't let me be too late. Please. I have to help him.'

The shadows swarmed around her but she kept running, using her hands to pull herself along on the yew hedges. Branches tore at her, but she kept going. She had to. The pungent smell of the trees almost overpowered her. But she couldn't stop. Not now.

She had to save him. Before it was too late.

David, her David, knelt in front of the well, gazing up at the moon. On his head he wore a woven crown made of yew. He didn't move, not even when she called his name. Tears silvered his handsome face, and as she reached him, trying to pull him away from the well, to shake some sense back into him, she could see his eyes moving frantically, as if he was watching something she couldn't see. He looked terrified.

'David, what's wrong? Please. Talk to me, look at me. David! What has she done to you?'

'Ellie?' he whispered, his voice hoarse. His eyes struggled to focus on her. 'Ellie, you can't be here, love. Run, you have to run.'

'David?'

But the voice that replied wasn't David's.

'Do you really want to know?' Gwyar chuckled. It wasn't Mary. Not any more.

'Tell me,' Ellie snarled.

'I'm showing him the future, Eleanor. His future.'

'What do you mean?'

Gwyar clicked her fingers and suddenly the world changed around them. Spitfires and Hurricanes spiralled through the blue sky, leaving trails of smoke behind them. The Luftwaffe's Messerschmitts burst out of the sun and the bombers followed. Pilots screamed as bullets tore through them. Some were blown out of the sky entirely. Others burned as they tried to escape crashing planes. Some bailed out only to come down as broken, twisted flesh. Others ploughed into the earth like meteorites.

The scene shifted. London burned. St Paul's stood out in a sea of flames like hell's own. The city was a wasteland of rubble. The broken shells of buildings, once fine and beautiful, stood in mute testament to the destruction. Ellie saw bombs falling even on Ashleigh, the pub and the vicarage no more than smoking holes in the ground. Death after death after death.

It was the destruction of all she held dear.

Tears stung her eyes as the smoke of so many fires and explosions choked her, the stench of gas and burning bodies. She saw camps full of emaciated men and women who barely looked like people any more, wide eyes staring from skeletal faces in constant horror, striped clothes their prison garb. The graves, the mass graves, ash hanging in the air like smoke.

'Stop,' David gasped and Ellie wanted to sob in agreement. 'Please stop. Ellie, please, go. Please. You can't do this. I can.'

What was he planning to do?

He was seeing it too, all of it, images of the war as it would unfold. This was why Megan had looked so horrified when Ellie told her the date. She knew this. She knew what was to come and she'd tried to warn Ellie. And Ellie had told her not to say anything.

Battle after battle was bad enough. The children and the prisoners, the bombs crashing down on the cities, ships on fire off the coast, men crowded onto beaches with nowhere to go, no hope. No hope left at all.

But if that was true, if all ahead was death and destruction and subjugation, where had Megan sprung from? Ellie couldn't imagine she had come from a Nazi regime or a world of death and pain such as they were trying to bring into being.

Not Megan, so full of hope and fighting spirit.

'It can't end this way,' Ellie whispered. 'David, believe me. It *won't* end this way.'

'It doesn't have to.' The vision cleared like the smoke of a battlefield clearing with a breeze. She was back in the maze, holding David close, but he didn't respond. His eyes moved frantically, watching another bout of horror, still trapped in Gwyar's spell. 'Not if you do as I say.'

'You're torturing him.'

Gwyar grinned back at her, defiant. 'Yes. I am.'

She was enjoying this, damn her, loving every second of it. 'Why?'

'This is his fate, Eleanor.'

What could she do? She released David, who returned to the same position, a man enchanted, kneeling in front of the well. But the horror on his face bled away to quiet insensibility. Gwyar grabbed her arm in a painfully tight grip and pulled her away.

Ellie gave a cry, but no one came to help her. David flinched, but he didn't move.

'Your *champion*. Not very heroic, is he?'

Yes, he was. If this woman was still Mary, if she had ever really been Mary, she should have known that. What she had shown him, the horrors of war all rolled in together like a terrible newsreel… who could see such things and not be overwhelmed? But still, he was trying to fight it, to make Ellie leave, to keep her safe.

'He's all he needs to be,' said Ellie.

'They're all the same,' Gwyar replied. 'All of them, down through the years. Look.'

The shadows surged around him again and his uniform changed. Ellie recognised it from photos of her father's comrades in the Great War. And then again it changed, to the garb of one of Wellington's men. Time acting backwards on his clothing, folding back the ages, back again and again. David took on the appearances of all the champions back through the years, until he knelt there wearing armour. It gleamed in the moonlight, like something from a fairy tale. The wreath on his head was fuller and the bright red berries looked like drops of blood.

'Is this what you wanted? Your knight in shining armour?'

'That's not what he is to me. He's my… my fiancé. And he's my friend.'

'A *friend*,' Gwyar sneered. As if it meant nothing. As if it was somehow less than any other relationship. It wasn't. Ellie knew that. She could rely on David for anything. She loved him and always had done. She was his and he was hers. Their friendship had made all of that possible. It was the rock that was the foundation of everything else.

And he was hers. It was so much more important than anything else. *Her* David. He had always been her David.

'Let him go.'

'He's no hero, no knight. None of them were.' Gwyar waved her hand dismissively and the armour vanished. David knelt there, naked, his skin covered in whorls and spirals of blue paint, golden bands adorning his toned arms and a torc encircling his throat. His hands were bound behind his back. There was a noose made of rough rope around his neck as well. It hung there, ominously, the tail of it trailing down his back.

'They brought us the strongest, the bravest, the most heroic among them,' Gwyar murmured, her voice like a half-remembered song. 'They gave us their greatest hearts. Offerings, each and every one. Champions prepared to die for their people. For their land. And for us. And we gave them peace, prosperity and bounty.'

And that was what David was, wasn't it? A hero, a champion. That hadn't changed. He might fight in the air, but he was doing it for this land. And for her. And for something even greater than that. For their freedom.

And for that Gwyar would kill him.

'What do you want from me?'

'You're a scion of an ancient bloodline. That makes you… well… unique, destined for greatness.'

'I don't understand.'

Gwyar huffed in frustration. 'Don't you? You're special, girl. A line descended directly from my sister, the Vala Gwynhyfer, the blood of the first Lady of Foxfield who should have been the greatest amongst us, who shouldn't have been having mortal children with anyone. And that light should have been dedicated to the Vala, not this petty world of men. You could change everything. *Everything*. You can save countless lives. You can stop this war. The power of one light is untold. All you have to do is take that final step, commit yourself to the Vala. Become one of us. All it takes is to kill him.'

'No. I…' All that death. All that destruction.

You can't do this, David had said. *I can.*

He was willing to die, if he thought it meant sparing the world from the savage vision Gwyar had shown him. But Ellie couldn't let him do that. She wouldn't.

'You'll have to kill me instead.'

That was what Gwynhyfer had done, wasn't it? She'd taken her beloved's place to save him. Ellie stared at David, her eyes burning with tears.

'You could take his place, it's true,' Gwyar almost purred. 'But think about it. You can take *her* place instead, become Gwynhyfer, and keep the powers of the Vala alive. Think of all those you could save. Not just one, millions. I want you to be a Vala, child. To take your place among us. I won't kill him. I want *you* to do it. Make a sacrifice. A loving hand and a willing victim are so much better.'

Ellie tore herself away, staggered back a couple of feet. But there was nowhere to go. She couldn't leave him.

'No. Never. Not David.'

'Ellie,' said David, his voice so soft, ragged. 'It has to be me. Please, love.'

Did he even know what he was saying? He seemed out of his mind. Enchanted or… or something… She tried to wipe her tears away with the back of her hand.

'Listen to him.' Gwyar crooned the words like a terrible lullaby. 'He dies willingly. A threefold death, in the oldest ways. A hero was strangled to the verge of death, then his throat cut, and then drowned. He'll barely know it's happening, I promise. You'll be doing him a kindness.'

'I will not.' Ellie recoiled from her, and Gwyar's patience snapped. She shoved Ellie towards him again.

'Kill him, or take his place as my sister did. Become one of those sad little lights, flickering in the maze forever. It's all the same to me. You don't want him anyway. Or you won't, not after this war. He's broken, Eleanor. I showed him what his future holds and he doesn't want to live. Who else would you have given the champion to? I left them for you – the maiden and her champion. I know you took them. I know you, Eleanor Fairfax. I've made it my business to know every iota of your life. Who else do you have for a champion? You sealed his fate the moment you handed it to him.'

It was as if her words awoke Ellie from a nightmare of panic and despair.

The corn dolly from the first night in the maze? But she hadn't given it to David. He hadn't been here.

It was as if by just beginning to think of her, Ellie summoned her. Just like that first night.

A figure came from the maze but this time, instead of the clothes of her own time, Megan wore the same shining armour Ellie had seen for that brief moment on David before it vanished. The armour of the champion, the armour of a knight not from reality but from that realm where imagination and belief were made real, the world of the Vala, the space within the yew walls of the maze.

Megan stepped into the moonlight, decked in shimmering armour, wondering at the transformation of her clothing, and then saw Ellie standing there.

She looked exhausted, worn, but defiant. And her voice was a miracle.

'Ellie? What the hell's going on?'

Chapter Twenty-Eight

The maze, at night

Megan stumbled at the entrance of the maze and dropped down on her knees as if someone had sliced her legs out from underneath her. The scent of yew trees flooded through her followed by a wave of terror and heartache, horror at something she couldn't see or identify. But that didn't make it any less real. She felt queasy, as if something was pressing down on her face, a sweet and cloying herbal stench that smothered her. The smell of the yew intensified, that aroma she had come to associate with the magic of this place. Juniper and musk, blood and death.

With all the will she possessed, she struggled on.

'Ellie?' she called and pushed herself on. She had to be here. She had to. Megan had read in the book that Ellie had left the village in 1939 and come back to the Hall with Mary. The green lights pulsed in front of her, urgent and desperate, telling her to hurry up.

Well she was going as fast as she could.

'Megan! Stop!' It was Faye. She was still behind her, and getting closer. 'Megan, please. Please listen! I understand now. You're a champion. It will destroy you if you go in there. They will destroy you.'

Megan dodged down the narrow path of the maze, determined to leave Faye far behind her. And running full tilt, she entered the centre of the maze and stumbled to a halt.

Just like the other night, no sign remained of the archaeological excavation. The grass was unturned, the well still fully intact. The benches were in the same arrangement that they always were, encircling the well like the seats for an audience. Whatever time this place inhabited, it wasn't her time. It wasn't Ellie's either, she understood that now. Maybe it wasn't any time at all.

But Ellie stood there, tears silvering her face in a mask of horror. And a man knelt at the well, his hands bound, his throat bare, crowned with a wreath, waiting for death.

'Ellie? What the hell's going on?'

Faye stumbled out of the darkness behind her and Megan swore, turning to face her. That was when Megan realised she was decked in armour, shimmering like mist around her own form. It wasn't real, couldn't be real, and yet she could feel it, hampering her movement and weighing her down with all the things that could mean.

'What's happening to me?'

'She gave *you* the Artrí?' the masked woman sneered. '*You?* What nonsense is this?'

'Come back, Megan,' Faye whispered, trying to grab her arm and pull her back. 'This is no place for you.'

'On the contrary,' Gwyar said. It had to be Gwyar. 'She's the champion. She's just where she should be.'

Faye circled Megan, trying to put herself between them. Trying, Megan realised, to protect her. 'Sister, what have you done this time?'

'This time? Oh, that's rich. I have brought all times together. This is *my* time, Muirgen. The black moon. My power is strongest of all here. Stronger than you. Will you test me? Come on.'

Rage crossed Faye's features as she took in Ellie and David, as she realised what was happening.

All times are one time, all places are one place.

'I thought it was Megan's interference changing this world, but it was you. This is not our way. This is sacrilege. Stop it, Gwyar. You're undoing everything.'

'Then it should be undone. You always followed the stream, didn't you? The status quo. But I am the end. I banished you from this place once and I will do it again.'

'It's over, Gwyar. Our sister has been brought home. Let her be at peace.'

'Peace? There is no peace, not for us, not for her. She is not home. You brought back a corpse and nothing more.'

Not true, Megan wanted to say. She'd seen the ghost, seen it trying to control Nora, seen it trying to help her break the hex. The ghost was real. Of that she was certain.

'She is free. That is enough.'

'Never. Never enough. We can make her whole again. We can be as strong as once we were. There must be three of us. She only needs a vessel. I failed so many times.'

'You destroyed so many lives.'

'And yet they are still here. In the lights. All of them. Even Eleanor.' Gwyar waved her hand towards the young woman. 'I won't fail this time. You've set her free of her old body. I can offer her a new one. Sister, listen to me for once in your wretched existence. We will be whole again.'

Faye hesitated. It was just a moment but Megan saw it in her eyes, the temptation, the desire for this to be true. For Gwyar to be right.

She faltered, for just a moment, and Gwyar struck. Faye staggered back as the night foxes swarmed over her, dragging her into the darkness at the foot of the towering yew walls.

A deep silence fell over the maze, desolate and terrible. Megan stared at Ellie, on her knees beside David, her face silvered with tears.

Green lights surged from the ground and among them, spilling, dancing, came a troop of red foxes, real foxes, scurrying ahead of a girl in a sage-coloured dress carrying a cloth-wrapped bundle like a baby.

'There you are. I've got it. Where do we start?' Her long hair trailed loose down her back and her face – her beautiful, clever face – carried the hint of sharp vulpine features. Her eyes were blue like lapis lazuli instead of hazel.

As quickly as they appeared the foxes were gone, another mirage or enchantment perhaps, but the young woman remained. She was real. Megan wished she wasn't. That she wasn't here. That she wasn't involved.

It was just as Megan had feared all along.

'Nora?' she whispered. Her heart beat with a slow, dull thud that threatened to shatter her.

For a moment Nora just stared at her, open-mouthed. She looked so confused it would have been comical in other circumstances. 'Megan? What are you doing here?'

She wore a gown of green like spring leaves, and she walked barefoot on the grass, which sprang back up behind her, leaving a trail of delicate flowers, although she hardly seemed to notice. She looked like a fairy-tale princess, a goddess of spring.

'Sweet Nora,' Gwyar crooned. 'And here is your champion. Just a little sacrifice. Then you can take your place among us.'

'Yes, the champion.' Nora blinked, as if dazed. She unwrapped the bundle in her arms, revealing an elaborate corn dolly, a man, crowned, his arms behind his back, his knees bent. A woven image reflecting the way the man knelt at the well, awaiting his death. It was like the corn maiden back in the hotel, beautiful if you didn't know what it represented. There was a scarlet ribbon tied around his neck which trailed down his spine towards his bound hands. 'I made it. Just like you said.'

Gwyar smiled, baring all her teeth. 'And you have done well. The magic has worked. Here he is, made flesh.' She held out the reaping hook and indicated the man kneeling at the well, in the same position as the figure Nora had woven. 'Take it. Strangle him, cut him. His blood in the well will complete your transformation.'

'No!' Ellie screamed. 'You can't. Don't touch him.'

Nora turned, her eyes wide, noticing Ellie for the first time. She moved like someone in a dream, like she had been drugged. Her pupils were too large, filling her eyes. 'Who are you?' she whispered. Then she looked back at Megan. 'What's happening? It's not… it's not meant to be like this, is it?'

'It's all real. He's real. Please…' Ellie cried.

Shadows surged up, terrible black vines coiling around her.

'Stay quiet, Eleanor,' said Gwyar. 'Or I will make you quiet for good.' Then she glared at Nora. 'What are you waiting for? It's time. This is your quest, remember? None of this is real. We talked about it. It's all symbolism, but they simply take on a solid form under the black moon. None of it is actually real. Just do it. Take your place.'

'I don't…' Nora shook her head, confused now, her doubts getting the better of her as she faced Ellie, David and Megan. She hadn't expected them here. Whatever she had been told to expect, it was breaking the spell. 'Hattie? What's going on? This is mad.'

Hattie. The final piece slotted into place. Megan recognised her now, even with the golden mask. The voice, the stance, the cruel humour. Mary Hatten, Hattie, Morgause, Gwyar…

Hattie had all but raised Nora and so Nora trusted her implicitly. Had she been using her all along? Changing her?

You risk changing everything. You've changed things already. You can't mess about with time. If you go in there, you could kill David as well. Nora wouldn't ever be born. Do you want that?

And then it hit Megan. The quicksilver flashes of differences she'd been seeing in Nora, all this time. Not just her eyes, but her confidence and her manner, the woman she was when they first met and the woman she was now…

Megan looked from Ellie to Nora. There were elements she recognised in both their features. The hair colour of course was all Nora's own, that riot of red and gold, fox fur in firelight, that had bewitched Megan from the first time she set eyes on Nora Grainger.

But her eyes…

There was David, right there in Nora's face. Megan could see his long lashes, the cheekbones, his mouth…

She had kissed lips with a quirk of a smile hanging in the corner, just like that.

David Grainger lived. Of course he did. That was known history. He had led a life after this and Nora was his descendant.

But now?

Any moment now he would die. Because Megan had changed things. Because Ellie wasn't being given the option to kill him any more. Nora was.

And if Nora did that, she would be killing her own ancestor before he ever had the chance to have children.

Sudden understanding surged over Megan, a sense of clarity that made the horror of it all the more sharp and bitter.

'Nora, she's lying to you. It *is* real. He's real. He's David Grainger. He's your great-grandfather.'

Gwyar, Mary, Hattie – she lived all her lives here in Ashleigh, watching the bloodline of Fairfax and any number of others, living and reinventing herself with each lifetime.

But someone had to pay for all that life, someone had to give their life instead. All those Fairfaxes. All those lights.

And those whose lives they touched. Ellie had died to save David. It had broken him to pieces. He'd lived, but his life had been a shell. He'd fathered a family that had never had a moment's luck, that had all been men until Nora. So she'd had only Hattie to guide her.

Gwyar has preyed upon our line, squatting like a toad in our place of power since then.

This was a trap. Some kind of sick and twisted trap.

Gwyar persuaded the women of the Fairfax family to try to become Vala, to fulfil some kind of destiny. But to do so they had to make a sacrifice. If they failed, or refused, they died and joined the ghosts of Foxfield Hall, the green lights haunting the maze, drawn there by the Green Lady, their ancestor.

'Be silent,' Gwyar snarled. She pulled the mask off and threw it in the air. It twisted in an instant and then disintegrated. A force surged up against Megan, holding her there as surely as it held Ellie. Both of them, helpless, useless.

'No.' Nora's voice shook the ground beneath them. 'Don't hurt her. Don't…' Her eyes were wide, and now they looked just like Ellie's eyes, Megan was certain of it now. Before they had been hazel, but now they were the exact same shade of blue.

Hazel eyes could appear to change colour, couldn't they? The way the light struck them, something about the pigmentation, any manner of things that would explain it. But this was more than that. So much more. Megan knew that in her heart of hearts. Nora was changing before her eyes.

'Megan… what do you mean? Who is he? Who is he really?'

'He's David, my David,' Ellie shouted. From somewhere she found her voice and her strength, for her beloved David. Or perhaps the effort of holding Faye, Ellie and Megan, all of them, and enchanting David at the same time, was finally weakening Gwyar. 'Don't you touch him. Don't you dare.'

'Ellie,' Megan said. Gwyar's power raged against her like a tempest, but she couldn't give up. Not now. 'Nora's your descendant, yours and David's. She has to be. She wasn't, not in the world in which you go missing at the Harvest Festival in 1939. But we changed things. You changed things.' And she turned to Nora, to beautiful, powerful, mysterious Nora.

Ellie glared at Nora and Nora faced her, defiant, fascinated. Those eyes, the colour of the summer sky. They had the same eyes.

A different Nora, stronger, more self-assured. A Nora who hadn't been dismissed and neglected, who had come out to people who cared about her, supported her. A Nora who had been built up, instead of torn down.

'If she kills him she's wiping out part of her own heritage.' Faye's voice came through the smothering darkness, echoing around Megan's mind like a ghost's lament. 'She'll cease to exist. Time, like magic, always finds a way and it found Nora. She shares the Fairfax bloodline.'

Megan had to do something. She had to find a way to stop this. To stop Nora. Because she didn't know what she was doing. She couldn't do this. Not the Nora that Megan knew.

From somewhere Nora found her voice again. 'I won't hurt them,' she said.

Gwyar snarled at her and drew back her arm as if to strike her. Nora's bluest of blue eyes widened in shock and betrayal.

Megan couldn't help herself. She stepped between them, ready to block the blow.

Gwyar froze, her arm raised high. She lowered it slowly, with meaning, and then she sneered. 'So determined to be champion, Megan? Or would you make a sacrifice of your own?' The cruel glint in her eyes sent a chill through Megan's body.

'You tried to kill me, didn't you? You planted the hex and framed her.'

'You thought I did it?' Nora interrupted, her shock giving way to outrage. Megan ignored her. This was no time for hurt feelings. If it was, they'd never stop.

The world raged around them, the hedges of the maze thrashing with a roar like the ocean.

Gwyar smiled, a wide, toad-like smile. 'You shouldn't leave your belongings just lying around or expect anyone else to look after them for you. Anything could fall into a pocket. And Nora was so good as to carry it back for me, bringing it to you without even a thought. Such a good girl, always so obedient. Until you came along.'

'What have you done to David?'

Gwyar spread her arms wide, her expression a mask of innocence. 'I showed him the war to come. That's all. The future. The future awaiting him if he lives.'

'But they win! The Allies win!' Megan snarled at her.

'Do they? *You* don't know that. Not any more. Anything can happen from this moment. We've been changing things, haven't we? Just by meeting Eleanor Fairfax, you've been changing her life, and those around her. Changing everything. Changing Nora. You made everything unstable to begin with. You and your meddling. But I can make sure that *they win*, whatever that means, that your world remains as it should. In fact, I'll sweeten the deal. You see, I know what you want more than anything, Megan Taylor.'

Gwyar lifted her hands again and the shadows spread out in front of her like a dark mirror. And in that mirror…

A cave, dusty and dry, where men huddled together. Wounded and sick, their eyes desperate. And one face, his sun-darkened skin crusted with blood and sand, his eyes dull with pain. A face Megan knew as well as her own. Her brother.

Megan took a step forward before she remembered that this wasn't real, that it couldn't be.

Hattie laughed at her. Megan glared back with hate twisting her heart like a rag. Gwyar. Not Hattie. Not that she had ever felt comfortable around Hattie anyway. There had always been something lurking under the supposedly affable surface. She knew what it was now. This.

'That's it, isn't it?' Gwyar said. 'Your brother. The thing you want more than anything in the world. Staff Sergeant Owen Taylor. They blew up the armoured transport he was travelling in but didn't get him. Not at first. He's hurt though and it didn't take long to capture him. He fought all he could, but in the end… well…' She leaned closer, whispering her poison in Megan's ear. 'He's going to die there, Megan. Not even a soldier's death. The long slow death of a prisoner. Every moment a torture. And worst of all is knowing that he has no hope of seeing you or your family again. That's draining his will to live.' Her smile grew wolfish, all her teeth showing. 'But you can stop it.'

The air left Megan's body. She could feel it, everything her brother was experiencing, the desolation, the loneliness, the cold ache of abandonment. It ate away at him. 'Me?'

The smile that twisted its way over Gwyar's face made Megan's skin crawl. 'Of course. With my help. I can change his fate, Megan. It's what I do, after all. I cast the fates of men and weave them together. Of course I can change the pattern. I can bring him home to you.'

Yes, she wanted to say. *A thousand times yes. Anything for Owen. Anything.* But she couldn't speak. Gwyar wasn't finished yet.

'For a price.'

Ah, there it was – the barb Megan had been waiting for, had known deep down inside her was coming. 'What price?'

Gwyar's smile grew wider still, too wide to be human. She had too many teeth. It was a smile that would feast on souls. 'You know what price. Give up. Leave them to me.'

Megan's throat tightened to a barbed wire. Give up, just let Gwyar do as she would, walk away from this madness, and have her brother returned to her.

That was all she had to do.

She'd have her brother home. She'd have her life back. Her mum would smile and sing again. Her dad would hug them both. And Owen would laugh.

And all Gwyar asked in return...

Her eyes met Ellie's. Ellie, of all people, the tears on her face reflecting her own. 'Megan,' she whispered, devastated. Megan didn't need to hear her voice. But it was her brother...

Gwyar stepped closer to her, her voice gentling to a purr of triumph. 'You're no champion, Megan Taylor. Just a glorified gardener. You know that.'

Megan's armour evaporated, like morning mist in sunlight, unable to stand up before the truth of Gwyar's words. She was not a hero. She never had been. She hadn't been able to stay at home and deal with the grief of losing Owen. She hadn't been able to stand the pain all around her. So she left. Time and again she left. All she did was run away.

That was all she had to do now. Give up. Go back to her life. She looked into the mirror of shadows again, seeing again her brother's broken face.

Make a sacrifice, Gwyar had said. This sacrifice. If she left Ellie and David behind, at Gwyar's mercy, she would be sacrificing them.

She couldn't. Not even for her brother. Because what would Owen say if she ever told him? What would Owen do in the same position?

He would fight. Of course he would fight. Like he was fighting now. He wouldn't give up or give in. Not like this.

She might not be a hero. But Owen was.

I'm sorry, Owen. I can't do it. I can't save you and you… you wouldn't want me to. Not like this.

Make the sacrifice…

Each Harvest Festival the people of Ashleigh made the corn dollies as tributes. Stand-ins to appease the witch, the maiden, and the crone. A forgotten rite. They threw them in the well to placate a ghost, or empower a goddess. Once upon a time…

Before it was corn dollies, it had been people. Real people. Real lives. People with hopes and dreams. With friends and family who loved them. Sacrificed to the Vala.

People like David, like Owen. People like her.

And the one that really mattered here was the champion. And how willing they were.

There was another sacrifice.

Megan threw herself forward, onto Gwyar's hooked blade, felt it slide inside her. There was no armour, just her own clothes, and they didn't even slow something so sharp. She felt the point dig deep into her body. Too deep.

When she fell away, sprawling on her back, her shirt was soaked with blood. Her hands came away red.

Strangely, there was no pain. Gwyar had said it wouldn't hurt. Maybe she hadn't been lying.

Nora screamed her name, grabbing her, dropping the corn dolly she had made, the champion, and Megan seized it. Her blood mingled with the straw and stained the red ribbons. Her own blood from her own hands.

Without hesitation, she hurled it at the well.

'Gwynhyfer!' she shouted. 'Gwynhyfer, help us. Please.'

'No!' Gwyar screamed. 'You stupid fool. What have you done?'

Light burst from the well, green and glorious, threaded with sparks of silver. Glorious, blinding, light spilled everywhere, light that burned into Megan's retinas and turned the world to agony.

Chapter Twenty-Nine

The maze, at night

A storm of light spilled from the well, filling the air with static, with the pungent smell of yew and churning water. Megan gazed at it, as if looking into the origins of magic itself. It burned her eyes with wonder and reverence. For a moment she was lost. Painfully lost. Her heart cried with the knowledge that she was witnessing something beyond sense and reason, something she would never see again, and something she would never understand. And there it was. If she could reach out her hand, she could touch it. She could grab it and pull it inside her to hold forever, where it would burn and transform her into something of wonders and terrors. But her arms felt like lead, too exhausted to ever hope she would lift them again.

The light ripped its way through the shadows Gwyar had used to build her illusion, in her attempt to entrap Megan with the promise of her brother's freedom, eating away at it with hungry iridescent lines like fire on a page. Owen's face vanished and Megan sobbed, knowing now that she truly would never see him again. He was gone. Raw magic swept towards her like a firestorm.

Nora held her, calling her name, trying to staunch the flow of blood with her hands. She wasn't even looking at the magic, just at Megan.

Ellie, still trying to help David, stood silhouetted by this wild magic. Transfixed by its feral beauty.

She was one of the daughters of Gwynhyfer, one of the bloodline. Gwyar had wanted to make her a Vala by killing David. Perhaps she still could.

The magic of the Green Lady would claim her. It would destroy her. It would tear her apart and change her forever.

'Ellie!' Megan yelled. 'Move!'

But she didn't hear. She couldn't. Someone else did.

David launched himself up from the ground. Megan had thought him unconscious, insensible, but now he moved like an animal, his legs coiling beneath him and throwing himself bodily at Ellie. He snatched her up and pulled her aside. They landed heavily and rolled across the grass in each other's arms.

'No!' Gwyar screamed again in rage. 'What have you done? What have you unleashed?'

The light stopped above Megan. It held its place, twisting, whirling, and then it vanished, like a puff of smoke which had been inhaled.

The centre of the maze plunged into darkness. Megan collapsed back, her head thudding against the ground. The harvest moon hung overhead, high and distant, unattainable, Ellie's moon, not the black moon from her own time. But the stars were too bright for a moonlit night. The Milky Way splattered across the heavens.

There were two skies. Two times…

Megan didn't feel any different. There was no magic inside her. No Vala taking possession of her body.

Slowly she dragged her gaze back down to earth. She could only stare at the place where the light had vanished because she knew… she knew what had been there, in that exact spot. *Who* had been there…

The woman who had been holding her.

Nora rose slowly from the shadows, drifting up from the ground like a puppet. She opened her eyes – neither hazel nor blue now. Green light poured from them. The crackle of ozone filled the air around her.

'Gwynhyfer,' said Gwyar with uncharacteristic reverence. 'Sister.'

'What is it?' Ellie gasped. 'What's happened to her?'

'It's the Green Lady.' Megan's voice trembled and terrible things scrabbled up inside her chest, clawing at the base of her throat. 'And Nora. She's in Nora. She's taken Nora.'

Megan tried to struggle to her feet again, but stopped before she could manage it. Not that it was actually likely she'd make it up. The stab of pain was enough to drop her back to her knees instantly. Oh it hurt now. It really hurt.

Ellie and David came to her side, still clinging to each other. 'Stay down,' Ellie told her. 'You're wounded. You're bleeding.'

Megan's hands felt sticky and warm, but there was a coldness in her stomach, spreading out in every direction.

'Ellie?' David whispered, his voice still dreamlike and distant, but shaken. 'What's happening? I saw... I saw such destruction. I saw the planes blown out of the sky and...'

'It's not real,' Megan said quickly, firmly. 'It's a nightmare. A lie.'

He didn't look convinced but he stopped arguing. Whatever magic or potions Gwyar had used on him, they were wearing off. They huddled by the well as the earth beneath them trembled and shook.

'Is this what you had planned?' Ellie asked.

'That implies I had a plan to begin with,' Megan whispered.

'What did she show you?'

She could barely heave the words out. 'My brother. He's gone. He's really gone. And so is Nora.'

'That's Nora? Your Nora? But that's…' Ellie's voice trailed off, finally understanding.

David wrapped his arms around her, pressed his face into her hair as if it was the only thing real left to him. And what did Megan have left? Gwynhyfer possessed Nora, and Owen was gone forever. What had she done?

A sacrifice. It sounded like so small a thing. But it wasn't. It was everything.

In throwing herself on Gwyar's sickle, Megan had turned things around and sacrificed herself. Her own blood on the champion figure, thrown into the waters of the well, released the power of the Green Lady. Her body might have been gone but the spirit in the well was finally free.

Nora, or rather Gwynhyfer, studied them for a long moment and then turned away, her grave expression draining Nora's beauty away to something austere. And yet, she was still beautiful. Beautiful and terrible in the same way as a volcano or a hurricane. Awe-inspiring. She radiated that fierce green-gold light.

'Sisters,' she said, and it wasn't Nora's voice. Not any more. It was old and shook its way through Megan's vital organs, crushing and remaking them with each syllable. 'Sisters, what have you wrought?'

Gwyar stared at her, with eyes wider than ever. For the moment, her voice failed her. Gwynhyfer, the Green Lady of Foxfield, stretched out one hand and the shadows smothering Faye evaporated.

Faye Seaborne lifted her ravaged face. Blood covered one side, made her eyes glitter and her teeth look even whiter.

'Gwynhyfer.' It was like a prayer, a sigh of relief and at the same time a warning.

Gwynhyfer moved as gracefully as a dancer, a study in elegance. Every tone, every gesture was an admonition. She paid Faye no attention at all, bearing down on their eldest sister.

Gwyar cleared her throat and put on a semblance of reason and common sense. 'Come now, little sister…'

'You…' and suddenly Gwynhyfer's voice was cold as an arctic wind. 'You stole the life I would have had. My future, my fate. Stole my husband, stole my children. You stole all I would have been. I never forget.'

'We brought you a hero. It can be just as it was before. We can be all-powerful again. Just as we were in the times long ago. You can make yourself whole again. Just finish the job. Kill her.'

Gwyar stretched out the hook.

Shadows leaped up from the ground, seizing Megan before she could evade them. Ellie and David tried to grab her, to pull her back, but the force against them was too strong.

Vines tightened all around her, binding her feet together, her hands to her sides. They forced their way into her mouth and down her throat, gagging her, smothering her. They lifted her from the ground and stretched her out between Gwyar and Gwynhyfer, her neck exposed. Gwyar wove another crown of yew out of shadows and spite. She placed it gently on Megan's head. Then she dipped her finger in Megan's blood, with surprising reverence, and pressed it to Megan's lips. Megan could taste it, salt and copper on her tongue.

Her pulse fluttered, the desperate heartbeat of cornered prey. Despair filled her, flowing from Gwyar's touch and smothering her spirit, stealing all hope. She couldn't fight them. She couldn't escape. She'd die here and anything she ever wanted out of life would be lost.

The silver hook nestled on her throat, her frantic pulse beating its staccato rhythm against it. The point bit at her skin, drawing a fresh drop of warm blood.

Gwyar sucked in an appreciative breath and licked her own lips.

'A hero's blood,' she said, as hungrily as an addict. 'And here she is, already devoted to the Fairfax line, questing, seeking truth and wonders. Oh Gwynhyfer, you were always the most cunning of us. You called her, didn't you? You seduced her, made her fall in love with the girl who would be your host. You chose her, brought her here to die. Like the kings of old who were brought to us, long before the Normans, long before the Saxons or the Celts. Long before any of them had names beyond clan and family. We were raw power then, as you are now. We were the Vala and we walked as goddesses among men. Do you remember, sister? Do you recall what it was like? Is it the same for you now?'

Gwynhyfer gazed down at Megan, her ageless eyes illuminating Nora's face with that strange green light. A small frown appeared between her eyebrows, just a line, nothing more. That familiar quizzical expression. Just Nora trying to solve a problem.

The hook pressed closer, its edge smooth as ice.

Megan tried to struggle, tried to cry out, but she couldn't. The shadows were too powerful. They pressed closer around her, tightening until she couldn't breathe. She could only wait for the sickle to bite.

Fingers closed around the blade, knuckles pressing against Megan's throat, protecting her. Blood splattered on Megan's face, Ellie's blood. She gave a hiss of pain and shock, but didn't let go.

'You won't touch her,' Ellie snarled, standing over them, blocking the blade. The edge cut into her hand, but she held on, even as Gwyar tried to wrench it away and the sharp edge sliced deeper. Ellie gave a gasp of pain and Megan tried to wrench herself free.

Rage engulfed her, turning the world black and red. She could feel it racing along her veins, pounding with her heart. Her own… and at the same time not her own…

It was so much greater than that. It was ancient, and ageless.

Gwynhyfer's. And Nora's. Twisted together like knotted, woven straw…

A wave of light and sound engulfed them, hurling them apart. Megan crashed to the ground, the shadows holding her disintegrating. Agony lanced through her, holding her down as surely as Gwyar's enchantments had. Ellie crashed to her knees, clutching her bleeding hand.

Gwynhyfer loomed over them, now shining through every pore of Nora's body, a form solid and real but drenched in light.

Megan looked up into her terrible face, a mask of grief.

'My child,' Gwynhyfer whispered and her voice raged like the storm. 'My blood.' She rounded on Gwyar, enraged. 'You've spilled my blood, murdered my children and stolen their destinies. My daughters, all down through the ages. You've tricked and manipulated them, tried to make them murder their loves, or die in their defence. You lie. Even when you tell the truth, you twist it into lies. You ingratiated yourself into their lives and lied to them, to all of them. To Eleanor, to Nora, and all the rest. You lie at every turn.'

Faye dragged herself to Megan's side and she was shocked to see grey and white streaks in Faye's dark hair. She pressed her trembling hands to Megan's stomach and a fluttering pulse rippled through her, deadening the pain.

'You have to get out of here, Megan. You need to get away. When Gwynhyfer is enraged, no one is safe.'

'I'm not going anywhere, Faye.'

'Hold still a moment. I may still have enough magic in me to heal you completely.'

She wasn't listening. It didn't matter. Healed or not, Megan wasn't leaving. 'Not without them.'

'Them?' Faye looked up at Gwynhyfer and the ferocious light that illuminated her. Tears like stars flowed down her face. 'I'm not sure Nora's ever coming back, not after this. She wouldn't listen. She wouldn't be warned. But who of our line ever has? I tried to stop Gwyar, time and again. She changes her name like her disguises but she's always here. I've tried and failed too many times. I thought by finally bringing Gwyn back to the Hall it would appease her, let her rest. But I never thought Gwyar would go this far.'

Gwyar advanced malevolently on Gwynhyfer. 'You ungrateful little trollop. I did everything for you.'

Gwynhyfer didn't move. 'You killed the unwilling.'

'I killed the unworthy.'

'You never recognised the worthy. Your lust for power drove you.' Gwynhyfer turned her brilliance on Megan again. 'Look at her. Is she not the most worthy?'

Gwyar lifted her chin imperiously, without even offering her a glance.

'I see only a mongrel child. She has no bloodline, no Vala blood in her veins.'

Gwynhyfer smiled. 'That's all you will ever see, old woman. I see the future, the *real* future. I see a beautiful creature born from our land, carrying within her the blood of many others. A perfect combination. Stronger than we could ever be alone. You could never see the beauty I see. She is a champion. *My* champion. My Artrí, come again.'

She reached out with an elegant gesture of greeting. Enthralled, Megan reached out in spite of herself though she couldn't hope to reach the Green Lady now. She didn't even have the strength to stand. That didn't seem to matter. It felt as if her fingertip caressed her lips where Nora had kissed her. Ice and fire trailed after her touch.

Megan gasped for breath, dizzy with the sensations of magic and blood loss. The pain ebbed again, and she knew that was not a good sign.

'Nora?' Her name was a prayer on her lips.

'She's here,' said Gwynhyfer softly. 'Sleeping. Safe. But I see her dreams. She dreams of you.'

'That's impossible,' Gwyar snarled. 'And she cannot be a champion. That's a sacrilege!'

'Sacrilege?' Gwynhyfer said, and her voice was stronger somehow, her voice and Nora's voice combined. 'What you did, down through all the ages... *that* was sacrilege. What should have been a sacred exchange became a blood-letting, an obsession with purity and worth. No more, sister. It ends now.'

The shadows, so long constrained, manipulated and used for Gwyar's foul intentions, fell on their former mistress like a wave of malice. Her voice rose to an inarticulate shriek as she vanished beneath them.

There was silence. Then the Green Lady spoke again. 'Muirgen? You are diminished. Your power fades. What did she do to you?'

Gwynhyfer reached out and Faye hesitated a moment. But then she too reached out to her sister, her fingers forming elaborate patterns in the air, green sparks glimmering there like Christmas lights. Faye sucked in a breath, her body rigid with shock, and then she too glowed, green light moving beneath her skin.

Megan fell back again, her body failing her.

Ellie caught her, cradled her, but she looked up at the Vala, her expression furious. 'Megan's your champion, isn't she? Nora's and mine too? A champion for all of us. Our Arthur.'

'And she has not failed me,' said Gwynhyfer. She smiled Nora's smile and Megan shuddered with recognition. And grief. Pain flooded back through her.

'Then you have to help her,' Ellie said, stubborn to the last.

'Do I? Have I not done enough?' Her voice sounded so tired. 'Can I not be free even now?'

'Hush, sister,' Faye murmured, the strange light in her fading now. But she looked more herself now, strong again, reverberating with power. 'You are free. You just have to let go now. I'll take care of everything else.'

'It will not last, Muirgen. Not this time.'

'I know. But it will be enough.'

Their fingers joined. Faye Seaborne smiled, her face reflecting the glow of the Green Lady. The light turned to a swirl of stars which rose to the sky overhead, merging with the moonlight.

Nora's body fell forward and Faye caught her, lowering her gently to the ground.

'Rest, child. It's over.'

Chapter Thirty

The maze, at night

Ellie fought to breathe, her whole body shaking. Megan had lost too much blood, she was sure of it. Her skin looked like parchment. David pressed his hands to her friend's stomach, trying to staunch the flow of blood, telling her to hold on, to breathe. He must have had some training from the RAF, she thought. But it would take a miracle to heal this.

'Help her!' Ellie shouted at Ava, whoever and whatever she really was. 'You're still a Vala, aren't you? Heal her.'

Settling the unconscious Nora on the grass, Ava came towards them.

'Oh hush, Eleanor. Handing out orders like that. Your family would be so proud. Gwyn has granted me enough magic for this, I believe. Let me through, Flying Officer Grainger, if you will.'

For a moment David didn't move, staring at her as if she would attack them and he wasn't sure if he would be able to defend them from her if she did. Ellie closed her hand on his arm, surprised to find his uniform reappearing as she did so. His muscles felt like iron beneath the coarse fabric, but he relented. Illusions… everything Gwyar had done was based on illusions and lies.

Everything but stabbing Megan.

Ava pressed her hands to the wound and hissed, closing her eyes. For a moment nothing happened and then Megan started as if waking from a nightmare.

'There now,' said Ava. 'Better? Just enough magic left. I underestimated you, Megan. I should have seen that you too were a light.'

'What's a light?' David asked, his voice tentative. His arms wrapped around Ellie. She didn't want him to let go. Leaning back against him, even sitting in the dark, in the mud of the maze, was heaven.

'Someone with a future,' said Faye. 'Someone with a destiny to do great good in the world. A light has a gift of some kind, a destiny.'

'I don't believe in destiny,' said Megan.

'Unfortunately, Megan, destiny believes in you,' Ava replied, not unkindly.

'What about Nora?' Ellie pulled forward but David's arms tightened. He was just as reluctant to be parted as she was. 'She's our granddaughter? How is that possible?'

'Great-granddaughter, I think,' Megan replied. And then a terrible fear passed over her features, the same visceral fear Ellie had felt when David was enchanted. 'Oh God, is she…?'

'She's just sleeping,' Ava assured her. 'She may not remember anything at all. Be careful, Megan. You're newly healed.'

'I'm fine,' she protested. 'I'm… I'm not even going to ask about that. Let me go, Faye.'

Unable to hinder her any more, Ava Seaborne looked to Ellie for assistance. Ellie couldn't help herself. She smiled.

'Go to her. She'll want to see you when she wakes up. A familiar face and all that. Someone…' Ellie glanced at David. 'Someone who loves her. Someone she loves.'

'At least let me help you,' Ava said, exasperated. 'Make sure it's taken. The last thing you want is that reopening.'

Megan looked as if she was about to argue. But instead she just nodded. She didn't even glance back as she all but ran to Nora's side, only slowed by Ava's insistence in helping her stay upright.

David took her hand and Ellie winced, sucking in a breath. She didn't mean to. She'd forgotten the cut.

'Ellie? You're hurt.' He turned her hand over in his so tenderly. The cut was deep and there was blood everywhere. That was when she realised she was shaking from head to toe. Couldn't stop. She curled in against David's body, feeling his warmth, his strength, needing him.

'Yes. But we're alive,' she whispered, as he took out a handkerchief and wrapped it expertly around her hand, tying it firmly. 'That's got to count for something. Are you…' She sucked in a breath to try to gain some composure. 'Are you quite well?'

The lines around his eyes deepened. 'I'm not… I'm not sure what just happened here. What I saw… the things she showed me…' His hair, so slick and perfect the night before, fell over his face, just the way she loved it. 'I'm going to catch hell for this. I think I might be AWOL. How long was I here?'

Ellie couldn't help herself. She pulled his face down to hers and kissed him thoroughly, taking her own sweet time. 'David,' she said when she was good and ready. 'We should get married.'

'Now?' He laughed, bewildered.

'Not now.' She smiled softly, fondly. 'But soon.'

'If I'm not up on a charge, there's a war to fight. And it won't be over by Christmas. You know that.' His eyes grew distant with memory, with nightmares, with all he had seen. 'We both do.'

'As soon as possible, love. I don't want to waste another day.'

She glanced over at Megan who was holding Nora in her arms, stroking her hair while the newly woken red-haired girl apologised over and over again. She'd been tricked too. Hattie had been as much a part of her life as Mary had been to Ellie and she had betrayed them both.

'But we don't know if we'll even make it through,' said David.

Ellie cradled his face in her hands.

'Look at her, David. Really look at her. She has your mother's hair, and my eyes. She has my father's nose. She's a Grainger and a Fairfax. We know we live because… look at her. She's our descendant. So we have to survive.'

His smile was quizzical at first and then transformed to something full of joy. When Megan kissed Nora, and she returned the gesture with such passion and pleasure, he looked a bit bewildered again. That was David. Never the quickest. But Ellie loved him for it.

'Things are different in the future,' he said at last.

'Are they?' Ellie asked. And showed him the same sort of kiss, the same sort of passion.

Ava Seaborne, Muirgen, or Morgan le Fey if that was what Ellie chose to believe, was waiting for them by the well. The lights had gone and the water was still and dark. Any moment, the magic would be broken and this maze would be just a place in her garden once again. Megan and Nora would return to their time, and Ellie and David to theirs.

And time would flow on again, as it must. Like a river, righting itself, correcting its course.

'Well, Lady Eleanor Fairfax,' said Miss Seaborne. 'You never listened to me.'

'And you never lied, did you?'

Ava smiled. 'I truly was trying to protect you. But I doubt that I would have succeeded as you and Megan did.'

'What will happen to you?'

'To me? Who knows? This is a new dawn. I've never seen its like. No one has.'

'Why did she haunt us?'

'Gwynhyfer? She couldn't move on. She was trapped here, trying still to protect her children. You. And Gwyar stayed here, looking for the next light to extinguish, to feed her own magic.'

Ava looked over at Megan and Nora, huddled together now, whispering, wrapped in each other's arms. They were each other's world now.

'Gwynhyfer had her own plans perhaps. She played with time, changed what she could. Perhaps she stood enough outside of time to manipulate it. Slowly though. A cockstride at a time. She brought you and Megan together, I'm sure of that. But Gwynhyfer was always clever. People overlooked that, overlooked her. They dismissed her, diminished her, forgot how powerful she really was. Even me.'

'And the future that woman showed us?' David asked, his arm still warm around Ellie's shoulder, a comfort and a support.

'Will happen.' Ava tried to give a smile of comfort as his face fell. 'She doesn't lie. That's her greatest trick, you see? But she never shows everything. And time is always fluid. The smallest change in one place can transform the future, or perhaps just nudge things in a different direction. Don't lose heart. You know you survive. I can't tell you more than that, not without impacting the future myself. We've already changed too much. It was necessary. But…'

David tilted his head to one side as he watched the two women from another time. 'But a world run by Nazis could never produce the two of them, could it?' he asked, his tone solemn.

Ava smiled, finally content with his understanding. 'Well said. Do you want to make your goodbyes?'

Seeing Megan there with Nora, Ellie couldn't bring herself to interrupt. Or to say the words she didn't want to say, that she was never going to see her friend again. Their times were just too far apart. Chances were, she'd never live long enough. Even without a war and goodness knew what in between their times. She'd be an old woman, even if she did. And if she sought Megan out before they first met… well, she might never come. And then what would happen?

Temporal disruptions, Ava had called it earlier today, when Ellie had been trapped with her, trying to figure out a way to stop this. Physics. She would have to explore that. There were so many things she needed to work out. And she needed the time to do it.

She had all the time in the world now.

'No,' she sighed, the bitter realisation that she would never see Megan again burning at the back of her throat. 'We should just go.'

'Ellie.' Ava seemed shocked. There was a certain thrill to that, to be able to surprise her. 'Are you certain?'

Ellie smiled. 'I'll find another way,' she whispered.

'I know you will. You already did.' Ava smiled, a genuine smile of admiration and respect that made Ellie beam.

'I should have listened to you.'

Ava sighed. 'Sometimes I know a lot less than I think I do. If you had, this would have ended very differently. With David's death perhaps? Or yours? You are a rare and wonderful person, Eleanor Fairfax. And I see a bright future for you. One which changes the lives of millions.'

'I'll settle with just having a life of my own. With David.'

Ava smiled her enigmatic smile. 'As it should be. But there's still a war to fight. David will do it from the air. I want you to use your mind, young lady. You are brilliant, and, to be frank, utterly wasted here in

Ashleigh. There's a group your father and I are bringing together, very hush-hush, but I think you would be a perfect fit. You like puzzles. Have you ever thought about breaking codes?'

Chapter Thirty-One

Saturday 2nd November 2019, All Souls Day

The main function room buzzed with excitement. Most of the village was in attendance, accompanied by more academics than you could shake a PhD at. The press were out in force and the whole thing was being live-streamed to the university website so the entire world could watch.

And all for the Green Lady. She had come home to Foxfield Hall.

It had been over a month. Megan couldn't actually believe that.

They'd tried to talk about what had happened that night. Nora was the only one she could talk to.

Nora had known Hattie all her life, a friend of the family, babysitter and everything else. She had become a confidante when Nora had felt like an outcast in the village, and she shared a love of local legends with Nora's father. She had always been there with a story, a tradition, and then, when Nora came back from university, she had told her that the Vala were real. She had offered her a chance to become one of the cunning-women of Ashleigh, the daughters of Gwynhyfer.

And Nora had seized that opportunity without ever thinking about what it meant. She hadn't even believed it, not all of it. It was superstition to her. She regretted that now. But what was done, was done.

Megan knew that whole conversation hadn't gone terribly well but at least they were in it together.

Faye Seaborne, along with most of the team, had finished up the archaeological dig and followed the body of the Green Lady back to the university soon after that night in the maze. There hadn't been many other finds. Faye didn't mind. She had her headline moment for her show, she said. She had found her Green Lady and that was what people would want to see. It made for a simpler narrative.

Hattie had completely vanished, sending a terse letter of resignation to the hotel trustees, which she hadn't even bothered to sign. Sahar regularly muttered her name and a string of curses while redoing all the staff rotas. Megan didn't dare tell her what had really happened. Or that the letter had probably come from Faye Seaborne.

The maze had been painstakingly restored to glory. The mature plants she had introduced married harmoniously with what had already been there, reclaimed from overgrown beds and tangles of ivy and briars. Megan couldn't take all the credit, she decided. It was as if the maze itself wanted to thrive, and while much of the effect was waiting for spring, the autumnal colours were breathtaking.

The rest of the work on the grounds could keep her here in Foxfield Hall for a lot longer. And not just the work.

Nora had kissed Megan again, a lot more thoroughly, a lot more times.

A ripple of applause greeted Faye as she stepped onto the podium, all cool TV charm and academic lecturer poise. The grey had been banished from her hair again, although Megan suspected the hair and make-up department for her show had a hand in that rather than magic. Faye didn't seem quite as indomitable as before. And yet, in another way, she seemed so much more comfortable in her own skin. Herself at last, without other expectations or duties.

'Ladies and gentlemen, thank you so much for joining us here. In the course of the evening we'll be going through our discovery, describing what we've found so far and the various results of the tests we've been running. Afterwards we will invite you to explore the incredible maze, newly restored by landscape gardener Megan Taylor. But first of all, we'd like to give you some background on the remarkable work which first brought us here. And, of course, pay tribute to its author.'

Faye clicked a switch and a black and white photograph appeared on the screen behind her of a young woman, in her late twenties, her hair carefully styled and her clothes neat and fashionable. She was smiling at something just beyond the camera. Or someone.

Megan knew that smile. Sometimes she saw the echo of it on her girlfriend's lips.

'Lady Eleanor Fairfax is no stranger to the people of Ashleigh nor, indeed, is this, her home of Foxfield Hall. A bright and inquisitive young woman, she studied mathematics in Oxford and during the Second World War she worked with the now legendary codebreakers of Bletchley Park – one of the youngest women ever to work there. She became part of the code-breaking section located in Hut 8, and later joined the Secret Intelligence Service, following the footsteps of her father, the Earl of Ashleigh. The work she carried out in Bletchley, alongside the brightest minds in Britain, is credited with changing the course of the war, shortening it and saving millions of lives.'

Faye clicked something on the podium and the next image appeared. Ellie again, older now, with David, handsome in his RAF uniform, and a young boy. Her family, Megan realised. She had a family.

Megan glanced at Nora. Well, of course she did.

'She married her childhood sweetheart, David Grainger, a hero of the Battle of Britain, one of those valiant men known as The Few. David himself developed something of a legendary status among his squadron, leading them on countless missions, reputed to have an unearthly sense for oncoming danger, and the reputation of always bringing his men back alive.

'Following the war, Eleanor was heavily involved with the establishment of the Prisoner Repatriation Programme as part of the Red Cross, and later her work with *Médecins Sans Frontières* saw her changing the lives of men and women all over the world to this day.

'Her legacy is multi-faceted. She returned to Oxford to study theoretical physics and authored groundbreaking work on temporal mechanics and relativity. You know, the easy stuff.'

Faye paused, giving time for the laughter to ripple around the room. She smiled, letting it die away before continuing.

'Following the death of her father, Eleanor returned to her love of archaeology, travelling all over the world, delving into the unusual, the obscure and the forgotten. Her many publications have been reprinted countless times. Today we are grateful for one in particular: a small book published in 1946 as *Tales of Foxfield and Ashleigh*. It contains her meticulous work uncovering the lost legends surrounding the Vala, the Green Lady, and much older beliefs and rituals which survive here, and the links to later Arthurian legends, possibly their very inspiration. It was this very book I read so long ago, which sparked my own interest in archaeology. With it as a guide we were finally able to recover the body of Eleanor's ancestor, called Gwynhyfer, the first Lady Fairfax, or the Green Lady. Right where Eleanor speculated she would be buried.'

It went on. Megan could only listen as Ellie's glittering life unfolded before her in more pictures. All the places she went, all the things she discovered, her growing family and her smiles. She always smiled. That meant she was happy, right?

'Ladies and gentlemen, the university and this research group would like to present a portrait commissioned especially for Eleanor's family, and we are lucky to have with us today, to accept it, Eleanor's great-granddaughter, Nora Fairfax-Grainger.'

Nora got to her feet and joined Faye on the podium, saying her thanks and looking both thrilled and excited.

Megan gazed at her girlfriend and the image behind her, the portrait in her hands, and she could see the way their features mirrored each other. Not the same but echoes, glimpses of one in the other. Nora and Eleanor… even their names.

She had never mentioned her great-grandmother, but who did? Megan didn't even know who her great-grandparents had been. Mum occasionally mentioned her grandparents, but more in a distant summer memory kind of way. Owen remembered Grandma, but Megan didn't.

Even the thought of Owen made her insides twist. Could Gwyar have saved him? She never told the whole truth, that was what Faye had assured her. There was always a trick. But what if…?

Megan pushed the thought aside forcibly.

This wasn't a time for dark memories and what-might-have-beens.

Nora was, and always had been, a Grainger, one of David's family, and now she was a Fairfax-Grainger. Somehow, everything had changed. And Nora's life and family history had changed with it. Had she always been related to Ellie? Or had that changed when Ellie survived? Was that even possible? So many questions whirled around Megan's head, questions to which she knew there would probably never be answers.

No wonder Ellie had turned to theoretical physics. According to the few articles Megan had managed to read on it, time was an illusion, perceived only by passing through it. But perhaps if you stood outside it, like the Green Lady, it was all one, just as she had said. All times were one time. And perhaps time could be changed. Perhaps it corrected itself, flowing however it would.

Or something. Megan's mind twisted itself in knots trying to work it out until she gave up and just decided to accept it.

Nora left the stage to rapturous applause and came back to her seat, clutching the painting. Faye spoke about her own research, the excavation which had led to the discovery and the results of the tests. The preservation of the body was remarkable and would allow them to study her life, and everything about her. Years of work, years of marvellous discoveries and wonders.

When Faye's presentation finished, and the crowd mingled, Nora caught her arm and drew her aside.

'I need to talk to you,' she said. 'About Ellie.'

Megan wasn't about to argue. If Nora wanted to talk, that was good. It wasn't that they had actively avoided the subject. Not exactly. But they swerved around it a few times. They made their way outside but she didn't say anything. Nora slipped her arm around Megan's and they walked in silence until they reached the maze.

When they were in the centre, the grass and the well repaired now, the scars of the excavation hardly visible any more – and not a trace of magic remaining – Nora sat on one of the benches and Megan settled herself beside her. The new flowering garden, with its nooks of wildflowers and heritage roses, elements of planting which echoed a knot garden, soothed her soul. It was her finest work.

But Nora just stared at the well and fidgeted.

'What's wrong?' Megan asked.

Nora handed her a letter. 'From Eleanor,' she said. 'Another one. She didn't hide it this time. Just gave it to me years ago, before she died, and said I'd know who to give it to. I promised her I wouldn't read it and I've always kept my promises. I didn't even realise it was for you until afterwards. Well… I'd forgotten about the letter to be honest. Or maybe… I don't know… maybe she only wrote it after… Look, it doesn't make sense. It never occurred to me that it was any more than… I don't know. Not dementia – she was sharp as a tack right to the end – but maybe a game she played? Anyway, with all this talk of Eleanor and her papers, I suddenly remembered it existed. Took me ages to find it in the attic. Here.' She thrust the letter at Megan. 'It's between the two of you.'

'She died?' Megan had never asked. She couldn't bring herself to until now. Because she knew the answer. Otherwise Ellie would have been there.

Nora shook her head. 'She died seven years ago, only a few years after Grandpa David. They were so kind to me. When I came out to her, it was like she already knew. She was so accepting, because, well, she *did* know, didn't she? She saw us, she knew you. She was amazing, Megan. But you know that, don't you? She passed away, quietly, in her sleep, with all the family present. They weren't making up any of that stuff about her, you know? She lived life to the full, every day, every second. Like she was trying to squeeze in everything.'

'Everything she missed before, when she died so young.'

'Yes. I guess so. I think she tried to explain it to me when I was old enough but she didn't say everything. Perhaps she didn't know, or maybe she didn't want to scare me. Or change anything. She always said time couldn't be rushed. It didn't really make sense until now.'

'But how?' Megan asked. Just trying to figure out all the aspects of it made her brain hurt. 'Did you know all along? Was she your great-grandmother before we changed events? Or have we always changed them. Did you—?'

Nora lifted a finger to her lips.

'You think too much, do you know that? I can't explain it. I only remember bits. It's fading. All of it.' Nora studied her for a long moment. 'Eleanor… Granny Ellie…' She shook her head, smiling sadly. 'I half-remember other stories. David must have married someone else, but it wasn't a happy marriage and it didn't last. I remember trying to tell Dad I was gay and… it didn't go well. But now, I know that's not what actually happened. It's like a really vivid dream fading after you wake up. Sometimes it lingers for a day or so, just fragments of it, but it drifts away, you know? It gets harder to remember as we go on. And it's only a small part of my genetic make-up that would have changed, after all. My eyes and my nose, I think. I'm better at maths than I ever was. Timelines readjust themselves after a divergence. I've been reading up on it. Her papers on it are brilliant and she set off a whole line of research. It could be a closed timelike curve, or perhaps a wormhole linking then and now through the maze, or maybe even— What? You're smiling. Am I rambling again?'

Megan laughed. 'You're dangerous when you get hold of theoretical physics, that's all. Must be genetic too. You leave me in the dust in seconds. I bet David had the same problem.'

Nora kissed her, lingering with her smiling lips against hers, eyes closed. Megan held the envelope against her chest, tight in her hand the whole time, and when they parted, Nora looked down at it. 'I'll let you read. I should be getting back anyway. People to schmooze. If we leave it to Alan he'll sell the hotel out from under us or something.'

Megan nodded, and waited until she was alone before opening the envelope.

Dearest Megan, she read. Ellie's hand, still unmistakable even after a lifetime.

I have given this to Nora because it is partly for her I write it. Once you have finished I hope you will give it to her as well to read. She is a good girl, but I think she believes I am rather strange. So many do.

I have no regrets. I lived a life, loved my family and did everything I ever dreamed of. All those times I was told a girl could not do that, I did it anyway. All those things I wanted to find out about, I went and discovered the answers. And it is thanks to you. You and Nora.

So be good to her, as I know you will be. I pray you will have the kind of life I led. I think you will. You are a light as well. If David and I could love and experience so much, just think what the two of you could do together.

Among other things I have made sure that some wrongs are righted. I cannot change the future, but I can be sure fate pays back what is owed. And I will see to that, for you. And for as many others as possible.

I am an old woman now. So I can use the tone of the old to the young, because I remember when we were both as young as you are now. And something magical happened. So be good, be kind, be… who you have always been. And discover your own fate.

All my love
Ellie.

A cool breeze touched the tear tracks on Megan's face. She hadn't even been aware that she was crying until she'd finished reading. She sniffed loudly, and imagined the look of disgust Ellie would have turned on her for that. She'd have offered her a tiny lace handkerchief and then refused to take it back. But no handkerchief was forthcoming. Ellie wasn't there. Megan wiped her face with her sleeve instead. And imagined the look she'd get for that too.

She folded the letter up like a precious relic and tucked it safely away. She'd show it to Nora, of course, though what Ellie's great-granddaughter would make of it she couldn't imagine. Back at the Hall, Nora was waiting.

*

Later that evening, Sahar poured extra-large glasses of wine from her never-ending supply of Pinot Grigio, and they sat on the patio outside the apartment watching the waxing crescent moon rise over the maze.

Nora curled in against Megan, her head on her shoulder and the long fall of her hair spilling down Megan's chest. She was almost asleep when the phone rang.

Megan knew the ringtone and everything lurched into dread as she grabbed it and brought up the screen. It was a video call from her mother. They hadn't spoken since that awful phone call about Owen, and them finding his DNA.

She almost dropped the glass as she tried to put it down. Nora caught it and took it from her.

Megan hit accept and the screen came up. But it wasn't home, and it wasn't her mother. The room was that kind of military waiting room she knew too well. They all looked the same. Her free hand flew to her mouth when she saw the man looking back at her. His cheeks hollow, his brow lined, his skin weathered, but that didn't matter when you saw his smile… his wonderful, beautiful smile…

He wasn't as broad as Megan remembered. The uniform hung a little oddly on him, as if he'd lost too much weight too quickly. His darkly tanned skin made his eyes and his teeth so very bright.

He was real.

Gwyar had said he would die if Megan didn't do what she wanted. That he was a prisoner and that he'd never come home. Gwyar had not lied, but she had always twisted the truth. And everything had changed.

Megan thought back to Faye's presentation. Ellie had set up a Prisoner Repatriation Programme. Megan's hand went to the pocket with the letter in it, her letter.

I've made sure that some wrongs are righted, she had written. *I can be sure fate pays back what is owed.*

Megan opened her mouth and closed it again, unable to find words through her disbelief. The joy bubbling up inside her choked her.

Owen grinned. 'We thought we'd surprise you. Didn't expect it would be that effective though, Meg.'

She found her voice in joy. 'Owen, you're alive!'

She didn't know what they talked about. There was only pure, radiant happiness and tears. Their parents had been called that morning and hurried down to the RAF base as he was flown in, repatriated following his rescue by a NATO-led squad. It had all happened so quickly that by the time the news had reached her parents he was already in the UK. They had been so busy getting to him themselves they hadn't been able to ring her until now.

He was home, he was safe. Like Faye had said, Gwyar never told the whole truth. She used it, manipulated it, made it suit her own ends.

*

Faye Seaborne was standing beside her car by the time Megan found her, rooting in her designer handbag for her keys.

'Did you do this?' Megan asked, her voice too loud with excitement and emotions.

To her surprise, Faye smiled. 'Not at all. I think you'll find that you and Ellie did.'

'Gwyar offered to free him, but I said no, didn't I? That was the sacrifice. I gave him up, left him for dead, and now—'

'No, Megan. That was never in my sister's power, no matter what threats and promises she made. You chose Eleanor and Nora. And Eleanor lived every moment of life you gave back to her. She filled it with good work, with joy, and with love. I wasn't lying when I said she saved lives. Not just during the war, but afterwards. She founded the Prisoner of War Repatriation Programme, dedicated to finding those lost souls everyone else had given up on and getting them back home. People like your brother. She's still saving lives.'

'She sent me a letter.'

Megan held it out, crushed in her fist, and Faye looked at it but didn't make a move to touch it.

'That's for you, Megan. Not me. Ellie and I made our peace long ago. We worked together for many years. I did everything in my power to help her. Always.'

Megan thought of David, the pilot Ellie had married, the man she'd loved. 'Was she happy?'

Faye smiled fondly. 'Oh yes. Very happy. So was he. He became a doctor, you know? After the war. If Gwyar had killed him who knows what would have happened. When she killed Ellie there was a hole in his life he never filled.'

'Nora says she half-remembers someone else? An unhappy marriage?'

'Yes. It will fade, those ghost memories. Another timeline. Time always rights itself. You saw the changes in Nora as they were happening, didn't you? She's a happier soul, especially now.'

Especially now. Megan blushed. 'Ellie and David?'

'They would have approved. They did. You know that. They were a perfect partnership, those two, complementing each other. They made everyone's life better. Still do. Speaking of which…' Faye looked past Megan, back to the house. When Megan glanced over her shoulder, Nora was walking towards them. 'You should go back to your friends, Megan. Make plans to see your family now, all your family. Introduce them to Nora. They'll love her, you know they will. Because you do. It's time for me to go.'

'What will happen to you? What are you going to do now?'

Faye opened the door of her car and slid inside, gripping the wheel. But she didn't move. She smiled up at Megan. 'Anything I want to. Schedule permitting. I'm heading back to Crete next week.'

'Another labyrinth?'

'They are rather special. You never know what's waiting in the middle, do you?'

Megan didn't know what to say to that. And she didn't want to think what Faye might stir up in the palace of Knossos.

'I was wrong about you, Faye. I'm sorry.'

The archaeologist grinned up at her as she closed the door. 'I got so many things wrong myself. Always did. But here we are now. It worked out in the end. Goodbye, Megan. Have the best life. You deserve it.'

She waved as she drove off.

Megan turned back towards Foxfield Hall. It was floodlit now, and beautiful. Such a strangely beautiful place.

A fox crossed the lawn. It stopped, staring at her, studying her.

'Megan?' Nora reached her side. 'Is everything okay?'

'Yes.' And it was. She knew it finally was.

Megan reached out for Nora and their fingers tangled together. From there they were like lodestones, drawn together, each touch a promise, an endearment. Nora's lips moved so delicately against hers, and her sigh rippled through Megan in mysterious ways. She kissed lips with that familiar quirk of a smile hanging in the corner, a smile that had come to her from the love of Ellie's life. 'Everything is fine now. Someone is still watching over us.'

But when she thought to look for it again, the fox was gone, vanished like a ghost into the darkness of the maze.

Perhaps it was a sign, or a mystery. Perhaps it was just a fox. But it didn't matter. There was nothing to worry about any more. Not with Nora in her arms, beneath the spreading boughs of the great yew tree.

A Letter from Jessica

Dear reader,

I want to say a huge thank you for choosing to read *The Lost Girls of Foxfield Hall*. If you did enjoy it, and want to keep up to date with all my latest releases, just sign up at the following link. Your email address will never be shared and you can unsubscribe at any time.

www.bookouture.com/jessica-thorne

Writing *The Lost Girls of Foxfield Hall* was always a labour of love. In many senses, this was the book that would not leave me alone and would not die. It's a prime example of never giving up on a story. Like Megan, it took a while to find its place, and a wonderful editor like Ellen to help me bring it back to life. These characters are like family and I'm so delighted to see them out in the world. I hope you love them as much as I do.

I would like to thank everyone at Bookouture, my editor Ellen, and my fabulous agent Sallyanne, who always had faith in the story of Foxfield Hall. I am also very grateful to my writing friends for their help and advice, Susan Connolly, Catie Murphy and especially Sarah Rees Brennan for reading it for me and sharing her excellent thoughts.

More madness awaits in the Lady Writers Quirk Club in the tiniest office for 2021.

Thanks also to Helen Corcoran, Karina Coldrick, Suzanne Hull and to my ever-supportive Naughty Kitchen of romance writers, Janet Gover, Imogen Howson, Alison May, Kate Johnson, Annie O'Neil/ Daisy Tate and Jeevani Charika/Rhoda Baxter (we of many names). Writing this during a pandemic was only possible because of all your support, and your friendships mean so much.

Thanks and love as always to my family – Pat, Diarmuid and Emily. At least now they're able to burn their own pizza while I write.

I hope you loved *The Lost Girls of Foxfield Hall* and if you did I would be very grateful if you could write a review. I'd love to hear what you think, and it makes such a difference helping new readers to discover one of my books for the first time.

I love hearing from my readers – you can get in touch on my Facebook page, through Twitter, Goodreads or my website.

Thanks,
Jessica Thorne

JessThorneBooks

@JessThorneBooks

www.rflong.com/jessicathorne

Printed in Great Britain
by Amazon